ORDINARY
MAYHEM

Visit us at www.boldstrokesbooks.com

ORDINARY
MAYHEM

by

Victoria A. Brownworth

A Division of Bold Strokes Books

2013

ORDINARY MAYHEM
© 2015 BY VICTORIA A. BROWNWORTH. ALL RIGHTS RESERVED.

ISBN 13: 978-1-62639-315-8

THIS TRADE PAPERBACK ORIGINAL IS PUBLISHED BY
BOLD STROKES BOOKS, INC.
P.O. BOX 249
VALLEY FALLS, NY 12185

FIRST EDITION: FEBRUARY 2015

A PORTION OF THIS NOVEL FIRST APPEARED IN A DIFFERENT FORM AS A SHORT STORY, "ORDINARY MAYHEM," IN NIGHT SHADOWS: QUEER HORROR EDITED BY GREG HERREN AND J. M. REDMANN, BOLD STROKES BOOKS, 2012. "ORDINARY MAYHEM," THE SHORT STORY, WAS AWARDED HONORABLE MENTION IN ELLEN DATLOW'S BEST HORROR OF 2012.

EXCERPT FROM MARY OLIVER'S "THE USES OF SORROW," FROM THIRST, BEACON PRESS, BOSTON, 2006. USED BY PERMISSION

CREDITS
EDITOR: GREG HERREN
PRODUCTION DESIGN: STACIA SEAMAN
COVER DESIGN BY SHERI (GRAPHICARTIST2020@HOTMAIL.COM)

For my smart and sexy wife, Maddy Gold, who shares the Grand Guignol with me, along with everything else. You make life at the cat farm a true adventure.

and

For Greg Herren, who makes me laugh—make that howl—every day. You push every literary envelope and have helped me do the same.

"I felt the urge to reassure him that I was like everybody else, just like everybody else."

—Albert Camus, *The Stranger*

"I used to think I was the strangest person in the world, but then I thought there are so many people in the world, there must be someone just like me who feels bizarre and flawed in the same ways I do. I would imagine her, and imagine that she must be out there thinking of me, too. Well, I hope that if you are out there and read this and know that, yes, it's true I'm here, and I'm just as strange as you."

—Frida Kahlo

"To reach something good it is very useful to have gone astray, and thus acquire experience."

—St. Teresa of Avila

Part One

PROLOGUE

I.

I was six.

It's a young age. Impossibly young, really. We think we remember six until we *see* six and then we see what six is. We say, *No, that's not six!* And we think it must be five or even four, and that *this* child is just big for her age, but really—that *is* six.

Six is small. Six is vulnerable. Six needs protection.

Six is A. A. Milne and Winnie the Pooh and Piglet and really just a bit past *Goodnight Moon*, which I never liked much, even if it *was* written by a lesbian with her own truly tragic story. Milne knew about six, that's why Christopher Robin is six and imaginative and yet has a robe with a hood and gets tucked into bed at night.

Now We Are Six is a classic because it resonates. We are old enough to read it ourselves—often our first "real" book. Even now, with kids and their tablets, parents and grandparents still give that book as a gift on a sixth birthday because *six* is right there, telling the child who gets the book, *This is about you, this is your life, here, in your hands. This is you, this is who you can be—adventuresome, an explorer, a friend to small, interesting creatures. This is your world, now you are six.*

My grandfather—Grand, I called him—gave me that book.

Grand gave it to me right after I saw my first dead bodies.

Now I was six.

The 100 Acre Wood and Pooh Corner were not my world, though, much as I wanted them to be. My world was somewhere else. Under the rocks of the 100 Acre Wood, perhaps. In the thick, rotted, fungal branches on the ground of the 100 Acre Wood. In the mouths of owls that ceased, by nightfall, to be intriguing intellectual characters with dyslexia and became instead marauding predators with a taste for small, vulnerable, bite-sized creatures, creatures whose blood was a delectable sense memory for them. My world was there, among them, small and bite-sized, in the leaves, scurrying, fearful, heart thumping, blood pulsing, head pounding. My world was the undergrowth, the mossy, lichen-covered ground, the place that always smelled a bit of dead things.

My world was not the 100 Acre Wood, or Pooh Corner. Death had touched me too young. Death had touched me at six. Death had touched me, and in touching me, owned me. It was my first "brush with death," as the phrase goes. It was my introduction to death, to mayhem, to the implacable, relentless ordinariness of pure horror. Hannah Arendt built her philosophical career on knowing, and stating with trenchant, defining clarity, that evil, in the end is, banal. Maybe. But if that's is true, then so, too, is horror.

Banal. From the French. *Ordinary.*

I knew at six that horror—real, true, hand-over-the-mouth-screaming horror—was ordinary. I knew that mayhem, that word we use for the most violent, most chaotic, most awful horror, was indeed ordinary. *Ordinary mayhem.*

I saw it first at six.

I've seen it ever since.

II.

They burned to death.

My parents burned to death.

Now you are six.

It was snowing, it was cold, fire met ice and they burned to death. While Christopher Robin imagined a coterie of cute, if somewhat wryly adult animals in the 100 Acre Wood, I imagined my mother's desperate, piercing, agonized screams from within the flames of our car. I imagined her arms flailing, clawing at the windows. I imagined my father shoving his athlete's body against the door over and over like a scene in a movie, trying to break through to the world without flames, the world in which they would both survive, unscathed, to be reunited with their young daughter in a snapshot of familial perfection.

But neither would escape. The car would be nothing but a burnt-out shell, an image in a photograph on the metro section of the newspaper I would, many years later, be taking photographs for myself—photographs like that one. Photographs of something awful. Obscenely, irrevocably awful.

Mayhem.

I imagined my parents dying, agonized, in our car, the car in which I would ride, curled in the corner behind my mother's seat, face pressed to the window, looking out, cataloguing, always cataloguing everything I would see. The greenish-brown rush of the river. The bright bursts of daffodils, forsythia, azaleas. The vivid yellow, scarlet, ochre of the turning trees. The snow—fat flakes falling as we rushed home to beat the storm.

Sometimes there were things I wished I hadn't seen—an animal killed in the road, guts spread in a thick red smear, a child crying hysterically while its mother slapped it repeatedly, nowhere for it to run or hide, a man hitting a woman on a street corner, people turning away, not intervening, allowing the brutality to go on and on way past when we'd driven by.

I still see all these images, all these years later.

I can't recall my parents ever telling me not to look, ever telling me to look away.

When you are six you begin to remember.

When you are six, you can no longer forget.

III.

I couldn't forget my parents burning alive. I couldn't forget the words: *burned* and *alive* or how they became inextricably linked in my consciousness so that whenever I heard *burned* it was immediately followed by *alive* and the images of my parents resurfaced, even if

I hadn't thought of them in forever, because after a while, I almost never thought of them. After a while I had to pull out photographs to remember them. After a while they seemed like people I had only met briefly, who I had never really known.

After a while. But not in the beginning. In the beginning I thought of them all the time. In the beginning, I felt their loss more deeply than anything I had ever felt. I felt their loss and the loss of everything familiar to me. In the beginning all I could think about were those words *burned alive.*

In the beginning, when I was living with my grandparents, I would turn on the stove while my grandmother wasn't around and hold my hand in the blue flame, hold it as long as I could, hold it in the flame, counting. I never got past five before I had to pull my fingers out and run them under cold water, tears pricking the backs of my eyes. *Burned. Alive.*

It stays with you, *burned alive.* It stayed with me.

Now you are six.

I imagined my mother and my father—such a beautiful couple, everyone said so—incinerated. I imagined them like I would later imagine Joan of Arc burning at the stake when I read about her at St. Cecilia's in religion class. I imagined them as I counted, my fingers in the blue flame, and tried to imagine not screaming, not pulling my hand away until it was like the long ash at the end of my father's cigarette as he sat outside, only half-smoking, staring at something, I never knew what, because I was only four, five, not-yet-six then, and my memory of my parents blurred so quickly, even though it should have been so precious.

But then so many things happened after they died, after my parents died, after they left me.

So much more.

After they died, I saw my first dead bodies.

They were not my parents.

They were not anybody's parents.

But the memory of them was seared as brutally, as grotesquely as my parents were in that car on that cold, heartless, icy night.

My grandfather handed me the little book of poems. Short little bits he knew I could read. Inside he had written, *For Faye, who would never go down to the end of the town, love Grand.*

The inscription referred to a line from A. A. Milne's poem, "Disobedience," in which the mother of a small boy goes down to the end of the town and is never seen or heard from again. There are condolences for the child, James James Morrison Morrison Weatherby George Dupree, but we never know what happens to him. Or where his father is. Or what became of his mother. It's a cautionary tale, of course, like most fairy tales and nursery rhymes, but it's a particularly unsettling one for a small child and its almost jaunty sing-song rhyme does nothing to mitigate the awfulness of what has happened to this small child, orphaned and alone.

I still have the book. I still have everything Grand ever gave me.

Most of all, I still have death.

That was his first gift to me. I was, you see, his apprentice. It took a long time for me to figure it out. It took till that night, at the gallery, when I saw him again. All the faces, all the bodies, all the stories I had seen and told and remembered came flooding back in that moment. In that moment, death touched me again—touched me like it had that first time.

I was, you see, no longer six. Now I knew what it all meant. Now I had that clarity, like Arendt must have had as she watched Eichmann in the dock and made her now-infamous declaration about the banality of evil that still shocks. Now I understood the gifts, all of them. And where I stood, in that moment, that knowing moment, the blood draining from my face, my heart beating out of my chest, was in fact, ironically, so very ironically, at the end of town.

CHAPTER ONE
OPEN IN RED LIGHT ONLY

The fascination began when Faye was a child. The darkroom, the red light, the big black and white timer that made a loud ticking noise as it wound down, the trays of liquid that turned the paper into pictures as her grandfather moved them back and forth with his fingers or a pair of big wooden tongs with plastic on the tips. She would sit on the high stool in the darkroom and watch as the paper came out of the big yellow boxes and then slid into the white pans of fluid that had that slightly acid smell that reminded her of the dead mice they sometimes found near the basement door.

Her grandfather never spoke to her when they were in the darkroom. He just moved from tray to tray, making the papers swim gently in the liquid that glowed red in the light. When the timer went off, the images would begin to appear on the paper: jagged pieces of clothing, a half-formed face, a disembodied leg, the flail of an arm. When the completed pictures finally came through, he would pull the photographs out of the fluid and hang them by the corners with little wooden clothespins on a thin piece of rope that ran the length of the darkroom.

Then he would take a magnifying glass and look at each picture. Sitting behind him, Faye would see an eye bug out, or a mouth go askew, or the side of a face puff up. In the hazy cast of the darkroom light, everything looked red, everything looked as if it had been soaked in blood.

Some of the photos her grandfather would mark with a silver pencil that came out white in the corner of the pictures, which were still wet— she could see they were wet, which made the images swim together. Some he left alone. There was a small black fan that ran all the time, back behind the trays. The photographs would move ever so slightly on the line, but they never blew around, never touched each other. When they were all hung up and all checked, or not, with the silver pencil, then the red light would go out and the door would open, and he would tell her they had to wait for the photographs to dry. Sometimes she would look back to see what was there, but the room was dark without the red light and she could see nothing at all. It was all black inside.

Later, they would sit at the kitchen table together and her grandfather would set things out on a big piece of yellow oilcloth. It was still the era of the Polaroid, and had been for several decades. Color photographs aged badly. People's eyes glowed like demons. Everything turned a kind of red the color of dried blood. People came to Faye's grandfather for portraits, for a classic photo that would withstand whatever time they thought they would have. Faye's grandfather's photographs were the next best thing to a painting. He was known as an artist as well as a photographer and Faye understood that what he did was two different things—take the photographs and then do the art.

❖

The art was a different kind of magic from the darkroom. On the table Faye's grandfather laid out a dozen or more little white glass pots with heavy, dark, oily paint in them. Reds, magentas, purples, and blues that looked like small organ meats with their thick, gelatinous consistency. The greens and yellows seemed like mold or fungus, but without the thick furring at the edges Faye had seen sometimes on rotting food. The paints smelled sharp, a smell she could never place because it wasn't like anything else.

Her grandfather would give her little pieces of his canvas board and a pencil and three pots of her own and some Q-tips. He let her draw and paint while he sat bent over the black and white photographs, slowly turning them to color. He would twirl tight little pieces he tore off cotton balls, dip them gently in the thick paint, and paint the photographs with the delicate details their owners wanted.

Faye would always watch him before she started her drawings. Watch the slow, meticulous way he twirled the cotton and how carefully he worked on the linen photographic prints. Sometimes he would take a cotton ball and rub it over a photo to make the color softer and lighter. She always noticed how red the lips were. From where she sat they always looked like wounds in the faces of the people. Deep gashes that would never, ever heal.

They could do this for hours—sit at the table with the white pots and the cotton and the photographs—without speaking. When the photographs were finished, he would slide them into sleeves of parchment paper and put them in the cabinet behind where the cameras and tripod were kept until whoever's photographs they were came to pick them up.

Sometimes, when no one was watching, Faye would open the door to the darkroom and turn on the red light. She would set the timer and slide pieces of paper from the yellow boxes marked with big letters, OPEN IN RED LIGHT ONLY, into the trays of fluid. She would sit on the stool and wait, but no images would appear in the trays. She would think about what images they would be: She would squint her eyes the way she had seen her grandfather do over and over and she would imagine the pictures.

The images she saw always looked like slices of bodies, half-finished faces, torn shreds of clothing. And always, they were bathed red, like the darkroom light, like blood, like the gashes of mouths her grandfather painted on the photographs. When she closed her eyes, they were still there: the charnel house images that were the bits and pieces from the pans of liquid. When she closed her eyes, the red light still burned behind her eyelids and pulsed, like a vein, until she turned off the light and left the room.

Chapter Two
The Grotto

Later, when Faye was sent away to the convent school for girls, she was often called to Mother Superior's office for this or that minor infraction. At first, in the early days, she felt fear, but soon she began to like the trips from the building where her class was over to the one where Mother Superior's office was. She liked the solitude, she liked the opportunity to explore. She would walk across the schoolyard, stopping briefly at the grotto with the sleek, despondent Virgin Mary standing within the hewn gray stone recess. Faye would stare up into the face of Mary and wait to see if she would speak to her like she had to the children at Fátima or to St. Bernadette at Lourdes. Sometimes there would be leaves at the feet of the Virgin and other times she would find small dead things—rodents or birds, because the grotto was set into a wooded area and there were feral animals, foxes and raccoons and cats, that came out from behind the trees to kill.

When she found dead animals, Faye would pick them up with leaves or sticks and take them to the bushes and lay them on the ground. She kept a notebook of sketches and each time she found a dead animal, she would draw it later, trying to remember exactly how it had been when she'd found it—if the neck was broken, if the mouth was open in a final scream, if it had puncture wounds or missing parts, if it was stiff and cold, or still limp and warm. Sometimes, when there was more than one, she would arrange them together on piles of leaves, sort of like a burial pyre she had seen in a book. She wasn't sure exactly what it was she was cataloguing with the drawings, but she knew they were important and she knew they meant something, so she was meticulous about them and would look at them later to be sure she had gotten everything right. She never killed anything herself, but she was always grateful that it was she who had found the dead things and not someone else. It was like a secret between herself and God. Or so she imagined it was.

After Faye left the grotto, walking back down the slate path and on toward the high school building where Mother Superior's office was, she sometimes heard crying. She was never sure exactly who it was, but it always seemed to come from the same place, the music rooms where one of the nuns, Sister Anne Marie, would compose different kinds of music for the girls to sing at the regular musical events that were held at the school. The place was named for St. Cecilia, the patron saint of music, and so music was a major part of the school's activities. Faye thought Sister Anne Marie was probably the person she heard crying. She thought it must be hard to love music so much but never be able to choose what music you listened to because nothing here was a choice, it was all up to God, or so they were told every morning in catechism class.

Sometimes Faye would walk closer to the place where the music rooms were—the small, two-story cottage across the stretch of lawn from where the grotto was—because she liked Sister Anne Marie. Faye thought she was nice, but sad, and there didn't seem to be anything that made her less sad. It was always the same—the sadness. Sometimes, when the nun played the piano for them in music class, she looked different. Not happy, exactly, but something else—glowing. Like the angels in the pictures in the catechism books. Music made her glow. Faye knew that there was something else, she just didn't know what it was. But she was sure that was who was crying, because another time she had seen Sister Anne Marie in the grotto, on her hands and knees in front of the Virgin Mary, her forehead touching the ground. And she was crying then, too, and hitting the slate of the grotto with her hands, slapping it over and over again, pounding it with her hands flat against the rippled gray slate. She was saying something, but Faye could only hear certain words. The only ones she was sure she heard were "sacrifice" and "terrible" and "killing."

Faye had stood behind a bush near the grotto and watched. When

Sister Anne Marie got up, there was blood on her hands, and little bits of leaves and twigs had stuck to them. She had looked at her hands and then she had turned and looked back at Mary. When she turned back around, Faye could see that the expression on her face was exactly the same as Mary's—sad. Very, very sad.

After Sister had walked away and gone back to the music rooms, Faye had gone up to the spot where the nun had been. The slate apron in front of Mary had smears of blood where Sister Anne Marie had been. Faye could see the mark of her hands on the slate—a thick, dark-red gore. She had bent down and touched it, had rubbed her fingers together, feeling the consistency of the blood mixed with dirt and a little bit of leaf matter. Faye had taken out her notebook and pressed the blood onto a page, wiping the blood off her fingers onto the paper. Then she had closed the book and stared up at Mary for a long time.

There was a fire escape that ran down the side of the building where the music rooms were. Once there had been a fire drill and Faye had heard the alarm and one of the girls hadn't known it was a drill and she had started to cry, saying that they were all going to be burned alive and it would be like going to hell. Sister Anne Marie had looked at Faye with a look Faye didn't quite recognize—some kind of distress. Faye thought she was upset because Faye's parents had been burned to death in a car crash. The words *burned* and *alive* stung when she heard them come from the mouth of the girl in her class, but they seemed far away, those words, masked by the sound of the alarm. It had been the first time she had heard those words since she'd left her grandparents' house. They were strange, somehow, and Faye heard the faint echo of them in her head, like they were being said from the end of a long hallway, another place, the place where no one knew exactly what those words meant.

Faye knew all about *burned alive*. Knew what the girl did not. Knew about the blood and the smoke and the flames in the snow and of course, especially, the screaming. Faye was always sure there had been screaming, because one day she had turned on the stove in the kitchen at her grandparents' house and put her hand in the flame and held it there for as long as she could, until she started to scream, involuntarily. Her grandmother had come running in and grabbed her hand out of the blue flame and put it under the cold water of the tap, then she had put ice on it. Faye's hand had turned red and there had been blisters on her fingers and the blisters had split open and underneath the skin was raw and bloody like meat and she had thought how terrible it had been for her parents in the car, screaming, with no one to come and pull them out. But now she knew what it would be like, the fire. Now she knew.

Faye had turned to the girl and said, "There's no blue flame. There's no smoke. There's no blood. So we won't die. And it won't be like hell, because there would be snow, too, and flames in the snow, and there's no snow."

The girl had stopped crying, but she still looked scared. Sister Anne Marie had stared at Faye, then. Her eyes seemed wider than before. The look on her face was strange, Faye thought. And not much different from that of the girl.

CHAPTER THREE
THE THINGS ON THE SHELVES

Outside Mother Superior's office, the big parquet off the closed door of the room had a row of hard, straight-backed chairs along the wall. Faye was supposed to sit and fold her hands in her lap with some semblance of the contrition she never felt, but instead she would walk up the steps to view the alabaster statue of St. Cecilia that lay on a white marble slab at the landing of the stairs, beneath a stained-glass window depicting the appearance of the Virgin Mary to the children at Fatima.

The body was life-sized and lying on what looked like a stone coffin of the sort Faye had seen in the old cemeteries she'd gone to with her grandfather. She was mesmerized by the statue of the fallen saint, and never failed to touch it, even though that was forbidden and the nuns would slap you if they caught you. The young saint lay on her side, as if she had merely fainted, like some of Faye's classmates did when they were fasting, and someone had placed Cecilia on the closed tomb and arranged her body there, as if she were sleeping. But Cecilia, the patron saint of the school, wasn't sleeping, Cecilia had been struck down by an infidel—there were three deep slices in her neck. She was supposed to have lived for three days like that, sliced open and lying there, her wounds exposed.

Faye always slid her fingers into the crevices where the wounds were, wondering, because she was fascinated by the lives of the saints and read as much as she could about them, what it had felt like to die that way, to have your head nearly sliced off, and to have fallen dead so openly, with the wound of your death exposed to everyone who passed. Her parents had died that way and Faye always thought death should be more private. That's why she always moved the little dead animals she found near Mary's statue in the grotto to a more secluded place.

There was no blood on St. Cecilia, of course. Just the vast whiteness of her body. The lovely face, eyes closed, the folds of her garments, and the three telltale wounds spread open on the neck, open so wide that a young girl's fingers could slip into the spaces, but not quite fill them. Faye would wonder if Cecilia had tried to hold the wounds closed. She didn't think it was possible, but she wondered.

Other times Faye would forgo the statue for her other fascination: the science library that was always open and empty whenever she was there—she had never seen the high school students inside, even though she knew it was used for the biology lectures. She had several years to go before she was in the high school. She wondered if the mysteries of the science library would be revealed then.

The room was very large, yet had no windows. Faye thought maybe they had been closed up, like in one of the Edgar Allen Poe stories, because the things in the room shouldn't be seen in the light, or from the outside by someone peering in. There was a smell that layered itself over the whole room that would make you gag after a while and she thought that was why the room was always empty and the sliding wooden doors were always open. She knew what the smell was—it was formaldehyde, the same smell that she remembered from the funeral home when her parents were killed. It was a smell that got caught in the back of your throat and lay there, until it was really hard to breathe and you had to get as far away from the smell as you could because the smell was always attached to death and it might be able to take your breath with it. Or so she thought.

In the room, on one side, the floor-to-ceiling bookcases were filled with books, all stacked neatly with the edges out to the end of the shelf the way the nuns had taught them books must be shelved. But on the other side were the jars. These were stacked from the floor to about a foot or so above eye level, so that none of what was inside could be missed, yet not all could be seen. Most were of a uniform size—about a gallon, Faye thought, envisioning the plastic milk jugs at home. Some were smaller, like the jelly and jam jars her grandmother would put up at the end of the summer.

All the jars were filled with a murky yellow-green liquid that looked like the bottom of the creek near her house where she would take the dog on Saturdays after confession and where you could see the small fish swimming under the flat rocks. But though the liquid was the same, the contents of each jar were different.

Faye thought of this as the experiment room. The jars were the most compelling thing in the school, to her—after Mary in the grotto and St. Cecilia on the marble slab. She often thought Mary or Cecilia could easily come back to life if the right miracle occurred, the kind of miracle they were always talking about at school. But Faye was certain nothing in the jars could come back to life, and uncertain if they had ever even been alive. Faye was surprised these things were even allowed in the school, since they all seemed as if they came from Satan and could never have been created by God.

All the things in the jars were dead, of course. Some she knew what they were—frogs and toads, some split apart and floating, their eyes open and staring out from the jars. She also knew the nematodes, because she'd studied about them and about the salamanders. There were some other slithery things—large, fat worms and little garter snakes. But the other things, she wasn't sure. One looked like a baby with a huge head that curved away from the body that seemed shrunken and too small—how could it ever hold that gigantic head up? The eyes of the big-headed baby were a milky blue and were set into a too-pink and somewhat bloody socket. There was something that looked like a tiny pig that had been skinned or had never grown a skin, Faye wasn't sure. Like the frogs, it too was splayed open and the eyes had rolled back in the head, exposing only the whites. The legs stuck out in front, like it was reaching for something, and the mouth was open, and Faye could never tell if it looked like it was smiling or screaming.

The most disturbing jars held things with more than one head. A rat, a frog, a kitten, another animal that looked like a fox, but wasn't. A baby alligator. A squirrel. These had all been sliced open and had an eerie comedy/tragedy look to the different heads. In the kitten, an eye had come loose from the socket and floated out a little on a shred of skin that looked like a stalk. If you moved close to the jar, the eye would move and turn a little toward you. Faye didn't like to think about the two-headed kitten with its floating eye.

Faye could never tell what was in the jars on the highest shelves and she had never dared to drag one of the big chairs over to stand on it to see what was in them. The higher the shelf, the more horrifying the contents of the jars, so she always imagined that the ones she could not see were the ones that held the things that weren't meant to be seen, the things that she was certain had not come from God *ever*, but which were like the bits and pieces of bodies she had seen in the photographs in her grandfather's darkroom: Things that it was best never to know about. Things that held mysteries it was better not to have revealed.

Faye wondered why there were never any students in that room, and she thought maybe it was because those things weren't really meant to be seen, but were there as a warning, just like the statue of St. Cecilia. All those things were meant to warn the girls at the school to be careful, to do what they were told, to stay away from places where blood-drenched body parts and kittens lolled with two heads and floating eyes, and someone could strike you down with their sword and slice open your neck so deep, you could never close it up ever again.

Whenever Faye thought about these things, she would stop looking at the jars and walk over to the chairs and sit, positioned so that she could see both the jars on the bookshelves and St. Cecilia lying, bathed in the colored light from the stained glass, and wait for Mother Superior to call for her.

Chapter Four
Taking Pictures

It never seemed like a big leap from those early days in the darkroom and running her fingers through St. Cecilia's wounds and cataloguing the science specimens to where she was today. Faye Blakemore was born to photograph carnage—or at least that's what she would say to slightly appalled friends and colleagues from the time she was in college until now. Once she was on her third drink it was easier to explain how she'd been mesmerized by the red light of her grandfather's darkroom or transfixed in a kind of religious fervor by St. Cecilia and her Reliquary, as she had come to refer to the science library, and how both had propelled Faye to her career—or her fate. Faye was never exactly sure what she should call what she did. She knew there was nothing else she *could* do; she'd never tried, but she didn't have to. She was meant to do what she did from the very first time she'd sat on the stool in the darkroom. She was meant to do what she did from the very first time she had felt St. Cecilia's wounds or gazed up into the contents of the jars in the science room. Some of the girls she had gone to school with had become nuns. Not many, but a few. She had become—this— but it was a calling, nevertheless. Of that, she was certain.

The squeamish were put off early by the baldness of Faye's statements about her work and why she did it, but others were, naturally, intrigued. The wrong sort of men and the wrong sort of women were drawn to Faye, although Faye had no interest in the men. Unsurprising, she supposed, given her past, given what she knew even before she had gone to St. Cecilia's. Faye supposed it was classic and Freudian, but she didn't care. She wasn't afraid of men, despite her history, and she had several close friends who were men, gay and straight, but she had no desire for men. Her desire for women ran as deep as her desire to take pictures and tell stories.

Women—Faye had always given herself up to the women, ever since Faye had fallen in love with Sister Anne Marie. Faye had realized, much too late, that she had been in love with the beautiful and mysterious nun from that very first day she had seen her in the grotto, prostrating herself before the Virgin Mary. But that Faye had loved her and would always love her also stood between her and intimacy. Or so she knew the shrinks would tell her, if she ever decided she should go to one. Sister Anne Marie, with her deep blue eyes and creamy Irish skin and dark hair and that hint of something in her voice—Sister Anne Marie was her first true love.

That wasn't something Faye told any of the other women. Not the ones at St. Cecilia's—well, there had just been the two—or the ones in college or now. But it was always there, haunting her, like a tune she couldn't quite get out of her head. Some film theme from an old movie or a new one that just lingers in the back of one's consciousness. Faye always thought of that haunting Jerry Goldsmith theme from *Chinatown* or the equally haunting Hans Zimmer theme from *Inception.* But she knew that if there were a soundtrack to her own life it would be that psychotic Clint Mansell score for *Black Swan,* which could so easily have been her own theme music—dark, frenetic, frightening, beautiful. That music, Faye thought, remembering Natalie Portman pirouetting through insanity, that music was indeed her own.

She wasn't crazy, though. Faye knew that about herself, even if some thought otherwise. Yet Faye herself had no flair for the normal, so she dove in, wondering sometimes if she was looking hard—perhaps too hard—for the kind of end that had befallen St. Cecilia, looking purposefully for the wrong woman. Faye wondered if she was destined to ignore every bit of what the nuns had taught her about circumspection and restraint. When Faye thought *restraint* she thought of people bound and gagged and waiting for something terrible to happen. She never thought of holding herself back from whatever it was she wanted to do.

Restraint was a form of punishment, it was sitting waiting for Mother Superior, it was *not* going home with the woman with the switchblade in her boot, it was choking back everything.

Faye had spent many years choking back everything, from tears to words to—so much.

Then, perhaps, Faye would simply end up like her parents— burned alive in a drunk-driving accident on New Year's Eve, blood and flames running hot red rivulets into the snow, the car crumpled like leftover gift wrap from Christmas.

Faye tried to care about what might happen to her, tried to think about the danger, tried to lean more toward normalcy, but it seemed counterintuitive to what she wanted from her life and the work that she also considered her art and which was inextricably linked to what she did when she wasn't drawing or photographing. Faye wanted to catalogue those things on the upper shelves, the hidden horrors she had never been able to fully glimpse. Faye knew there was more than the two-headed kitten with the floating eye or the flayed-open pig with its hideous gaping mouth. There was how they got there in the first place. She had known all along those things weren't created by God. What she hadn't known was that it was people, not Satan, who had filled those jars and thought nothing of it as they did so. Once she understood that, Faye wanted to be the artist who shocked and appalled and drove people from galleries with their hands over their mouths, unsure if they were going to scream or vomit or both because she had shown them something of themselves that they wanted to see, couldn't wait to see, were in fact desperate to see, and even excited to see, but which revolted and horrified them nonetheless.

❖

Just as Faye's fascination with her grandfather's darkroom and the dead things she found at school had started soon after her parents' deaths, Faye's career had followed a similarly clear-cut path. After college, Faye had started on her quest simply enough, doing the kind of photojournalism that won awards and which no one thought of as voyeuristic because it had purpose and meaning. Art was always her end game, but she wanted that foundation of sincerity first. She wanted to tell her stories, but she never wanted to be perceived as a monster just because she wanted to roll back the rock to see what slithered underneath. After all, Faye was merely moving the rock and showing what was beneath it—she was doing what she had always done, recording the deaths of the little creatures with as pinpoint accuracy as she could, but she wasn't doing the actual killing. Faye didn't create the things no one wanted to see—and it wasn't because of her that they couldn't keep themselves from looking. Everything Faye had photographed from the time she had gotten her first camera at eleven when the notebooks and drawings were no longer enough had led her in the same direction: show the wounds deep enough to lay a finger in, examine the jars on the uppermost shelves, see if the bodies really do come together in the trays of developer, or if they were never whole in the first place, if it was always the fleshy, gore-streaked, blood-soaked shrapnel of human carnage, of what people can do to each other when no one else is looking.

In an interview after her first big award, after she had chronicled the impact of an arson fire on a small town where several hundred people were trapped in a theater for a children's Christmas pageant and the charred bodies had been laid out on the snowy sidewalk like some horrific holiday display, Faye had told the reporter that it didn't faze her to detail what people were capable of because she knew everyone, given the right circumstances, could do the most unspeakable things and have no conscience about it whatsoever. Faye had leaned forward and looked directly into the face of the interviewer as she explained how the person who had set that fire had done so deliberately, had put two-by-fours through the door handles, had poured the accelerant all around the building and then lit the match—knowing there were three hundred people inside, more than a third of them children, and that it was a week before Christmas and everyone in the town would be touched by the tragedy.

"We're all capable of killing," Faye had told the reporter, who was older than she by at least a decade and clearly unnerved by what he had hoped was merely her youthful candor and artistic bravado.

"The question is, *why* would we kill? To save ourselves? To protect someone we loved? Or just because we wanted to know what it was like to watch the blood or breath run out of someone else? Or because we've come to love the sound of other people's tormented screaming?"

That first award had led to others, because the stories had gotten grislier and more provocative and sometimes it seemed that only she had the stomach to tell the tale—the stomach and the interest. Faye was always interested.

Faye covered other terrible events—fatal fires, multiple killings. She had been the first photographer on the scene of a freak accident when an 18-wheeler carrying steel pipe had lost its load on the West Side Highway where it wasn't even supposed to be. Lengths of pipe had flown off the rig, doing damage as they went. Two lengths shot through the windshield of the cars directly behind the truck. One driver had been decapitated instantly, his head flying into the seat behind him. The EMTs had found it later, on the floor. In the other car, a passenger had been impaled. The steel pipe had gone through his chest just above his heart, skewering him to the car seat. It had taken over an hour to cut him free, and even then a piece of the pipe protruded from his chest as he was lifted onto the gurney. Five other pieces of pipe had flown over onto the sidewalk, killing three dogs and fatally injuring their owner, who died later at the hospital.

The paper's photo editor had looked at Faye's photographs and then at her.

"Good stuff," he'd said, then added, "for a horror movie. No way we can use these. What were you thinking? Decapitation? Impaling? Dead dogs? Really, Faye? We'll use the first one. The rest you can take home for your scrapbook. And remind me never to look at *that*."

She *had* taken the photographs home and filed them. The paper had gone with her first shot of the truck and the splayed pipe with the windshield behind the truck smashed through, the headless body obscured. But before the other photos had left the paper, the buzz had gone out about them. Everyone on the city desk had made sure they got a look at them. Just as Faye knew they would.

That was why the darker assignments had continued to go to her, because everyone knew she'd photograph anything. Then her editor changed. He thought her photos had a whole other level of potential and he wanted to let her run with her gut and his own voyeurism. "People's right to know, Faye, people's right to know."

That was how she'd been sent to do a series she thought might get turned into a book about children dying in the San Joaquin Valley in central California. A piece had come over the wire about a disease cluster and deaths linked to pesticide poisoning from run-off into the well water in the towns surrounded by the lush, endless fields of cotton, soybeans, strawberries, grapes, almonds, limes, roses, and carnations that spun out in a little hub of perfect produce and collateral damage from Fresno.

"Fresno is a hellhole of a town," her editor had told Faye. "But it's one of those places where a lot happens off the page. Let's get it on the page. There's something there and I know you'll find it."

The story was going to be in the paper's magazine section. Nothing like dead and dying kids when you were having your Sunday breakfast or coming home from church. As she tracked down her sources for the pesticide poisoning exposé, Faye was caught in the endless web of contradiction that was the Central Valley: unremittingly beautiful and gut-wrenchingly grim. It was blazingly sunny every day and by eight a.m. it would be 100 degrees as Faye drove from one small town, Pixley, to another, Wasco, and then onto a series of other small towns. Then she would go over to Bakersfield, then back to Fresno. Eighteen-hour days cataloguing things that would make most people scream and run from the room. In each place Faye went there were dead or dying children, their parents' faces always uncomprehending, unable to cope with the idea that the only work they could get hired to do was killing off their children, slowly and terribly.

Faye had sat in a tiny oven of a house where a shiny little white coffin festooned with gaily colored woven crosses was displayed in the center of the room. Its tiny occupant was a bald and wizened four-year-old girl in a white frilly dress reminiscent of the First Holy Communion dress Faye herself had worn at St. Cecilia's. This girl in the coffin was the third child in her family to die from the cancer that came from the work her parents did in the fields.

When Faye had taken the photographs of the weeping mother and inconsolable father as they sat next to the tiny coffin, the father's arm draped protectively around it, she had remembered being at the grave site after her parents' deaths. Her father's assistant, a trim young woman with fluffy blond hair and big, dark sunglasses, had been standing in the snow with a friend, visibly weeping. But when Faye's parents' coffins—side by side—were being lowered into the frozen ground, the woman had cried out and run to the edge of the big, gaping hole with the green, fake-grass tarps next to it, and had called out Faye's father's name over and over, a white rose in one gloved hand and her arms outstretched, as if she were trying to grab the coffin to her. The friend who was with her had tried to pull her back, murmuring to her to calm down, but the woman had pulled away, slipped on the muddy side of the hole, and fallen onto the coffin. She had gashed her cheek on one of the brass hinges, and blood gushed from the wound and onto Faye's father's coffin as she lurched into the open grave.

A collective gasp had gone up among the mourners and the priest had looked around as if someone else might be able to fix what had gone wrong at the burial and make everything proper and sedate again. He had glanced at Faye, who had been in a kind of shock since her parents had been killed and she had been staying at her grandparents' house, waiting to go back home, not knowing that would never happen.

Faye's grandmother had put her hand over Faye's eyes like a kind of visor—not tight, but just like a shield, as if she were keeping a too-bright sunlight away from her, even though the day was gray, and she had whispered, "Poor girl," and Faye had wondered if her grandmother had meant her or the woman who had been hurt. But before the woman had been lifted out of Faye's father's grave by some of the men at the grave site, blood coursing down her cheek and onto the front of her ivory coat, Faye had seen the look on her grandfather's face as he watched the sad, macabre scene.

It was excitement. He had licked his lips and his eyes had sparkled, but not with tears, like her grandmother's, but a different kind of sparkle. And Faye had been glad her grandmother had covered her eyes. She hadn't wanted to see more.

CHAPTER FIVE
DECOMPOSITION

After Faye had photographed the little girl in her coffin, she took photographs of the boy with no arms or legs, whose mother had tended the roses and carnations in the fields near Wasco until just a few days before her son was born at the hospital in Fresno. The woman had gone mad when she had seen her egg-shaped baby, all round and sweet, but missing so many of his parts. The boy's father had fled back to Mexico, clutching his rosary and the thick cross around his neck, hoping God would forgive him for whatever it was he had done to create a monster even the Chupacabras would be frightened of. The grandmother had told Faye the story while the boy, now five and very lively, rolled around in the dirt and laughed, crawling on his stomach like a lizard in the hot sun and telling Faye funny stories in Spanish while she took his picture. Faye had thought, just briefly, that he could have been one of the things in the jars back at school, floating dreamily in the murky yellow-green fluid in a perpetual limbo state while St. Cecilia's mutilated body watched over him from her alabaster slab.

After Faye had photographed the little lizard boy, she had driven back to Fresno, heading to the morgue to photograph the bodies of children waiting for autopsy. According to the coroner, seven children between the ages of two and eleven lay on trays in the morgue, all allegedly dead from the cancers caused by the pesticides. Their bodies could not be released to the families until the investigation was over. And that could take weeks.

It was late—after nine p.m.—when Faye arrived at the morgue. The coroner had agreed to meet Faye at nine, and as she grabbed her bag and cameras out of the car, she was suddenly aware that it was nearly fully dark and that the parking lot was empty of all but a handful of cars. Faye wasn't one for foreboding, but she didn't want to stay. She didn't like this place, and she hadn't even gone inside.

There was no security at the door and Faye just walked through, following the black signs with arrows sending her in the proper direction. It wasn't a large building and the heat of the day hung in the halls. Faye had been so aware of the heat on this trip. The blazing sun, the lack of shade anywhere due to the omnipresent fields of this or that crop. Fresno was a small city and towns around it were hamlets with nothing but convenience shops and beer outlets and dollar stores here and there. The poverty was like the heat—oppressive and endless, rolling over everything.

The morgue building was the hottest place Faye had been that day. Hotter even than the little house with the corpse in the dining room. As hot as the dusty yard where the boy with no arms or legs had slithered in the dirt. She had hoped for the chill of institutional air-conditioning, but there appeared to be none. She felt like heaving.

The building smelled like most morgues Faye had been in—a heavy layer of formaldehyde covered everything, but underneath you could still smell the semi-sweet acid stink of rotting bodies. She knew that smell.

Decomposition. It had been with her since childhood. Since the mice at the door of her grandparents' basement. Since the basement itself, that one time she had gone down and found all those things, right before she'd been sent off to St. Cecilia's for school.

As Faye got closer to the autopsy room, she began to gag. The rotting smell had overtaken everything. She wasn't sure she could stay. She couldn't imagine how anyone could work here.

The double doors in front of her opened, and a middle-aged man with graying hair and glasses greeted her. Classical music—Brahms, perhaps—played at a moderate volume, though not loudly enough to drown out the sound of the refrigeration unit that banked almost the entire wall across from where Faye and the coroner stood.

The room was that institutional yellow—the color of a faded manila envelope, meant at some point to be cheery, no doubt, but in the glare of the fluorescent lights, with the black squares of night-dark windows set up above the sight-line, it just looked raw and ugly, the color of oozing pus.

The morgue itself was a surprisingly large room, yet still only a third of the size of the morgue in New York, but then there would be fewer bodies here. A scale like you'd see at the produce market hung from the ceiling in the corner next to a blue-cushioned examining table of the sort in doctor's offices. Faye wondered what live person was being examined here. On the white paper sheet sat an open book and a cup of coffee. Perhaps it was for the living after all.

The other wall held an array of sinks and cabinets, and in one there were jars like the ones that had been at St. Cecilia's, only these held organs that she recognized right away. Organs for dissection. Organs to explain what should be inside each body splayed open in the Y-shaped wound that exposed it all. Organs that held nothing but knowledge—no hidden message, like those jars at St. Cecilia's.

The coroner introduced himself and led Faye to the opposite corner where there stood a series of stainless steel tables with sheets covering what lay beneath. Flies buzzed in the room and occasionally sizzled in the blue light of the bug zapper that hung in a far corner. Too far away from the bodies, Faye thought.

It was time to start taking pictures. She started to put down her bag when the coroner grabbed her arm and shook his head violently. "Don't do that!" he exclaimed, grabbing her bag before it touched the floor. Faye looked at him quizzically and he pointed down at the floor. As she looked, the floor, a dull yellow-gray linoleum, appeared to move. Everywhere there were maggots—so many, that Faye wondered how she hadn't heard the squish as she stepped on them, walking through the room. The music and the refrigeration unit had drowned out the sound, but now as she stepped back, involuntarily, she heard it, and it made her feel nauseous.

The coroner led her outside the double doors to a bank of chairs eerily reminiscent of those outside Mother Superior's office. He took her bag and placed it on one of the chairs. He explained that the excessive June heat had caused a worse outbreak than usual of maggots.

"I had to leak the story to the news," he told her. "They're everywhere. They're in the walls, inside the tiles on the ceiling. It's better now, at night, but during the day they drop on us from up there while we're working. They're infesting new bodies, there's so many larvae. It's interfering with autopsies, time of death, that kind of thing. We don't know whose maggots are whose."

We don't know whose maggots are whose. Faye turned to look at him when he said this—so extraordinary a statement—and saw a small white worm inching across the collar of his lab coat. She reached out and flicked it off with her finger without thinking.

"There's probably more inside," he said, his face unsmiling. "I don't even look anymore because I feel them crawling on me all the time, whether they're there or not. Should we go back in? I think you should leave your bag here."

Faye stood, took out the camera she wanted, and zipped the bag closed. She checked it for maggots. Nothing. They went back in through the double doors. She began taking pictures of the floor, then the far wall, which was alive with maggots. She looked up, but couldn't see any on the ceiling. "They tend to withdraw at night," the coroner told her. "I never see them on the ceiling then—just on the floor and the walls."

The coroner led Faye back over to the tables and he drew the sheets back as she took shot after shot of the children. Every small body was crawling with maggots. On the smallest, a girl of twenty-eight months who had died of neuroblastoma, maggots crawled in the incision in her skull and all along the Y-shaped cut in her chest. Faye could tell they were eating the flesh because the areas near the stitching were raw and macerated and pulling away from the thread, showing bits of bone beneath.

A little boy of about five had maggots coming out from under his eyelids and, as Faye photographed him, maggots crawled out of his nostrils. The coroner stifled a sound and Faye turned to look at him. He told her, "It wasn't this bad earlier. They start with the softest flesh, the maggots do. So the eyes and the mucosa go first."

Faye turned back to the tables. The oldest child, an eleven-year-old girl who had died of kidney cancer, was the only one of the children with hair. Maggots crawled along the black ringlets, like some obscene beading. They came in and out from inside her mouth. The coroner moved to pull the sheet down further, but Faye put out a hand to stop him. "We know what's happening down there, I think," she said, somewhat brusquely, and continued to take shot after shot of the children on the remaining tables.

The coroner re-covered each body, then took Faye over to the corner of the room, where a cabinet filled with more jars stood.

"These are the organs of the victims," he told her, as he opened the cabinet. "We had to preserve these to keep the maggots away. We'll need them if there's a lawsuit, and I'm sure there will be. But you can see the effects of the cancers. These are the organs of old people, not children. These are monstrous. It shouldn't be like this here—" and he had waved his arm out toward the tables with the sheets. Faye saw a maggot moving along his belt, under his white lab coat when he raised his arm.

Faye had stopped shooting for a moment when he had said that—*monstrous*—and had looked at him for a second before she resumed photographing the oddly shaped and discolored organs in the jars. *Monstrous.*

When she was finished, Faye thanked him for his time, and for showing her the organs as well as the bodies. She added, as a courtesy, that she hoped an exterminator could kill the maggots.

"You know what we say here," he told her as she was leaving, "the worms crawl in, but they don't crawl out." Faye thought of the childhood rhyme. She couldn't smile, though. She just needed to leave.

She said good-bye and strode to the car. In the bushes next to where she'd parked, she vomited several times. She stomped her feet on the ground to loosen any maggots that might have traveled onto her shoes or the cuff of her pants, then wiped her feet hard on the grass, getting as much of the squashed maggots off as she could. She walked further into the grassy area to a bush and pulled some leaves off, leaf after leaf, tearing them raggedly and holding the torn bits up to her nose to smell them. *Fresh, green, living.* She stifled the urge to put the leaves in her mouth.

She walked back to the car, the smell of macerated leaves pushing out the scent of death.

CHAPTER SIX
THE PRICE OF BEAUTY

As she worked on the story, there were more children—dead and alive—one almost dead. Too many. In the end, Faye put together a disturbing tale told in a montage of photographs about more than twenty sick, maimed, and dead children. She had juxtaposed them with the beautiful flowers, lush fruits, and pristine bolls of cotton that were the other side of the pesticides. She had a jar with maggots in the center, the white worms crawling over the side, moving toward the food and flowers. Perfection always came at a cost, she wrote in her copy. Because there is always collateral damage in any war and this one, the war on bugs and fungi, was killing kids.

Faye had spent nearly six weeks on that story. After it was complete—or as complete as it could be, since it was a story with no ending—Faye had driven up to San Francisco before she flew back to New York. She needed to get away from those lush but deadly fields and from the oppressive heat.

Her editor had told her to take a week, "Get some R and R, you need it after this. A tough one, I know."

But he hadn't known. He'd had no idea.

CHAPTER SEVEN
IN THE DARKROOM

It was night and the house was quiet when Faye left her bed and went downstairs to the darkroom. She had a little flashlight that she kept under her pillow so she could read under the covers after she was supposed to be asleep. She almost never fell asleep without reading. And she often woke from bad dreams, dreams about her parents' accident, dreams in which her grandfather's photographs were moving on the thin clothesline, dreams in which the clothesline itself was drenched in blood and the black fan was on fire and the darkroom filled with smoke the way she imagined her parents' car had done when it crashed, down near the river on New Year's Eve, and then caught fire. Faye would try to scream in the dreams, but no sound would come out.

Faye opened the door and turned on the red light. Photos hung from every part of the clothesline. She knew they were dry because the little fan was going and it had been hours since her grandfather had been in there while she did her homework at the kitchen table and he had done all the work alone, without her, and her grandmother had been down the street, at the church with her friends. It was, she had told Faye, bridge night.

Faye went over to the photos and shined her flashlight on them, one by one. The photos were all black and white—her grandfather hadn't gotten to the color part yet. But as she looked at them, she wasn't sure if or how he would color them.

The first photo was of a woman with half a face. It was what Faye's grandfather called a portrait shot: Just the woman's head and shoulders.

Or part of her head. It wasn't the kind of half-face Faye saw when she looked over her grandfather's shoulder as he brought the magnifying glass up to the still-wet photos, or the bits and pieces she saw when the paper was beginning to become a picture in the tray of developer. In this photo the woman only had half her face. Her forehead and eyes were normal—smooth and with sleek eyebrows and eyes that looked like they might be blue or maybe gray, like Faye's were. The lashes were long. Her hair wasn't light, but wasn't dark, either. Faye thought it was probably light brown or maybe a darker red color.

The rest of her face wasn't a face anymore. There was a big hole where her nose should have been and then her teeth were half there and half missing, like when you saw a skeleton in a book. Around where her mouth should have been was a lot of muscle-y flesh. It looked raw and open, like it had just been sliced, like meat. It looked like the lambs' heads that hung in the Italian Market at Easter when they went down to get the roast. If the photo hadn't been black and white, it would have been red like that meat, Faye was sure, but there was no blood, just the raw, wounded, cut-open parts.

The next photo was the same woman, but this time her eyes were closed and Faye could see that there were cuts over her eyes on the eyelids and there were streaks there, like blood, and the one socket looked hollow underneath, like her eyes had come out, too, like the bottom of her face was gone. The other eye socket looked squishy somehow, like the eye had been rubbed out and little bits of it had pushed out and been left on the eyelashes, which looked thick and matted on that side.

The photograph after that was different—the eyes were also closed and flat and in this one both had been squeezed out and there were more pieces littering the eyelashes. The flesh of the face was all there in this one, but the mouth was open, wide, like the woman had been singing, or maybe screaming. And the tongue was out, but in pieces, like a snake tongue—cut down the middle so that it went in two different directions.

The next few photos were of different women, all with their eyes closed and all with cuts on their faces and pieces taken off—a nose, lips, a piece of cheek. One had slices all up and down the face with chunks of flesh taken out, kind of like bread from a loaf. All the faces looked raw and meaty, like the first woman, but there wasn't blood running in the photos. It just all looked dark, like when Faye would open the white pots of paint and it looked like thick blood in the pot.

Faye didn't know why these faces were like this, and they scared her, but she couldn't stop looking at them.

The last six photos were of more women. The first one had her eyes open and her mouth was open, too, like she was surprised. She was standing outside somewhere—on a street, but not really near anything. There weren't any stores around, just a big long brick wall with writing on it that didn't say anything and then the sidewalk and it looked like it was night, but it was really bright where she was standing.

The woman was wearing a really tight dress and had her hair up on her head and she had big white earrings on and really high heels and a little funny short jacket. She looked frightened and she was half-turned, like she was going to run away.

In the next photo, it was the same woman, but in this one she was against the brick wall and she looked like she was crying. She had her hand up to her face the way people in movies sometimes do, with the back of her hand against her mouth and her palm out toward the camera, like the way women scream sometimes. This picture was more of a head shot, but you could see down to her breasts. In this picture you could see her dress was torn a little in the front and one of her earrings was gone, and her ear looked bloody where the earring should have been. It looked like it had a little rip in it, like the skin was torn.

In the next photo, the woman had a big cut on her face, like some of the other women, and her one eye was closed and looked darker than the other one. She wasn't on the street anymore, but was in a room somewhere, and she was sitting on a small bed. She was still wearing the short dress, but there was a rope tied around her ankles and her hands were in her lap and she had rope around her wrists. She was sitting really still and her mouth was closed because there was something tied over it and there was also a big cut on the front of her dress where her left breast was. It was dark in the spot there—her dress was a light color—and it was flat, not like the other side. There was something round and dark on the bed next to her. It looked like it might be her breast, just there on the bed, instead of on her chest.

Now the photographs really scared Faye and she wanted to stop looking at them. They were like pictures out of a scary movie and she wasn't usually allowed to watch those, because she had the bad dreams and her grandmother said they reminded her of *the trauma*, but she wasn't exactly sure what *the trauma* was, just that it had something to do with her parents dying and her coming to live with her grandparents in the little house with the darkroom and the sign out front about the photographs.

Faye didn't want to see the other pictures, and she thought she should go back upstairs to bed, but now it was like she was reading a story and she wanted to know how it ended. But after she had looked at all of them, after she saw everything that was there, and all the bits and pieces and all the dark spots and all the things that were lined up on the bed like when you fold the laundry and put it away in your drawers only this wasn't anything like laundry, Faye wished she hadn't looked. She felt funny—scared and sick and like she might throw up. She went to the door and turned out the red light. She closed the door behind her and turned off her little flashlight. She went into the kitchen in the dark and got a glass of water. She drank all of it and it sloshed around in her stomach and she thought she was going to throw up. She stood over the sink and made a little choking sound, but she didn't vomit.

When she turned to go back upstairs to bed, she saw her grandfather standing in the doorway, in the dark. She stopped and stood still and waited.

"It feels that way at first," he said, his voice soft and low, because it was night and dark and Faye's grandmother was sleeping. "Sickening. But then it feels different. So different. And when you sit here"—and he pointed to the kitchen table—"when you start the painting, it seems good. It seems really good. And you feel proud of the work you are doing. Because it is, you know, art. And art is always beautiful and important, no matter what the subject. No matter—" He stopped speaking for a moment and stared at her, then he said, "One day you'll understand, even if you don't right now."

Faye didn't speak, didn't say anything. She never asked about the photographs or what they meant or why the women had lost their faces or their eyes or their breasts or why one had been cut open on the little bed and everything inside her had been taken out and laid around her like—like something Faye couldn't quite describe.

Faye just stood there, looking at her grandfather standing in the doorway. She wondered if her father had known about the photographs. She wondered if her grandmother knew. She wondered if someone else should know about them. Someone other than her.

And then her grandfather had stretched out his hand to Faye and she had walked toward him and they had gone upstairs together, each to their own rooms. Faye had lain in her bed and thought about the pictures for a long time, especially the ones where the pieces were on the bed, laid out around the body, and the way the woman's legs were spread apart and the thing that had been between them. She thought about what the pieces were and what it meant that they were there, on the bed. She still felt sick, but not as sick as before. She thought about what her grandfather had said and how she didn't understand what it meant. Then she rolled over on her side and she had gone to sleep.

CHAPTER EIGHT
CHINATOWN

Faye had taken that week's vacation her editor had offered, staying in San Francisco the whole time. She'd settled into a boutique hotel on Post Street where she was near enough to everything that she could walk, take a cable car, or, if she absolutely had to, drive. She'd driven up from Fresno on a Friday and taken a long nap before ending up in the Castro after eleven, drinking gin martinis because she'd never liked vodka all that much and she really liked gin, and waiting for this one or that one to sidle up to her as they always did. Faye liked women, liked them a lot, and they liked her even more. They liked what they thought she was—they liked what she had learned to project since her days at St. Cecilia's, since her days in the darkroom, since…

Calm. She'd patterned herself after the saints she'd read about in those early years. Not the acts so much as the demeanor. Faye was always unfazed. In the clubs, Faye was always just sitting on the bar stool, looking, watching, seeing. She didn't need to be eager. Not being eager drew people to her.

The ones who liked her most were the tough ones, the ones who wanted to pin someone pretty to the wall or the bed—white, black, Latina, and Asian butches with shaved heads or fauxhawks, with body art and piercings everywhere that mattered. In San Francisco, Faye had spent her first three nights in three different beds, but hadn't found what she was looking for. She had walked through the Mission District and Pacific Palisades and back. She'd gone from bar to bar, beginning and ending at the Lex, beginning and ending with the same kind of women.

On the fourth night, Faye had stayed away from the Castro and the Mission and had worked her way from her hotel toward Chinatown. She'd had a fruity, too-sweet drink with the clichéd umbrella and pineapple and cherry skewer in it at the tiki bar off Union Square with the Asian hostess. The place was a combination overpriced tourist trap and mob hangout. When Faye had walked from her hotel to the bar, she was pretty sure she was looking for more things to photograph, or some kind of trouble, she just wasn't sure which. Time felt like it was standing still for her since she'd left the dead and dying children behind in the San Joaquin Valley, with the bougainvillea landscaping along the highways between one pretty little coffin and another.

Maybe she just needed to get back to New York.

She'd walked down Market Street late the night before, after two, closer to three, after she'd exited the bed of the scrappy little Latina butch she'd left the Lex with around eleven. She'd gone to the Tendernob, the most crime-ridden place she could find in San Francisco, because it wasn't New York and there wasn't enough danger for her—or at least she hadn't been to the city enough times to know exactly where to look for it, although everyone said the same thing:

Stay away from the Tenderloin, stay away from the Tendernob. And so she had taken her camera down Market, over to Sixth, then back to Little Saigon, but there was nothing to see—homeless men, addicts, transgender prostitutes looking for dates or just money, a man who said he was a priest trying to talk people off the streets and into shelters. She watched an older Chinese woman trying to catch one of the night pigeons that were always down there whenever Faye had been in San Francisco, but she hadn't caught it and both she and the woman gave up that game.

Faye had walked around for a few hours, until it was getting light. This was the place, the Tenderloin, now working its way into gentrification like everywhere else, that Dashiell Hammett had written about in *The Maltese Falcon*. How could it be less dangerous now than it was then? Or had Faye become inured to danger because after her parents' deaths, her grandparents' house, and St. Cecilia's, everything else had seemed so close to normal, even children burned to death in a Christmas pageant or children poisoned in their mother's wombs?

Faye had left and gone back to her hotel to sleep, the only

photographs from her sojourn those of a petite Asian prostitute with a knife strapped to her thigh, the Chinese woman chasing the pigeon, and in the dark recess of an open doorway, the man dressed like a priest getting a blow job from a Latina trans woman.

❖

Faye and the Asian hostess, Shihong, had sat talking and then left the tiki bar together and headed to Chinatown. Faye had always liked it there—had liked the smells and the guttural sounds of languages that weren't English or Spanish. It was big and strange and seemed more like Hong Kong than San Francisco. It wasn't like New York's Chinatown—it was its own city, the biggest Chinatown in North America, the most foreign place Faye could find stateside. The rolling night fog, the closeness of the water, the hilly streets—all added something, an aura, an atmosphere, Faye couldn't quite place, but she liked being there. She liked feeling completely anonymous.

Shihong had led her through the maze of alley-like streets off Grant Avenue, after they had walked through the Dragon Gate. Shihong had pulled her into a darkened doorway and kissed her, hard, and Faye had felt the sleekness of the satin dress she wore as she ran her hands down Shihong's body. Then Shihong had taken Faye to a place where she had ended up buying several animal netsukes, a dark little shop where no one spoke English and where she was the only customer. She had wondered briefly if it was a front for something else.

Afterward they had stopped for more drinks and Shihong had told Faye about Chinatown, *her* Chinatown, the Chinatown she'd come to as a young child, with her grandparents, after something terrible had happened to her mother back in China. But it had been a passage through darkness. A passage she only knew bits and pieces of. "My story," Shihong said, "tattered. Shredded. You know—not a whole thing. Lots missing. Here"—she had waved a somewhat dismissive hand toward the street—"same story, repeat, repeat, repeat."

As Shihong described Chinatown, Faye thought it sounded a little like St. Cecilia's. Insular, self-protective, wary of outsiders.

"No *Joy Luck Club*," Shihong had continued, her soft voice surprisingly rough, reminding Faye of her friend Rosario back at St.

Cecilia's one night when they had talked about the place they'd both spent their whole lives. It had been a night of revelations. This was another. Faye sat and listened. She wanted to know more about this woman, about her story.

"No PG movie," Shihong said. "Look around you—no money, many secrets, lots of darkness. So much, I could never leave. The secrets become you, don't they?"

Shihong had looked straight at Faye and stretched out her hand and Faye had taken it, wanted to kiss it. She stroked the palm lightly with her fingers. Shihong tightened her fingers around Faye's, made a little pumping gesture, intensely sexual. Faye looked at her, Shihong slid her leg between Faye's under the tiny table. The feeling was more intense than the sex Faye had had the past few nights.

The secrets become you. Faye decided to tell Shihong a story about secrets, a story she had only told one other time, to Sister Anne Marie. Shihong listened, without moving, except to sip from her drink. But she held on to Faye's hand and when Faye finished telling the story, Shihong had looked at her, stared with an expression Faye, who was so good at reading other people's faces, who photographed those faces every day, couldn't quite discern. Then Shihong told Faye about a black market shop she thought Faye might want to see, "a shop that sells secrets," she said, "a shop not"—she had briefly turned away from Faye—"for everyone. There are two Chinatowns, you know. One for tourists, one for us. I take you to the one for us."

They had left the bar, wending their way through the fog and a series of alleyways. Along the way Shihong would stop and pull Faye into a doorway here, an alcove there, and kiss her, hard. The kisses were hot and violent and Faye's mouth felt bruised from the force of them. But she didn't pull away. There was a kind of heat emanating from Shihong that Faye didn't quite understand, but she wanted to see where it went. Even if it took her to a place she didn't know.

The two women kept walking, Shihong slightly ahead, her hand in Faye's, almost as if she were pulling her along, until they reached a small shop on a tiny street, the name of which Faye had not seen—the streetlight over the sign was out. The name of the shop was written in Chinese characters—no English translation. Shihong had rung a bell and an elderly woman in traditional silk pajamas had answered the

door. She and Shihong had spoken in whatever dialect they spoke—
Faye had no idea, some kind of Cantonese, she assumed. She knew
nothing about Chinese, other than there were endless dialects.

Faye also could not discern the tenor of the conversation—was
it friendly or rancorous? Shihong had lowered her voice while the old
woman had raised hers. Faye had thought for a moment that she should
leave right then—run, in fact, since the door was still open and she was
fairly sure she could find her way back to Grant Street and out of here.
The Castro was one thing. She had felt equal to the women she had
bedded in the past few days. The Tenderloin had been the same—she
spoke that language, always had. But here—here she was in a foreign
country and one where she stood out; she was nothing like anyone,
here, especially not here in the old part of Chinatown where some
things clearly had not changed in the hundred and sixty-odd years since
this place had been established.

Faye edged back toward the door. It was definitely time to go. She
needed to be back in New York. This was not the place for her. She was
used to intense situations, but she couldn't read this. She wasn't sure
she wanted to.

But just as Faye half turned to leave, the old woman reached into
the folds of her trousers and pulled out a key, pressing it into Shihong's
hand and folding the fingers over it. She then turned toward Faye,
bowed quickly, and shuffled away. Faye had been disarmed by the
bow, chiding herself for being nervous. This was an old woman, not a
threat. She remembered the feeling of dread she'd had at the morgue
in Fresno. And in the end that had just been heat and maggots. Nothing
dangerous. Nothing irreparable. Just an unpleasantness. Plus, she and
Shihong had had that chemistry over drinks and those kisses—that was
real, not fake.

Faye looked at the woman as she disappeared up a staircase to the
side of the shop's interior and wondered for a moment whether her feet
were bound—it had only been a little over fifty years since that barbaric
practice had ended. Faye wished she'd paid closer attention. She knew
that was a photograph she would like to have, although she wasn't sure
she could have asked for it.

Shihong shut the door behind them and locked it with the key in
her hand. She took Faye's hand and Faye shook off her momentary

fear as Shihong pulled her forward into the dark recesses of the shop. A dim amber light glowed beyond the doorway as they walked through a room made narrow by high stacks of shelves on one side of the pathway they were walking. On the other side were glass cases, like in a jewelry shop. Faye couldn't really see anything in the dim light. Everything was dark—the wood of the shelves, the things on the shelves. The lights in the glass cases were off. She couldn't discern where she was or what was there. Shihong stopped suddenly and turned toward her.

"You saw her," she told Faye, referring to the elderly woman. "Now you see why I cannot leave this place. This will always be my home."

Faye nodded, but wasn't sure what Shihong meant. Was this woman related to Shihong? What *was* this place, exactly? Did Shihong live here? Faye flashed for a moment on the classic Roman Polanski film and wondered if perhaps she had stepped too far into the wrong story by coming here, to Chinatown, with this woman she'd known for barely three hours who had picked her up at a mob bar and had now locked her into a shop with no English name, a shop that held God-only-knew what.

Shihong reached up above the two of them and switched on a small light. It illumined the shelves directly in front of them. On the shelves were rows of jars. For years Faye had never seen anything like that room at St. Cecilia's. Now, in the space of a few days, she'd been treated to the anomalous organs in the Fresno morgue and whatever this was. Just as at St. Cecilia's, these jars were above Faye's head, not at eye level. The fact that she could not see them made her anxious suddenly, and she thought again that she should leave. She looked at Shihong, questioningly. The woman tossed her head back, her black hair whipping behind her, her long earrings making a light tinkling sound as she did so.

"You said you like to uncover secrets," Shihong said in a tone Faye could not decipher. "Here are secrets. Secrets from the other Chinatown. My Chinatown. What do you think now?"

Faye had stepped back, away from the shelves, and looked up. She stared at what was arrayed all along the shelves. Faye, who was never fazed, had gasped, her hand flying up to her mouth, stifling the scream that threatened to escape. She turned toward Shihong, but she was no longer there.

❖

Faye had left the unnamed place many hours later, her left wrist sliced raw and open with a rope burn and bruises and dried blood. Her bag was heavy and full as she heaved it over her shoulder. In her right hand she gripped the netsukes and her jacket, both smeared with what looked like blood and something else—maybe little bits of flesh. She remembered what Shihong had told her when Faye had asked what her name meant in Chinese.

"The whole world is red," Shihong had told her.

❖

When Faye got back to the hotel, she changed her reservation and packed. She stopped at the post office on her way to the airport and mailed a large package. Then she flew home to New York.

CHAPTER NINE
THE SECRETS BECOME YOU

After the first time, Faye would creep downstairs to the darkroom in the middle of the night when she was certain even her grandfather could not hear her. She had begun to wait for the nights when she had seen him take the little pill from the bottle in the kitchen on the shelf over the sink. She had learned to make the trip without her flashlight, so that even that weak whisper of light wouldn't disturb her grandparents—although it was her grandfather she didn't want to wake.

She would go into the darkroom and close the door before she turned on the red light. The photographs were always the same: Women. Several at a time. The progression of the pictures was always the same—wounds to the face, smashing of the eyes, torn pieces from the lips, nose, cheeks, ears. There was always one with the frightened look who ended up tied on the bed in the room Faye didn't recognize. But each new time she came down to look, now, there were more pieces on the bed. And this time, there was something new.

It was the ninth photograph on the line. Faye wasn't sure why she always counted the photographs, but she did. The ninth photograph had a woman in a chair at a table. She was wearing a dress and the skirt was pulled all the way up, to where her underwear should be. She had something over her eyes and something over her mouth and the thing over her mouth had a big dark spot on it. Her head was down, like she had fallen asleep at the table.

She was tied to the chair at the ankles and her legs were open the way Faye's grandmother told her never to sit. Where her underwear should be was a dark spot and that spot was on her dress right there, too. On the table was a plate and a fork and knife and a glass with something dark in it. The plate had something on it, too, but Faye wasn't sure what it was.

All the other pictures were of plates on the table and each one had something else on it, something Faye had never seen before. It all looked like meat, but not meat they ever ate here. The last photograph was back at the little room with the bed. The woman who had been sitting at the table was lying on the bed and her dress was ripped and there were pieces taken out of it all over. On the bed next to her were the plates, all of them with the things on them that looked like meat, but Faye wasn't sure.

She stared at the photos for a long time, going back and forth and looking at all of the things on the plates. Then she knew what it was she was looking at: the things on the plates were the things that were inside her operation doll. They were the organs—the heart, the liver, the kidneys, the intestines, some other things she didn't think were inside the body in the operation doll.

Faye looked at the photographs again. Then she turned off the light and shut the door. She went into the kitchen and sat down at the table. The light from the back porch was on and a small shaft of it came through the window onto the table, onto her pajama legs as she sat in the chair and thought about what she had just seen.

She got up to go back to her bedroom. When she got to the door of the kitchen she turned and looked at the table and chair again. It was the same as the one in the photographs. Suddenly, Faye felt really hot and her heart started to pound fast, like when she was scared. Then everything went dark as she fell to the floor.

CHAPTER TEN
ESPERANZA

Another Christmas, three years after the arson fire and six months after Faye had taken the photographs of the children in the Central Valley, a young woman, distraught over a bad breakup and too upset to head home for the holiday, had thrown herself from the subway platform in front of the train. She'd been sliced nearly in half, yet remained alive beneath the train. Faye had been only a few blocks away, still at the newspaper, and gotten the call from the city desk to go down and see if she could get some shots. The city desk editor was always looking for the story that no one else had, and he and Faye got along really well because those were the stories she wanted, too. He always saw Pulitzer on everything and he'd say to her, "This has Pulitzer written all over it, if you've got the 'nads. Whaddaya think? Can ya do it?"

He liked talking like that, like it was 1940 and she was Weegee being sent down to take flashbulb shots of dead gangsters lying in the street in the meat-packing district with the kind of equipment her grandfather had once used, instead of the small Nikon with the SIM card that was even more like magic than everything that had been in her grandfather's studio when she was growing up.

So Faye had gone. In fact, because it was two days before Christmas and a Friday night, she'd been the only one around for the shots. The EMTs and firefighters who were cutting away at the train car above the woman wouldn't let the TV crews down—too much equipment, too dangerous. But Faye, lean and lithe and agile enough to leap down onto the tracks without getting in anyone's way, had been there with her little camera. She'd crawled down to chronicle what the woman thought—prayed—would be her final moments as rescuers worked above to free her. Faye had talked to her the whole time, talked while the whine of the torch and the crunch of the shears had cut and cut and cut around her and the woman, whose name was, in an irony too bald for Faye, Esperanza, told her the story of why she jumped in front of the train and how much she wanted to die.

Faye had photographed the aftermath, too. She couldn't catalogue the sucking sound as what was left of the young woman was pulled off the tracks, or the smell of charred flesh and other offal that rose up off the place where the woman had been under the train, but Faye took shot after shot as the EMTs got Esperanza onto the backboard and strapped tourniquets and put pressure bandages on her, hung the IV that they hoped—or maybe didn't—would keep her alive, and pushed morphine into the drip.

Faye just kept shooting—the IV bag streaked with blood, the blue and yellow vial of morphine, the silver-foil warming blanket to try to prevent the shock that had set in an hour before, the expressions of fear, pain, and something else Faye couldn't name on the face of Esperanza and the faces of the EMTs.

As Esperanza had been lifted up onto the platform, Faye had kept on shooting—photographing the EMT whose job it was to collect the body parts left behind in the hope—*esperanza*, Faye thought—that something might be re-attached if the woman made it into surgery before she died. An arm sheared off at the shoulder, a leg in two pieces, a slab of flesh with shredded muscle and mangled bone, something else red and pulpy that Faye couldn't identify. All of these went into plastic bags and coolers filled with cold packs, then were handed back up onto the platform, like this was some creepy Christmas tailgate party, and all the while, Faye kept shooting photo after photo.

The woman hadn't died. Esperanza had lived, missing an arm, a leg, part of her shoulder, several ribs, and a section of pelvis on the side where she'd been sliced apart by the train. The excisions had left her with just a sheer covering of skin over that half of her body, so that some of her organs—a lung, a kidney—could almost be seen through the bluish-pink layering of muscle and flesh that resembled uncooked chicken. The woman's hideous deformity remained a constant reminder of her momentary misery and sudden desire for the obliterating death that never came after all.

Grateful that Faye had been down there on the tracks with her, Esperanza had allowed Faye full access to her recovery, and the photo essay, *A Cry from the Tunnel: Woman on the Tracks*, had become a coffee-table book that one critic called "art of the creepiest, most intrusive, most voyeuristic, most repugnant sort. Even Nan Goldin or Diane Arbus wouldn't touch this stuff. We really don't need to see everything, just because it's there," he had written. Faye had smiled a grim smile when she had read that, telling her assistant, Sonja, who had brought the review to her with trepidation, "But that's the whole point—no one wants to touch it. Yet the organs are still going to be pulsing just below the skin, aren't they, whether we want to see them or not? This is what happens when we leave people to die and they don't die. Why can't we tell their stories? Where's the empathy for *their suffering*? Just because we don't want to see it doesn't mean it shouldn't be seen."

Other reviews had been laudatory, but had more than hinted at the dark side of Faye's artistry and one had gone so far as to mention Faye's parents' deaths as a possible foundation for what the critic had called Faye's "addictive and addicting response to the grisly and profane."

There had been a book signing downtown, which was well-attended, and Esperanza had been there in her wheelchair, with a cousin and some guy she had met in rehab. There had been a big party after at Locande Verde, in the Greenwich Village Hotel, that had packed the restaurant, but Esperanza had left after the signing and Faye hadn't tried to stop her. Faye and Esperanza both knew she should have died. Faye wasn't sure how long it would be before Esperanza tried to kill herself again. Faye only hoped this time she would be successful if it was what she really wanted.

After the party, there had been the inevitable—some had gone home and others had wanted to keep partying. Faye had taken a cadre off to dance at Henrietta Hudson because even the boys were welcome there, although she never went for the boys, just the tough girls.

The night at the club had gone late and Faye had wanted to see the river when she left, not quite drunk, but barely sober, after some quick and unexpected finger-fucking sex in the bathroom with an assiduous publicist from a rival publisher. She'd taken a cab to the meat-packing district. Faye didn't live down there anymore, but when she had, on Horatio Street, she had woken up nightly when the trucks had rolled in and some nights she'd gone to the window and stood, just to watch the big hunks of flesh and bone travel from one place to another, bodies of animals hanging from big racks, just like clothing in the garment district.

This night Faye got out of the cab near her old apartment and just walked. She wasn't sure what she wanted to see—the river or the meat—but she wanted to see something that wasn't there at the book signing or the party or the club. The meat-packing district was all trendy now, with the High Line and the Hotel Gansevoort and the old slaughterhouses turned into lofts. There were only eight or nine meat-packers left and none of the edgiest S&M bars that used to be there, like the Mineshaft. And yet she still wanted to go, still wanted to think about what it had been like when she did live there, before gentrification took over. It hadn't been that long—not even ten years.

She pulled her camera out of her bag and walked away from the river and toward where the trucks would be unloading the meat. It was almost four a.m. and she was looking for flesh—dead flesh, cut slabs of flesh, chunky, meaty flesh, and the commingling smell of blood. And something else Faye couldn't quite name. Maybe, if she kept looking, she would find it.

CHAPTER ELEVEN
MEAT

Faye's grandmother had found her on the floor that night, awakened by the sound of her small body falling, catching the side of a chair as she went down. She had lifted Faye up off the floor and as Faye came to, had asked her what had happened. Faye just stared at her, but said nothing. She knew she should tell, but what was there to tell, really? She sat in her grandmother's lap on one of the chairs where the woman had sat. Which one was it? Which one had she been tied to? Which one had her organs on the plate in front of her? And how could she live without her organs? Faye's operation doll was empty when the organs were out on the floor when she played with it in her room. Was the woman empty, too?

Faye couldn't think about any more of it. She wished she hadn't looked at the pictures because now that was all she could see—the pictures and the table, the chair and the woman, the plates and the organs. Were they the same plates that her grandmother put down at breakfast and dinner? Was the meat they were eating the organs from the woman?

Faye felt hot again, and sweaty. Her face was burning hot, like she was in the sun. She wanted to go to sleep. She wanted to forget about the pictures. Her eyes started to burn and she felt tears coming down her face.

Her grandmother felt her forehead and whispered, "Oh, you're burning up. No wonder you fainted. Let's get you to bed."

She had carried Faye upstairs herself, then, not waking her

grandfather to come and get her. Her grandmother had laid her on the bed, on top of the covers, and gotten clean pajamas and told her to put them on. She had left the room and come back with a washcloth. She wiped Faye's face and the cloth felt cool and now Faye was sleepy and not thinking about the pictures anymore. Her grandmother got her into the bed and covered her up, still wiping her face with the washcloth.

"Are you feeling better, dear? I know this is all very hard on you. I'm not surprised you're sick. Things will be better when you go off to school. It will be new and strange at first, but it will be good for you, you'll see. How do you feel now?"

Her grandmother had looked at Faye, her face full of concern and caring. Even in the dim night-light, Faye could tell she was worried.

"I think it was the meat," Faye said. "I think the meat from dinner made me sick. I don't want to eat it anymore. Please don't make me." And Faye's eyes had filled with tears and her grandmother had stroked her hair.

"Well, we'll have to find something else to feed you, then, dear, won't we? But for now, no more meat until you are better, okay?"

Faye had slid down under the covers and put her head on her grandmother's lap.

"Thank you," was all she said, and then she fell asleep.

CHAPTER TWELVE
JUST SO MUCH KILLING

After Esperanza and the book and the controversy, Faye had more cachet at the paper. She went into the editorial meeting a week after the book party and asked if she could do something really different. Faye wanted to do a two-part series on women in Congo and Afghanistan.

"These wars are endless," she had said. "And the women are the primary victims. Our readers know about these places—think of all the African immigrants here in New York," she had argued. "And we're still in Afghanistan. Even if we leave, nothing will have changed there for women. It will still be the most hellish place on Earth after the DRC. Give me three weeks. I'll get you something no one else has. Hell, I may do the stuff in Afghanistan in a burka, so that people will know what it's like to live life seeing everything through a tiny mesh screen."

Faye had detailed the stories of gang rapes and acid burnings. She pulled up the page of facts from her iPad that she'd compiled with the help of a woman she knew at an NGO and read off the string of ritualistic mayhem: 15,000 rapes a month in Democratic Republic of Congo. Hundreds of acid burnings and mutilations in Afghanistan. Women raped and eviscerated on their way to get water in the bush. Women raped and then stoned to death. Women flayed alive. Child brides dying on their wedding nights because they were under thirteen and the men were adults—their bodies torn, their cervixes and uteruses and rectums punctured, bleeding to death before they ever got to the hospital. Women tortured with unspeakable brutality and no one paying attention. No UN sanctions. No invasions. Nothing.

Just so much killing.

Faye had relayed the stats slowly, emphasizing the horrific details. *As if they needed emphasis*, she had thought. *As if words like* acid *and* mutilate *weren't explicit enough.*

"You understand," Faye told her colleagues, leaning forward and looking at each of them, "these are going to be photographs no one else has, stories no one else has. But it's going to be ghastly and hideous and no one in this room is going to want to look at these photographs, let alone our readers. But we have to make them. We have to make them."

Faye had felt every bit of the passion in her voice. She looked around the table. There were eleven people there, including her, nine of them men. These were people she respected, but she was afraid to discover just how far their liberalism extended—if it went as far as concern for nameless, faceless women in the developing world.

When Faye had finished detailing all the ways a woman could be mutilated in the service of war, she knew the assignment was hers. Not for the right reasons, of course, but hers, nevertheless. She could practically see the word light up on everyone's forehead: *Pulitzer.* It was a done deal. She had hoped it would be.

She'd had to choose, though: Afghanistan or Congo, it could not be both. She'd chosen the DRC because so little had been written about it, and the photos were even fewer. Faye knew in the global village of social media, photos were everything in winning a war of conscience. She wanted to jump-start that however she could for the women and girls of DRC.

Faye had hoped if her work on the DRC was a success, she could come back and ask for Afghanistan again. She already had an idea for a story here, in New York, while she prepared to go to the DRC. When she pitched that, her editor said, "Seems like a lot, back-to-back, Faye. But if you can get the permission of the girl and the family, then okay," and she had pursued it. Faye was sure she could do the story before she left for the DRC and just as sure that it would resonate in her absence, leaving a taste for more while she was traveling through the Congo.

The Afghan girl had been thirteen when she was married to a man who was thirty-four. *Sold.* By her father. To pay off a debt. Lila, a friend of Faye's who was a social worker liaison for a domestic violence agency that dealt specifically with immigrant women in the boroughs, had told Faye about the young woman's case.

"Americans know nothing about child marriage and what it does to these girls," Lila had said, pleading with Faye to do the story. "You know what happened to me, what's happened to other women here in the city. They've been sold. Not just in their own countries, but to men here. Western men buy these girls, bring them here, and then all kinds of things can happen to them. But this girl—it happened to her in Afghanistan. She's just lucky someone saw her, took an interest. How many never get seen, never get help? So many of these girls, they just become easy prey. Poverty is a great motivator for evil."

When Faye had been forced to choose between Afghanistan and Congo, she'd thought a photo essay of the young Afghan woman would at least be an alert, would at least highlight what was happening in Afghanistan—that there was much more than the war. As Lila had said, "American taxpayers are pouring money into these countries where this kind of brutality is commonplace. *Commonplace.* Faye, please—this girl, she's been through so much, you can't imagine."

Lila had taken Faye to meet the young woman, her host family, and her doctors. It was a grim story and not for the first time Faye had wondered how long she could keep doing this. How much was penance for her past, how much was commitment to the victims, how much was her own flirtation with danger and darkness? Each new story she covered peeled away a layer of her own story. Each new story made her just a little more raw, closer to that look of Esperanza's side, with the bluish skin barely covering the organs that were meant to be hidden and protected.

Maybe, Faye thought, *some things weren't meant to be seen.* Maybe there was a reason the jars were kept on the uppermost shelves.

Lila had given her the numbers to go with the pictures. More than sixty percent of Afghan girls were married by the time they were sixteen, many of them sold to pay off family debt. There had been a law passed in 2009, the Elimination of Violence Against Women, but it had never been implemented. It covered rape, domestic violence, and child marriage, but as Lila explained, "Nobody cares whether a girl is fifteen or eighteen. They want her gone. She's a drain on the family resources. And more often than not, daughters get sold. Sold, Faye, *sold.* That's what happened with this girl. And when he didn't like what he bought, he cut her up like a paper doll and threw her away, making sure no one else would want her."

Faye had read over the stats and had gotten angry, remembering what it was like to be that young, how she could barely leave St. Cecilia's, let alone be ready for marriage. Lila had explained that the Afghan parliament not only ignored the EVAW, but in 2013 had passed a law that outright prevented girls from testifying against forced marriages, against being sold by their families. There was no place for them to turn. Even students at Kabul University had protested the EVAW as recently as this year. It was "un-Islamic," according to the students.

But what about these girls being married off, probably before some of them had even had their first period? The more Lila told Faye, the more Faye wanted to meet Asifa, the young woman having her face and body reconstructed after her husband had hacked at her with a shearing knife. She'd been brought to the United States to receive medical treatment a few months earlier by an NGO that cared for victims of catastrophic injury from Afghanistan. Most of the people they had brought were women and girls, victims of acid burnings and mutilations.

Asifa was seventeen, now. She'd had five surgeries in eight months, including a procedure where her new ears—her husband had cut hers off—had been grown under the skin of her thighs, like some crazy science fiction experiment. There would be another six or seven surgeries over the next eighteen months. Asifa's foster family had petitioned for asylum for her to stay in the country on humanitarian grounds.

Asifa was learning English, but her sponsor, Mashal, was there to translate for Faye. Lila told Faye Asifa wanted her story told and that she was no longer ashamed of how she looked.

"Of course, the shame does not rest with her, does it?" Lila had said, angrily. Lila herself had been sold at sixteen by her stepfather into the bride market, like many other pretty teenagers from the Eastern Bloc nations. When her American husband tired of her, he'd abandoned her. With little English and fewer skills, she'd ended up a prostitute in Brooklyn, barely eighteen, until she'd been rescued by another woman she'd later become lovers with. That had been almost twenty years ago, but Lila still bore the scars, even though, unlike the young woman they were going to see, hers weren't visible.

Lila was driven. She made Faye feel driven. Faye knew Asifa's story was so different from Esperanza's. Asifa believed she had another chance, another opportunity, that her life had started over as soon as she had landed in the United States, as soon as the doctors had looked at her mutilated face and told her they could build her a new one.

Faye wasn't sure what she had expected. What she *hadn't* expected was to see a young woman straight out of one of her grandfather's photographs. What would have been a pretty, even beautiful face was disfigured by a missing nose and diagonal cuts along her upper lip. Her ears had also been cut off, but these had already been reconstructed and replaced. Faye was impressed by how they looked, there was just the still-red scar where they had been attached to indicate something had been wrong. She was even wearing earrings. "One of the nurses made them for me. They clip on, see?" She had taken off one of the delicate gold earrings and handed it to Faye.

Yet for all this semblance of normalcy, as Faye looked at Asifa, she couldn't help but wonder, if this was Asifa *after* surgery, what had her face looked like before? Part of her wanted to leave. This was taking her to a place she wasn't sure she could go. *What made some men fixated on cutting up women?*

Lila must have sensed her discomfort. She reached out a hand to take the earring, an excuse to touch Faye's hand lightly, a whisper of reassurance without speaking, without unsettling the delicate balance in the room. Asifa was telling them she would never be able to have pierced ears again, but that she didn't want them. "I am not wanting any more cutting," she said, and looked away for a moment.

They had spent three afternoons together, Faye, Mashal, Lila, and Asifa. The first afternoon they had just talked and Asifa had told Faye her story over a strong tea sipped through sugar cubes and translated by Mashal. The next two afternoons Faye had taken the photographs, first with Asifa's veil across her face, highlighting her beautiful eyes and the wave of brown-black hair that crept out from beneath it. The final afternoon, the veil had come off.

And yet despite the disfigurement, Asifa's warmth and generosity shone through in Faye's photos. She laughed a lot, a light, tinkling sound that was clear and childlike and utterly devoid of sadness, and Faye had photographed her laughing, as well as looking near tears. By the third day, Asifa was telling Faye and Lila stories from her childhood. Faye was desperate to somehow capture that contrast between her mutilated face and her buoyant, girlish affect.

This story wasn't an exercise in voyeurism, it was a story about the transformative nature of survival. Faye had stopped herself from thinking about how this had been what her grandfather had done to women and had begun thinking that some women could survive no matter what the odds, that some had a resilience that was almost impossible to imagine. Asifa was one of those women. Faye still wasn't sure whether *she* was one or not. When she watched Lila watching Asifa, she wasn't sure about her, either. Maybe neither of them had been saved early enough. Faye hoped Asifa had been.

Faye and Lila left together that last afternoon and went to have a drink which turned into several. They'd both been shaken by the past few days; it had felt deeply personal. But Faye knew it was different for her than it was for Lila. She didn't want to contemplate what Lila would think if she knew Faye's story. Suddenly, she could see Grand slicing up the face of Asifa, tying her down in the little basement room meant to replicate an apartment, a cozy series of rooms, when it was anything but.

Faye felt nauseous, she told Lila she'd be right back. "Too much tea and beer," she said, giving Lila's shoulder a quick squeeze. Then she went to the ladies' room, threw some water on her face, and some more. She stared at herself in the mirror. She needed sleep. Even though the light was a comforting candlelight yellow, not glaring—that would have sent customers running for the streets, instead of thinking they could definitely have one more—she looked wrung out. The past few days had been harder on her than she'd expected. She'd need to rest for a few days before she left for the DRC. Maybe doing Asifa's story before she left had been a mistake.

She closed her eyes for a moment, breathing deeply, saying a Hail Mary. Then she headed back to the table and Lila.

❖

Lila was texting when Faye got back to the table. The bar was filling up with the happy hour crowd. Faye was grateful for the noise.

"I'm not ready to go home," she said to Faye. "Some nights I feel too messed up by the days, from everything they tell me, to go home to her. She's"—Lila stopped, made a little gesture—"outside of all this. I want to keep her safe. Someone should have kept all these women, all these girls, safe." She took a long sip of her drink. Faye saw she'd gotten another one while she'd been in the ladies' room.

Faye reached across the little table, took Lila's hand.

"Asifa's a strong young woman, Lila. She's like Malala. She's going to shine a bright light on this horror, you'll see," Faye comforted Lila, hoping her words were true and what she had seen in Asifa would be seen by others, as well.

Lila started to cry. The bar was dark enough to hide silent tears, but even with the larger crowd, probably not loud enough to drown out actual sobbing.

"I see my lost life in her, Faye. My lost life. I can never have that part of me back. And it's so painful—so painful, I can hardly breathe." Lila had covered her face with her hands for a moment, then seemed to pull herself back from whatever precipice she had been on.

"Maybe I should go home," she said, after tossing back the last of her drink. "Tomorrow is a long day. There are always more wounded women, always more. And our wounded must be tended to."

It was a sad, jangled note to end the evening on, but Faye got Lila into a cab, kissing her on both cheeks, then walked home. The brisk air sobered her up. She was surprised to discover, several blocks from home, that she was crying.

❖

Preparing to go to the DRC was easier than Faye had expected, except for the unsettled feelings Asifa's story had left her with. The main thing was the vaccinations and buying some long scarves and that burka, just in case she could go directly from the DRC to Afghanistan, just in case Asifa's story had so much impact on her editor that he told her, "Faye, this is great stuff, we need more just like it." It had happened before. It could happen again.

Buying the scarves and the burka had been a bizarre experience in a small shop in Jamaica Heights. The shop window was filled with mannequins that were dead white, covered in various dark-colored burkas, some with fabric that had a pattern woven into it that could only be seen up close. Inside the shop, the mannequins were just the same: Only the white slit where the eyes should have been showed, giving each mannequin an eerie look, as if the burkas clothed ghosts. An unconscious metaphor, Faye thought, considering that under the burka, all women became invisible.

Faye left New York for Kinshasa just over two weeks after the editorial meeting. Standing in her apartment a few hours before she took the cab to the airport, she thought, this was the last one—the last story. Or if she went on to Afghanistan, that would be. But when she came back to New York, it was over. She was going to leave the paper. She was going to put together a show that would be a retrospective of her work, *all* her work. Faye already knew what she would title it: *Ordinary Mayhem.* She was already writing the copy for the book that would follow it.

Faye walked into the small room that served as her studio and shut the door behind her—force of habit. She closed the blackout shade on the window over her work table and walked to the old apothecary cabinet she'd found on eBay that stood against the far wall, behind the door. There were curtains over the glass doors in a deep burgundy red. Inside the cabinet, on the six shelves, were a series of jars in different sizes. She stood and looked at them for a time, then reached in and touched one, then another. She took out one of the largest jars, walked to the table, and put it down. She sat in the chair, looking at it, then reached for her notebook and wrote a few sentences.

On the wall opposite her table were photographs—rows and rows of photographs. She stared at them, then made more notations in the notebook. The book about Esperanza had just been a start. Soon she would have that show. The gallery exhibit—that was going to reveal a completely different side of her work. Not just the photographs, but the other things. It would definitely be mixed media. She had already had several offers from gallery owners. She had chosen one at the edge of SoHo—still trendy, but enough money to get her what she wanted in the end. The notoriety and the attention. She had another story to tell, after all. And that story was hers.

For a brief moment she thought of her grandfather, the darkroom, the other things. She thought of Sister Anne Marie. And of that night in Chinatown, with Shihong.

Faye felt cold. She looked at her watch. Then she got up and put the jar back on its shelf. She closed the cabinet again, locked it, and left the room.

It was time to go to the airport.

CHAPTER THIRTEEN
THE TRAUMA

It was summer before Faye went into the darkroom again at night. Her grandfather would invite her in during the day, but Faye only went in after she had seen people in the studio and she'd seen the photographs being taken. Then she knew what would be on the floating pieces of paper in the trays. Then she knew she wouldn't be sick. She wouldn't see the women, or the table, or the pieces of the women on the beds and on the plates. She thought about these things all the time, but there was no one to tell about them, no one to talk to. When he went into the darkroom, her grandfather would wink at her, like they had a secret between them. And they did—Faye knew now that if her grandfather had taken those photographs, it was like everything else he took photographs of: the weddings, the graduations, the prom pictures, the family portraits. He arranged everything. She could almost hear him saying to those women, "Now lick your lips and tilt your head up."

And then what had he done? And where had he done it? And why?

There was something so strange for Faye about the secret. She knew it—she'd figured it out that night at the table, and then she fainted, because it made her sick to think about it. Yet she wasn't afraid of her grandfather. Every night he would kiss her before she went to bed and it didn't scare her, it didn't even make her feel creepy. Sometimes she thought she'd made it all up in her head, that it never really happened. But then he would wink at her and she would think that it had to be because of the secret, because he knew she knew and that it was something they shared.

He told her over and over that he would give her a camera in a few years so that she could take her own pictures. "You'll see things, and you'll want to photograph them," he told her. "You'll want to see them over and over again. Because even though you have the memory of something, seeing it again, having the picture—it's just like being at that place or doing that thing all over again. And it makes you feel—" He had stopped talking for a moment and she saw the look on his face. He was remembering. He was remembering the women and the parts and the table. And she had to look away. It was better if she looked away.

But he had started talking again, and had told her that until she had a camera, she should draw pictures of things she saw that meant something to her. She should keep a notebook. And he had given her some special pencils that were very sharp and in a little box. They were different colors and he had told her to try to make the colors match the things she saw. He had also given her a little notebook. It had thick white paper in it with no lines and it had a spiral binding so she could tear out the pages if she wanted to.

Then he had taken her out back, into the yard, and he had said, "Look at this, you should draw this," and he had pointed at the edge of one of the flower beds.

Faye had looked and there was a small dead shrew there. Its eyes were open and so was its mouth. It looked like something had surprised it all of a sudden. Then Faye looked closer and she saw that it had a tear in its stomach and some of the guts were out on the ground. She didn't want to look at it anymore, but her grandfather said, "Now go inside and draw the shrew. Draw everything you saw. Because then, when you want to remember it, it will be right there for you to look at."

Faye couldn't imagine when she would want to remember this, the little animal with its screaming mouth and torn stomach.

Faye's grandfather had been looking down at her as she bent over the flower bed, and as Faye looked up, she could see his face, all excited. What she didn't know was whether he was excited about the dead shrew or about her drawing it.

❖

Faye still remembered the night when she had fainted in the kitchen and her grandmother had taken her upstairs. It had been cold on the floor, but she had still felt really hot. She'd stayed in bed for almost two weeks after that. There had been a trip to the doctor who had told her grandmother that Faye was suffering from trauma, just as her grandmother had been saying all along to her, to everyone. The anguish over her parents' deaths, plus being uprooted from her home—it had all been too much, the doctor told them. Faye's immune system was worn down, the doctor said, and she was prey for infection. He had given her grandmother a prescription for some pills that Faye had to take for two weeks, to make the infection go away, and before they left the office, a dark-skinned woman in a bright pink uniform with little smiling animals on the shirt had taken three glass vials of blood from her arm.

The doctor had also said that Faye needed to be back in school. That too much time had passed—"It's been several weeks since the accident"—and she might end up being left back a year if she didn't return. He recommended tutoring if there were problems adjusting to the new school in a different borough.

"I know Brooklyn is like a foreign country to her," he'd told her grandmother, "so whatever we can do to help the transition. This is, you know, compounding the trauma."

He also recommended a therapist. "She needs to talk to someone, talk it out," he had said, while he rubbed Faye's shoulder like she was a cat.

Faye had started at St. Cecilia's on Valentine's Day. The school was different from her other school—there were only girls, and nuns in habits taught all the classes. A priest came every morning and gave Holy Communion to the girls who were old enough. Faye would have her first Holy Communion in May. She was sorry her mother wouldn't be able to see that, because she had wanted to make Faye's dress. They had talked about it at Christmas, before the accident.

St. Cecilia's had girls who went home and girls who lived at the school. Faye wasn't sure why some girls lived there and the rest of them did not, but she thought maybe it would be nice to live there, with all the other girls and the nuns. Maybe it would be different from her grandparents' house. She hoped it would be. She hoped it would be more like home. Or at least different. She was ready to leave her grandparents' house now. She was ready to go someplace else.

The school year had gone quickly. Faye hadn't fallen behind like the doctor had said; in fact, she was recommended to skip a grade. She'd had her First Holy Communion and had stood at the altar rail with the other girls in her white frilly dress and thin white veil. Her grandmother had given her a rosary with pearly beads and a little white Missal as a present and her grandfather had taken her picture and she had watched him develop it in the darkroom after.

She had spent part of the summer at a camp for Catholic girls and she had made things and gone hiking and caught frogs and let them go again. In the mornings there was Mass and then there was swimming and lunch and activities in the afternoon. Faye had made some friends, including a girl, Rosario, who would be in her new grade at St. Cecilia's in September. Rosario didn't have a father, either, although her father wasn't dead. She just didn't know who he was. Rosario lived with her grandparents, too, because, she said, her mother was "sick on the drugs" and she couldn't take care of Rosario anymore.

Faye was looking forward to seeing Rosario again. Now it was late August and Faye had been back at her grandparents' house for more than two weeks. It was another week before school would start again. It was hot in her little room, which used to be her father's room when he was a child, and the fan just whirled around, but didn't make anything cooler.

Sometimes Faye would go downstairs and lie on the floor in the kitchen because the linoleum was cool and her grandmother kept everything so clean, she didn't mind being on the floor. She would take the pillow from her rocking chair and put it under her head and sleep there until it got light.

This time when she went downstairs, she stopped outside the darkroom door. She stood still for a minute. She could hear the black fan whirring inside. She could imagine the photographs moving slightly on the clothesline. She could imagine the cut-up women in the pictures, too.

Faye went into the kitchen and put her pillow on a chair. Then she went back to the darkroom and went inside.

CHAPTER FOURTEEN
IT IS ALL THE SAME HOUR

The story in Congo was different from anything else Faye had done. The place was hot and steamy and breathtakingly beautiful. That was the text. The subtext was like all subtexts—something totally different. The war that wasn't a war in Congo was an unending nightmare from which no one could awaken, least of all the women whose lives Faye had come to chronicle. Everything had been shunted off to East Congo, so that people could act like nothing was happening in the rest of the country.

Faye had never seen things quite as terrible as what she saw in Congo and she had to find ways to make the story new, to make a war-weary readership care about the women and girls who were being gang-raped and eviscerated on their way to get water or wood for fire or just right in their own homes, as they lay sleeping. Faye was keeping notebooks again—this was no place for an iPad or a cell phone vlog. As soon as she got there, she knew there was another book here. A big book. *An important book.* Because Faye knew that even though people didn't really care what happened to these women, they'd still want to pore over their suffering and examine every hideous detail. She could see them turning her photographs this way and that to see every bit of the horror and still feeling just a little disappointed that they couldn't see more.

It was just like when she had taken those photographs of the rig that spilled the steel rods back in New York. Everyone wanted to see the decapitated driver, blood and spinal fluid spurting from the place where his head should be, jagged bits of bone and spine and strings of sinew all splayed out like rebar twisted in cement when a building is demolished. Everyone wanted to see the guy screaming, pinned to the seat of his car with the steel pipe, his mouth open in one continuous howl as he tried to pull himself free. Or the dogs, flattened next to their owner, intestines protruding from one, brains spilled out from another. Everyone wanted to see mayhem juxtaposed with the most tranquil of settings. A simple weekday dog walk turned into carnage. That's all there was in Congo—the simple walk turned into carnage, set against the most postcard-beautiful background.

Faye had met with a woman, Martine, in Kinshasa. Martine worked for the NGO Women for Women and Faye had talked to her on the phone while she was still in New York, setting up the itinerary for her trip. Martine was very dark-skinned and slight, but elegant—she seemed much taller and more imposing than her actual height implied. The scarf wound around her head was a muted blue fabric with black flowers outlined in it. Her skirt, which fell almost to her ankles, was of the same material and she wore a white blouse that looked like a T-shirt, but was a thin linen with white embroidery. She wore no jewelry. Martine told Faye to remove her earrings, watch, and the thin silver bracelets she wore on her left wrist.

"They will tear the earrings from your ears, should they catch you," Martine said, almost matter-of-factly, as if it were a foregone conclusion that Faye would be ambushed and injured. "They do that. And the watch and the bracelets they will notice first. Just put them away. You don't need to know the time here, anyway. It is all the same hour."

Martine had traveled with Faye to eastern Congo, which was, Martine said, the rape capital of the world. "We give out numbers, but we can't really count. On one weekend, 16,000 women were raped. So many of these women have been raped more than once. By the time they come to us, it is all over for them, they believe. So much has happened. They feel destroyed, like ghosts, yet still drawing breath."

Faye and Martine had gone to South Kivu province, then to a rural refugee center outside Bukavu, where rape victims were cared for by Catholic nuns and medical personnel from Doctors Without Borders. The building was low and flat and spread out over a wide space that was lush and green. A low-hanging mist furled around the center and in the near distance Faye could see the hills of Rwanda rolling out over the horizon. Below them lay Lake Kivu. It was an incredibly beautiful landscape. If only you didn't know what lay beneath as well as beyond, for the legacy of the Rwandan genocide was what had bled over into the DRC.

As they entered the building, Faye felt dread take her over: it was like the morgue in Fresno—a bad feeling, a grim, heart-pounding foreboding. She began to sweat; a slight faintness gripped her briefly. Maybe this trip had been a bad idea. Maybe she wouldn't be able to do what she had hoped. It was only a few days and the handful of people she'd talked to had made her sick with their stories. And how to explain such extremes of violence against such a serene—no, breathtakingly beautiful—landscape? This was exponentially worse than the pesticide poisoning story. Worse than Esperanza. After all, Esperanza had tried to take her own life. Tragic as it was, that young woman had been driven by her own demons, not someone else's. This was like Asifa, only more—more Asifas, so many more Asifas.

Martine led Faye down a wide, open hallway to a very large room that served as a ward for women recovering from gang rapes and the surgeries required after. As they neared the room, a hideous smell began to waft toward them. Faye coughed and Martine said, "I know, I should have warned you. The smell—it is awful, you see. I would give you something to put under your nose, but it does not help. I have tried all of it…"

"What is it, the smell?" Faye asked, trying not to gag. She had stopped walking down the open hallway toward the room. She wasn't sure what was beyond the doorway. The place was surprisingly quiet. Too quiet. Preternaturally quiet. She reached in her bag for an Altoid. The intensity of the mint would help deaden the smell—and calm her gagging.

"Urine, feces, blood. There is always some rotting flesh, no matter what the doctors do. The gangrene, it can set in quickly, the wounds are so severe. That is the smell that lingers most, the smell of what is already dead. The things that have been done to these women—" Martine drew her hand across her face. It came away wet. "What they tell you when they get here, what they describe—"

She turned toward Faye, looked directly at her. Martine's eyes were the deepest brown, almost black; Faye could hardly discern the pupils. Martine reached out her hand, placing it on Faye's shoulder. Her grip was shockingly tight. Painful. Faye wanted to shake it off. She was reminded of Shihong, in Chinatown.

"Make them show you," Martine said, her voice almost a whisper, her face moving closer. "Of course, that means you will have to look, but make them show you. People must see what goes on here. It is hell here. It is the very worst of hell. Make them show you. Make them take you to that hell."

They had entered the room and Faye had steeled herself, biting into the mint and feeling the burning heat of it on her tongue. It would keep her focused, that mint. She'd keep putting them in her mouth as long as was necessary.

The room was long and open. The ceiling was low. Windows ran the length of each side of the room. It reminded Faye of the dormitory at St. Cecilia's. Only this was a ward and the paint wasn't the bright white of St. Cecilia's with its tidy little stenciling of blue crosses near the ceiling. The paint here was shiny enamel of the sort that had been used decades ago, and was probably filled with lead. It was a pale blue and here and there where the paint was scraped off, a sweaty effulgent plaster showed through; it looked like infection. The floor was painted concrete. There were drains in different places. In more than one spot, blood pooled on the floor, flies and other insects buzzing over it.

Everyone on the ward was hovering just this side of death. Twenty-four beds—cots, really—twelve on each side, lined the walls. The beds were low and very flat—thin mattresses with no pillows. Each had a colored sheet but nothing else.

Some women lay in a fetal position, others lay completely flat. Still others lay as if they had been thrown onto the beds, their legs and arms askew. Most had IV bags, a few also had bags with blood. There were none of the accoutrements of a twenty-first-century medical ward for what Faye presumed was the intensive care status of these patients. No heart monitors, no oxygen, no nurses, no call buttons.

Some of the beds had another person tending the woman. A mother, a sister, an aunt. No men. No children.

No one seemed to speak, but there was, Faye realized, a low susurration throughout the room—a collective sighing between patients and their care-givers. Occasionally there was a moan.

Martine explained what Faye would see when she got closer. They began with a woman named Jetta. She was one of the women sprawled on her cot. She had not one but two IVs, each running into the place where her arms should have been.

Martine spoke to Jetta in a language Faye did not know, and then the story began to be repeated—Jetta looked at Faye and Martine repeated in English what Jetta told her.

They had come for her at night, late, after midnight. She was alone, her husband had gone to care for his ailing father. It was just Jetta and her younger son and daughter. The older son was with his father. There were five of them—*five, imagine, five*—she said. Jetta started to cry then, and Martine, who was sitting close to her, where her family should have been, began to stroke her forehead.

Jetta continued, explaining how they had threatened to rape her daughter and her son—*they are only children, they are only children*—and so she consented. Or so they told her husband, later. But what she had done was beg them for the lives of her children. There was never any consent. Never.

They made her children watch—time after time, in all the places. She was torn apart. And when it was over, they cut off her arms. *"One for each child,"* they told her, and had tossed the arms at the feet of each child. She could still hear their terrified screams. She could still hear her own screams. *"We were like animals, in our pain,"* Jetta said. *"Like animals in the bush, tearing each other to bits."*

Two neighbors had crept up because of the screaming and had slipped into the house after the men had left. *"I owe them my life,"* she said, because they had kept her from bleeding to death and had brought her here.

Six more women consented to talk to Faye, to let her take pictures of them. The stories were each of unbelievable torture. Two women had also lost limbs, five had lost their uteruses, because of knives being used on them, or the barrels of guns. All would need catheters for the rest of their lives because of the damage that couldn't be repaired.

One woman, Yvette, had lost part of her bowel. She had been pregnant when they took her, and so they had cut her open after they raped her and killed her baby, hacking it to pieces in front of her.

"I will never have a child, now," she cried. *"I will never have a husband. I will only have this—"* and she had pulled up her shirt and revealed a webbing of raw, red scars against the dark skin and at the center, a tube leading out to a small bag filled with a thick dark fluid. *"This is the baby I care for now, now that my child is dead, my husband has gone."*

Each woman had allowed Faye to photograph the scars, the missing pieces—one woman's breasts had been sliced off. Faye had them turn their faces away, so they would not feel humiliated, but Yvette had said no, she wanted to be seen.

"Let them see what they did to me. Let them see the pieces of me that are missing—my baby, my heart, my soul. They think they saved me here at this place. And they are kind, they want to help. But I died with my baby. I am a ghost, just a ghost—but a vengeful ghost. So show them, show them my face. Let me haunt them for all eternity."

Faye thanked each of the women, one by one. And then she and Martine went outside where Faye walked as far from the center as she could, put both hands over her mouth, and screamed.

Chapter Fifteen
What Is Left of Me

There was another woman Martine wanted Faye to see, but she wasn't on the ward. She was in a cottage off the main building with three other women. Faye said she wasn't sure. She felt shaky and something else, she didn't know what it was. *Déjà vu*, yet that wasn't possible.

Martine was talking to her. "We have to keep the worst ones separate," Martine told Faye. "Sometimes it is better if they do not share their stories. These women are so fragile, and some of these stories—well, you will see."

Faye wasn't sure what could be worse than the evisceration of Yvette and the murder of her baby. What could be worse than having your arms cut off and tossed at your children's feet while they—and you—screamed? What could be worse than five men, or seven men, or nine men and your insides coming out of you?

Vandana sat in the corner of the small room in a straight-backed chair. There was no one else in the room, which held a small cot, a plastic dresser, and a fan. There was a thin pillow between her and the chair. She was looking out the window, which faced the Rwandan hills. It would soon be dusk and a spiral of insects whirled in a column just outside the window.

Vandana didn't turn when Faye and Martine came into the room. She said, *"It is so beautiful here, but I never want it to be night. I want to be where it is never, ever night."*

She didn't turn until they were standing next to her and Martine said something softly, and Vandana turned toward them, then.

Her face was in two halves. On one side, a pretty, twenty-something woman with full lips, high cheekbones, and a dark, sparkling eye. On the other side, a reddish brown welt of a scar ran from an inch above her eyebrow, through where her left eye should be, and down to her mouth, which had been sliced at the corner, leaving another scar that ran from the corner of her mouth, up her cheek, to her ear, which was gone, sliced clean off. She was missing part of her hand on that side as well. Her eye socket was concave and the scar ran in a Y-shape over it.

Faye began to feel hot. Her heart was pounding now, too, and the blood rushed in her ears.

"I've been waiting for you," Vandana said, *"I've been waiting to tell you everything, since I have so little to show you. You cannot photograph what is no longer here."*

Like all the other women, they had come to Vandana's house at night, the soldiers, or whatever they were, she wasn't sure. *"They all call themselves soldiers, but what are they really? Just monsters. Nothing but monsters. They are the things you feared as a child, that you begged your mother and father to protect you from in the dark, in the night. But there is no protection now. The monsters, they are free to do as they please. They are free to be monsters, monsters."*

As Vandana began to tell her story, Faye felt herself recede from the room—this story had a familiarity to it that at first she could not place.

Vandana's entire family had been home the night the men came. They had broken through the door and there had been no time for hiding. Vandana, her husband, her mother, her two small children, her brother and two sisters—eight of them in all—had been asleep.

Her husband had been trussed up right away. It was, they told her, his job to watch. They had tied him to a chair with rope, Vandana said.

"And then they made a meal of us. I am the only one left—what is left of me."

Faye looked at Martine, but Martine said, yes, that was what she had said.

Faye had been half sitting on the edge of the dresser across from Vandana. She stood up, but felt unaccountably dizzy. Martine reached out her hand to steady Faye, a look of concern on her face. Then Vandana said something which Martine translated as, *"I understand. I wanted to run as well. I still do, but there is nowhere to go, no escape from this—"* and she had gestured over her body with the mutilated hand.

Faye moved to the cot on the other side of Vandana, the side where her eye was missing and her face raw. She sat at the edge of the hard little bed, thinking that anyone who had been through these things deserved more comforting places to rest. She wanted to lay Vandana in a thick feather bed, let her be comforted by the enveloping softness.

The story continued. There had been eleven soldiers—eleven monsters. They had been young and particularly sadistic, Vandana told Faye. They had begun by killing her mother outright.

"They took her head off." Vandana said it succinctly. A tear rolled down her face on the side where the eye was. It had happened quickly, but not without suffering.

"They said nothing. They just pulled everyone up from the floor. They tied up my husband, put something in his mouth so he could not speak—or scream. Then the one soldier—" Here Vandana stopped speaking. Faye leaned forward. Vandana had closed her eye. Her mouth was tight. She was clenching and unclenching a piece of the fabric of her skirt in her remaining hand.

She opened her eye and her lips parted, then she began to speak again.

"This one, this one who looked like someone's lost child, he just took the butt of his rifle and hit her so hard in the side of her head that her eye came out, it fell onto her cheek. And then as she grabbed for her eye, she didn't even have time to scream, really, another one, a taller, bigger one, older—he took a machete and sliced right through her neck. He did it with such force that her head came off—completely off. The children were screaming, my brother and sisters were screaming. My mother's head landed near my husband's feet—his bare feet. Her hair had fallen over one foot. You could see my husband's mouth try to scream, but he couldn't, because of the thing they had stuffed inside."

Martine coughed several times at the end of this part of Vandana's story. Faye continued to sit at the edge of the cot. A reel of pictures flashed through her head. Outside the little cottage, the sounds of the compound could be heard—as if this were any other place, as if this were any normal day, as if the stories Faye had heard, the stories Martine must have translated into English and French several times over, were not the stuff of sheer unmitigated horror, did not call up, as Vandana had said, the childhood images of monsters.

"They silenced my brother first. A third soldier grabbed him from behind and slit his throat like a goat's. The blood just pumped out like I have seen at the well here. After that, well—it became so ugly."

Vandana leaned forward, then stood. She turned toward Faye, but spoke to Martine, asking her if Faye was ready to take the photographs. Faye picked up her camera and Vandana untied the fabric that was knotted at her left shoulder but draped around her body like a long sarong.

The light green fabric was embedded with a faded blue and red print—flowers, maybe. Faye wasn't sure. But as Vandana's garment drifted to the floor, Faye bit hard on the mint in her mouth.

Under her left arm, the arm without the hand, chunks of flesh had been removed. Inside her thighs, more flesh had been cut away, as had part of the soft mound where her pubic hair should have been. Vandana turned around, as if she were showing Faye a new outfit she had gotten, and Faye saw that her buttocks also bore the marks of cutting, and her back had been flayed open and sewn back up, inexpertly, as if in a great hurry.

Vandana moved closer to Faye, who had been taking shot after shot. Vandana stopped and looked at her and said something. Faye looked to Martine, who said, "She wants you to look closer. At the wounds."

Faye stayed where she was, as the naked woman moved toward her. Faye thought about all the times naked women had come toward her in just this way and how none of those times had been anything like this. She wondered if she would think of this the next time she was with another woman. She hoped not.

Vandana was right in front of her now and she began to point— *"La, la, la,"* she said as she pointed to her thigh, her arm, her pubic area. It was then that Faye saw. The chunks of flesh hadn't been cut away, they had been torn away—by teeth.

"I told you," she said, *"they made a meal of us. This is only part of what they did. There is so much more."*

Chapter Sixteen
The Other Side of the Door

Faye wasn't sure why she wanted to go into the darkroom again. She already knew she didn't want to see whatever it was that was hanging from the clothesline. But she opened the door anyway and went inside.

The red light came on when she flipped the switch. She saw that there were photographs, but she didn't look at them. She held her left hand at the side of her eye like she was blocking bright sunlight. She didn't want to see what was there.

Faye had never been in the basement of her grandparents' house before. The door had a big bolt across it and there was usually a chair in front of the door. Once, Faye had asked her grandfather what was down there and he had said, "Mice. Mice and the furnace. And darkness. There's a lot of darkness. It can swallow you up, you know. You don't want to go down there. Trust me. It's not a place for little girls."

As Faye began to move the bolt back, she could feel her heart pounding again. She hoped she wouldn't faint like she had in the kitchen that last time. But she wanted to go down to the basement. She wanted to see what was there. She *needed* to see what was there. Something one of the older girls had said when she was away at camp had made her think about the photographs and her grandfather, and now, the basement.

The bolt didn't make any noise when she pulled it back, which surprised her. She had thought it would be loud and make a grating noise or a clanging sound like the black iron gate in front of the house that she would sometimes swing on until her grandmother would come out and just say her name, "Faye," and she would stop and come inside.

On the wall at the top of the stairs was a big white light switch. It was round and ceramic. When she flipped it, a light went on at the bottom of the stairs. It wasn't a bright light, but it wasn't red, either.

The stairs were made of a rough-looking wood. Faye went down two, four, six steps, and then stopped. She could see into the basement now if she crouched down and looked to the right, where it was open.

There were boxes all along the walls and the tiny windows that Faye recognized from where the garden was. There were some other steps that led up to the door that was on a slant that was in the garden, too. It had a big bolt across it like the one upstairs. She could also see the heater—what her grandfather called the furnace. It was silver and black metal and had big round tubes coming up out of it.

In the center of the room was a table, like the one in the kitchen. There were two chairs, one on either side, and the table was set, like there was going to be a meal. In the center of the table was a jar—a really big one, like the one her grandmother had that was blue and white china and had "flour" written across it in pretty writing. Faye couldn't see what was in the jar from her spot on the stairs.

In the corner there was a long wooden table—Faye knew it was a workbench because her father had had one in her old house when her parents were still alive. At the end of it was something Faye couldn't quite see.

She got up from the step and went down the rest of the stairs and over to the workbench. There was a chain above it that turned on a light. Her heart was beating really fast now and she wasn't sure if she should pull the chain or not.

She put her hand on the chain, closed her eyes, and pulled. When she opened her eyes she saw it.

At the very end, near the wall, in the darkest corner of the basement room was a vise. It was just like the one her father had at his workbench. But her father's had always had pieces of wood in his, wood being pressed together for something her father was making—a shelf or a little table or bookcase. Once, there had been the leg of a chair that kept falling out of the socket in their dining room.

Her grandfather's vise was turned tight, just like her father's had been. But inside the two metal pieces there wasn't wood. There was a lady's head, pressed between the two metal pieces at the sides above the ears.

Faye thought she was going to scream, but she didn't. She felt hot and her heart still pounded and her face got flushed and sweaty. But now she wanted to look at it. She went closer.

The skin wasn't like skin anymore. It was all dried up and wrinkly. The hair wasn't soft-looking, either. It was long and a reddish color and some of it was wound around the part of the vise that gets turned. Where the eyes should have been were just holes that were black around the edges and the mouth was all sewn up, like the mouth on her Raggedy Ann doll that Faye's mother had made for her.

Faye reached out to touch it, but changed her mind. She pulled the chain and the light went out. She walked toward the table, to see what was in the jar, but decided she didn't want to know. She wished she hadn't come down here, but at least she knew what was here now. It was one of the places where the pictures got taken. Because as she was going back toward the stairs, she saw the little bed against the far wall, behind the stairs. The little bed where the women in the photographs would be.

She had seen enough. She went back up the stairs, turned out the light, pushed the heavy fat bolt back across the door, and left the darkroom without looking at the pictures.

She went into the kitchen and washed her face and hands, then she got her pillow and went back upstairs to bed. It was just beginning to get light.

CHAPTER SEVENTEEN
AFTER IT GETS DARK

Vandana had put her garment back on. Faye watched as she managed despite the missing hand to deftly twist the fabric around her mutilated body and tie it over her shoulder using her other hand and her teeth. She sat back down in her chair and resumed her story. Faye wasn't sure she could hear more, but Martine was looking at her with the look she had given her before, when she asked her to "make them show you."

The story Vandana recounted was pure nightmare. Her brother's body had been cut open and his organs had been cut out. The men had shoved the hot pieces of flesh into the hands of everyone in the room—her sisters, her children, her. They had been ordered to eat—the liver, the kidneys, the heart. And when they didn't or couldn't, the soldiers had begun to do their worst. Atrocity after atrocity. Vandana's four-year-old daughter had been raped, then killed. Her sisters had both been disemboweled while they were still alive, one soldier raping her youngest sister while her guts pulsed onto the floor. Her six-year-old son's head had been cut off, like her mother's had been. Her husband had choked to death in front of her when he vomited into the rag they had stuffed in his mouth.

Vandana had been the last. They had sliced at her back when she had tried to run and cut off part of her left hand. She'd been raped by all of them, her rectum ripped open, her vagina prolapsed outside her vulva. They had torn bites out of her flesh as they assaulted her—tearing bits of her buttocks and breasts and vulva. They thought she was dead when they left—everyone else in her family was. She wished she had been, but she was still writhing in her own blood, feces, vomit, and urine when her aunt found her the next day. She'd been brought here, barely alive, and saved. Although for what, she could not say.

"They took everything. What you see here is all that is left. They wanted us to eat each other and when we wouldn't, they made their meal of us. I scream every day as it begins to get dark. Every day I relive the nightmare as dusk falls. Now that you know my story, perhaps I will not have to live much longer. I miss my husband and my children. I miss my family. I know they are waiting for me. I only hope they are in the light, and there will be no more darkness."

Vandana pointed out the window to the setting sun, an incomparably postcard-beautiful sunset that bled out onto the lush greenery beyond the cottage, and said, *"Soon it will be dark and I will live it all over again, until dawn comes. So you see, I was not saved. Not saved at all."*

She began to weep and as Martine went to her, a woman came in dressed in a white nun's habit, murmuring softly in the same language Vandana and Martine had been speaking.

Martine whispered a thank-you to Vandana for her time and her story, and kissed her on her good cheek, while the nun prepared some kind of medication for her. Martine and Faye left. As they drove back to Bukavu proper, Faye was silent. Martine talked a little, explaining how these were actually common stories. Many of the soldiers now tried to force cannibalism on their victims as a way to defile them and shame them, making them unfit for this world or the next.

Faye listened, but said nothing. She kept hearing Vandana saying, *"They made a meal of us."*

She and Martine rode the rest of the way in silence. Martine said they would spend the night there, in Bukavu, at the hotel.

"We cannot drive around at night, you see," she said, looking away from Faye. "It would not be safe. This is not a place to be a woman. Not at night. Not on the road. The roads have been bad since the war, and it is easy to break down, and then…" Martine's voice trailed off.

"Tomorrow we will go back west. I will arrange for us to get to Kinshasa. I think you have your story, now, don't you?"

That night they had stayed at the best hotel in Bukavu, the Orchids Safari Club. The place was small, but lovely. Faye thought it could have been in any resort town in the Bahamas or the Virgin Islands—someplace where the only horror outside the hotel grounds might be the poverty of the island residents. The view of Lake Kivu was extraordinary, even as it had gone almost dark, and for a moment in this place filled with European and East Asian tourists, one could believe that nothing bad was happening outside its walls.

But peculiar rules reminded Faye that all was not right in Congo. There was no eating outside, despite the gorgeous view from the veranda. There was no room service. The rooms were simple, but luxurious compared to what Faye had just seen. Yet there was an atmosphere that reminded Faye of the Graham Greene novels she had read in college. Why was there even a hotel in a place like this, with so much happening beyond the gates, just down the bad road Martine had spoken of, all rutted and gnarled? Faye recalled the scenes from *Hotel Rwanda*, and remembered how the deadly legacy of colonialism lingered. She wondered, as she watched the other guests in the dining room, most of them speaking either French or some kind of Arabic, if they knew that somewhere not far from where they ate, later that night, people would be forced to eat the still-pulsing organs of their families just before they were murdered in their own homes.

❖

Faye had not expected to have Martine walk toward her bed in the hotel room and stand there, as if waiting to be invited in, but it was not an unwelcome surprise. As she stood, dropping her thin robe onto the bed, Faye saw her perfect, unmarred body, the skin smooth and dark, devoid of scars or burns or teeth marks. That was more of a relief even than the orgasmic sex itself. Faye wanted to look at Martine, feel every bit of her body, the wholeness of her. Faye hadn't had sex with anyone since the night of the book launch and the release felt good, surprisingly intense, given the day they had shared. Neither of them cried, though. Faye thought perhaps the sex took the place of tears.

Later, as they lay in Faye's bed, Martine told her that she had been gang-raped three years earlier, by four men who had stopped her at a roadblock when she was driving from one care center to another. "They didn't cut me, they didn't burn me. They let me live. I didn't get pregnant. But I could never imagine being with a man ever again after that. Because, you see, I had seen these men before—many times. They ran this same road block for nearly a year before they raped me. How could they see me all those times, how could they smile at me and let me pass and then one day pull me from my car and drag me into the bush until I was bloody and act as if it was simply expected? How could I be sure that another man might not turn into a monster before my eyes? How could I risk having a child with a monster?"

Faye had held her, stroking her arms and making the small susurrations that are not actual speech, but which sound like comfort. Faye had thought about telling Martine a story, but then she remembered Shihong in Chinatown, and said only, "It's good that you told me. Someone else told me that the secrets become you. And they do. That's not always a good thing."

❖

In the morning they had dutifully pretended nothing had happened between them beyond a comforting exchange. After having a meal in the dining room and then walking out onto the veranda and looking at the lake, they had gone on to the airport and flown back to Kinshasa.

But that night, the night she had spent with Martine, Faye had had a series of progressively more terrifying dreams. The dreams had stayed with her after she awoke. Even when they had reached Kinshasa, the images still lingered. Faye wanted to go back to New York. She didn't think she could go on to Afghanistan now. She called her editor. She'd have to do the second part, Afghanistan, later. This was a lot to process and she wasn't feeling all that well, she told him—water, developing world, she knew he understood. She tried to keep the shakiness out of her voice. She wanted to get out of this place. The contradiction of the physical beauty and what she knew lay beneath was too extreme, even for her, the photographer who never cringed, never flinched, never stopped recording the darkest of images.

Faye booked her flight, then she called Martine from her room at the hotel. She had asked for a room on the top floor—for some reason she felt safest there, as if soldiers would work their way up the flights if they invaded in the night, and it would be easiest to attack on the first or second floor, rather than the tenth. She asked Martine to spend the night with her before she left.

"You understand—I don't feel safe. It's not that I expect you to protect me, and we're in Kinshasa now, anyway, and this is a big city, as big as New York, and I know I'm being paranoid. But I just don't want to be alone."

Martine had talked to her on the phone, trying to reassure her. Telling her the kind of historical facts one tells a tourist—that Kinshasa was the second-largest city in Africa. That it was the largest French-speaking city in the world—that legacy of colonialism, again. That Faye should try to absorb the lush beauty and not be fearful because Kinshasa was civilized, truly. It's not like they were in the bush. And anyway, tourists came all the time to see the gorillas. She was safe at the hotel. She really was.

But Faye knew Martine was reciting from childhood memory and that knee-jerk thing that Faye herself always felt when people talked about the dangers of New York. But this was not New York and she had just spent days looking at the torn-apart bodies of several dozen women. Faye was beginning to understand why Vandana began to scream as night fell.

❖

Faye fell into a deep sleep after the sex with Martine. This time it was Martine who held her and Faye felt that sense of safety she had hoped Martine would give her.

Then the dreams came.

CHAPTER EIGHTEEN
ANIMAL SACRIFICES

After that first summer, Faye had been grateful when school started and she could see Rosario again. She liked being out of her grandparents' house. She liked being in the crisp blue blouse and navy blue skirt of her uniform. She liked the music at the school and she liked running her fingers through the cuts in the neck of St. Cecilia as they walked down the steps to the assembly every morning after Mass. If she couldn't be in her real home with her parents, she could be here. In the afternoons she would go to the grotto and pray to the Virgin Mary to make her parents come back, even though she knew God didn't give people back once he took them.

Faye started to bring little gifts to Mary—a flower, a pretty leaf, a drawing. She knew that in the Bible there were animal sacrifices, but she didn't want to kill anything. She wondered if the lady's head was still in the basement and if that would count, but she didn't want to go down there again, she didn't want to touch it, and somehow she knew it wasn't the right thing to do—that God might actually punish her for that. If not for stealing, then for whatever had happened to the lady, because Faye never told anyone and she knew, she really did know, that she should have told someone.

If she'd told anyone, it would have been Sister Anne Marie. Sister had been very kind to her since she had come to St. Cecilia and Faye felt like she could tell her things.

It was October when Faye was helping Sister Anne Marie at

lunchtime by clapping erasers outside on the fire escape and sweeping the leaves that gathered around the door to the little music cottage where they had choir every other afternoon.

Faye could tell Sister Anne Marie was trying to get her to talk about her parents, but Faye didn't want to. She had already talked to Rosario at camp that summer about her parents and Rosario had been really strange to her afterward. So Faye hadn't said anything else and Rosario had stopped being weird and Faye began to understand what her grandmother meant when she said, "We don't share family things outside the house, Faye. It's not proper. You understand what proper means, don't you?" And Faye hadn't. What she did know was that secrets were supposed to be kept, not shared. That's what her grandmother meant.

But Sister Anne Marie wanted her to share secrets with her and Faye thought it would be different, because Sister was a nun and Rosario was just another kid, like she was. Rosario had her own family secrets and always felt bad after she told them to Faye. But Faye was better at listening than Rosario was, so she always knew to look solemn and nod her head and not say anything but maybe just put her hand on Rosario's shoulder like her grandmother did with her. That always seemed to work. So Rosario kept sharing her secrets and Faye just kept listening.

Faye liked autumn. She liked the leaves and the crisp air and the way everything smelled. She liked that it was mostly gray outside and windy, and that she had to wear a jacket and that her hands were always cold. She liked Halloween and Thanksgiving—or she used to.

She stood by the door with the broom in her hands and she was surprised to feel the tears running down her face. Sister Anne Marie came and took the broom away. She shut the door and led Faye to a small bank of chairs behind the music stands and they sat down. Sister asked Faye what was wrong, but Faye didn't say anything. Then she said, "I would have brought the things from the basement to the Virgin if I thought they would bring my parents back, but I don't think they will. I don't want to kill any animals, but that's what they do in the Bible. I'll kill something if I have to, to bring my parents back, but I really don't want to. I brought other things, but I think I'm supposed to kill something."

Sister Anne Marie had looked away for a moment and her hand had flown up to her face in the same way as the women in the photographs Faye's grandfather had taken. She turned back to Faye and said, her voice a little funny, "Why do you think you have to kill someone, Faye?"

"In the Bible there's always animal sacrifice. A lamb or a goat. Or a calf. Or some doves. I don't even know where you get those things in Brooklyn. I don't think it's the same if you get them from the Italian Market where they are already dead and in the butcher shop. But I would get one if I knew how. I would do what Abraham did if it would save my parents, the way it saved Isaac."

Sister Anne Marie had looked different then—the scared look on her face had changed to a worried look. She had talked to Faye about her parents and said that they couldn't come back, but that Faye would see them later, in Heaven.

Faye had told her that she wished she had died with them, that she wished she could live at St. Cecilia's with the girls in the dorm. That she had liked being at camp, that she didn't want to be at her grandparents' house anymore. Then she told Sister about the photographs and the table and the things on the plates and the head. She knew this was what her grandmother had meant about not telling secrets, that it wasn't proper. But Faye knew that even if the table and the plates and the things on the bed weren't real, the head was real. And now that Sister knew, maybe she would let Faye come and live at St. Cecilia's all the time with the other girls who were orphans, like she was.

Faye hadn't planned any of this. She hadn't planned to tell Sister Anne Marie about any of the things she told her. And now she couldn't take it back. All she could do was say again, "I think I should live here. I think it's what my parents would want. I think that's why I am supposed to go and pray to Mary every day. Because then she will intercede like the priest says, and if my parents can't come back, then I can come here, instead."

❖

It was almost Halloween when Faye had first seen Sister Anne Marie slapping her hands on the slate outside the grotto until they were bloody. It was almost Thanksgiving before she told Faye that she was going to talk to Faye's grandfather and "get to the bottom of this."

That day, that first fall day when Faye had been crying, Sister had asked her again and again about the photographs and everything else. She had asked Faye about the doctor and the medication and when Faye had fainted and been in bed and all of that. She had asked Faye if she understood what she was saying and Faye had told her yes to everything and said that she didn't go into the darkroom anymore now that she knew what the photographs were, because they frightened her and sometimes they made her sick and that she didn't eat meat anymore because of what she saw on the plates and she thought that was what was making her sick—the pieces from the ladies in the photographs that her grandfather took that were on the plates and then maybe in the refrigerator and then on the plates. Their plates, the plates they ate from every day.

Sister Anne Marie had left the room then. She had told Faye to stay there and she'd be right back, but Faye had heard her in the lavatory outside the music room, throwing up and making gurgling noises and running water in the sink and when she came back her face was red and she looked like she had been crying.

"We'll find a way to fix this," was all she had said then, and she had put her arms around Faye and held her really tight. Then she had sent her back to class.

CHAPTER NINETEEN
THE LAST NIGHT

In the dreams Faye had on her last night in Congo, she was running through the lush rainforest of Kivu, trying to save Martine. Faye had been in the Land Rover with Martine, but then they had hit something—a great gaping hole in the road—and Martine was no longer in the car with her. It was late in the afternoon, nearly evening, just as it had been when they had left the care center after talking to Vandana, and the shadows had begun to fall as the sun set. Faye had gotten out of the Land Rover and had gone searching for Martine. She had tried to call her name, but no sound would come out of her. So Faye ran, looking near where the car was stuck in the big hole in the road, then further and further into the rainforest.

In the dream, Faye was out of breath from running, and she could hear her own breath and her heart pounding in her ears as she ran. She was frightened, as frightened as she'd ever been, because there was no one near where she was and she couldn't find Martine and she knew she had to find her, had to find her, something had happened to Martine, *where was she?*

Faye had fallen, then, as she whirled around in a circle trying to see everything she could before it got dark, trying not to lose sight of the road so she didn't get lost among the trees and plants. She could hear the insects and the birds and some small sounds of shrews or weasels or whatever ran along the ground here in this place she knew almost nothing about.

She had fallen, tripped over some plant or root or something and when she fell, everything around her was wet. But it was always wet in the rainforest, that was why it was called rainforest, she told herself, as she tried to get up out of the wetness. It was then that she realized the wetness was blood and the ooze of entrails and damp, gory pieces of bodies—hands, feet, ears, a head, then another head, all crawling with maggots and worms and other slithery things she couldn't identify, didn't want to identify.

She had tried to scream, had put her blood-drenched hand up to her mouth and seen that maggots were dripping from her hand onto her legs. She had felt the pressure in her lungs of screaming, but no sound would come out. She could feel her lips pulled tight across her teeth, her mouth wide, as wide as it had ever been, but no sound, no sound at all came from her, none at all.

❖

It was after that when Faye began to get sick. Very sick. So sick that it took her over a week once she was back in New York to understand how sick she was. She was sick with images that would not go away, sick with remembering. She lay in her own bed, in her own apartment, paralyzed with fear, paralyzed with the photographs in her head that just kept flipping by like when she was at school, back at St. Cecilia's, and the nuns would run the little round carousel slide projector that had been there forever and the girls in her class had all giggled because it seemed so old-fashioned. The images in Faye's head ran like that—over and over, clicking past, and then starting again. She was literally reeling from the intensity and how many pictures there were in her own personal memory card—hundreds, hundreds, how had she taken all these photographs, how had she seen all those things?

It wasn't just Bukavu she was remembering.

It was Chinatown, it was Fresno, it was Asifa, it was Esperanza lying under the train, it was the accident with the decapitated man, it was the fire in the theater at Christmas and all the incinerated children, it was St. Cecilia's. It was her grandparents' house. She was remembering it all now. And then, one night, she was awakened by her own screaming.

CHAPTER TWENTY
AN ACT OF CONTRITION

Sister Anne Marie had made up the little bed for Faye at the end of the row in the junior dorm at St. Cecilia's. There was a small table next to the bed that had two little drawers in it. On the table was a little wooden crucifix, but it was just the cross, there was no Jesus on it.

The bed was small. A single bed with a flat wooden headboard. It was low to the floor and Faye thought there wasn't even room for there to be someone her size under it, let alone a monster.

There were fourteen beds in the room, which was on the top floor—the fourth floor—of the dormitory. All the girls in the junior dormitory were twelve years old and younger. In the senior dormitory, the girls were teenagers. There were more of them—thirty in all. The first floor had a big living room kind of room with chairs and sofas and a TV and there was a kitchen and a dining room.

When Sister Anne Marie made the little bed for Faye, she told her that she would be staying there from now on. She said that she had spoken to Mother Superior and that Faye shouldn't worry. She was going to see Faye's grandfather "This very day," and from then on, Faye would be what she called "a ward of the State."

She patted the end of the bed when she had finished with the sheets and the dark blue blanket and Faye sat down and Sister sat next to her. "We will pray now," she told Faye. "We will pray for your parents, who are in Heaven, and for your grandmother, for Jesus's forgiveness, and we will pray for the salvation of your grandfather's soul. And we will pray for…those women in the photographs."

Faye wasn't sure what Sister meant about her grandparents, but she said the three Hail Marys and the two Our Fathers with Sister, out loud.

Sister pulled a little box out from under the bed—it was cardboard, but flat. She put it on the end of the bed and opened it and inside were pajamas and underwear and a pair of slippers and a thin robe.

"These are for you. They are yours now. You can wear them tonight when you go to bed. In the drawer here"—and she had opened the top drawer in the little table—"there is a toothbrush and everything else you need. I'll have Theresa show you everything tonight. You know her, she's in the fifth grade. She sleeps in the bed next to yours."

Sister Anne Marie put the underwear in the second drawer, along with the robe, which she folded very flat. She put the pajamas underneath the pillow and put the slippers on the floor under the bed, by the table. She looked at Faye, still sitting on the bed, and then she came over and put her arms around Faye.

"St. Cecilia will watch over you, Faye. She will. She was brave, like you."

Then she had taken Faye's hand and they had gone downstairs. Faye had sat in a window seat with her notebook and watched as Sister Anne Marie walked down the walkway to the end of the driveway and turned down the street, toward the bus stop that went to the subway that went to Faye's grandparents' house.

Faye never saw her again.

CHAPTER TWENTY-ONE
AFTER THE DREAMS

More than a week had passed since Faye had returned to New York and she had barely left her apartment. She had stayed away from the newspaper, she had stayed away from friends, she had stayed out of her own studio. Faye had told her editor she was ill, really ill, some kind of parasite, she never should have eaten that food, and that she was being treated, but that she was too weak to come in.

Faye said she'd email him photos to look at in a few days, but he told her to rest, they had time before the story ran, two weeks, maybe more, wiggle room, don't worry. Faye told him she had a rough draft of the copy, but thought she might need help from rewrite. "The pictures don't tell the whole story," she'd said as she thought of the chunks of flesh torn out of Vandana's body and what Vandana had told her. "For the first time, the pictures really don't tell the whole story."

On the eighth night after she was back, Faye woke up drenched in sweat and screaming. She picked up her iPhone, Googled a number, and called the suicide hotline.

"I want to be dead," she said to the woman who answered the phone. Her voice was flat, monotonal. It held none of the hysteria she'd awoken with. She repeated, "I want to be dead. I *need* to be dead." And then she had hung up before the woman could say anything at all.

CHAPTER TWENTY-TWO
ON THE UPPER SHELVES

Before she had left for the DRC, Faye had been planning her exhibit. Every night she had spent a few hours in her studio, ambient music playing as she sorted through boxes of notebooks, memory cards, negatives, and actual photographs. She had gone to the cabinet time after time, taking out this jar or that. She had been writing the copy to go with the exhibit, knew exactly what she wanted, had already settled on the gallery, signed the contract, knew that very little was missing. When she returned from this assignment, she'd have everything she needed.

It was time to reveal the upper shelves, time to tip the jars open and let the contents spill at the feet of the those who came to be titillated by mayhem, time to show what happened when St. Cecilia didn't die, yet the wounds didn't close, either. Time for the screaming to begin.

CHAPTER TWENTY-THREE
MISSING

Theresa had shown Faye around the dormitory that first night. Faye had thought it would be scary, but it wasn't. The girls in the junior dorm all laughed a lot and threw things at each other and then Sister Mary Margaret had come in and told them to "simmer down" and "get ready for bed," but she was kind of laughing with them and then said, "I mean it, now," and tried to look stern but it didn't work, but the girls started to get ready for bed anyway, because they didn't want Sister Mary Margaret to get mad.

Faye had fallen asleep right away, before she even finished all her prayers, and she hadn't woken up until Sister Mary Margaret came back for them in the morning.

The police had come to St. Cecilia's just after dinner two days after Sister Anne Marie had left to go to Faye's grandparents' house. Sister Anne Marie had never come back to St. Cecilia's, and Mother Superior had reported her missing.

The police had sent a detective over to the dormitory and Sister Mary Margaret had come to get Faye because the detective wanted to talk to her, to ask her what she had told Sister Anne Marie.

They had all gone into a little room off the living room in the dormitory, the room that Sister Mary Margaret called the office. There was a desk and three chairs and a lamp and a big, plain crucifix on the wall over the desk. Mother Superior sat down behind the desk and Sister Mary Margaret sat in one of the chairs and had Faye sit next to her. The detective, who said, "Call me Tom, Faye, my name is Tom," asked her about different things—her parents, if she was sad, if she was angry.

Faye said she prayed a lot for her parents to come back, but that she knew that couldn't happen. She said she wasn't sad as much, now that she was at St. Cecilia's. Then she said she knew she should be sad about not being at her grandparents' house anymore, but that she really didn't like it there, that at first it was okay, because of the darkroom and the people who came to get their pictures taken, and painting with her grandfather in the kitchen. But then there had been the ladies in the photographs and the things on the plates and the head in the basement and she didn't want to eat meat anymore and it just got harder and harder to be there and easier and easier to be here, at St. Cecilia's, and that since she was really an orphan anyway, she should be here, it's what her parents would have wanted, she was sure of that, really sure, because there was never anything but wood in the vise at her parents' house and there was that lady's head with the sewn-up lips and no eyes in the vise at her grandparents' house and Faye just knew, she really just knew, that wasn't at all right.

Detective Tom had been writing things down on a little notepad. Sister Mary Margaret had been holding Faye's hand while she talked, but after Faye started to talk about the photographs, she had squeezed Faye's hand really hard and then let it go. Detective Tom was leaning against Mother Superior's desk and Faye couldn't really see Mother's face. But Detective Tom had stopped writing after a while and had just looked right at Faye while she talked.

"I never looked at the jar on the table," Faye said, at the end. "I just really didn't want to see any more. Sister Anne Marie said she would get to the bottom of things. She said it would all work out."

Detective Tom had turned and looked at Mother Superior then and tilted his head toward Faye as he said, "We need to talk now, without the child."

CHAPTER TWENTY-FOUR
NOISE

A fter Faye had called the suicide hotline, she had gotten out of bed, gotten dressed, pulled on her coat, and left the apartment. It was nearly two in the morning, but it was New York on a Thursday and even though it was biting cold, there was always somewhere to go, places where there would be people. Faye needed people. Faye needed noise and music and even though she hated it, maybe even cigarette smoke. Faye thought if she just had a drink in a bar with a lot of loud music and people shouting and laughing and dancing and smoking and drinking, she wouldn't kill herself.

At least not tonight.

She wouldn't go to the river and drown herself, which was how she had decided to die. She already knew from a myriad of stories she'd covered what *wouldn't* work—she couldn't throw herself in front of a car or a subway. She couldn't take pills or hang herself. She couldn't jump from her apartment window. She didn't want to take anyone else with her, anyway, not now, not tonight. She had enough blood on her hands. Faye just wanted a drink and some inane conversation and someone to give her a reason not to die, even if it was just temporary. She needed to stop seeing the slide show that wouldn't stop running in her head. She needed someone else's story or pictures to run for a while. She was prepared to be the best listener ever. If only for this one night.

❖

When Faye woke up, it was nearly dark again. She looked at the clock—quarter to five. How had she slept so long—ten, twelve hours? She didn't remember coming home, but she also didn't remember dreaming, so she didn't care if she'd gotten plastered or even with whom. She hadn't slept without nightmares since that night in Bukavu nearly two weeks ago with Martine. She lay in her bed, trying to think. She vaguely remembered being in one of the Irish bars near Penn Station. She'd liked those bars when she had first been working at the paper. A lot of retired cops hung out there, along with a few errant IRA types, and some low-level criminals and mobsters. It was as good a place as any to get a drink, or get drunk, and she got to listen, because she was always looking for a new story then, or even an old story that could be brought to life in a new form—a story that could best be told in photographs.

Faye knew she'd been in a cab, though going to or from the bar or even what bar, she couldn't recall. Faye sat up slowly—she felt slightly dizzy, as if she'd had way too much to drink. She had an awful taste in her mouth and what felt like pieces of food. Ugh—had she gone to sleep with food in her mouth? Or had she vomited from drinking? Her lips felt dry and cracked. She walked—staggered was more like it—to the bathroom, turned on the light, and looked in the mirror.

Her mouth was crusted with blood and there was blood on her left cheek and blood on her neck and ear. She spat into the sink and bits of what looked like meat splattered the porcelain. *Meat?* Faye hadn't eaten meat since she was seven and living at her grandparents' house. She felt like she was going to vomit. Faye turned on the faucet and as she did, she saw she had blood on both hands. Her nails had blood under them and as her heart began to pound, she saw she had blood on her shirt and blood on her thighs. She turned off the faucet and got into the shower, still in her shirt and underwear. But as she reached for the faucet there, she saw blood on her feet, blood pooled on the floor of the tub, blood leaking from somewhere behind her.

Faye felt hot and dizzy and she could feel the air pressing up out of her lungs, but she didn't scream, couldn't scream. She turned and pulled back the shower curtain.

There, behind the shower curtain, up against the edge of the tub, lay the crumpled body of Sister Anne Marie. Her throat was slit and gaping, the blood thick and gelatinous around the wound. Her habit was cut apart in different places—one of her breasts had been cut clean off. Her side was open, just like in the pictures of Jesus, and her liver had been cut out. Her habit was pushed up to her waist and blood was congealed on her thighs and between them. Her face had not been cut, but her eyes were open wide and had the blue fish-eye film of death over them. Her mouth was open and askew and there was blood on her teeth and lips, but Faye did not see a wound. As she leaned closer, though, she saw that Sister Anne Marie's tongue had been cut out. Inside her mouth was filled with clotted, pudding-like gore.

Faye stood there, her feet covered in the pooling blood, staring at Sister Anne Marie's body, at what had been done to her. She reached over to pull down her habit, to cover her up, automatically crossing herself as she did so, but as she moved forward, making the sign of the cross, she slipped in the blood and fell into Sister Anne Marie, Faye's face up against hers, her lips almost on the dead nun's.

It was Faye's own screaming that finally woke her.

CHAPTER TWENTY-FIVE
HAIL MARY, FULL OF GRACE

Sister Mary Margaret had taken Faye out of the office in the dormitory and led her back to the living room. Theresa had gotten up and come over and asked if she was okay and Faye had just nodded, but hadn't said anything. Faye knew something was wrong, she knew that something had happened to Sister Anne Marie and she was afraid— afraid it was her fault and that she would never see Sister Anne Marie again.

After a while, Detective Tom had come out of the room with Mother Superior and they had walked to the front door together and walked out onto the enclosed porch. They were talking very low and both of them looked serious. Faye couldn't hear anything they said. From where she was sitting, Faye could see Mother Superior put her head down and put her hands on her face and shake her head. Detective Tom put his hand on her shoulder and said something. Then he left. Mother came back in, motioned to Sister Mary Margaret, and they went into the office together and shut the door.

❖

Sister Anne Marie never came back to St. Cecilia's. There was an assembly and Mother Superior spoke to everyone and said there had been an accident and Sister Anne Marie was not coming back to St. Cecilia's. Mother told them that they might hear things, other things, but that was what had happened. There had been an accident. She said it was very sad and it was all right for them to feel sad and they could cry if they wanted to, but they should remember that Jesus was taking care of Sister Anne Marie now and that she was safe and loved and in Heaven.

There was a big rustling in the room and murmurs and Faye could hear the sounds of some of the girls starting to cry and there were whispers among the older girls.

Mother Superior looked very pale and tired as she stood on the little stage where Sister Anne Marie had put on the recitals and musical events. Faye knew that people weren't supposed to lie, but she knew Mother Superior was lying. She knew that there hadn't been an accident. She knew that Sister Anne Marie had gone to her grandparents' house to make sure that Faye never had to go back there and now she was gone. Faye thought about Sister Anne Marie praying with her in the dormitory, sitting on her bed with her and hugging her, and she wished she had never told her about her grandfather and the photographs and the lady's head. Faye didn't want to cry, but she did anyway. She wanted to see Sister Anne Marie. She didn't want to think about what had happened to her. She couldn't think about what had happened to her.

Mother Superior told them they should all pray for Sister Anne Marie. Right now, they were going to pray for Sister Anne Marie, "Hail Mary, full of grace, the Lord is with thee, blessed art thou among women…"

All Faye could hear was crying.

CHAPTER TWENTY-SIX
TRYING NOT TO DREAM

Faye hadn't quit the newspaper and now she knew she wouldn't. She'd intended to when she got back from the DRC and Afghanistan, but she'd never gone on to Afghanistan as planned—it had been too much. That story was still waiting for her and she still wanted it. She'd learned that ordinary mayhem was her *métier* and she knew she had to follow it, no matter what.

It had taken nearly all the pre-production time they'd had for Faye and her editor to lay out the Congo story. He had looked at the photos— she'd culled just under a hundred for him to look at—and he had looked at them for about fifteen minutes and then had abruptly gotten up and left the room.

When he came back, he hadn't looked directly at Faye, but had gone back to the light table and said, "Powerful stuff, Faye. More powerful than I expected. I have to think about what we're going to use here. Give me some time—go do more work on the copy. It needs to be pristine for this one. I don't want rewrite involved. This is all you here. All you. I want to showcase this. People remember the other stories— that girl in the subway and the kids being poisoned. The Afghan girl with the cut-up face. That—well, it got a lot of play while you were away. You haven't even seen it, have you? Really good. Doesn't say much about where we've put all that tax money, though, does it? Anyway, Faye, they want to hear from you. And you were there, in the DRC—rewrite wasn't there. So just tell it. Lay it out for us. The part that's not here, whatever that is. You know, I don't. You don't have to turn into a writer—just short descriptions. Just the story behind the photos."

Faye had gone home to write, but had ended up crawling into bed and trying not to dream.

CHAPTER TWENTY-SEVEN
PRAY

Faye had stayed on at St. Cecilia's until she graduated. A decade of moving between the floors of the dormitory. A decade of leaving talismans for the Virgin Mary in the grotto. A decade of being friends with Rosario and Jessica, Tamara and the three Theresas. A decade of prayers. A decade of photographs. A decade of running her fingers through the slices on St. Cecilia's neck every morning on her way to Mass. A decade of knowing she was Mother Superior's special project, because Mother Superior knew what no one else had known.

Mother Superior and Detective Tom had told her that Sister Anne Marie had had an accident when she had gone to Faye's grandparents' house. They had told her there had been a fall down a flight of stairs, a broken neck, a twisted body on the basement floor. Things like this happen sometimes, Mother Superior had told her in the little office, while Detective Tom had looked off to the side, not meeting Faye's eyes. But Mother Superior had looked like she had been crying. Mother Superior, who was in charge of everything, had looked scared.

That night Faye had prayed until she fell asleep. Prayed for Sister Anne Marie, who had been her friend, and who had protected her. Prayed for Mother Superior, who had told Faye lie after lie because she knew the truth was too awful to bear. Prayed for Detective Tom, because he had found Sister Anne Marie, and Faye knew what that meant. Prayed for her grandparents, because she was afraid they would go to hell and never see Jesus. Prayed for herself, because as she had sat in the little office, she had felt like Detective Tom and Mother Superior were both afraid of her, and if they were too afraid, Mother Superior might not let her stay at St. Cecilia's. Mother Superior might call Detective Tom, and he might put her in jail. Because they knew she knew. They knew Faye knew about everything. Maybe, Faye thought, maybe they thought that she was part of it.

And maybe, maybe, maybe, she was. Which was why she had to pray.

CHAPTER TWENTY-EIGHT
PREDATORS

The day after she'd had the nightmare about Sister Anne Marie, Faye had finalized the date with the Tribeca gallery owner she'd signed the contract with for her show and had begun to put it together. Now she had a clear picture of the show in her head. She was ready. She went down to the gallery and met with Nick Allingham, the owner, and his assistant, a young woman with fluffy, white-blond hair and dramatic tattoos who went by the unlikely name of Persia, just Persia.

Nick was clear: He wanted a gag order on the show until the opening. Only he and Persia were to see the photos and what Faye was calling "mixed media" pieces. There was also a video installation piece that Persia had put together of Faye's previous work. It was going to be fantastic. For the first time since she'd returned from the DRC, Faye felt okay. More than okay, actually. Maybe the nightmares were over for good. Maybe that was what the work was for—to keep the nightmares at bay.

Nick and Faye both knew the show was going to generate the kind of attention that Andres Serrano's *Piss Christ* and AIDS artist David Wojnarowicz had garnered. Nick was calling Faye "the new Mapplethorpe" in press releases and on the gallery's website, which made Faye cringe. She didn't want to be derivative of anyone else. Faye reminded Nick that Mapplethorpe never developed his own photographs and that they were all staged, whereas hers were real— *cinema verité* of the most visceral sort. She knew she sounded petulant when she said it—a diva artist of a type she'd never aspired to be. But it was out there.

Nick shrugged. But Persia, who despite her studied vacant look was clearly brilliant, the video installation was spectacular, said that they—Faye, Nick, the gallery—needed to be prepared for backlash. And also to expect it.

"Sure, this mayor isn't going to go all Giuliani on everyone and try and shut the place down, but this is intense. People always think they really want to know," Persia said, her unnaturally green eyes sparkling with something Faye thought was pure rage. "Oh yeah—they all think they want to see what's hiding underneath the rocks or what's hidden behind those blue drapes at the scene of an accident or behind the yellow police tape at a crime. They think it will broaden them and expand them and put them more in touch with humanity, but they really don't want to know because they really can't, you know, *process* it. They're really just voyeurs and can't admit to it. They just want to get off on the sickness of what's in the darkest recesses of everyone's twisted psyche. I mean, think about how many people buy the artwork and memorabilia of serial killers. *Serial killers*. Imagine."

Faye had begun looking at something in one of her portfolios while Persia was talking, but when she said *serial killers*, Faye had snapped to attention and looked directly at her. But Persia was just spewing—she hated the insincerity of the majority of what she called New York's "art predators" and just kept ranting.

The rest of what she said, Faye had always known. She'd known it since the very first time she'd actually looked at the photographs of the women hanging on the clothesline in her grandfather's darkroom. She'd known it when she had been unflinching on the subway tracks with Esperanza. She'd started to feel it, really feel it, when Shihong had shown her everything in the little shop in Chinatown. That still made her shudder. The story with Asifa—that had made her feel like her grandfather had been right there, in the room with her.

But Faye had never felt it as deeply as she had when she had been in the DRC. That feeling, which she'd had every day and night since, was the feeling that Persia was talking about. Once you knew for sure what other people were capable of, once you knew the horror was more than nightmare, once you knew what *true* horror was and that there was nothing supernatural about it—no vampires, no werewolves, no things that went bump in the night—but that it was as real as it gets, that it was what Vandana meant when she said "monsters," then you could never look away again.

Ever.

All three of them—Faye, Nick, Persia—wanted to be prepared for whatever the response was, but they also wanted the initial shock to be dramatic. Persia said she wanted people to feel like they'd been hit hard when they first came into the gallery. Nick knew the kind of reviews Faye's other work had received and he was hoping for an even more dramatic response to this show. He was hoping for a sellout opening where all Faye's work was sold and people put in orders for more.

Faye was exhibiting the most brutal of the DRC photos—ones that the paper said they simply couldn't run, even in the magazine. And then there was everything she had gotten from Shihong when she'd been in Chinatown, and the contents of her apothecary cabinet at home. There were the photographs she had taken years before, of the jars at St. Cecilia's and of St. Cecilia herself, lying on her alabaster slab, with her neck sliced open. Those were the photographs she had taken with her first camera and developed herself, they were her own private retrospective, she realized now.

But there were also the other photographs, the ones that no one had ever seen, that even Nick hadn't seen yet and which would be in the show as a surprise. A stunning surprise, Faye thought.

❖

The nightmares had stopped after that last dream about Sister Anne Marie, the one that had been so intense, so real Faye had actually tasted blood in her mouth, but then realized she had bitten the inside of her cheek from fear in her sleep. When she woke up there was fresh blood on her pillow.

Faye had called Martine a few days later. They had talked for a while and Faye had felt better. She realized that getting back to work was the best thing. She was already planning her trip to Afghanistan.

She could still go, she knew she could. She just had to recover a little bit more. Have more nights of dreamless sleep. She was sure of it.

There were other stories to tell there—stories beyond Asifa's story. That had been distanced from the place, because she was here, applying for asylum, working to put her life back together. Asifa had closed the door on Afghanistan. But Afghanistan was still an open door for the rest of them.

A soldier had just gone nuts over there and killed over a dozen civilians, some of them children. He was decorated, but on his fifth tour of duty. He'd already had a traumatic brain injury in an IED attack. The day before he went out at night and shot up a series of homes in the village near the base, he'd watched a friend get blown up in front of him. Body parts had landed in his lap. If he'd been a foot closer, it would have been *his* body parts strewn across the roadway.

Faye had called a friend, a reporter, over in Kabul and asked what else there was to know. He'd told her that there had been some "unpleasant stuff" at the base where the soldier had been—another soldier had gone home on leave and lit his wife on fire and killed himself. A few other suicides, really grisly ones. Another couple murders. "It's a bad situation—you just can't keep sending these guys out to kill every day for years and years and think they're going to stay anything like normal, you know? They become killing machines. Put them back in their own society and they can't cope. They *need* to kill. If you want stories, I've got stories. Let me know when you're coming."

And Faye, who had been so sure before she'd gone to the DRC that she was leaving the paper, leaving the images behind, had felt the lure again. This time she would be prepared, though. She knew that. This time she'd be safe from the carousel of images. The gallery show would take care of all that—it would be cathartic, an exorcism. It would lay it all out. The ordinary mayhem she'd lived with since the night her parents burned alive in their car in the snow on New Year's Eve. Faye thought she was okay now. Faye thought she was safe.

CHAPTER TWENTY-NINE
THE BOX

A few months before the end of her senior year, Mother Superior called Faye into her office. Faye had watched different classmates brought in for what other girls had always called the "separation" talk. The girls who were orphans—they all qualified, even though Faye was the only one left who actually had no family—could stay at St. Cecilia's throughout the summer after their graduation, but they had to keep working and they had to find a place to live if they weren't going to college in the fall. St. Cecilia's gave every girl a stipend when she left the school. Still, over the years a few had ended up staying at the school and working there. Three girls who were in the high school when Faye was in eighth grade had actually gone on to become nuns.

Faye was going to college. She had gotten financial aid to NYU. But she was not eager to leave St. Cecilia's. She felt safe there, protected. She had let herself be sheltered. There were the things she knew and the things she didn't want to know. There was nothing Dickensian about St. Cecilia's. She loved it there. She loved Sister Mary Margaret, who was like a den mother to the girls in the dormitory. She loved the strength and calm of Mother Superior. She even loved the Latina nun who had taken Sister Anne Marie's place with the music, Sister Fatima Dolores.

In the ten years Faye had spent at the school, she had never climbed on a chair or a step-stool to see what was in the uppermost jars outside Mother Superior's office. She had never gone into Manhattan to search the newspaper files at the public library with the stone lions out in front to see what she could find out about Sister Anne Marie's death, or even about what had happened to her own grandparents. Mother Superior had told her, after Sister Anne Marie's disappearance, that Faye wouldn't be seeing them again, that legally she belonged to St. Cecilia's now. She had told Faye that there were some rules that her grandparents had broken and that there would be some punishment involved, just as there was at St. Cecilia's. That was all she said, and over the years they had never spoken about it again.

Until the day Faye went to the office for what she thought would be the separation talk.

It was a chill gray day in early March. The daffodils had come up early, due to a short spurt of warm weather, and they were in full bloom by the grotto as Faye walked that same path she had taken every day she had been at the school. She had stopped and said a small prayer to Mary just as she always did. She listened for a moment, as she had continued to do all these years later, listened for the sound of Sister Anne Marie crying in the music room when she thought no one could hear. Sister Fatima Dolores never cried. She was relentlessly cheerful, always humming, always smiling. Faye never thought of her as Sister Anne Marie's replacement. She just thought of her as someone else. But Faye still listened for Sister Anne Marie. She couldn't help it.

Mother Superior opened the door to the office and another girl, one of the Theresas, slipped past Faye. Her head was down and she only murmured "Hi" to Faye without looking at her as she walked hurriedly away. Faye looked after the retreating girl and then turned to Mother Superior, a questioning look on her face. Faye hadn't thought the separation talk was going to be that bad. Her stomach flipped a little as she walked into the office and shut the door.

She'd been in this office many times over the years. She'd memorized it—from the spare black crucifix to the small glassed-in cabinet with the prayer books to the oval print of Raphael's *Madonna of the Streets* that hung opposite Mother's desk.

"You know we have a separation talk with all the senior girls who live here, right, Faye?" Mother began. Faye nodded and Mother continued.

"Ours will be a little different, dear." Mother had reached across the desk then and held out her hand toward Faye. Faye reached back. It was strange and somewhat unsettling. Faye had never remembered

Mother touching anyone except shaking the hands of parents. Mother only grasped her hand for a minute, then let go.

"I have something for you. I don't want you to take it to the dormitory and I am not altogether sure I should even be giving it to you. But it belongs to you, so you should have it. And since you will be leaving here soon—" Here she paused and looked toward the small window, then back at Faye. "You need to have it before you go...out there." Mother waved her hand in the direction of the world outside the window, the Brooklyn neighborhood outside St. Cecilia's protected little enclave.

"We've never talked about this, but now we have to," she continued. "We have to talk about Sister Anne Marie and your grandfather."

Faye hadn't realized how straight she'd been sitting in her chair, her hands folded in her lap the way they'd been taught by Sister Mary Margaret. Now she gripped the arms of the hard wooden chair. She could feel her heart racing.

"I don't want to talk about that, Mother, if you don't mind. I just don't..." Faye had that hot, dizzy feeling she'd had so many years ago at her grandparents' house. She didn't want to feel like this. She wanted to leave. She had actually started to get up out of her chair when Mother said, "Please sit down, Faye. We have to talk, whether either of us wants to or not."

And then Mother began. She bent over and picked up a white cardboard carton, the kind that Xerox paper came in, with a lid on it. Neatly printed on the side was FAYE ELIZABETH BLAKEMORE and Faye's old address, the one she had with her parents. Faye felt tears pricking behind her eyes. She didn't want to cry. She wanted to leave.

"I haven't looked in this box, Faye," Mother Superior said, and Faye believed her, although she couldn't imagine how Mother had kept her curiosity at bay all these years. Maybe, like Faye, she really didn't want to know what was inside. "I'm sure there are things here that could be upsetting. And I would prefer, given what happened with Sister Anne Marie, that you not discuss this with your friends, even though you may want to. It's especially important that you not say anything to Rosario Lopez or Theresa McCann, as they are both already in a somewhat unstable situation." Faye thought about how Theresa had been when she had left Mother's office a few minutes ago. She wondered what was wrong.

Mother continued, "Whenever you want to look at the contents of this box, let me know, and I will provide a space for you to do so. I think that it would best if you do that here or across the hall in the biology lab."

Faye thought about the appropriateness of the jars of horrifying things as she looked through whatever it was that was in the box.

"We have never discussed this, but I think you have known this whole time that Sister Anne Marie did not have an accident." Mother looked at Faye and got up from behind the desk, came around, and stood in front of Faye.

Faye could feel a fine film of sweat break out over her whole body. She felt clammy and cold and her teeth started to chatter uncontrollably. She didn't want to hear this. It was time to go. She got up out of the chair and moved toward the door, but Mother was faster and put her hand against the door, keeping it shut, before Faye could open it.

"Please…" was all Faye said, her hand still on the doorknob, her back to Mother.

"You must hear this, Faye, because you cannot leave here not knowing. Other people know. They know out there. They know and it's quite possible when they hear your name or where you went to school, that someone will say something to you. Someone will ask you if you are the girl whose grandfather murdered the nun and…well…"

It was out now. There was no taking it back. Faye didn't even feel it when her body hit the floor. She was already unconscious.

CHAPTER THIRTY
VICTIMS

Faye lay flat on her bed in the dorm staring up at the little blue stenciled crosses. She was still in her uniform. It was almost dark and the only light was the small one on the little table near the door that led to the landing at the top of the stairs. She hadn't wanted to take the box Mother had given her. She hadn't wanted to look inside. She hadn't wanted to remember the things she had spent ten years—most of her childhood—trying to forget.

But Mother Superior had wanted her to take it. She had waited more than ten years to give it to Faye. And she clearly wanted Faye to have time to recover before she went off to college. But how could she ever recover from this, from what Mother had told her? From what was in the box?

After she had fainted, Mother had brought her around with smelling salts. Faye remembered that her mother had had the same old-fashioned bottle on her dresser. Faye had wanted to take the bottle from Mother and hold it, the sense memory of her own mother, her dead mother, her burned-alive mother, was so vivid in that moment. But instead she had pulled herself up off the floor and sat down in the chair in front of Mother's desk and started to cry.

It hadn't been what she had wanted. She had spent all these years being brave and controlled and leading as close to a normal life as she could for a girl whose grandfather had killed women and whose grandmother had known and said nothing. She had tried to be a good student and pray every day and make friends and not seem like the displaced orphan girl who kept herself cloistered like a nun behind the walls of St. Cecilia's. But Mother had blown that safe façade apart with her box of who-knows-what and her declarative statement that Sister Anne Marie, Faye's first friend, her protector, her second mother, had been murdered by her grandfather.

And now all she could do was weep. Ten years of weeping. She wanted to wail and claw at her own skin and tear her clothes, like some biblical hysteric, but she didn't. She just sat, her head on her arm on Mother's desk, weeping.

Mother stood over her, stroking her hair. They stayed like that for ten, fifteen, twenty minutes. And then as suddenly as she had begun to cry, Faye just stopped. She pulled a tissue from her uniform pocket, wiped her face, blew her nose, and stood.

"I'll take the box now, Mother, and go across the hall if no one is there." Her voice sounded hollow and scary, even to her. Mother walked around the desk, picked up the box, and handed it to Faye.

"I would say perhaps now is not the time, but I don't think there will ever be a right time, my dear. I am sorry. Please knock on my door when you are finished and I will keep the box here for you." Mother opened the door for Faye and led her across the hall to the creepy room that had fascinated and repelled Faye since she'd first come to St. Cecilia's. Faye put the box down on one of the marble tables next to some beakers and turned toward Mother, who said, "I'm going to pull these doors shut, Faye. Please don't let anyone in. And remember, you have done nothing wrong, and God loves you as His own."

With that, Mother had pulled the double doors out from the wall and closed them, leaving Faye alone with the shelves of jars filled with horror and the box filled with still more.

Faye had involuntarily made the sign of the cross before she opened the box. But when she looked inside, at first it all seemed anticlimactic.

Inside there appeared to be nothing but a big stack of thin, opaque paper envelopes of the sort her grandfather used to put the finished photographs in when he gave them to clients. But as Faye began lifting them out, she saw what they were. Strips and strips of negatives. Hundreds of them. Perhaps as many as a thousand. And at the bottom of the box, several small notebooks and a small stack of the little paintings Faye used to do at the kitchen table when her grandfather was coloring the photographs. Faye looked at the first few envelopes and saw that they were labeled in that silver pencil that her grandfather used. She sorted through the pile until she found the envelope she was looking for, the one she knew would be there, even as she hoped it wouldn't.

The photographs of Sister Anne Marie.

Faye thought about whether or not she should look at the pictures, thought about whether or not she should read the notebooks. But she was seventeen now, not six and a half, and she had experienced more than most adults ever would—she knew that, even though she had spent all these years pretending that those things had happened to someone else, a different Faye, not the Faye who had always lived at St. Cecilia's.

She slid the negatives out from the envelope and the whispery crackle of the paper sounded shockingly loud in the sterile quiet of the science lab. She closed her eyes for a moment and thought of Sister Anne Marie as she had last seen her, angry and determined, beautiful and strong as she had walked away from St. Cecilia's for what would be the last time, intent on protecting Faye from her murderous grandfather. Faye had loved Sister Anne Marie. Without her, Faye knew she would be dead, knew she would never have learned that she could ever be safe, that there would always be women to protect her and hold her and keep her from the kind of harm the women in the photographs her grandfather had taken could not be protected from.

Faye held the first strip up to the light, and the gasp that escaped her was involuntary. She had known what she would see, but still it shocked her, and she lowered the strip to the table, took a deep breath, and slipped it back into its envelope. She didn't need to see more. She knew what was there. The box was a catalogue of mayhem. Ordinary women, ordinary mayhem. They hadn't known what would happen when they encountered the mild-mannered, attractive older man with the camera who just wanted to take a picture of a pretty girl. Faye could imagine her grandfather—out walking, or driving in the car—coming up to each woman. He was striking, her grandfather. Tall, his hair still dark, with only a little gray at the temples. He was handsome, with good, strong features and sparkly eyes that were a very pale blue that made them stand out against his dark hair and skin that always seemed to be somewhat tanned, no matter what time of year it was. Faye could imagine how the women felt comfortable around him because she had seen him calm crying babies and soothe nervous prom dates and talk easily with client after client, as if he had known them for years.

Faye could imagine a girl getting in her grandfather's car because it was too cold or too hot or just because her feet hurt and she wanted a ride and thought it would be safe, with this calm, attractive older guy. And then they had ended up in the basement, cut open, cut apart, other things, the things Faye couldn't think about, done to them on the little bed down there.

Faye didn't want to think about how that had happened to Sister Anne Marie. She hadn't thought of Sister Anne Marie the way she had about those women in the photographs. But Sister Anne Marie was beautiful. She had told Faye she was black Irish—that her family had come over from Ireland and settled in Brooklyn only one generation ago. That both her parents had strong accents and she herself had had one when she was Faye's age, but the nuns had drilled it out of her, the brogue, she called it.

So when Faye saw the beautiful Sister Anne Marie tied up on the little bed with the marks that Faye now knew were mutilations on her body, with her habit pushed up past mid-thigh, she had been shocked, saddened, sickened, angry. She didn't want to think of what had happened to Sister Anne Marie. Most of all, she didn't want to think that it was her fault.

Faye whispered *Mea culpa, mea culpa, mea maxima culpa*, and put the envelope back into the box. She took out one of the small notebooks, slipped it into the pocket of her uniform, put the lid on the box, opened the double doors, and went back to Mother Superior's office. She balanced the box and knocked on the door. When Mother opened, she handed it to her, turned, and walked away. She heard the door close, but she didn't look back.

Instead Faye looked up the stairs at St. Cecilia and then quickly ran up, touched the three slashes in her neck, ran back down, and walked quickly to the door that led to the grotto. All she could see was Sister

Anne Marie, mutilated, in the basement of her grandfather's house. Only Mary could help her now. St. Cecilia was just another victim.

❖

That night in the dorm room, everyone seemed subdued. There was none of the usual laughter and pillow tossing and fake shoving that went on most nights. Even Sister Mary Margaret seemed to know that the realization that soon they would be leaving the safe enclave of St. Cecilia's, the place that had been their only real home, had hit them all, hard, with the separation interviews. From this day until the day each of them left St. Cecilia's, it would all be different. They would have to toughen up, prepare themselves for battle with the world outside this cocoon of studies and prayer and nuns who loved them like the families they never really had. From now on they were on their way to the outside, and whatever that held. Faye knew better than most what lay beyond the ivy-covered walls of St. Cecilia's. And that knowing frightened her more than she could say.

When the lights went out, Faye could hear the muffled crying of Rosario, Theresa, and several other girls. It made her feel less alone as the tears fell onto her pillow until she finally drifted off to sleep.

CHAPTER THIRTY-ONE
IN THE CABINET

A couple of nights before the opening, Faye was lying in bed, trying to sleep, trying not to think, trying not to worry that it wouldn't be a success. She had begun taking sleeping pills ten days after she'd gotten back from the DRC. The morning after the night when she'd wanted to kill herself, when she couldn't remember what had happened and she'd awakened from the terrible dream about Sister Anne Marie, she'd made an appointment with her doctor, gotten some Ambien and hoped that it would work. And it had—she'd slept through night after night with barely a dream.

Until that last night.

Faye wasn't sure at first if she was awake or asleep as she sat on the floor of her studio, the sharp halogen beam of the little gooseneck lamp beside her the only light in the room. On the floor around her were bits and pieces of things she was taking to the gallery—the last-minute touches she'd been considering and reconsidering since the last exhibit and the book about Esperanza. These were things she'd been putting together since she'd first decided on what she wanted the exhibit to be. These were, she thought, the subtly horrifying nuances that would complement the photographs.

Faye turned her head—she thought she heard something in the other room—and she saw the apothecary cabinet was open and the contents were in different places around the room. Not turned over, but out from their shelves. Faye didn't remember taking them out, but she knew you could do things on Ambien that you didn't remember.

Her doctor had even warned her about that before she had written Faye the prescription. Faye's friend Dorcas had taken Ambien and ended up driving to Connecticut to an ex-girlfriend's house in her underwear and almost getting arrested.

Open in front of Faye was her oldest notebook—the one she had kept that first year at St. Cecilia's. On the verso page was a drawing—a really good drawing, actually—of a dead squirrel. Faye stared at the details: the throat had been torn apart, probably by one of the feral cats that roamed the school grounds and the woods just beyond. The squirrel's eyes were open and in the drawing, the mouth was open, too, and the teeth were bared in what Faye now knew was the death scream. It was a child's drawing, but it had a surprising verisimilitude to it. So much so that Faye thought back to Detective Tom McManus and wondered what he would have thought had he seen it. Would he have reconsidered letting her stay at St. Cecilia's?

On the opposite page there were several rough dark smears and at the bottom of the page, in Faye's careful, looping, second-grade cursive was the notation: *Sister Anne Marie's blood from in front of the Virgin Mary at school.* Faye could still remember the day she had seen Sister Anne Marie at the grotto slapping her hands on the slate until they bled. She could still feel the texture of the blood mixed with dirt and leaves when she had touched it on the cold, slate path.

Faye closed the notebook and stood up. She walked to the window and opened the blackout drapes. She looked down onto the street six floors below. Would she die if she leapt from the window? What if she went out backward? Was she more likely to smash her head irreparably if she went that way? Would she be more assured of "dying instantly," as they said? She thought about the people jumping from the towers on 9/11, their bodies ablaze. She thought about the immigrant girls jumping to their deaths from the Triangle Shirtwaist Factory, their hair and skirts on fire. She thought about those little parchment Amaretto papers that flew up at the end when you lit them in a restaurant after dinner. Maybe she should set herself on fire first. Maybe someone would take a photograph of her as she sparked through the air to the ground below. Maybe she would set the timer on one of her own cameras first, before she did it, so it would be recorded in real time.

Faye opened the window. A rush of cold air hit her. The air smelled like snow, but there had been very little snow that winter. She sat on the edge of the sill, listened to the sounds of Manhattan below her, and thought about just leaning back, how easy it would be. She thought it might be like falling backward into a pool. She thought it would be quick. She thought she should just close her eyes and do it. But when she closed her eyes and started to lean back into the air, into the cold embrace of the winter night, she felt a hand, strong, on her arm, pulling her back. She opened her eyes, startled. There was Shihong.

"I don't think you want to do that," Shihong said in her low, whispery, slightly accented English as she pulled Faye back into the room. "Not when I've brought you these for your exhibit." Faye half-stumbled back into her studio and looked toward where Shihong was pointing.

On the long table across from the window were four jars—four of the same jars Shihong had shown her in that black-market shop in Chinatown. And now when she saw them, just as she had then, Faye couldn't keep from screaming.

This time she did not wake up. She wasn't dreaming.

CHAPTER THIRTY-TWO
DISPLACEMENT

Faye couldn't forget the box. She couldn't forget what she had seen or what she had yet to look at. *How could she?* It was, she realized, her legacy. Her brutal, violent, blood-soaked, ravaging legacy. She remembered Mother Superior telling her that the box was not about her, that it was about her grandfather, and to a degree, her grandmother, and that it was in no way *her* personal story.

But every time Faye had thought about it, she had gotten sick. Literally sick. She had had to go into the lavatory—the nuns always used that institutional word—and retch. She would look at herself in the mirror afterward as she threw water on her face. Her eyes red and teary from the violent retching, her pale skin a little blotchy. She would stare at her face and wonder if somewhere in that visage there was a killer waiting to be born. *How old had her grandfather been when he had begun his career as a killer? Had he been her age?* Everything she knew about serial killers she knew from TV. It was a subject she had stayed far away from as a student, a subject she had had no voyeuristic desire to learn about, even though TV and pop culture put murder and murderers front and center in her consciousness. She had known the big names—Son of Sam, John Wayne Gacy, Ted Bundy—yet she wasn't even sure *how* she knew them. TV, most likely. Jeffrey Dahmer was more recent. Just a few years ago. What grade had she been in when he had been arrested, his gruesome story detailed on the evening news in their communal living room at St. Cecilia's? But Faye had walked away when the stories had come on TV. She hadn't known details. She hadn't *wanted* to know details. Details would have demanded comparisons and she feared comparisons. Because some memories she had been unable to forget. Even in the quiet and safety of St. Cecilia's—because it had always been quiet and safe for her—there were still some things she could not forget and some days and more nights they invaded her thoughts and seeped insidiously into her dreams. *The things on the plates. The dark spaces on the ladies' dresses in the photographs. The head in the vise. The way the basement had smelled. The bits of hair everywhere—dead hair, hair that smelled like a two-day-dead mouse in a trap.* Those things, those memories, those images were always there, somewhere in her mind. She didn't think about them, but sometimes they came back, uninvited, unbidden. *Unforgettable.*

And now there was the box. So all of it—those things, those images—would come back again and again and again. Now Faye would *never* be able to forget. *Never, ever, ever.*

❖

Faye had, of course, caught snippets about the Dahmer case unfolding on the front pages just as she was beginning to recall specifics about her life with her grandparents, specifics that would resurface in half-remembered dreams. In her sleep, her past always seemed to meet her present in some unknown and, Faye thought, possibly unholy way.

Faye had of course seen the newspapers in the living room at St. Cecilia's and they couldn't be ignored. "Body Parts Litter Apartment." "Horror Unfolds: 11 Skulls Found." "The Cannibal: Madman Admits Killing 17, Eating Some."

How old had she been? Eleven? Twelve? Impressionable, certainly. Faye wondered now, a few years past and with memories of what was in the box flashing through her mind like the old carousel wheel the science nun, Sister Catherine, used in class, why the nuns hadn't kept those papers away from the girls. Had they been scattered around as carelessly as Faye remembered? Or had they actually been hidden and it was just her memory that made them stand out? She wanted to go downstairs now and look to see where today's newspapers were, just to put her memories in perspective. Just to calm herself.

As if she could gain perspective now about any of this. As if she would ever be calm again after being given the box by Mother Superior.

And yet the memories were there. *Had she actually read those papers?* Had she sorted through the recycling at the back of the kitchen and pulled out the forbidden pages and read the stories of the murdered animals, the teenager who escaped, the heads in the freezer, the body parts cooking on the stove? It was all suddenly so vivid.

Or were those memories a conflation of the images from the box? Images emerging from the sheaf of negatives in their slightly opaque glassine envelopes? Images from her own history, not a news story vaguely remembered?

Faye wasn't sure. She didn't know how to be sure.

❖

There were things about which Faye *was* sure. She knew from the contents of the box that her grandfather—her flesh and blood—was one of the most notorious of the killers. But unlike the others, or at least some of the others, he had eluded capture. According to newspaper clippings in a manila envelope Mother Superior had handed her with the box, he was on a Most Wanted list, but in the decade Faye had been at St. Cecilia's, he had not been caught. Which meant, as far as Faye could discern, that he would never be caught.

Maybe her grandfather was like Jack the Ripper or the Zodiac Killer and would just never be caught because no one knew how to catch someone like him.

Or maybe he was dead. Maybe they both were dead. Faye could only remember her grandmother now in the context of her grandfather's crimes. Even if her grandmother hadn't known what was going on before Faye's grandfather murdered Sister Anne Marie, she knew then. She knew after that killing. And she had still chosen to go with him—a murderer, a rapist, a serial torturer whose bloody work had gone on in their house for years. Had gone on—had been staged and photographed and then he had climbed into bed with her after. He had always been with her *after.*

Faye could feel the sickness wash over her along with a wave of memories of the darkroom, the basement, her grandmother, her grandfather. How could she separate the way they had treated her from what they had done? She couldn't do it. They had been so kind to her. Had treated her so gently. She could recall her grandfather putting out the pots of paint for her and giving her drawing lessons. A notebook. A camera. Everything that had defined her in the days when there was nothing to define her, when she was just *the orphan* or *that girl whose parents were burned alive* or nothing at all. A nameless, faceless, being-less girl. A cipher. Her grandfather had given her the tools that kept her from disappearing altogether. Faye knew, knew deep in the core of her, that without what her grandfather had given her, she might be dead now. That she might have taken her six-year-old self out into the snow late one night after her parents' deaths and just lain down, covering herself over and over with icy whiteness until the numbness set in and she was gone. Instead of burned alive, like her parents, she would have been buried alive, in the snow, a refuge of cold and quiet and most important to her then, oblivion. There would have been nothing else.

But that hadn't happened because of her grandfather. Faye's grandmother—the woman who had held her while she cried, and put cold compresses on her forehead, and let her stay home from school for months because she just wasn't ready to leave the house, leave the yard, go further than the corner store—Faye remembered her grandmother as incredibly gentle. She had taken care of Faye after her parents' deaths, after the awfulness at the cemetery, after Faye burnt her hand and after her discovery in the basement and her fainting and begging never to eat meat again. How could *that* woman, Faye wondered, be the same woman who got into bed every night with a man who did such unspeakable things to *other* women?

Faye couldn't figure it out. She couldn't make sense of any of it. She hadn't realized just how protected and sheltered she had been at St. Cecilia's all these years. That had been altered irrevocably by the box and the envelope and Mother Superior reaching across the desk and taking her hand, Mother Superior standing in front of the door to her office and barring Faye's escape, Mother Superior keeping the knowledge of where Faye had come from to herself all these years and then revealing it, suddenly, so that the literal breath had gone out of Faye.

Faye thought about how she had fainted. But she also thought about how Theresa had left Mother Superior's office crying, shielding her eyes and her face from Faye as she left. How many secrets had Mother Superior hidden from her charges? What revelations were being quietly exposed behind her office door, St. Cecilia's prostrate form just out of earshot, the things in the jars floating in silent witness to all the horrors that could be imagined that Mother Superior might have to tell to each and every girl as she prepared to exit into the "real" world from what Faye had always thought of as a fortress of protection and safety and kind of gentle oblivion?

Yet Faye had wanted it that way—to be in that state of unknowing. She had kept it that way. And now Mother Superior had handed her Pandora's Box—with her own name written on the side—and made her open it. What had spilled out into the world—into her world—could never be put back. Secrets can never be untold, Faye knew now. She'd realized that the first time she'd gone into the darkroom alone and seen the photos hanging, the bits of bodies strung along the clothesline, fluttering like ghosts in the slight breeze of the black fan. She'd realized it when she had been in the kitchen vomiting, like she had done over and over since she'd been given the box, and her grandfather had surprised her and had told her that it felt like that at first, but then it changed and it felt like art.

He had said that. Faye remembered it clearly. *It was art.* He had thought of his killing as a form of art. Suddenly she wanted to run and get her notebooks and tear them to shreds, all her drawings, all the dead animals, the smears of blood from that day she had come upon Sister Anne Marie in the grotto. *What had she been thinking, recording all these things? What did it mean that she had touched someone else's blood and put it in her book? How far removed was she really from her grandfather? Was this how it had begun for him? With a smear of blood? With drawings of dead animals? Had he carried small dead bodies and placed them on woodsy pyres like she had done?*

Now she *was* going to be sick. She ran to the bathroom outside the dorm room. The long white bathroom with its thick white sinks and fat spindled faucets opened before her. Faye thought it had never looked so preternaturally white. Yet as she practically fell into a stall, vomiting up her lunch, a film of sweat breaking out on her face and neck, she remembered the first night she had stayed at St. Cecilia's, how Sister

Anne Marie had brought her to her bed and given her pajamas and a robe and shown her the little table next to her bed with the crucifix.

That night Sister Mary Margaret had brought her six-year-old self into the fourth-floor bathroom that was just like this one, and the light had been a scary white. The window had been black at the end of the long row of stalls and showers and their reflections had wavered on the glass and when Faye had seen it she had suddenly let go of Sister Mary Margaret's hand and she had screamed and screamed. The watery, moving shadow selves of her and Sister Mary Margaret had reminded her of the ladies in the photographs as they came alive in the pans of liquid in her grandfather's darkroom.

The door to the bathroom had banged open and a white-clad figure had come rushing in. Faye had seen flashes of girls' faces, hair splayed out all around when the door opened and the flash of white had rushed toward her. The disembodied nature of the faces had just added to her terror. Everywhere there were bits and pieces of bodies. There was nowhere for Faye to look, so she just screamed.

Sister Anne Marie had gathered Faye up in her arms and held her tightly, pulling Faye into her lap on the cold, white-tiled floor. She had whispered words Faye couldn't understand. *Were they prayers? Was it Latin? Or was it just the soft susurrations of someone comforting a child in the universal language of soothing?*

Sister Anne Marie had been dressed only in a long white nightgown, her feet bare. There had been a scapular and a sparkly rosary around her neck, both askew, and Faye had felt the imprint of the crucifix on her cheek. Sister Anne Marie's hair had been incredibly short, cut close to her head. Faye had thought it looked like silky black feathers.

The nuns had looked at each other and Sister Anne Marie had asked Faye what was wrong, once she had stopped screaming, but Faye hadn't been able to explain, had only shuddered and Sister had looked at her and asked her if she was cold and Faye had shaken her head no. Both nuns had gotten Faye ready for bed—bathing her and helping her brush her teeth. Sister Mary Margaret had sent Sister Anne Marie back to her room on the floor below the dormitory. Faye had seen her put her arm around Sister Anne Marie and give her a sort of hug, then she had said something low that Faye couldn't hear and had tucked the scapular and the rosary back inside the neck of Sister Anne Marie's nightgown, her fingers brushing Sister Anne Marie's cheek. Sister Anne Marie had reached for Sister Mary Margaret's fingers and had held them, briefly, just for a second or two. But long enough for Faye to record the moment. Long enough for her to remember everything that had gone on that night, in that room, among the three of them.

❖

Thinking about that night, now, Faye began to cry. She slid to the floor of the stall, tears running down her face, her shoulders heaving, rubbing her arms, trying to soothe herself however she could. *What time is it?* She needed to get back downstairs, or at least out of here. She didn't want to run into any of the other girls while she was still so upset. She especially didn't want anyone to come looking for her. But she couldn't move. She couldn't stand up and most of all, she couldn't stop crying. She kept thinking of Sister Anne Marie running from her room when she had heard the young Faye screaming, running barefoot, running without a veil or wimple or anything to make her look like a nun. *Running to save me.*

❖

Faye heard someone coming up the stairs to the room, walking past the bathroom door into the dorm. She gulped air, swallowing, gasping, trying to get control. She slid back up to her feet, straightening her uniform. She left the stall and stood over one of the thick white sinks, the *cold* faucet turning in her hand, water blasting out of the tap in the way they had all been instructed never to do. Faye bent over and splashed water onto her face over and over until she felt like she was drowning.

She *was* drowning. She was drowning in all the memories that would not stop flooding over her. She was drowning under the weight of knowing Sister Anne Marie was dead because of her. First she had been pulled out of her room in her bare feet, shorn of her nun-ness, and now she was dead—dead for ten long years, but Faye was mourning her like she had just died because for some reason, before seeing the clippings from Mother Superior, Faye had always believed Sister Anne

Marie would come back. She would come back, she would be okay, she would forgive Faye.

Most of all, she would forgive Faye.

Now that would never happen. Now the best Faye could hope for was that they would meet in heaven and Faye would be forgiven there.

Faye looked in the mirror. Her eyes were puffy, her pale face streaked with bits of red. She turned and let out a small shriek. Involuntarily. It had gotten dark since she'd come into the bathroom and when she turned, her ghost self moved on the blackened window at the end of the room. Her heart beat fast in her chest and her stomach churned again. She felt the bile in the back of her throat. She felt the loss of Sister Anne Marie as if it were something she could touch and taste, something that was making her sick with its viscous, acid poisonousness.

Her world would never be the same. *She* would never be the same. All Faye could think about was that, now, as she dried her hands and face on a rough paper towel and left the room. She would never, ever be the same.

CHAPTER THIRTY-THREE
A NUN'S STORY

When Faye had first come to the school it was still both school and *orphanage*, but that name had been changed when Faye was eight. Then it became *home*. St. Cecilia's *Home* for Girls, not *Orphanage* for Girls. Less Dickensian sounding, although St. Cecilia's had never been that for her—Dickensian. It had always been *home*. While other girls had stayed out past curfew or done other things that broke the rules, Faye had always been the good girl, the girl that no one could ever complain about or find fault with. After her earliest years in that revolving door to Mother Superior's office, sitting on the hard chairs and looking between the jars on the shelves and St. Cecilia lying above her, she had learned how to stay within the lines, to be as she knew, now, smart without being smart-assed. She would push the envelope in class, but not too far. She had found that invisible boundary line that should not be crossed and she had been grateful for it. She hadn't wanted to disappear, to be a cipher, but she also hadn't wanted to cause trouble.

Perhaps it was an innate sense she had from that day she told Sister Anne Marie her story that she had to be extra good, extra careful, that everyone would be watching her for signs of evil, that made her so compliant. But Faye thought it was more that she had just wanted to stay behind the wrought iron gates, close to the grotto and the little chapel and the music room, and not venture too far into the world she had already known way too much about before she even had her First Holy Communion. Part of Faye thought it might be best for her to stay behind the gates forever. Part of her thought going too far past those gates might end in mayhem—the kind of mayhem that had been in that box Mother Superior had given her.

The box. The box with her name on it. Her box. Her life.

There was no end to the misery of her knowledge, now. Faye was trapped by knowing, trapped by the box and the notebooks and the drawings and the negatives in the little glassine envelopes. Trapped by the clippings Mother Superior had so carefully cut out for her, so carefully saved. The clippings that said, unequivocally, that it didn't matter that Faye had learned to walk the line so carefully. She was forever marked by what was in those clippings. She was forever in the thrall of evil. It didn't matter that she had prayed every day since her parents had been burned alive—and had prayed before that, her mother sitting on her little bed while the young Faye knelt on the floor on the pale blue rag rug her mother and dead grandmother had made— what had happened to that rug, Faye wondered with a pang of loss and longing—her small hands clasped in prayer, pointed up to heaven, her eyes tightly shut, imagining God and angels and the Blessed Mother drifting above her on fluffy clouds in her child's vision of Heaven. It didn't matter that she had embraced God and Mary and the saints and had felt a deep and abiding love for all of them. There was rarely a Mass now that she was older where tears didn't come to her eyes as she thought of Christ in his final days, more human than God, unable to escape the fate laid out before him. Or all the saints, particularly the ones she had developed an early affinity toward, like St. Francis with his love for animals or St. Teresa of Avila and her brilliance or St. Joan of Arc, who fought battles against evil in her armor and who had been burned alive.

Faye had taken St. Joan as her special saint at her confirmation. In Faye's mind, St. Joan was the patron saint of those who had been burned alive. And although she herself had not been, only her parents had, Faye felt an affinity for Joan of Arc that was all about the fire.

But now the saints could not help her. Mary could not help her. She didn't dare think God could not help her, because she knew all about the sin of hubris, but here she was, seventeen, about to leave this haven of safety and solace in a few months, and there was the box, and all that was in it. How could she ever wash her grandfather's sins from her? There was no absolution for this, was there? Sister Anne Marie was dead because of her. What was the penalty for killing a nun? Who would she pray to, now?

Faye saw the clippings in her mind's eye. Each one more horrifying and irrevocable than the next. There was no escaping this new knowledge. Mother Superior had protected her for years, but as she had said when she had waved her hand toward the office window and referred to the world "out there," it was likely that others might know. Might know who Faye was. What she had done. It was likely that Faye would never be safe again, once she left St. Cecilia's.

❖

Faye thought about Jeffrey Dahmer. She thought about killers. She thought about her grandparents. She thought how fortunate she was to be safe at St. Cecilia's and unnamed in all those clippings. She wondered how long that safety would—could—last. The clock was ticking on her life behind St. Cecilia's gates. The clock was ticking on her anonymity, her girlhood, her protection. The clock was ticking on what it was she would do next. It was ticking for *all* of the girls in her class, but it ticked loudest for her. So loudly that Faye thought the sound of it might drown out everything else.

Until it didn't.

❖

Three days after Mother Superior had called her in for what she had thought was the usual separation talk, Faye had gone back to see her. It had been three days of watching the other girls in her class— there were so few of them, so few of *us*, she thought—walking around like zombies, trying to come to grips with the fact that soon, in just a few months, they would be out on the street. Literally. *Out*. Like that scene at the end of that film from a long time ago, *The Nun's Story*, that she and Rosario had watched one Thursday night at a local repertory cinema, because Rosario had told her, suddenly, out of nowhere, that she was thinking she wanted to stay at St. Cecilia's, that she wanted to enter the novitiate, that she wanted to be a nun. Rosario had told Faye the film was going to be playing, just two nights, and asked Faye if she would go with her. Faye, who didn't go out much, had said yes, and they had gone together. Rosario had wanted them to go in their uniforms—to be obviously Catholic school girls out to see a movie about a nun. Faye had thought it was weird, but she had complied. Rosario was her best friend, had been her best friend for a decade.

How could she refuse this one request, no matter how odd she found it?

Faye had loved the film. Loved it. *The Nun's Story* had touched some deep part of her, she wasn't sure what, but she knew it was a good thing she had come to see it with Rosario and she understood why Rosario had wanted to sit in the old re-conditioned theatre that smelled of popcorn and dust, where the occasional mouse (Faye had hoped they were mice) ran down the aisle beside them, and see this film from another era of nuns, an era Rosario and maybe Faye herself would have liked to be part of. She knew then that Rosario had wanted to stay in her uniform because she had wanted to feel like she was part of the world of the film, part of the world of the convent. *Part of.* The thing Faye knew neither of them had ever truly felt: *part of.*

At the end of *The Nun's Story*, Sister Luke, the nun of the story, leaves the convent, leaves her nun's family behind and goes out into the world alone, by herself, with nothing but the clothes she is wearing and a little suitcase. The door latches behind her and that click sounded so ominous to Faye. It was the sound she knew all of them, every girl in the senior class at St. Cecilia's, was dreading—the sound of the world they knew closing behind them, shutting them out, pushing them out. Faye had been surprised to find she was crying at the end. *For Sister Luke? For herself?* For the emptiness in that little street when Sister Luke leaves her life in the convent for whatever it is that awaits her on the outside after Sister Porteress locks her out forever?

All Faye knew was that she and Rosario had sat in their seats, quietly sobbing for different—or maybe the same—reasons while the credits rolled before they could get up and leave the theatre. Faye had felt something in her break. She hadn't felt that feeling for a long time. It was the feeling she had had when Mother Superior had told them all that Sister Anne Marie had had an accident, that Sister Anne Marie was not coming back. Faye felt her breath catch in the back of her throat like it had then and felt a wave of fear, like if she cried even a little bit more, she would be crying forever, wailing and screaming and would have to be locked away like the crazy woman they called the Archangel in *The Nun's Story* who nearly kills Sister Luke when she's working in the mental ward of the hospital. Nearly kills Sister Luke because she disobeyed.

Rosario put her hand on Faye's arm and had squeezed hard. So hard that it hurt. Faye was sure her arm would be bruised later, but she didn't care. In fact, she was grateful. The pain had snapped Faye out of whatever was happening to her. It had brought her back from the brink of something terrible.

Faye looked at Rosario, making a little cry and yanking her arm away, rubbing it through the pale blue sleeve of her uniform. "What the hell, Ro?"

"I had to stop you," Rosario had said. "I had to stop you from going there."

Faye had stared at her, tears still streaming down her face, but she hadn't said anything else. She hadn't asked what Rosario meant. Faye knew what she meant. And even as she rubbed her arm, she was grateful.

❖

Faye and Rosario had gone to McDonald's after the movie and sat in a booth. They had both been ravenous. Faye had eaten fish—she'd never eaten meat again after her grandparents' house, but the nuns had made her eat fish, telling her, "Growing children need protein, dear"— and French fries and Rosario had eaten a Big Mac, which Faye had tried not to look at. The juicy meat looked like guts to her. She didn't know how else to describe it. She was never able to look at meat, even meat as altered as Rosario's Big Mac. Faye always thought, whenever she saw it, like when she had been on kitchen duty at St. Cecilia's and had watched Sister Claire cutting up chunks of red beef for some kind of stew, that the meat had once been human. That the meat had been cut from some woman somewhere and delivered to St. Cecilia's for them to eat. She knew this was crazy, but she couldn't help it. She'd read somewhere that children get imprinted early with all kinds of things. She'd been imprinted with the belief that all meat came from humans.

As they sat there in what was the blatant irony of the McDonald's booth, as Faye saw it—could there be a more obvious symbol of worldliness?—Rosario had poured out her story to Faye. Her new story, because Faye already knew her old story. Rosario's new story was that she couldn't leave St. Cecilia's. That she knew if she did, she would die. Just like Rosario had known that Faye was careening toward some invisible edge, ready to pitch forward into a void that would have taken her away from everything, forever, Rosario knew that if she left St. Cecilia's she would die. She would just *die*. She would become a drug addict like her mother and a gang member like her father and all she could see in front of her was a lifetime of razor blades inside her cheek to cut anyone who might surprise her and scary sex and taking lives and having babies she would never want and never be able to care for properly and she just couldn't, she just couldn't do that.

Rosario had leaned forward across the booth in a movement that had reminded Faye of when Mother Superior had taken Faye's hand and said to Faye, *"Esto es lo que soy."*

This is who I am.

"Which is who you are, Ro?" Faye had asked her. "The gang member drug addict or the nun? 'Cause you know I'm not seeing you as either."

Faye told Rosario she was surprised by her revelation. She knew more about Rosario than anyone else, maybe even than herself, because Faye didn't have to pretend not to know things about Rosario and she *did* have to pretend not to know things about herself. But she didn't say any of that. She just said she was surprised and that she wasn't sure that Rosario had thought it through and that there was more to being a nun than maybe she had considered.

"They give up everything. You can see, they give up everything. You don't have to give up everything." Faye was surprised at both the passion in her own voice and at how suddenly selfish her words sounded.

"I have nothing already, *amiga*. We—all of us at *the home* got nothing. You know that. We both know that. It's no secret. It's no accident, either. What's out here for us?" she waved her hand around "Just more nothing. Lots more nothing."

Faye was stunned by the venom in Rosario's voice, the way she said *the home* instead of *St. Cecilia's*. There was anger and hurt and Faye wasn't even sure what else in Rosario's voice. How could Faye have thought all these years that Rosario was as contented at St. Cecilia's as she was, when she was now so clearly roiling with rage? Roiling with it even as she was telling Faye that she wanted to stay there forever. While Faye, who wasn't ready to leave, didn't know if she could handle leaving, hadn't even considered becoming a nun. Even after whatever it was that happened to her in the theatre happened to her, she still wasn't thinking about becoming a nun. But Rosario not only was thinking about it, it was why they had come to the movies tonight in the first place—come out in their Catholic school uniforms and sat in the darkened theatre and watched Sister Luke take her vows and then break them again.

So of course Faye had thought Rosario was happy at St. Cecilia's, felt safe at St. Cecilia's. Faye thought she knew everything about Rosario before they left for the movies. Now—she wasn't sure. But then Faye knew all the things Rosario *didn't know* about *her.* They both had their secrets. And now Faye wondered how many other secrets were hidden at St. Cecilia's that no one had ever spoken aloud, that no one dared to speak aloud. Faye wondered what would become of them all once graduation happened and the summer reprieve they had been given, the months between May and September, were ended. Then what?

Faye wondered how many of the nuns she had known her whole life were actually like Rosario—women who had wanted to be something else or do something else, but who had been too afraid of what could go wrong or too desperate about the life they had left and had decided to stay within the controlled confines of St. Cecilia's where nothing bad could happen unless you went beyond those gates in search of that something else. A madman who killed women in his basement perhaps. Or something worse—if there *was* anything worse.

❖

They had finished their meal and walked to the subway, the chill air enveloping them. Rosario had linked her arm in Faye's and Faye had leaned into her. Rosario had squeezed her arm then, in response. It was companionable, this walking arm-in-arm. It felt old-fashioned and old-lady-ish, but Faye liked it and it helped to take the edge off how she was feeling. Unsettled, even frightened. Everything Rosario had told her had made her feel like the ground was shifting beneath her feet. Like a sinkhole was opening, threatening to swallow her and everything she had built for herself—because she realized now that she had built St. Cecilia's as a fortress, as a safe space that was inviolable and which no one could breach and now all that had crumbled after one old movie in too-vivid color and one conversation in a too-loud McDonald's with the girl she thought was her best friend, but who she now thought she might not know at all.

❖

They had missed a subway and had to wait a long time for the next one, huddled together on the bench in the brightly lit station where everyone waiting kept themselves separate, distanced. No one wanted to interact with anyone else and Faye was glad of this. She didn't feel up to fending off strangers. She also didn't know how Rosario might react. They were both the fragile young schoolgirls they looked like, tonight. But everyone was in their own state of contemplation. Faye and Rosario didn't speak, they just sat, pressed close together against the cold and the night, their arms still linked. Rosario was shaking a little, pumping her legs up and down in her seat.

"Man, it's cold," she had said, barely above a whisper, her breath puffing out as she spoke. Faye tightened her arm in Rosario's in response.

A white man down at the end of the platform was pacing and smoking and having a conversation with the voices in his head, his arms waving around occasionally as he gesticulated to his spirit world. At any other time Faye and Rosario might have giggled or made a joke or referenced *The X-Files*, but not tonight. Tonight they were somber, each caught in her own contemplation of what lay ahead. Each thinking about the film and how it had resonated somewhere deep inside them.

They had gotten back to St. Cecilia's late, past their curfew. Most of the lights were out on the upper floors and they had to go around to the back door, by the kitchen, where there was always a key for the girls who decided to break curfew or the ones like Jessica and Tamara, who each had already found part-time jobs in downtown Brooklyn at the Fulton Mall at Christmas and had been kept on past the holidays and worked from after school until the shops closed at nine, then had to make there way back here.

Faye had a job, too, had had one longer than anyone else in their class. But she never worked nights. Sister Elizabeth called Faye's job "an apprenticeship," but it was still a job. Faye worked at a local shop that sold cameras and developed film and gave workshops on taking pictures. The man who ran the shop, Angelo de Luca, was a friend of Mother Superior's—Theresa Flynn had told her that he was actually Mother Superior's brother, but no one was supposed to know that, because nuns weren't supposed to have much contact with their families. Jesus and Mary and the saints were their families, now, Theresa had said and rolled her eyes heavenward in an exaggerated way that had made Faye laugh.

It was a strange job—or not-job—but Faye liked it and she knew from the first day how lucky she was to have it and how this was one more example of how Mother Superior looked out for them, looked out for *her*. Faye didn't need to see too many people at the job, because she mostly worked in the back of the shop, developing photos and packaging them up. She made minimum wage—$4.25 an hour—but only for ten hours. The other four hours she worked each week she didn't get paid. Those hours, Angelo "Call me Angie—everybody calls me Angie, since I was a little kid, they called me that" had told Faye, were like taking a class. They were the hours that she was learning how to "do everything a photographer does."

And it was true—Faye was learning a lot from Angie. She had learned how to mix the chemicals, how to take out the film, how to make the photographs come to life.

"We're old school here, Faye. We do everything the way my uncle taught me to do it. And you know why we do it that way? Because we don't make mistakes that way. We don't make mistakes. And that's how you run a business. You don't make mistakes."

Faye had made few mistakes. Angelo—Angie—had given her practice film to develop, "So's you don't screw up anybody's baby pictures, or pictures of their dead mother. That would be a disaster."

It had been natural, easy, like she had always known how to do it. Everything she did in the little shop felt comfortable, an extension of herself. *This* was, Faye knew, *who* she was. This was her world. The images coming alive in the pans of fluid. The bits and pieces no longer scared her—because they had at first. At first they had taken her back to her grandfather's darkroom. But then that feeling had drifted away, replaced by a new feeling, a feeling of competence and achievement and something Faye wasn't quite sure what it was, except that it was intrinsic to *her*. It was in her guts and in her heart and it was going to be her life.

Angie had taken her to get a bank account for her checks. "Mother Superior, I know her, she does not want you girls just throwing your money away on nail polish and boys." He had winked at her—an exaggerated "We know better" wink—and Faye had laughed at that, knowing she wasn't interested in either nail polish or boys. But it had felt good to have the account, it had felt good to be able to have the little book in which her savings were recorded. It wasn't much, she knew, but it was a step for her. And most importantly, she was learning. She was learning how to be who she was going to be.

Saturdays were long days at the shop, and busy. This was her full day of work—nine of her fourteen hours, the others split between Mondays and Wednesdays after school. On Saturdays Faye was taking orders, working the cash register, and in the last two hours, developing film. Angie had told her that soon, he was going to take her out to "photograph the neighborhood, Faye. I want to show you how to see everything. All the little pieces of your life, so's it doesn't pass you by, you know?"

So Jessica and Tamara had jobs and Faye had her "apprenticeship." Rosario had searched for a job, but without success. She wasn't the only one of their class without a job, but Faye knew how much it bothered her.

"I guess I'm too street for Gap and Sack a Gold musta thought I was gonna steal their crap *jewelry*," she'd told Faye one afternoon after she had come back to St. Cecilia's, sneering and drawing out the word when she said *jewelry*. She had had a small wad of papers in her hand and Faye could see they were application forms. She had watched as Rosario shredded them into tiny bits of confetti and put them in the drawer of her little table.

"You never know when you want to surprise someone," she'd said, but Faye had thought Rosario would likely do something she shouldn't with that confetti, like throw it in Sister Elizabeth's face, since it was Sister Elizabeth who had sat them all down and talked to them about career counseling and finding jobs by May and how their exit stipend from St. Cecilia's wouldn't last long and how they needed to spend the summer saving money for when they left in September. Faye knew it had galled Rosario that both Jessica and Tamara had been hired by the Fulton Mall Gap store, but Rosario didn't say anything except, "Tamara's lucky she's so light-skinned. For a black chick, she's lighter than I am."

Faye had said nothing, because there really wasn't anyone paler than Faye in their class, and she was sure that like Tamara and Jessica, who were both pretty, if she had tried to get a job, which she knew she had to do soon, really soon, her looks would have helped, not hindered.

It was dark by the back door when they walked around. Inside, the kitchen light was already out and only the small night-light by the stove was lit, casting a pale bluish glow over the stove and the big double sink. Faye knelt down and lifted the flowerpot from its saucer and took out the key. When she stood up, Rosario was right next to her. She looked at Rosario and felt the key digging into her palm. Rosario grabbed her arm again, this time to pull Faye close to her—very close, right up against her. For a moment Faye thought she was going to pull a razor blade out from inside her cheek and slit Faye's throat and her heart started to race. She wasn't sure why she thought this—possibly because Rosario had put the idea in her head earlier. Or because it was so dark out there behind the convent that everything seemed strange and unsettling. The vines from the grapes that ran over the arbor in summer hung down behind the back porch and looked ominous to Faye in the darkness, lit only by that small, blue-white interior light and a light back by the garage beyond where they stood, which only served to elongate the shadows from the vines.

"We should go in," Faye whispered, her breath crystalline puffs in the chill night.

"*Lo dulce*," Rosario said, her voice different from what Faye was used to. Faye knew she should pull away, but she didn't, she couldn't. She just stood there, feeling Rosario pressed up against her, their breath commingling in the darkness.

Faye felt she should say something, but she didn't know what to say. She couldn't think of anything she should say. And yet she didn't want to move away, either. She had a flash of memory, of Sister Mary Margaret touching Sister Anne Marie's face that night, Faye's first night there at St. Cecilia's. She reached up and touched Rosario's face the way she had seen Sister touch Sister Anne Marie's face.

Rosario took her hand and kissed the palm. "Like this," she whispered and pulled her uniform up just enough to press Faye's hand up against the crotch of her panties. Faye felt her breath catch in her throat. *What was she doing? What were* they *doing?* And yet she had no desire to stop, to push Rosario away, to run to one of the nuns and confess. Instead she looked past Rosario to the long bench at the end of the porch. Half of it was stacked with recycled newspapers, tied neatly with string. Sister Claire's obsessive neatness. She pulled Rosario to the bench and they sat for a minute, just looking at each other in the semi-dark.

Faye wanted to ask Rosario what was happening here, what she expected, what she needed, but she said nothing. She just waited and as she did, Rosario leaned over and kissed her.

The kiss was both soft and deep and Faye felt herself falling into it, felt the heat rise between her legs. She squeezed her thighs together reflexively, surprised by the intensity of feeling. Rosario had opened her coat, then Faye's. She unbuttoned the two middle buttons on Faye's uniform blouse and slid her hand, her surprisingly warm hand, inside Faye's bra, twisting the nipple as she lifted her breast out of its casing.

Faye should have felt cold—it was freezing out on the bench in the dark, still-wintry air—but all she felt was the warmth of Rosario kissing her and touching her all over. Faye could tell Rosario had done this before, probably many times. She wondered for a moment who Rosario had done it with, but that thought passed quickly as Rosario slid the crotch of Faye's panties aside and began to stroke her clit. A small sound Faye didn't recognize escaped her and she felt herself moving in tandem with Rosario's touch, the heat so intense now she wanted to cry out.

Rosario stood up and straddled her lap, her legs spread over Faye's as she pressed and pulled and stroked Faye's clit. As Rosario lowered herself onto Faye, she whispered, "Stroke me, mama," and Faye had felt the heat course through her, hearing Rosario call her *mama* with her slightly accented English. "Like this, baby," Rosario said, and pumped her fingers up and down on Faye's clit.

Faye followed Rosario's lead and slid her own hand into Rosario's panties. The hair was wiry and different from her own and Rosario's lips were fuller, her clit bigger. Faye whispered, "I love how you feel," as she played with Rosario's clit as if she'd been doing this forever.

Rosario was talking to her in Spanish now, too fast for Faye to know what it was she was saying—or maybe it was just words she'd never heard before. Sex words. Words that she wasn't supposed to know. Secret words. Rosario was wrapping herself around Faye, touching her so fast. The words, the feelings, it all melded together. Rosario was so close to her, so close, so close. No one had ever been so close, she'd never felt so close, she'd never felt…so much.

Rosario kissed her at the end. Kissed her, re-buttoned her blouse, called her *lo dulce* again. She pulled Faye up from the bench and Faye could feel the imprint of the bench on the backs of her legs, the imprint of Rosario on the front of her thighs. Rosario put her arms around Faye, but didn't kiss her. She pushed Faye's hair back from her face, back from her ear, then whispered, "*Me gustas, mi bebé,*" in Faye's ear.

Faye took a breath. It was so much. Too much.

"*Yo también,*" Faye responded, suddenly deeply self-conscious of her accent. She put a finger to Rosario's cheek. Rosario took it, kissed the fingertip, put it against Faye's lips. Faye felt tears prick behind her eyes. She wasn't sure why. She shivered, suddenly cold.

Faye unlocked the door to the kitchen and replaced the key under the flowerpot. She was careful to lift up when she opened the door, remembering how it would stick. After she closed the door behind them, Rosario led her to the sink. "Wash your hands before we go upstairs, in case anyone stops us," she said, winking at Faye. The wink looked eerie in the bluish light from the stove.

Faye dutifully washed her hands with the lemon-scented soap Sister Claire loved. Now she felt a little dirty. Instead of a shared secret, or even a shared promise, Faye thought perhaps she and Rosario had shared a mistake. She didn't want to think of what had happened between them like that. She wanted to think of it as something they had done to make each other feel better after the way the film had riven them, after the revelations Rosario had made while they ate. She wanted to think of it as a bond, not a sin.

"A little salt," Rosario said, shaking some onto Faye's hands as she washed. "*Eres tan bella.*"

Faye felt the color rise in her cheeks. "*Gracias,*" she whispered.

They dried their hands and made their way through the semi-dark to the stairs and climbed to their third-floor dorm room. Faye took off her clothes, wrapped herself in her robe, and went down the hall to take a shower, willing herself not to think as she did. Rosario did not follow her, but when Faye came out, her hair still wet, Rosario was outside the door.

Don't worry, *chica,*" she whispered. "It will all be okay tomorrow. You'll see." She leaned in and kissed Faye lightly, then she went in to shower. Faye walked softly back to her bed, the sounds of her sleeping classmates enveloping her.

She pulled the covers over her, turned on her side, and began to cry. She had no idea why.

CHAPTER THIRTY-FOUR
INSTALLATION

The gallery looked perfect. The bottle-green velvet drape on the front window was pulled across. It would be pulled back only after the gallery opened at seven. In the window, centered in front of the drape, was the poster that Persia had done for the show. It was the photograph of the bodies of the children in the morgue in Fresno, with the maggots, along with Faye's name and the name of the show, *Ordinary Mayhem*, and the gallery and the dates. The photo was black and white and the titles were in a dark blood-red—Persia's idea, naturally. That this was the least disturbing of the photos in the show struck Faye as she walked into the gallery. There were small programs printed up in a stack with the same image on them, and inside, a statement by Faye about the content of the show and the meaning of the work.

Faye had hung everything herself early that very morning. She had asked that Nick and Persia not be there and they had agreed. A long red satin drape had been strung across the photos on each side of the gallery on a little pulley. The drapes would be pulled away once everyone had arrived at the gallery. Faye had also arranged all the other pieces on the series of tables that Nick had provided for her. The tables were covered with pieces of velvet in a dark claret and black. Even Nick and Persia had not seen what was underneath. The show was going to surprise them as much as it would the public. Persia had wanted to see, but Nick, who always seemed permanently bored, was obviously excited by the idea that here was something that might stimulate his jaded palate.

At the back of the long room was a table with various canapés of the most chic New York kind. The bar stood at an angle to the food. It all looked splendid. There was a display of flowers in dark reds, with a series of rather frightening-looking greens that reminded Faye of *Little Shop of Horrors*.

"When do you want to take the drapes off the tables, Faye?" Persia was sleek and alien-looking in a tight, black silk *Chinoise* dress with impossibly high black platform shoes and one long black earring that dangled to her shoulder. She looked magnificent, and not for the first time, Faye thought perhaps she should have invited her home before this. After the show, Persia might not be as interested as she had seemed during the preparation.

"What do you think?" Faye asked. "Should we have an unveiling after people arrive or do it now, for you and Nick and the wait-staff and then cover everything over again? We have a half hour. What do you think? Do you think people will hear the screaming from here?" Faye didn't laugh when she said this and she thought she saw Persia flinch involuntarily. For the first time, Faye felt apprehensive. She knew what was under the little drapes. She knew even the cynical Nick and the cool aesthete that Persia was would be unsettled. Maybe they should wait until there was an audience and do it all at once. Like ripping off a bandage.

"I say let's do it now," Persia said, looking around for Nick, who was on his cell phone in the back, a glass of red wine in his hand. "I want to see what's going to slither out from under the rock."

CHAPTER THIRTY-FIVE
DOPPELGANGER

Nick had decided to wait for the unveiling, and as Faye glanced at her, Persia seemed relieved. Faye suddenly wondered if the actual reveal would be as compelling as either she or Persia had anticipated.

Faye felt surprisingly calm. Preternaturally calm, in fact. Faye's whole life had built to this moment. She realized that now. Her parents' deaths, the first time she had seen the photographs in her grandfather's darkroom, some of which were arrayed in baroque frames on one of the tables in the gallery. Sister Anne Marie at the grotto. The day Mother Superior handed her the box of her grandfather's negatives and notebooks. And then all the stories she had covered, all the bits and pieces of horror she had collected and catalogued over the years since she had left St. Cecilia's. This, this exhibit, this wasn't a retrospective of her work so much as it was a retrospective of her life.

A line had formed outside the gallery an hour before the show was scheduled to start. It was clear that Nick's hype had worked. Plus, there had been a blog post on a local arts webzine that had suggested Faye had had a breakdown when she'd returned from the DRC. Faye knew people liked to see other people fall apart publicly. No doubt some of the people in line had done just that—come to see her, expecting her to be gaunt and wraithlike and muttering to herself. Except she wasn't. She felt fine for the first time in months. Even she didn't know why. Just last night she'd thought she'd never make it to the gallery, never get the show up, never be there for the opening. Last night she had thought it was over, that she would indeed kill herself. Last night she'd nearly lost it for good.

❖

It was only twenty-four hours before her own opening when Faye went to the book signing of her old friend, Keiko Izanami, who had just been nominated for a major literary award for the poetry collection she was reading from that night. The two women had gone to NYU together and Keiko had been one of Faye's first lovers during her freshman year. They'd both stayed in New York after college and had remained close over the years, but Faye hadn't planned on going to the event. She had kept most of her friends at arm's length the past few weeks, trying to pull herself together, trying to sleep without dreaming, trying, still, to keep herself from the urgent desire to kill herself that kept seizing her every other day. The only person she confided in was Martine, because the only person she thought understood was Martine. And yet even she didn't know Faye's secrets. No one did, except Shihong. But after the opening, after all the pieces of the exhibit were laid bare, then everyone would know. Then she would be free of secrets, she'd have exorcised all the demons. And maybe then she could either drown herself in the river or she could get her life back.

Keiko had texted her several times and Faye hadn't even responded, which was a level of rudeness she didn't like in herself, but which she couldn't explain. It was late in the afternoon of the book signing when Keiko called. Faye saw the number and this time, she picked up. Keiko was both worried and pissed, and said that while she knew Faye's big opening was the next night, that was really no excuse not to come to the signing, and Keiko really wanted her there. So Faye said she would go.

Keiko and her publisher had chosen one of the independent bookstores downtown for the big event. It was a nice shop and Faye had been there many times. The two old queens who owned it had patterned it after Shakespeare and Company and it had taken the place of several other shops that had closed in recent years.

Faye really wasn't prepared for so many people, but she promised Keiko she'd stay for the entire reading and that she'd hang around to meet Keiko's new girlfriend as well as another poet friend that Keiko thought would be a nice match for her. Faye said she was only doing anonymous one-nighters these days after she was on her fourth or fifth drink and when Keiko stared back at her, Faye laughed and said, "Just kidding. I'm currently single, but sure, I'd love to meet her." But Faye didn't want to meet anyone. Faye wanted to go home and sleep the dreamless sleep of the dead.

The poetry was heady. Keiko's entire book was dedicated to Japanese forms—haiku and tonka, with a series of poems toward the end that were done in tercets. Faye had felt a measure of pride as she listened because she knew how hard Keiko had worked over the years. Like Faye, she hadn't had an easy early life, and the two had bonded over that when they had first met.

The audience was a mix of Keiko's colleagues and students from NYU, other poets, and a group of those art predators Persia had been railing about, but Faye relaxed more easily than she had expected to and settled into the rhythm of the pieces as Keiko read in her lilting, mellifluous voice. Faye felt calmed and soothed by the cadence and Keiko's lush, sensual imagery. She was glad she had come and wondered now why she had avoided it.

When Keiko announced she was about to read her last poem, she explained that it was an older one, a haiku she had written in college for a close friend, but which she still had great affection for—as she did for the friend. She looked over toward Faye and Faye felt herself blush involuntarily as the audience responded with the light laughter that naturally accompanied such revelations from a poet as seasoned as Keiko. Then she read:

> *there is a way to*
> *cut a mango right*
> *no blood, just fruit, and you   you*

As the audience applauded and Keiko bowed, Japanese-style, with her hands clasped in front of her, Faye felt an unpleasant wave of dizziness come over her. She remembered the occasion of that poem—a morning when she had been preparing breakfast for the two of them and had sliced through the too-soft mango and into her finger, nearly to the bone. Something about the blood pulsing and the fleshy mango had made her almost hysterical and Keiko had rushed in, her long black hair flying out behind her. Keiko had helped Faye wash the cut and wrap it. They had gone to the student health office, which was closer than the hospital, and Faye had gotten six tight little stitches and an Ativan to calm her.

Faye had never told Keiko why she had gotten so upset, hadn't told her that the blood and the fruit together had made her think of the plates on the table in those photographs of her grandfather's, that somehow it seemed as if the mango were a pulsing, living organ there on the narrow counter when the blood spurted onto it.

The applause had subsided and Faye continued to sit while the rest of the audience rose and headed toward Keiko to have her sign their books. Faye wasn't sure how long she had sat there when Keiko came over and asked her to come upstairs, said that there was food and a surprise and the woman that she wanted Faye to meet.

Faye wanted to leave, but she let herself be led up the narrow little staircase to the large upper room of the store. Bookshelves lined the room and there were tables pushed to the side with more books on them. Chairs were scattered around the room, but everyone seemed to be standing, talking and laughing and milling about. A level of normalcy Faye had missed these past few weeks.

At the back of the room was the food table. Or what was passing for a food table. Stretched out on a red linen tablecloth on what Faye presumed to be a massage table was a young, naked woman covered in sushi. On a table next to her, bottles of wine were arrayed. People were standing around the table with the woman and as Faye and Keiko approached her, Faye could see she was Asian and impossibly fit, as well as beautiful. Faye felt the dizziness she'd experienced earlier return and she leaned over and told Keiko she really had to leave.

"It's a little too claustrophobic here, for me, and I really do have an intense day tomorrow," she explained, but Keiko wasn't having it.

"Oh, you can stay for a little sushi," Keiko said and nudged her, smiling. "That's my new girlfriend, by the way. Mika. She is, as you can see, delicious." Keiko laughed her wry little laugh and pulled Faye forward. As they came up to the woman, Faye could see that people were actually eating bits of food directly from her. Faye had heard this was a new trend, but she'd never actually seen it before. Something about it horrified her.

"She's lovely, but I prefer my food served on plates, and I

really have to go." Faye was feeling hot and dizzy and intensely claustrophobic. A woman came up beside Keiko, then, and she turned toward her, smiling and hugging the woman. Faye stared. The woman looked so much like Sister Anne Marie, it was eerie—no, frightening. Faye felt her heart start to race again. It was absolutely time for her to leave. She looked away for a moment and saw several men eating sushi off Mika's perfect body. She got a flash of Vandana at the Congo clinic, saying, "They made a meal of us," and thought she might vomit. A rush of images came into her head, each more terrible than the other. She had to get out of there. Faye turned back toward Keiko and touched her arm, "Now I do have to go, Keiko," she said, trying to keep the rising panic out of her voice, but Keiko interrupted her. She was pulling the Sister Anne Marie *doppleganger* closer, and introducing her to Faye. "Faye, this is Molly Sullivan—just wait till you see the spelling, Faye, her family went all in with the Irish. Go ask someone for one of her books and see their face when it comes up. Molly's the writer I was telling you about. We teach together. Molly, this is Faye, she's about to be the most famous photographer in New York, after her super-secret gallery opening tomorrow night."

"Super-secret? Sounds intriguing. I will have to come." Molly extended her hand to Faye and Faye took it, took Sister Anne Marie's hand, and held it fast. Molly looked at her quizzically.

"If you're going to hold on to it, you'd better at least read the palm." She laughed her Sister Anne Marie laugh and tried to turn her hand slightly in Faye's grasp. Faye let go.

"I'm sorry—you look like—you remind me of—someone I used to know." Faye wanted to walk away, but felt trapped, mesmerized by the dead woman in front of her.

Keiko turned to Molly. "Faye has been very reclusive lately, working on her show. Also, she just returned from a pretty harrowing trip to the Congo. Maybe you saw her piece last week in the Sunday magazine?"

Faye just stood there, she could look at the people eating the woman to her right or she could look at the woman back from the grave to her left. She felt faint. Molly said, "I did see that piece. It was very hard to look at. I can't imagine how difficult it must have been to actually be there. I admire your—fortitude. Some stories beg to be told, but it takes a certain guts to tell them."

A small group came up to Keiko then and she turned away from Molly and Faye to talk to them. The two women stood, not saying anything for minute. Then Faye spoke.

"I don't mean to be rude, but I really do need to leave. I have so much left to do and I only came tonight because Keiko and I are such old friends." She put her hand out toward Molly and said, "I hope we will see each other again. And I don't mean to stare, it's just you look so much like a—teacher I once had." It was so hot, Faye felt so hot. She wanted to sit down with this woman, she wanted to have a moment of Sister Anne Marie–ness before the opening tomorrow. She wasn't sure what it meant, meeting this woman now, right before her exhibit, but it felt important, somehow. And yet she couldn't bear to be in this room another minute, not with the people with their mouths all over Mika just outside her periphery. A wave of nausea came over her as she saw the plates with the pieces of female flesh and organs on them in her grandparents' house and now she could hear the sounds, the sounds of women's flesh being eaten.

"There's a lot of us black Irish girls here in New York," Molly was saying to her, "and we all look alike, with the black hair and blue eyes. I'm only second generation, myself. My grandparents were immigrants. My mother says the nuns had to drill the brogue out of her."

Faye swiveled around, remembering how Sister Anne Marie had said the same thing to her, years ago.

"Would you like to have a drink sometime, after you've recovered from your gallery event? Here's my card—now you can see that fun Irish spelling Keiko mentioned. Give me a call when you come up for air."

Faye took the card—-*Mallaidh Sullivan*—her hand brushing Molly's fingers. "That *is* some spelling," Faye said. "I had a friend at school, Niamh. I never understood how that spelling was pronounced Neave."

Faye was talking fast and not even sure of what she was saying. She wanted to stop seeing the slide show that had begun in her head when she'd first seen Mika laid out covered in sushi. Maybe she should have a drink with Molly now. Maybe it would distract her. Or maybe she'd wake up screaming in the middle of the night again, seeing Sister Anne Marie's mutilated body in her apartment, her mouth filled with blood.

"I will, definitely," Faye said, "but now I just really have to get going." She wasn't sure what she should do next, so she reached for Molly's hand again, this time turning it over, looking at the palm. "I've never read one, but perhaps if I get to examine it further—" Then she laughed, a forced little laugh that she hoped wouldn't actually sound forced and which would lighten the strange vibe she'd thrown over everything with her vision of Sister Anne Marie. It was past time for her to go. Faye did a half wave to Keiko, who was heading back toward them, and went down the stairs as quickly as she could, moving briskly through the store, then out, into the chill air. She wasn't sure what she should do next. The panic was washing over her in waves. She just had to get through the next few hours until she went to the gallery to hang the show. Then it would all be over. The exorcism she was hoping for would be complete. She would be free of all these memories, all these images. She would lay them out on the tables and hang them on the walls of the gallery. And then she could begin her life, free from all those ghosts that followed her, clung to her, night and day.

CHAPTER THIRTY-SIX
MATRYOSHKA

Faye sat on her bed in the dorm. She had been packing. The senior girls were all in full-on exit mode, now, although surprisingly—or maybe not—no one had left early. Everyone seemed to be feeling like Faye—waiting till the last possible moment to leave. Rosario was indeed staying, spending the next year working part-time at St. Cecilia's and studying to enter the novitiate. She and Faye had met one other night, after lights out. It had not been planned—not like the first time had been planned, either, though. Faye had heard Rosario get up from the bed across from hers and go down to the bathroom. She wasn't sure what had made her follow, but she had. Had she wanted a reprise of that night outside the kitchen in the freezing dark? Had she hoped Rosario would pull her close again, touch her in those ways new to Faye, at which Rosario was so adept?

It had been similar, but not the same. When Faye had gone into the bathroom, Rosario was waiting for her. How she knew Faye would come to her, Faye didn't know, but she was waiting down at the end of the room, sitting on the tiled window ledge, her bare feet on the radiator below. She was wearing pajamas and her legs were spread wide, but she wasn't touching herself. She was just waiting. Faye had been struck by both how sexy she looked and how alone. Faye had a sudden flash of how scared this room—well, the one a floor above, just like it—had once made her. She wasn't scared now.

Faye turned off the light and walked down to meet her, pulling her off the window ledge, wrapping her arms around Rosario, kissing her over and over.

It had been quick and exciting. It was also the last time they would ever touch each other. There had been an undercurrent of sadness to their touching that had almost overwhelmed the intensity of the sex. It had made Faye feel like something was opening up inside her—breaking, maybe—and she didn't want to break. She had spent years trying to piece herself back together. She didn't know if she could do it again. She was already broken when she got to St. Cecilia's. Losing Sister Anne Marie had shattered all that was left of her small, six-year-old self.

Faye had barely spoken for nearly a year after that, after Sister Anne Marie had left and never come back. Mother Superior had made Faye see someone, a nun who wasn't from St. Cecilia's who came to the school twice a week to talk to different girls about their problems with "adjusting." The nun, Sister Ofélia Márquez, was also a doctor, Mother Superior had explained. A psychiatrist who specialized in children who had experienced trauma. Faye had gone to a room next to Mother Superior's office every week for that year she wasn't talking much and met with Dr./Sister Ofélia.

Faye had talked to Sister Ofélia when she couldn't talk to anyone else. The first time they had met, Sister Ofélia had asked her why she didn't want to talk and Faye had said, simply, "Because the last time I talked, to Sister Anne Marie, she left here, she had an accident, and she never came back. Ever. I don't want that to happen to anyone else."

Faye had told Sister Ofélia that her grandfather had been a bad man and that she knew this because of the things she had found. "I can't tell you the story, because when I told Sister Anne Marie, she cried and she threw up and then she said she would 'get to the bottom of things,' but then she had an accident when she went to do that, and she never came back. And I want you to come back."

The words had rushed out of Faye. She had said them fast and soft and urgently and she had twisted a part of her uniform while she was talking. She saw it was all creased in the spot she'd been twisting over and over when she stopped telling her story.

Sister Ofélia had asked her a lot of questions, some of which she had answered, some she hadn't. She hadn't answered any questions about her grandparents. All she had said was there were things she had seen that she didn't like and she would never eat meat again because she knew where it came from and she didn't want to see that on the plate like it had been on the plates at home, at her grandparents' house. She also said that her parents had been burned alive and that she hoped she would get to see them again, but she was afraid she might forget what they looked like and she might not recognize them when she saw them.

"And what if their faces are all burned up? What if they look like the ladies in Grand's pictures? Will I still know it's them? Will I still know they are my parents? Can God put their faces back together again? Can God put the lady's head back on her body and put the pieces back inside?"

Sister Ofélia had gotten up and walked to the window and looked out. *It was happening again.* This was what had happened to Sister Anne Marie.

Faye had stopped talking, had held her breath, had counted, had said a Hail Mary holding her breath until she slid out of the chair and onto the floor.

When she woke up, Sister Ofélia and Sister Mary Margaret were there. She was on the floor, but there was something soft under her head. It was Sister Mary Margaret's lap.

She had looked up at Sister Mary Margaret and said, "I'm so sorry I killed your friend. I'm so sorry." And then everything had gone black again.

❖

This time with Rosario, there was a darkness that enveloped them. It was more than the room, the coldness of the white tile, the fear and pain they both felt. The first time had been a beginning. This—this, despite the release their bodies felt—was more of an ending. Too much of an ending for girls who were still girls, Faye had thought. Part of her wished she hadn't come to meet Rosario. But when Rosario pulled her into her arms, holding her so tightly it was hard to breathe, Faye knew it was the right thing. She hadn't broken. But Rosario—Rosario was on the verge of breaking. And while Faye thought staying at St. Cecilia's might save *her*, she thought Rosario staying there might be the thing that actually shattered Rosario into bits.

"You don't have to stay here, you know, *chica*," she whispered into Rosario's soft ear with the three little black studs. "You don't have to." She had pulled back a little, had stroked Rosario's face, had felt the wet cheek from the silent tears.

"You don't have to give yourself to this place. No one will hate you if you change your mind."

Rosario had put her fingers on Faye's lips and shaken her head. "*No mas*. I can't leave. *Esta es mi penitencia*."

"Your penance for *what*?" Faye asked.

"You wouldn't understand, *chica*. You wouldn't understand."

Rosario had kissed Faye one more time, so hard Faye's lips felt bruised, like she'd been slapped.

Maybe she had.

❖

In three weeks, the day after Labor Day, classes started for Faye and Theresa. They were moving into their apartment together in one week—one week until they left St. Cecilia's forever.

Faye felt nervous all the time, now. She felt unsure, unready. What lay before her was so open and vast and unknown. *What was she doing? How could she leave St. Cecilia's?*

She knew there was no choice for her *but* to leave. Still, she felt as if she were Sister Luke leaving the cloister, waiting for that ominous click as the door latched behind her, her old life inaccessible, her new life impossible to imagine.

The world *out there* was filled with people like Rosario's gang family and Jessica's brother the rapist and her own grandfather. She'd had so little contact with people *out there* since she'd been at St. Cecilia's. In the beginning the nuns had kept her cloistered because she was so young and, as her grandmother had said after her parents were killed, she'd been through *a trauma*. She was also one of only three girls who was an actual orphan. All the other girls who lived there—not the girls in the school, but the girls who lived at the *home*—had some kind of family *out there*, it just wasn't family that could take care of them.

Angie had helped her with people. He was friendly and avuncular and he liked Faye. "You're like another daughter to me, Faye. And I do everything I can for my kids."

Since the middle of her junior year, when he'd hired her after Christmas, after Mother Superior had told her that to be able to get into college as a photographer, she'd need a portfolio, she had been Angelo de Luca's underpaid worker and over-privileged student.

For a year and half he had helped her, taught her everything about the darkroom—his darkroom, not her grandfather's darkroom. He'd introduced her to camera after camera. "Remember, old school, you gotta go old school." The Saturdays at the shop had become half working behind the counter, half taking her out into the neighborhoods of Brooklyn to shoot pictures of everything, in every kind of light.

"Mother Superior says you need to have a lot of different kinds of shots, so we're gonna get you everything you need. You don't disappoint Mother Superior. But I guess you know that by now, eh, eh?" He'd laughed and nudged her in the arm with his elbow, then.

Angie would take her to lunch on these junkets. "Whaddya mean you don't eat meat? How d'ya get away with that with the nuns? Okay—no meat. We'll go Italian." And then he would laugh again and Faye would feel like she was going out with a favorite uncle who wanted to treat her and spoil her.

But he was also a strict teacher. Every trip Faye had to fill the roll and when it was done, she had to go back and develop it. He taught her a different kind of discipline than the discipline the nuns had taught her. And he'd taught her to see past the obvious view, to the more hidden, more mysterious one. She'd never have had that portfolio to take to NYU without him. He was one of the people she was most grateful for.

While she was packing, Faye found the *matryoshka*. It was buried in the bottom of one of her few boxes, wrapped in a Russian-language newspaper, the Cyrillic letters a swirl of beautiful but incomprehensible words she couldn't read or even guess at.

How could she have forgotten about this? She leaned back on her bed, the matryoshka clasped to her chest.

❖

The Russian girl had only stayed at St. Cecilia's a short time, less than a year. Sister Mary Margaret had brought her into the junior dormitory one evening as the girls were getting ready for bed. The Russian girl had stood in the doorway, slightly behind Sister. The light had framed her in a way that had made them all look. The girl's hair was very long and very blond and Faye was sure she wasn't the only one in the dorm who thought, *angel.*

There was always an empty bed there, in their dormitory. The bed right inside the doors to the hall that led to the long, old-fashioned bathroom with the big white sinks with the big white knobs that read "hot" and "cold" on them. Sister Mary Margaret said there always had to be space for "one more young soul." Faye remembered when that young soul had been her. There had only been one other girl in the dormitory since her. And now the Russian girl.

Sister Mary Margaret had introduced her to everyone. *Laryssa.* Sister had said the name rolling the *r* a bit, making the name sound like poetry.

They had all tried to be welcoming, but new girls always made everyone nervous. Faye had understood this when she had been given her bed and box of things by Sister Anne Marie that day. But the girls already knew *her.* Faye had gone to the school. No one knew the Dominican girl. *Ximena.* Or the Russian girl. *Laryssa.*

No one knew them. The nuns might have said there was space for more girls, but the girls themselves didn't feel as if there was. No one had space for them. Not in their hurt, often petty, nearly broken, little-girl hearts. Sharing had never helped them. So they were wary of it.

Faye thought of St. Cecilia's as a safe place, walled-off from whatever it was that was *out there*, as their science teacher, Sister Juliana, always referred to the world beyond their little enclave. "Once you are *out there*, girls," Sister Juliana would wave her hand with her long, tapered fingers in the direction of the white-curtained windows that ran alongside the classroom and she would turn slightly away, as if to shield herself from whatever it was she was imagining, "things will happen. These will not all be good things, girls. Not all. Not good." And then she would turn back to the book in front of her open on the desk and continue whatever lecture it was she was giving them.

But when Ximena and Laryssa came, from *out there*, Faye felt unaccountably afraid. It wasn't the girls themselves—at least not Ximena. Ximena's skin was a deep brown and her hair was long and fell in shiny black waves over her shoulders. She had a sly "hah!" kind of laugh that made the other girls laugh, too.

Ximena had somehow fallen just right within the unstated boundary between acceptance and denial, like a tightrope walker who managed to negotiate the slimmest of lines across the most devastating of caverns. Ximena had seemed part of them right away. Less than a week after she'd come, she had sat with Luz when she started crying for no obvious reason and held her hand and said soft things to her in Spanish which Faye didn't understand. Faye liked Ximena. Everyone liked Ximena. No one turned their backs on her or tried to freeze her out. There was space for "one more young soul" after all. Ximena slipped into that space.

Faye couldn't have explained why Laryssa conjured different feelings, but she did, and they were strong. They all felt it.

That first night when Laryssa had been brought into their dorm, they'd thought she was angelic, a blond, ethereal vision who maybe was going to bridge the gap between St. Cecilia's, Brooklyn, and, well, heaven.

They'd thought that, but Laryssa had an aura of darkness around her and it permeated everything in her path. Many of the girls were sad and depressed, but Laryssa was beyond that, past that, had come out the other side of that. Laryssa was angry, prone to rages. Faye had been almost ten when Laryssa had come. Laryssa was her age.

But Laryssa was nothing like Faye. Faye had learned how to follow the rules early on. Laryssa made her own rules and no one knew what they were, not even the nuns. Maybe not even Laryssa.

As she lay on the bed, holding the matryoshka, Faye wondered what some of the other girls would say, the ones who had been here when Laryssa had come, and when she had gone, if she had mentioned Laryssa's name. But everyone was unsettled enough. There was no reason to disrupt the uneasy balance more than it already was.

❖

There were events that had led up to Laryssa leaving. The first had been Sister Claire. All the girls had rotations in the kitchen where they were taught to cook. "This is a life skill, girls," Sister Claire had told them. "Everyone has to eat, and so everyone has to know how to cook. You will find when you go back to your families or out into the world, that you won't always have the money to eat exactly what you want. So I'm going to teach you how to make things that are very delicious and really good for you, that are also very inexpensive, so that wherever you are you can have food and not feel deprived—that is, not feel like you are missing out on what everyone else has."

Faye liked Sister Claire and she liked the cooking classes a lot. There was almost never any meat involved because Sister Claire said, "Meat is expensive. And there are other ways to get your protein. These are the ways you can feed your families that are healthy without spending too much money. Also, being able to cook, you can help make things easier on your families," Sister Claire would tell them.

Faye was always silent when Sister Claire talked about the importance of learning how to make "a good, substantial meal with not very much." Sister Claire was sensitive to the poverty most of the girls had come from, even if she wasn't sensitive to the fact that Faye would not be rejoining *her* family until she went to Heaven.

No one knew exactly what had happened that day in the kitchen with Laryssa. At each one of her classes, Sister Claire would choose a different dish to teach the girls, asking them what they liked and what dishes were familiar to them. Most of the girls' families had strong ethnic roots. Puerto Rican, Dominican, Irish, Italian, Polish, Ukrainian, Russian. Sister Claire herself was "half Ukranian, half Russian," as she had told the girls on different occasions, leaning in and whispering the information as if it were a secret.

"My grandmother used to make these *deruny*," she'd say as she taught them to make the fat little potato pancakes mixed with onion and garlic and topped with sour cream with a little bowl of sour cherries next to them.

"We didn't have a lot of money and they are inexpensive but, um—so delicious. They can be both dinner and dessert. Aren't they delicious, girls? And if you don't have cherries—and we didn't always have cherries—you can slice up apples very thin and fry them right in the pan with the *deruny*." She had shown them how to do it both ways.

Faye had loved the little pancakes with their sharp and sweet flavors. They weren't like anything else she had ever eaten and she wanted to know how to make them. She thought her parents would have liked them. She had wondered if there was food in Heaven, or cooking, but she hadn't asked Sister Claire.

After Laryssa had come to St. Cecilia's, Sister Claire had asked her what she would like to make for her family. She had asked Laryssa in what Faye had thought must be her own language, because Laryssa still spoke both Russian and English. When she was angry, it was mostly Russian, and she would yell words the younger girls didn't understand, although once, one of the older girls, who was also Russian, had grabbed her arm and said something back at her in Russian that had made Laryssa stop.

That day in the kitchen, Laryssa had said "blood soup" and Sister Claire had looked upset and some of the girls had made noises and some had said, "Ew."

"That's not a dish we can prepare, Laryssa," she had said carefully, putting her hand on Laryssa's shoulder in what had looked to Faye like a comforting way. "Can you think of something else?"

"I like blood soup," Laryssa had said, more loudly this time, her voice a kind of heavily accented hissing. She had pulled her shoulder away from Sister Claire sharply, and that had made some of the girls start whispering.

"We need to kill a chicken or a duck. I can do it," Laryssa said. "I know how to slit the throat and drip the blood into a bowl. I can teach the others," and she had half-turned toward the rest of them, but no one had said anything. Faye had thought her grandfather should have had Laryssa as his granddaughter. It was a thought she didn't want to have.

The kitchen went quiet. Sister Claire looked at Laryssa, then she said, calmly, "We won't be doing that, dear. That dish is what we call an acquired taste. We want to make dishes that everyone can make, everyone will like, and that are inexpensive to prepare. So we're going to make something else, today. Next time, you can choose the dish. You can think of something else between now and then." Sister Claire's voice sounded a little irritated, now, like it did whenever the girls made a big mess, or someone didn't clean up when they were supposed to.

Sister Claire said, "We're going to make a *tortilla española* with plantains. It will be really delicious. And you don't have to be Puerto Rican to like it. Let me show you."

Luz had clapped her hands and Sister Claire had turned to her, an eyebrow raised and Luz had said, "That is my Mami's favorite. I want to know how to make it for her."

Sister Claire had put eggs, onions, potatoes, and green peppers on the big counter near the stove and she had asked someone to get out the flour, and someone else to get the big mixing bowl. She had put the big black skillet on the stove and turned on the gas, explaining that the oil had to get very hot for the plantains and for the omelette. She had been talking, telling them how to flour the plantains and how to beat the eggs lightly, and how to chop the onions very fine, and cut the peppers in thin strips, because "everything is just so much more flavorful when you cut it thin and delicate."

Sister Claire liked to use the words *delicious* and *flavorful* when she described the food she was teaching them to make. Faye thought it was because everyone understood those words and knew what they meant. So far, Faye had thought everything Sister Claire taught them to make was delicious. And also flavorful.

Sister Claire had put them all at stations around the kitchen in little groups with tasks for each group, reminding them all to be careful with the knives. "Always be very careful with the knives, girls, you don't want to cut yourselves. Nobody wants bloody fingers in their food!" They had all gone, "Ew, blood in the food," in a little chorus and Sister Claire had laughed and then there had been the sounds of low talking and chopping and sizzling and Sister Claire humming a little as she sometimes did.

Faye hadn't seen what happened next. She, Luz, and Rosario had been cutting the plantains the way Sister Claire had shown them how to do. But suddenly there had been a strange noise Faye didn't recognize, then a crash, and a strange, scary scream. Faye had turned to see Sister Claire with blood on her big white apron. She was holding her one arm up in the air and blood was running down it toward the rolled-up sleeve of her habit and she was telling someone—one of the Theresas—to go get Sister Juliana, who was in the little office off the living room and to hurry.

The blood dripped on the floor and Sister Claire leaned back against the double sink, staggering a little. Faye had seen her lips moving and she knew Sister Claire was praying. She had wondered if Sister Claire had thought she would die. It looked like a lot of blood and it was very red. Then Faye had watched as Laryssa came close, a small white bowl in her hands. "Now we can make the soup," she had said quietly and she had stretched out her arms, holding the bowl under Sister Claire's arm. Blood had dripped onto the side of the bowl and Faye had felt sick and dizzy. She knew she could never touch that bowl again and she would have to ask Sister Claire to throw it away, ask someone to throw it away. She memorized the way the bowl looked, so she would be able to search for it herself, later. She would bury it in the garden. Like something dead.

Sister Juliana had almost run into the kitchen, telling the girls to go to the dormitory and stay there, someone would be up to talk to them. Everything would be all right, not to worry, she said, but she wanted everyone to say three Hail Marys, no, ten Hail Marys for Sister Claire. Sister Juliana had grabbed the bowl out of Laryssa's hands and muttered something that had sounded to Faye like, "You sick girl, you sick, sick girl," and she had pulled Sister Claire into the chair by the back door and told her to hold her arm up higher and put her head down to her lap and to "just breathe calmly, Claire, we're going to get you help, nobody's going to die here today, nobody."

Faye had stood silently just inside the door to the kitchen, watching everything, instead of going upstairs as they had been told. Sister Juliana had taken tea towels and wrapped them around Sister Claire's arm and Faye had watched the blood spread out like a flower over the towels as Sister Juliana went over to the phone on the kitchen wall and called the police to come and get Sister Claire before she died in the kitchen, bleeding to death because there had been "an incident with one of the girls."

❖

The other "incident" had involved Ximena and Luz, who had become good friends. Luz was a small, quiet girl whose mother had "fallen in with the drugs and the street business," as she described it. Luz and her older brother had gone to stay with their *abuela*, but then she had gotten ill and couldn't take care of them anymore. The brother had gone to St. Joseph's in the Bronx, and Luz had come to St. Cecilia's. Luz had been nice to Faye at both the school and the dormitory. They weren't close, but they liked each other and were kind to each other in the way little girls can be, but often aren't. But once Ximena came to St. Cecilia's, she and Luz were best friends. They would talk in Spanish out in the schoolyard, their heads close together, black hair shining in the sun. And while Faye sometimes felt left out, she was glad they had each other. She had Rosario, she didn't need two best friends.

Faye hadn't been the one who found Luz. Ximena had found her. Luz was at the bottom of the stairs between the third and fourth floors, on the landing below their fourth-floor dormitory, where the junior girls were. No one knew why Luz would have been upstairs when everyone else was in the living room, but Jessica had said she thought Luz had gone upstairs to get something, maybe her inhaler.

The railing was broken and so were some of the balusters. Several jagged, splintered pieces of baluster spoke had been sticking out of Luz's back, at her side. She was unconscious and there was blood on her uniform and on the floor around her. It hadn't been a lot of blood, but after she saw it, after she had taken in the whole scene, it had made Ximena scream and scream.

They had all come running from the living room where Mother Superior was talking to them about an educational TV show they were going to watch. Faye had hung back, not wanting to see whatever it was. The incident with Sister Claire had been enough for her. She knew enough to stay far away from screaming.

Luz wasn't dead, but she was badly hurt. She had a hairline skull fracture and they had to take out her left kidney. She had been in the hospital for several weeks and when she came back she had a big red welt-like scar on her side that was shaped like a half moon that she showed everyone. Luz said she didn't know what had happened, exactly, and she said that the nurses at the hospital told her that the mind sometimes covers over bad memories so that you don't have to keep re-living them over and over. The nurses told her this was especially true when someone got badly hurt.

By the time Luz came back to St. Cecilia's, back to tell her story and show her scar, Laryssa was gone.

Ximena had told them later that night, after Luz had been taken to the hospital and Laryssa was downstairs in Mother Superior's office, and they were all huddled together near Luz's bed in the dormitory, that when she found Luz, Laryssa was sitting on the stairs a few steps up from Luz's body.

"She was just there, in the dark, on the step. It was really weird."

Laryssa hadn't said anything or gone to get anyone to help. She just sat there. When Ximena saw her, she had asked why she didn't call anyone and Laryssa had just continued to sit there at first, silent. Then Ximena said Laryssa told her, "That's what happened to my mother. Just like that. But maybe more blood. More pieces of wood. Yes, there was more blood. I remember, now. A lot more blood."

And then Laryssa had gotten up and walked past Ximena and gone down to the living room with everyone else. She never said anything about Luz, they had just heard Ximena screaming. Ximena said she thought it was Laryssa that made her scream, not the blood.

No one knew what had happened—if Luz had fallen, or if Laryssa had pushed her. But a few days later Faye had overheard Sister Juliana talking to Sister Ofélia, who had been seeing Laryssa since she'd been at St. Cecilia's, and Sister Juliana had said about Laryssa, "She's a very sick girl. She doesn't belong here, she belongs in a hospital. Since she's too young for prison. She's going to kill someone. I want her out of here before it's one of our own."

They had gone into the office and closed the door and Faye hadn't been able to hear anything else. But she had told Rosario later and Rosario had said, "I heard Mother Superior talking to Sister Claire. Sister Claire said Laryssa cut her on purpose. Maybe her family is gang like mine. Maybe she thought Sister Claire disrespected her."

Faye hadn't responded. But she was pretty sure they were all too young to be disrespected. A few days later Sister Ofélia came with a man who wasn't a priest and they took Laryssa away. She never came back to St. Cecilia's.

❖

The matryoshka had been a gift from Angie, purchased one Saturday when they had gone to Brighton Beach. When Faye had come into the shop that day, Angie's daughter Tina was there and Angie had told Faye they were going out to Brighton Beach to "Little Odessa, so you can take some pictures of a different world. You're gonna like it. It's like another country there. You'll feel like you traveled somewhere far, but you just took the subway to another part of Brooklyn."

They'd taken the B train to the end and Faye had realized when they got there, she hadn't seen the ocean since before her parents died. She had wanted to take pictures of everything and Angie had let her, handing her five rolls of film. "Just remember, you gotta develop it all."

She had taken a roll of photos before lunch, focusing on the storefronts with their Cyrillic signs. She loved the way the letters looked—angular, foreign.

Angie had taken her to lunch where they'd had *blini* and *pirozhki,* then they had gone to the St. Petersburg bookstore where he had told her to pick out a matryoshka to memorialize the day. Faye hadn't known what a matryoshka was, and he had led her to a big case in the bookstore that was packed three-deep with the little wooden stacking dolls.

"Let me show you," Angie said, opening one up. "See—doll inside doll inside doll. I got these for Tina and Amanda when they were little. They loved taking them apart and putting them back together."

Faye thought the dolls were the perfect metaphor for her, for her life at St. Cecilia's—the same doll, but different, living inside each other. Faye told Angie she wanted him to choose for her, and he had. Angie picked out one with a black background that made all the colors on the doll stand out. The doll's face had blue eyes and red-blond hair and was covered in beautifully executed wildflowers. "Looks a little like you, Faye," Angie said.

They walked along the pier and Faye stared out into the ocean. It was beautiful. She could stay here. She could definitely stay here.

❖

The sounds, when they came, were unexpected and foreign. *Gunshots.* Faye and Angie had just had another small meal—"It'll be like the English do, a tea," Angie had said, and he had given her this quick, one-armed hug and laughed his big laugh. They'd eaten at the Café Arbat, which sounded nicer than it was, but the food was good and everyone was speaking Russian, which made Faye feel like she was somewhere else, not Brooklyn.

Neither she nor Angie had wanted to head back just yet. Angie had been telling her about when he'd come out to Coney Island with his family when he was a child, and Faye, had, for that brief time, as she listened to him recounting his excitement at the rides and the cotton candy and the ocean, felt as if she were part of a family, a real family, where people had stories that were funny and silly and had nothing to do with anything that could send them to prison or death row.

Angie had heaved himself out of his seat and said to Faye, "Gotta get you back home, Faye," and Faye had felt the word *home* differently—more like how Rosario had said it that night and less like how she had been feeling while Angie was telling her his Coney Island stories.

Out on the street they had headed toward the subway when the shots rang out. Faye counted seven, maybe eight, but she knew she had missed the first few. Angie had pulled her into a doorway and put his arms out, protectively, blocking her behind him, the way Faye suddenly remembered her father doing with her mother once, when they were driving in the car and he had slammed on the brakes because a dog had run out into the street, a little boy chasing after it.

The memory had stung, somehow—it was so long ago, and yet the flash of it was so vivid, almost palpable. Faye could hear her father call out her mother's name, then her own. Tears stung behind her eyes and she had felt so vulnerable in that moment, not from the threat of bullets, but from the threat of her past, her present, and the future that yawned so uncertainly and so dangerously before her.

There were sirens, then, and people were swarming toward where the shots were, near the subway. They had to go that way, they couldn't avoid it. Angie said to Faye, "I don't want you to look, okay? You don't need to see any dead mobsters. Promise me you won't look. And for God's sake, don't tell Mother Superior about this, okay?"

But Faye had looked, they had both looked, there was really no choice. Faye wondered how anyone could keep from looking. They had pushed through the throng of people, all talking in Russian, no one speaking English, a jangled cacophony of sounds and some anguish, as Faye could hear a woman sobbing uncontrollably and repeating something over and over again. It had sounded like "*Pochemu oni yego ubit*" to Faye and she had written it down in her notebook and later when she was back at St. Cecilia's had asked one of the Russian girls if she knew what it meant. Anya had looked at her strangely, then said, "It means 'Why did they have to kill him.' Who would be asking you that, Faye?" And Faye had said she thought she heard someone saying it over and over again and it must have been a song or something and had quickly walked away.

The dead man was lying on the sidewalk, like he had just decided to take a nap on the ground. Faye had thought being shot to death would look more—she wasn't sure what—violent, maybe. But it was just like he'd lain down in his suit and coat on the sidewalk. Except for the blood and the fact that his eyes were open. His eyes were very blue, and he looked straight up at the crowd. There was a thin line of blood coming out of the side of his mouth and underneath him there was more blood, a blanket of blood, so that it looked like he had decided to lie down on a big spread of blood.

The crying woman was on her knees in the blood, touching the man's face and saying things in Russian. She kept turning to the crowd and saying things, but no one answered her. Then as Angie was pulling Faye toward the subway stairs, the police arrived and one officer put his arm around the woman and told her it would be okay while the other called out, "Anybody see this?" and then people started to move away, back up, act like they didn't understand English.

The subway rumbled above them and Angie said, "Let's go, Faye. I think you've seen more than enough for one day." He had put his arm around her like he was her uncle or her father and he had led her up the stairs, away from their trip to a foreign country, back to the Brooklyn they knew, the Brooklyn without blood and dead men shot down in the street.

Faye lay on her bed until it started to get dark. There wasn't much else to pack. There was so little to mark more than a decade at St. Cecilia's. Just her few boxes. She stared at the matryoshka in the semi-dark. The doll really didn't look at all like her, except maybe the eyes. But Angie had wanted her to have it. And she realized that it was the only gift she'd been given since her grandfather had given her a little book called *Now We Are Six* right before she found out that he killed women in their basement. But like that little book, the matryoshka had a hidden story. Not a story about Coney Island and cotton candy like the ones Angie had told her that day. And all the stories Faye knew seemed to end the same way—in killing.

CHAPTER THIRTY-SEVEN
THE CLICK OF THE LATCH

The day Faye left St. Cecilia's there were only a few things to do: go to the biology lab and memorize the contents of the jars there, run her fingers through the slashes on St. Cecilia's neck a final time, and say a last prayer at the grotto to Mary for all that had come before and all that was ahead of her.

She had said her good-byes to the friends who were still there, and to Sister Mary Margaret and Mother Superior and the other nuns. She had said good-bye to the ghost of Sister Anne Marie as she stood at the spot where she had always heard her crying.

And then she had left. Everything she owned, what little there was from the decade she'd spent there, had been taken to the small apartment she was sharing with one of the Theresas for her freshman year. Theresa was going to Fordham, she to NYU. It was small, but what they could afford and they were used to sharing a far smaller space than this. It was their new life, but they were as scared as they were ready.

The second week she was living in Manhattan, Faye had gone to the public library and searched for her grandfather's case. She had gone back every day for a week and read everything she could stand to read. About how it had been Sister Anne Marie who had undone him with her murder. None of the other women—evidence of at least seventeen murders had been found in the house—had been traced to him, but Sister Anne Marie had.

They'd never found Faye's grandfather, or her grandmother. When the police came to the house, it was as if the two of them had just gone out for a walk. The car was there, parked on the street as it always was, in front of the house. They hadn't taken anything with them. All that seemed to be missing was her grandmother's purse, which she took with her every time she left the house, regardless of whether she was going to the store a block away or somewhere much further. The purse, and, it seemed, some camera equipment.

What the police *had* found, there, in the basement, had been Sister Anne Marie. Raped, mutilated, her tongue cut out, sliced into pieces, and stuffed back in her mouth. The medical examiner's report stipulated that she had been alive through all of it.

Other stories Faye read explained that the house had gone into foreclosure and been sold at sheriff's auction. There had been a granddaughter, who had been sent to the orphanage at St. Cecilia's in Brooklyn. Her name was not released to the press, but she was said to have been a witness to at least some aspect of the killings, according to homicide detective Tom McManus.

It was more than Faye had wanted to know. Especially the part that he was still out there, her grandfather, taking pictures of girls who were disarmed by his calm demeanor and simple charm.

She'd been safe at St. Cecilia's. Now she was on her own. And there was a murderer, a serial killer, who was the only one who knew for sure who—and where—she was.

CHAPTER THIRTY-EIGHT
EXORCISM

When Persia and Nick had each pulled the drapes on the photographs before a rapt and packed audience at the gallery, there had been a collective sound that had rippled through the men and women standing in front of Faye's work. When she herself had pulled the pieces of velvet from table after table, the sounds had been both louder and more—she wasn't sure what the word was—repelled? Awed? A few people had turned and left the gallery immediately, but most had, as Faye had expected, stayed to look hard and long at all the things they didn't want to admit they wanted to see.

Persia had come up to her after she had looked at the tables and had said simply, "I didn't expect this. I really didn't," and had moved on before Faye had had a chance to respond. Faye wasn't sure what Persia meant, but she had looked stunned and slightly sickened. Perhaps she wasn't as hard-core as she thought she was.

Faye overheard a flurry of comments as she walked through the gallery, a glass of red wine in her hand.

"Look at that, look at that, did you see what she had there, in the vise, in those jars?"

"It's not real, though, right? I mean that wasn't human, right? None of it was human, was it?"

"Did you see the pictures? The ones in the frames on the table?"

"Omigod—I've never seen anything like that in my life!"

"Why would anyone pose photographs like that? How did she do that? How *could* she do that?"

"Can you do that with Photoshop? Really? I mean it's different from those superimpositions you can do with characters from *The Walking Dead.*"

"It's creepy, the way she has these photos from her real work in with these fantasy photos—like it's all the same thing."

"What about those jars? Is it even legal to have that here?"

There had been a scream, suddenly, and Faye turned to see a woman float gracefully to the floor like an overblown petal, as if she'd been practicing that fainting scene for a while.

Persia rushed toward her, looking around for Nick as she did. Faye looked at what the woman had been looking at. Oh yes, Shihong's jars. That was worth screaming over. But then, to Faye, it was all worth screaming over. She'd screamed and even fainted over all of it herself. And yet, there was nothing that unusual here, really. It was all the work of other humans, and for some that "work" had a dailiness to it that made it absolutely mundane and ordinary. And despite what some in the gallery were saying, it was all real. Not one image was Photoshopped, not one was "fantasy." These were all "work" photos. She just couldn't explain that to the people who had come to the opening.

Faye thought of how her grandfather had explained his torture murders to her as work, work to be proud of. Explained it to a six-year-old whose parents had just been killed as if it was the most ordinary thing in the world to say. *Ordinary mayhem.* That was the very worst kind, Faye thought. Very. Worst.

Faye moved toward the door, then turned and looked back over the room. It was different from what she had imagined. There had been gasps and a few stifled screams. As more people had entered the gallery after the initial reveal, there had been other noises—other little shrieks, some choruses of "Oh no!" And then, mostly, silence. Much of the food at the back of the gallery had gone uneaten—or rather, people had taken little plates of food, but had left them all around the gallery, unable to look at her work and also eat. Everyone had, however, had at least one drink.

Nick had come up to her after the first hour to let her know that every photograph had sold and that there were orders for more, a surprising number. The installation pieces were not for sale, but that hadn't kept people from asking, from wanting them. No one seemed to understand that everything on the tables was real. It wasn't mixed media, it was found horror.

"Pretty grisly stuff you've got here," Nick had said, his look of perpetual ennui shaken off for the moment. "You'd never know it to look at you, you know. You seem so—demure, almost. It's a little shocking, actually. I guess I didn't expect it of you, even though I'd seen your work in the paper, and the portfolio. This"—he waved his hand to take in the exhibit—"this really is a lot more than I thought it would be. Persia's a bit upset, really. But still, brilliant, brilliant stuff."

Faye had listened as he spoke and wondered what it was that people saw when they looked at her. *Demure?* That was the girl who'd been raised by nuns. Well, nuns and a serial killer and his accomplice. Did those twin upbringings show in her work? Faye wondered what the people in the gallery thought when they looked at her, her work, and her again. It didn't matter, really. She just wondered, curious more than anything. She had the strangest feeling of both *déjà vu* and anticlimax.

Keiko hadn't come to the opening, but she'd called earlier and wished Faye luck and impressive sales. There had been an incident at the bookstore the night before, after Faye had left. Keiko didn't want to get into it, but someone had taken the sushi eating too far. She and Mika had ended up at the hospital later that night. Faye wasn't surprised. There seemed a very fine line between a sensual display like the one at the bookstore and the stoking of some primordial desire in men that turned women into prey. Faye had shuddered at the thought. She had tried not to think about it, about blood running into the sushi and strategically placed lettuce leaves and pieces of fruit. Tried not to think of Mika's perfect flesh marred by the jagged tear of teeth.

The opening had been a success. Seven or eight critics had come up to Faye and asked her questions. She'd been polite, she'd been vague. She'd revealed what she thought was useful, ignored the questions she didn't want to answer—or couldn't answer. When nearly three hours had passed and the gallery was still filled with people, new faces replacing the original ones, Faye had had enough. She told Nick she was leaving, she had to take a walk, she'd be back in a bit. He didn't try to stop her. He was in his element. He was the gatekeeper to the horror show and he was reveling in it. Faye wasn't sure if she should be grateful or appalled.

Faye stepped out into the brisk cold in this end-of-winter night, glad that it was clear. She wasn't sure what she felt. *Empty? Relieved?* She had put a handful of the least horrifying photographs of her grandfather's crimes in among her own art because it was part of her story—she was the one who had survived. She had displayed the jars Shihong had brought her because they, too, were part of her story, part of the endless horrors perpetrated on women. Faye wondered, for the first time in a long time, if her grandfather was still alive, and if he was, if he was still murdering women and cannibalizing them. *Would he have wanted to be there at the bookstore last night, eating from Mika's lovely body?* Or was solitude with his victims an essential part of the experience for him? Faye wondered if her grandmother was still sharing his bed every night, still pretending that the plates she set the table with weren't used to serve up the entrails of her husband's victims.

Faye took a deep breath of the icy air. She wasn't sure what to do now, wasn't sure what would happen when the reviews of the show hit, wasn't sure if it was all over for her now, if she was free to start over, or if she should start walking toward the river, as she had planned for so long.

She stood outside the gallery, unable to decide what to do next. Shihong was still in town, although she had not come to the opening. Nor had Molly come, or at least Faye hadn't seen her. She thought that was probably best. Maybe she should just go home and try to sleep a dreamless sleep.

Faye started walking, walking, then stopped, turned toward the curb, ready to hail a cab. As she put her arm up, she looked into the mass of traffic passing by. And then, several cars over, Faye saw something that made her stomach lurch. An attractive older man with gray hair and a camera, leaning out of the passenger side window of a taxi as it headed uptown. Her heart started to race, faster, faster, faster. *Is it him? Does he know I'm here? Did he see my name in the newspapers in the promotion of the opening? Has he come for me, finally, after all these years, when just the memories of him had stalked me? Will I become yet another of his victims?*

Faye dropped her arm, stepped back from the curb. No, it wasn't over. The exorcism wasn't complete, as she had thought. It wasn't over at all. Faye turned and began to walk. Back to the gallery, or toward the river, she'd know when she got there.

PART TWO

Someone I loved once gave me
a box full of darkness.

It took me years to understand
that this, too, was a gift.

—Mary Oliver, "The Uses of Sorrow"

CHAPTER ONE
UNDERWATER

E verything had changed after that night.
  I had known it would.

I had also known, after what I'd seen, throwing myself in the river was not an option. I had to somehow pull myself back from the brink. I could keep the river in reserve, like a gift I would give myself. The gift of oblivion. The oblivion I had imagined since I was six and had thought about burying myself in the snow after my parents were killed. I had wanted oblivion then even though I knew nothing yet, really, about how terrible the world was. My parents had been killed, but I hadn't seen it. Hadn't seen what *burned alive* looked like. I only imagined what it was like. I had only tested it with my hand in the flame on the stove.

Fire had never tempted me again. But the river—the river was a constant temptation. The dark, obliterating fathoms I had promised myself awaited me, but not yet. Not yet. Not now that I knew he was still out there. Not now that I knew I had to stop him. Not now that I was the only person who had a chance of stopping him. Not. Now.

It should have been the best night. It *was* the best night. It was also the most awful night since I'd been in the DRC. Worse even than the night I had nearly thrown myself out of the window of my apartment, pulled back only by Shihong's mysterious arrival that I still didn't quite understand. And which she had yet to explain.

A group of us had stayed at the gallery after it closed. Nick had prepared a second feast, one he'd been quite proud of. He'd had a friend's

Mexican grandmother make a series of platters filled with *calaveras de azúcar*. He thought I'd be charmed, not horrified, so I tried to look charmed. But the smiling little skeletons, the brightly tinted skulls—in the eerie light of the gallery, the light meant to create an atmosphere— the skulls reminded me of my grandfather's photographs, reminded me of the ghastly grins on the faces of the women whose flesh had been cut away. I could barely breathe. *He was out there, he was out there, he was out there, he was still killing, he had seen me.*

How long before I was one of those skulls, one more victim of my grandfather's murderous obsessions?

"I had to have them made especially for you—commissioned. My own contribution to the art world," Nick said, letting out his low British chuckle. "They're out of season." Nick put his arm around me and squeezed me like a child who had done very well. I'd laughed a little too loudly. *As if skulls were ever out of season.*

"*Día de los muertos.* That's November, Nick," I said, looking at the beautifully crafted sugar skulls and the *pan de muertos*—bread made into a skull and crossbones. There were other delicacies as well, but these—these were the special ones for me. *The food of death.*

The select group of invited guests included a few friends of mine, some colleagues, a handful of Nick's favorite clients, and three critics he wanted to impress. This was an after-hours party. I hadn't seen most of these people at the opening. They had clearly waited to come later, entering through the side door, little black-rimmed invitations with a small bloody fingerprint at the bottom, designed by Persia, in their hands, glad to be able to peruse the show Nick had promoted so heavily, at their leisure and without the crowd.

Persia had greeted everyone, offered them drinks, and led them into the now-low-lit gallery. The velvet drape across the window had been pulled closed and the combination of the drape and the lighting had a created a strange and different atmosphere in the somewhat macabre shadows from sconces and candles. I watched Persia take people to individual photos or pieces on the tables. I could tell she was enjoying unsettling Nick's guests.

So many secrets. What did Persia think when she looked at my work? Did I even want to know?

I wasn't sure how Molly had ended up with an invitation, but when

Persia led her to the first table, I had an idea it was Keiko's invitation that had been passed on to her.

She saw me talking to one of the critics and came toward me. I excused myself and went to meet her.

"I wasn't expecting you," I said, suddenly at a loss for words. I was glad she was there, I had hoped she'd come to the opening. But as I stood looking at her Sister Anne Marie face, a wave of fear came at me. I couldn't help thinking there was someone else who might see that same face and want to kill it all over again.

"I can see why you were anxious at Keiko's reading," Molly said, looking toward one of the tables where my work was laid out. "This is"—I could tell that despite being a writer, she was searching for a word, a descriptive that was diplomatic, that wouldn't insult me, but which would express her revulsion at what she saw—"stunning."

Good choice. Her face was unreadable in the half-light where we stood. Or maybe I just didn't know how to read her. *Yet.* I knew we would get a chance to read each other, if only I could survive what was coming, what I knew was coming.

If only.

I'd thanked her, explained I'd been working on the show quite a while, more than a year, really. That in some respects I'd been working on it since my childhood, when I'd first discovered photography and art. "I was an orphan, you see," I said, my tone as ironic as I could make it. "That colors things. A bit darkly, too."

I could tell she wasn't sure if I was making a not-quite-funny joke or if I was serious. We were interrupted by Nick with one of his clients. It was nearly a half hour before I was able to get back to Molly, more sales complete. I apologized for leaving Molly alone and she said, "It gave me the opportunity to really look at your work. It's really extraordinary. Hard to look at—like that magazine piece of yours. We don't like to think of these things, do we?"

She'd paused, then put her hand on my arm, looking at me, not past me, as she had been. "We are more like animals than we know."

I agreed—what she said was true, of course, but also oblique. It wasn't a catch-all. Did her "we" include the two of us? Or just me, the granddaughter of the serial killer who I'd just seen again for the first time in nearly thirty years? It had been less than two hours since I'd seen him and already I was feeling like a criminal, still implicated by his crimes.

We are more like animals than we know.

"Keiko thinks you need to get out more. After seeing this, I think maybe you need to stay in more. Why don't I make you dinner and we can talk about how evil is actually anything but banal?" The words came out of her in a rush. *Had the color risen in her face?* I couldn't tell in the muted light.

We made plans for dinner. She put her phone number into my phone and I put mine into hers. "I'll text you a time," she said, then gave me a quick noncommittal hug. "I'm glad I came. I wasn't going to. I thought it might be too much."

"Was it?" I asked, unsure what the hug had meant.

"Yes. But you'd be disappointed if I'd said no." And then she'd left, making me wish I'd left with her.

❖

The group at the gallery had stayed later than I'd expected and most of us had had too much to drink. I felt as if I'd drunk myself sober over the course of the night. When I left the gallery, Persia put her hand on my cheek and told me how much my work had impacted her, Nick told me, "You've made a lot of money here tonight, Faye, you should be thrilled. Brilliant, just brilliant."

I'd thanked them both and left.

I had walked to the river, leaned over the small iron fence, and stood looking down into the darkness. I could hear the sounds of the city behind me and the soft slapping of the water below me. *Had Grand been watching me all along? Was he there when I left? Is he here now, waiting to spring at me with a box cutter or a switchblade or something that would be sharp and swift and take me by surprise?*

I felt beaten by the night, by his return to my life, by what lay ahead of me. This felt like a saint's task, what I had to do. Fend off the infidels, the Visigoths, the men who would take women's bodies and attempt to take their souls. How many souls had he taken? I was not going to let him take mine.

That Nietzsche quote came into my head: "Whoever fights

monsters should see to it that in the process he does not become a monster. If you gaze long enough into an abyss, the abyss will gaze back into you."

I was embarking on a fight with a monster. I was gazing into the abyss right now—the yawning black maw of the Hudson River. I was also gazing into the abyss of evil, the evil that was part of me, that was, no matter what Mother Superior had told me, linked by DNA to my orphan self.

Yes, he was an old man, now. But that only meant it would be easier for him to prey on vulnerable women because they wouldn't fear him. I knew he was still handsome—even the flash I'd seen had shown me that. A slew of writers and artists, actors and musicians went through my mind—old men with wives half their age. Yes, if Clint Eastwood was still directing and acting in his mid-eighties, Grand could still be luring and killing women.

I tried to figure out exactly how old Grand was—how could I have so few facts about my own history? There had been no photographs of him in those clippings Mother Superior had given me when I left St. Cecilia's. But I remembered that neither his nor my grandmother's hair had been gray. Had they married very young? Had my grandmother been pregnant? My parents had been so young when they'd been killed. They'd met in college, married when they were in graduate school. They hadn't quite made thirty. I was already several years older than they were when they'd been killed. Maybe my grandparents were in their mid- or late forties when I went to live with them. Which meant my grandparents could be in their mid- to late seventies now. Which meant he—Grand, I had to start naming him, connecting him to me—could have another few years of killing left in him. Two of my professors from college were in their late eighties and still taking pictures. Another had turned ninety last year and just had a retrospective. And none of them were driven by maniacal obsession like Grand.

I could look him up on one of those genealogy sites. I didn't know how to search for my grandmother. In all the papers she had his name. *My* name. I could do a search of *our* name. Do it from the office so that it wasn't on my own ISP.

He already had me thinking like a criminal. When he was the criminal.

All this time I had thought he was dead. Why was he still alive? How was he still alive?

I looked into the river, pushed myself up on the railing. It wouldn't be hard to pitch myself forward—these railings were decorative, after all. Not meant to keep people from diving in. Not meant to keep us from the lure of oblivion. Not meant to protect us from the soothing, enveloping water.

When I was first working for the newspaper, I was often sent to Morningside Heights and Harlem to cover anything gruesome. I'd only been at the paper a few months when I was invited to go cover a drowning in East Harlem with one of the older beat reporters. His regular photog wasn't in—his wife was having a baby—so he took me to "show me a different part of the city."

He'd said, "Practice your Spanish on the way. Not much English, there."

There had been a drowning. Or so it seemed. When we arrived, it was a bad scene. Really bad. It had been a hot mid-September day and even now, nearing dusk, it was as stifling as any July day. As we pushed our way closer to the river, we could see the bodies there, lifeless, on the ground, water splashed out everywhere, two FDNY guys leaning against the low railing, one with his head in his hands, the other smoking a cigarette and looking out onto the water.

The bodies looked pitiful in the waning light, just there, on the cement, the sun setting beyond the river. A harbor cop was pulling yellow crime tape from one part of the railing to another and I had wondered if the whole river was a crime scene.

There were three of them. Two Latino kids—we couldn't tell if they were boys or girls from where we were—and a young woman, probably the mother.

There was a lot of screaming and yelling and people who were obviously family shouting and crying in Spanish. I had told the reporter I was going to try and get closer and he had shaken his head no and tried to pull me back, but I thought I might be able to look like a bystander instead of the press and might be able to get close enough to take some pictures.

I had asked a girl—she was maybe fifteen, she wasn't crying, but she looked distraught—if she knew what was going on. My Spanish had improved since St. Cecilia's, but I searched my memory for drown and swim. "*Qué se...ahogan? Estaban—nadando?*"

"*Nadar?*" she said, her face suddenly angry. "*Nadar? Que mierda los mató!*"

Swim? Swim? She fucking killed them.

The girl had gone into a tirade in Spanish which I could barely follow. As I told her I was sorry and asked if I could help her in any way, she'd punched me, hard, in my arm and spit at me. "*Puta de mierda blanca. Coño intromisión. Perra entrometida. Lárgate de aquí!*"

I backed away as she swung at me again and people around her turned to stare at us, one older woman pulling the girl back and shaking her finger at me. Everyone had heard what the girl had said.

Fucking white bitch. Meddling bitch. Meddling cunt. Get the hell out of here!

The girl was screaming it over and over and she was sobbing now, keening and practically collapsing as the older woman put her arms around her and tried to calm her. Suddenly, the reporter was next to me. "You're supposed to cover the story, Faye, not *be* the story. Let's do what she said and get you the hell out of here. We're not going to get any answers from these people tonight. They're too upset. Those kids—God—they're only four and five, the cops told me. What the hell was she *thinking*?"

We'd ridden back to the paper mostly in silence. He was going over his notes, I was just sitting there, my arm throbbing, grateful the girl hadn't broken it, even more grateful she hadn't punched me in the face.

It had taken me a long time to understand what I had done wrong. That I had been an outsider intruding on raw, intolerable grief. That my whiteness itself had been perceived as an intrusion, a kind of racist voyeurism, when I had just seen myself as doing my job. Asking any question, presuming any circumstance, had been not just awkward, but insensitive to the point of callous, I realized much later. The racial divide—a divide white people can choose to ignore at will but which people of color never have the option of ignoring—just added to the problem, and the perceived insensitivity.

I would play that scene over and over again in my head for years, wondering how I would have felt if a reporter had asked my six-year-old self how I felt, knowing my parents had been burned alive, wondering how I would have felt if a photographer had wanted to take a picture of me at the place where it happened, or beside the burned-out wreck.

Replaying the scene had made me cringe again and again. I, of all people, the orphan, the refugee from St. Cecilia's, should have known how wrong it had been, especially in my heavily accented Spanish. The bodies still there, clothes wet and stuck to them, water splashed out around them like the tiered halo around Our Lady of Guadalupe. They were a tragedy and I had been just another voyeur, a vulture ready to peck away at their inconsolable grief.

The girl had been the sister of the dead woman—the dead woman herself had been only nineteen, the little boy and girl four and five as the police had said. She had stood the kids on the other side of the railing, telling them to hold on, wait for *Mamá*. Then she had climbed over, too, taken one little hand in each of hers, said, "*Ahora salta!*" and they had all jumped, none of them able to swim. At least one of them not wanting to.

There had been back story, all of it ugly, which had just added to my revulsion at my own casual cruelty. Now, as I stood looking into a different part of the same river, thinking about how that river could end my own suffering in a matter of minutes, I understood that scene, all of it, with indisputable clarity. There it was before me, the "torn magnificent Hudson," as Jane Mayhall, a *New Yorker* poet, had described it in a poem I loved, called "Surfaces." There it was, laid out before me like a lover's promise, the glassy, splintered darkness. Would my life flash before me, or had that happened enough here, on the hard surface of land, to forgo taunting me anew in my final moments of life? Wouldn't the suffering just end the second my body disappeared below the surface? Hadn't I been partly underwater for a while? A long while? Maybe since my parents' car had incinerated in the snow by a different river. Maybe since I had never fully come up for air since then.

I stared out into the night, over the black expanse, so few sounds around me, even in this massive city, because it was so late. Those darkest hours, Martine had called it when we were in the DRC. And now, there it was, the river, my dream escape, the place Grand had both driven me to and kept me from. As I stood there, leaning over the little railing, hearing that light *slap slap slap* below me, I thought about the Latina woman in Morningside Heights and her children, I thought about the world beneath the Hudson's now-black surface. How many bodies had buried themselves there, rather than continue on, tortured?

I would not be one of them, tonight. But I was not ruling out forever. I could not, because I didn't know what was next, what would happen now. Everything had been so clear before tonight and now— now it was murkier than the river before me. Yet the Hudson was here for me, waiting, arms open, endlessly seductive, ready to pull me to her whenever I needed, whenever I wanted, whenever I had finally had enough.

Waiting for whenever I had ended the quest I had, unwillingly, oh so unwillingly, just begun. I turned my back on the water and headed home.

CHAPTER TWO
MAUL

That first night I had barely slept. After I'd gotten home from the river I'd stood in the shower for a long time, not caring how much water I was wasting, not caring about sustainability, not caring about the environment, just needing to feel the water run over me as I tried to scrub away the knowledge that I now needed a plan. A survival plan. An escape plan. I was in danger, other women were in danger, and I was the only person, truly, who could stop the trajectory of killing my grandfather had put in place probably long before I was born.

I had woken up after less than two hours of unremittingly nightmarish sleep. I was being chased, I was being beaten, I was being slashed. The images were dark, the dream-plots darker still.

I lay there, shaking again, thinking about him, about all of it. I felt queasy, my mouth dry. I got up and walked to the kitchen, took some seltzer and a lime out of the fridge, looked over at the gin as I cut and squeezed the lime onto the ice, watched it cloud the seltzer briefly. I couldn't drink anything but the seltzer. I couldn't afford even a brief spurt of oblivion. Not now.

Not now.

I went into my studio. I realized I hadn't been in here since the night Shihong had mysteriously appeared. The jars she brought weren't here, now. They were at the gallery, little red dots beside their names on the wall by the table where they were displayed. *Not for sale. Private Collection.* They were a private collection, all right.

I sat down at my work station, pulled out a notebook, began writing down some of the images from my dreams. *Was I already thinking of a new project?* How could I think of anything but Grand and his crimes and his having seen me? *He saw me.*

I played out the scene again: My looking across the lanes of traffic, my seeing him in the cab, his camera pointed at me like a weapon. *His camera.* How many photos had he taken of me, the adult me? Had he seen me before? Had he been watching me all along and I had just never seen *him* before? Had he been at the publication party for my book? So many questions. How many years would I have to replay? I was certain he hadn't hovered outside St. Cecilia's because I so rarely left there and that would have been the one place the police would have had under surveillance after Sister Anne Marie had been killed.

Or maybe this was the first time. Maybe he just had to see what he had wrought in me, had to see what kind of art *I* produced and how it mirrored his own.

I shuddered involuntarily.

Torture as art. Murder as art. The Nazis had catalogued their atrocities against the Jews as if it were art. ISIS was doing the same thing now in Iraq and Syria—staging beheadings as if they were performance art, the backdrops, the orange jumpsuits of the victims, the black outfits of the executioners. Staged for the camera. Just as my grandfather had staged his victims for the camera.

Sylvia Plath had said it, "dying is an art." *So was killing.*

I knew, whether I wanted to admit it or not, that Grand wanted to kill me. Had likely been planning to do so for some time. How could he not? He had wanted to groom me, to make me his partner in killing. To raise me for that sole purpose. I wondered why it had taken me all these years to come to this realization. And why it had taken *him* all these years to appear in my life.

That was what those days in the darkroom had been about— prepping his young apprentice. He had wanted me to understand the process. He had always sat me to the side when he'd taken photos in the room where he did the portraits. He'd wanted me to see how it was done: *Tilt your head up. Now tuck your chin a bit. Now lick your lips. That's good. Now say cheese. Perfect.*

I could hear his voice so clearly in my head, as I remembered him positioning people on the little plush-topped bench in front of the black velvet backdrop. There were two others—one wine-red, one a deep green. But mostly he used the black. "Everyone looks good against black. It doesn't matter what their coloring is, their race, their hair, any of it. The black, you see, Faye, acts as what we call relief. So the person stands out against it. It gives the portrait depth, a perfect outline."

Yes, he had been grooming me. There had been a black drape in the basement, too. I remembered it, now. I remembered everything, now. I was his apprentice. I wondered if he had seen me burning my hand in the flame on the stove. Or if my grandmother had told him. I wondered if it had excited him to imagine the two of us, out together with our cameras, me the young bait. Would he have passed himself off as a widower with me, his young daughter? Scenarios spilled over each other in my mind. I didn't know how to shut them off, make them stop.

I remembered something from the summer, there, at my grandparents' house, before I had gone to live at St. Cecilia's. I had been out back in the yard. It was off the kitchen and there was a small hill behind it, because the house was on a hilly block. It was one of those gruesomely humid days—New York in August. The sky had that storm-heavy yellowness to it, and I had heard thunder in the distance. My grandmother had called to me from somewhere inside the house to come in, but I hadn't gone in, I'm not sure why. I was back by the hilly part of the garden where my grandmother had a berry bush— blackberries, I think. And behind the bush was some small animal. I don't remember exactly. A shrew maybe, or a vole. Something bigger than a mouse. I watched as it began to skitter out from behind the bush and run down the side of the yard.

Grand had come out then, to get me, he was calling my name. And suddenly there was a flash, it was lightning, and it was hitting the little wrought iron fence that ran down the side of the yard. But the animal, the vole, was struck, too. I guess the lightning had gone into the ground right there and it had been tossed into the air by the impact and let out a little death scream. And I had involuntarily covered my eyes and Grand had pulled my hands away and said, "You want to remember this, Faye. This is how they die—there's a scream, and the body flops around like a fish, and then they are lying there, in repose. And you see, they are beautiful again."

But the animal had not been beautiful. It had been burnt underneath and its mouth had been open in that final scream, its eyes wide. Grand had gone inside and come out with a camera as the rain came down. We had stood there together in the rain as he took a series of photographs of the dead animal.

"This is life, Faye. You want to capture it in all its different guises. You remember that. It's important to remember that."

I had remembered it, of course. But it was a sense memory, rather than a memory of the moment. Until now. Now that memory was back. All the memories were back. They had come with Grand's reappearance. And I felt very much like that vole running out from behind the safety of the blackberry bush, not knowing that death lay just yards away. Sudden, terrible, and final.

Now all I could think was, *How many times did Grand see me that I didn't see him?*

I couldn't help going over and over the same thoughts, trying to recall every minute detail, closing my eyes like they do on the police procedurals. I tried visualizing the scene on the street and then in the gallery and then on the street again. *Had he been there? Had he been there?* I couldn't see his face at the gallery. But I could see him looking straight at me from the cab.

I went back to the notebook. What had my dreams told me? *Ragged bits of scalp. Trailing strands of hair. There were bones everywhere. And skulls. We (who is the we? Me and Molly? Me and Persia? Me and Nick? Me and Grand?) stood looking at them, on the long tables.*

It wasn't much. It had felt like much more when I first woke up. Now the images were still viscerally clear, but I couldn't grasp what they might mean—or if they meant anything at all. Now it seemed as if I was searching for meaning in everything and anything, that I needed a key to unlock all that had been hidden from me since I was a small child. I tried not to think about my parents, those strangers whose faces were known to me almost wholly through photographs—photographs my grandfather had taken.

I tried not to wonder if my father had known about his father's dark "art." I tried not to wonder if he had been a participant. Or even if, like me, he had just discovered the photographs and chosen to ignore them and what they meant. I didn't want to think about all the layers of complicity that wrapped my family tree in violence and death.

But where did that leave me? I wasn't a killer. I wasn't suppressing the urge to kill. I knew this about myself by now, for certain, after years of worrying that killing lay dormant in me, that killing would surface at some point. I would never be part of that gruesome work my grandfather had seen as his artistic endeavor. But I would be—I was—a chronicler of the kind of violence he and men like him wrought on the world.

I looked down at the notebook. The only other words I had written were *Grand in the taxi* and *Did Dad kill with Grand?* That last had a line through it.

I closed the notebook, turned off the light, and went back to bed. Hopefully sleep would not elude me the way the truth about my lineage had all these years.

❖

It was almost noon when I finally woke from what had felt like—and probably was—a drugged sleep. I'd taken a Xanax and chased it with a shot of gin, after all. It wasn't so much that I wanted oblivion as that I wanted a respite from my own endless loop of questions that had no answers. I'd needed sleep or at the very least to be unconscious and not thinking—a form of rest.

I lay there for a bit, pulling myself together, trying to figure out the next steps I needed to take. My life felt like it was in free fall. I had to stop that feeling. I had to cut out the emergency parachute for my own life before I crashed.

Grand's reappearance hadn't ruined me. I had to remember this. I still had plenty to hold on to. My work. My friends. The possibility of Molly, who despite what she had seen at the gallery, was interested in me. The doors were not all closed. I had to remember that.

I got up, had a semi-breakfast of fruit that was on the verge of going off, a super-frothy cappuccino with a ridiculous amount of sugar, and some biscotti I couldn't even remember buying. What had I been eating the past few days? I'd have to go out. I'd have to get food. *And I'd have to risk seeing him again.*

I did a brief check of Facebook and Twitter accounts. Lots of discussion about the gallery show, none of which I could focus on, so I posted nothing. I'd think of a generic post for later. My email was also full of well-wishes and raised eyebrows. I saved it all for later—not knowing when later might be.

Molly had sent me a poem. She said she had written it right after she had left the gallery, that the images of my photographs and mixed media had left her shaken, with a host of complex feelings. She said she wanted to make me dinner. Perhaps the next night, if I wasn't busy. The tone of her email was intimate, like we knew each other well, like we were close, like we had dinner all the time. I liked the tone. I was unsure about the poem.

Mauled
for F.E.B.
by Mallaidh Sullivan

At the gallery, your art
Stops hurts mauls
Breath held captive
Breath held before
An array of violence
On the walls, on the tables
A careful display of flesh torn from bodies
A careful display of all we do to each other
So careful, that display
More careful than we are with each other
The images ricocheted off the walls
Like arterial splatter
Their raw wounds, their riven scars
Their terrible, monstrous beauty
The beauty we find steeped in blood

The tables were covered
You did not see me
The tables were covered with food
I saw people talk, eat, stare
You were distant
The tables were covered in blood
I saw you, moving fast, untouched
A face in a crowd of your own making
I saw you, the tables were covered with you
I heard the voices, the screams
Not your screams, the screams of witnesses
Your witnesses
You were distant, from the witnesses
The tables were covered with blood
The tables were covered with you
Some of us have a need for savagery
Some of us have a need to be covered
To be distant
Some of us need
Some of us need you
To be distant
To not scream
Some of us have a need for savagery
We are more like animals than we know

Some of us have a need for savagery. Did Molly mean me? Did she mean everyone? I tried to imagine telling her about Grand, about St. Cecilia's, about what was happening to me right now.

I tried to imagine and couldn't.

I printed out the poem, tacking it up on the bulletin board in my studio. Then I got dressed to go out and buy food. *And hunt for a serial killer*, I could not help but think.

We are more like animals than we know.

Molly had no idea. I hoped she never did.

CHAPTER THREE
LIES OF OMISSION

A few nights after the opening, I was standing outside Molly's apartment building with a bottle of Portuguese white wine and a bouquet of delphiniums mixed with some rather creepy-looking ferns the florist had told me were ostrich fiddleheads. I knew they were ultra hip, but they added a dark edge to the delicate blue flowers that disturbed me the more I looked at them. Although the past few days—no, the past few months—it hadn't taken all that much to disturb me. Life was starting to require a trigger warning for me.

I was standing there thinking I should just pull the fiddleheads out and toss them on the curb, except you don't do that sort of thing in Manhattan or someone might call the police and that was the last thing I needed. In addition to the creepy ferns with their almost human heads, I'd also had the slow realization on the cab ride over that delphinium was embedded in my consciousness from A. A. Milne and that meant Grand, and I nearly left the entire bouquet in the taxi, but didn't.

There was something about the first-date aspect of the evening that had unsettled me. I'd changed clothes twice—something I rarely did. I thought about canceling—which I also rarely did unless an assignment came up suddenly. The truth was, I'd been so casual about sex and relationships for such a long time, I wasn't sure how to do this again, the seriousness. Because this—Molly—felt real and special and already started, somehow. As if we were already in a relationship, we just hadn't fit all the pieces together yet. We'd texted for an hour, maybe more, until we were actually falling asleep on the phone the night after the opening and it had felt so teenage—an hour? falling asleep?—that I wasn't sure whether to be delighted or sneering at myself. At the end of our conversation Molly had asked me if I had food preferences and I told her I had been a vegetarian since the age of six. She had said that surprised her, since I was so "worldly," as she put it. Didn't I want to try new foods in all the different places I'd traveled? I hadn't elaborated, she hadn't pressed it. Vegetarianism was more common now than when I was six, after all.

And yet—it felt like the first secret. *Why* I was a vegetarian was different from why other people were vegetarians. I had almost never said the word, but had Molly asked me I was certain I would *not* have said, even in some jocular way, *I was raised by my grandparents, who were cannibals.*

No, I would *not* have said that. But the simplest question of food preferences had already made me think that intimacy was forever out of my reach, that once I had left St. Cecilia's and other girls with shattered stories, I was less and less likely to find a woman with whom I could be honest. My past was inextricably part of me, but it was also unnamable. Could I start now, fresh, pretend I was an amnesiac, that I had no memories to tell because I could not remember any? Could it be like it was in my catechism class at St. Cecilia's, where if you recited a perfect act of contrition when you went to confession, you were absolved of all sins and your soul was clear and clean and fresh? Could it be like that?

My past was not something I could share or even wanted to share with anyone, least of all with the woman who looked so much like Sister Anne Marie, who had literally given her life for me.

I doubted I would ever tell that story—my story—to anyone else. I wasn't sure why I had been able to tell Shihong that first night we had spent together in San Francisco. Perhaps because I'd thought I'd never see her again and I just needed to talk that night. Perhaps it was because of all she had revealed to me, for exactly the same reason. We had bonded over our mutual horror stories. Like Martine, Shihong and I had been on the side of the world, and by world I meant this temporal world, that no one else I knew had been. The dark side, the side few ever saw and none wanted to see.

I knew Molly hadn't. I knew whatever her history was, there would be little horror in it. It was part of what drew me to her. It also made me question what I was doing with her. Where had she come from, now, at this point in my life when I was about to go under for the third time, when I was about to embark on a medieval kind of quest to subdue the monster, cut off the head of the gorgon? Why, other than her striking resemblance to the Sister Anne Marie of my childhood, had she struck so deep a chord in me? So deep that I felt as if I were already in love with her—deeply, irrevocably. Molly was, I realized suddenly, a lifeline for me, the person standing there by the water's edge tossing me the life preserver, begging me to hold on, not drown, save myself. When she had told me at the gallery that I needed to get out less, not more, she had meant I needed to spend less time in the midst of mayhem and more surrounded by normalcy.

Molly was, quite simply, a bridge to normalcy. No wonder this all felt so foreign to me. When had I, the orphan who had never been put up for foster care, never known more than St. Cecilia's and my grandparents' house—because really, my memories of my parents had dimmed so quickly, with no one to stoke those memories—when had I lived *normal*? Those beautiful people burned to death when I was six were more like people in some lost footage of someone else's life, not mine. That life *had* been normal, but it had burned up in the car with them, on that snowy night, and turned to ash. I could no longer even hear their voices. I could only see their faces if I looked at photographs. They were lost to me. My only family had been Mother Superior and Sister Mary Margaret and Sister Claire and of course, Sister Anne Marie. They were the women who had tried to give the foundling that was me, the changling that was me, a fresh start. I can only imagine what Mother Superior had prayed for every night when she thought of me. How much had I deepened her faith when I had failed to turn into a monster as she must have feared I would after all I'd seen? How much had I secured her belief in the power of prayer? If there was anyone who was responsible for my not becoming the monster my grandfather had hoped would grow up to commit untold atrocities with him, it was the nuns of St. Cecilia's. I owed them my life for maintaining that *home* in the 1980s when fostering out children or returning them to their families of origin was becoming the hard and fast rule. They must have known it wouldn't work for me, that I needed the cloistered life of St. Cecilia's that girls like Rosario had found claustrophobic but under which I had thrived and flourished until Mother Superior had sent me out to apprentice with her brother, where she knew I would be safe. I wondered if he had ever told her I had witnessed my first murder with him? Probably not. Probably that secret had been told in confession and nowhere else.

And now another woman was waiting to save me from my own history, even if she wasn't completely aware of that. Yet as I stood outside her door, my heart beating fast with anticipation and yes, even some inchoate fear, I remained unsure if I should hit the buzzer on the little pad of names or just keep walking and hand the flowers and wine to the first person I saw.

The closest I'd come to being serious with anyone in the past few years was whatever it was Shihong and I had been doing across the continent from each other for these past months. She and I knew each other's darkness. That was our connection. She had told me the stories of her being smuggled into the country, of how her grandmother, who had scared me that first night, had hobbled around, the last generation of women with bound feet. She had told me stories of horror and tragedy and violence that she remembered at least as well as I did my own. Shihong had used the word *mayhem* and she had known I understood. Her mother a single, never-wed young woman, involved in the political upheaval in the days after Tiananmen Square. Her father unknown in a story her mother had refused to tell until the day she died, when she was only a few years older than Shihong and I were now. Shihong's mother was killed in some accident shrouded in a political mystery Shihong had never been able to unravel.

Shihong's grandmother had been a refugee of torture and re-education, her grandfather murdered by Mao. They had fled together—the grandmother and young child, the only ones left. Shihong's grandmother had gotten them out of Fujian province through the Snakeheads—the *shé tóu*—and Shihong's grandmother had had to work off the debt in unsavory and illegal ways, including trading in horrific relics like those Shihong had given me. It was why Shihong had never been able to leave the secure and suffocating confines of Chinatown and wouldn't until her grandmother died.

Shihong and I were as bonded as we could be, given my whiteness and her indentured servitude as she viewed it, to America. But that bond between us was strong and would always be there, of that I was certain. We were destined to stay close, in an intimate way that transcended our being lovers. That closeness was born of our shared secrets. As she'd said, *The secrets become you* and ours had become us.

She had also saved my life. You don't walk away from that. Or at least I didn't. And she'd opened a door in me, a door to seeing where I'd come from and perhaps, where I was going. It was because of her that I was even able to be standing here, at Molly's door, able to consider a life with another person, able to envision sharing the future, even if the past had to remain hidden.

The evening with Molly was another door opening. I determined as I walked into her apartment, the scents of a serious meal redolent around me, that I would push all thoughts of Grand and what I would do next far away from me, if only for the night.

Molly charmed me, taking the wine and flowers, kissing me lightly on the cheek. ("Oh this is a nice wine—perfect for our first courses. I delved deeply into the vegetarian for you. I don't actually eat meat very often, but I do eat fish and fowl, so I guess I will have to do that out of your sight, in future. And these—I love any blue flower—how did you know? Delphiniums are so delicate. And these other things—hmm. Is that a nod to your work? Believe me, I'm not about to forget that. Anyway, thank you, darling.")

It was surprisingly easy, this casualness we'd fallen into so readily. The term *darling* sounded so natural. Not forced or affected. I felt as if I'd been hearing her say it forever, I was sure I wanted to hear her say it more. *How was it we'd only known each other such a short time?* I followed her into the tiny galley kitchen, standing in the doorway with a glass of the Portuguese white, watching her put together a plethora of little dishes.

Once I'd had a glass of wine and eaten half a plate of bite-sized crustini ("It's really not difficult to bake your own bread if you have a free afternoon") and three different bruschettas with tapenade ("I admit, I'm a bit of a foodie, but I try not to talk about it because it's so, you know, *obnoxious*.") I felt my life outside her apartment dissolve like an after-image. This was—or could be—my new life. Once I got the rest of it sorted. Once I let go of all the things that had led me to this crossroads in my life.

But I was not going to think about those things now. I was going to think about her, about Molly, about the delicious little bites of food she was putting in my mouth ("You'll want to taste this—I hope you like olives, not everyone does. There are five different kinds in there. I love the Italian market, don't you? Oh and these—I usually make these with salmon, but not tonight. Tonight it's charred vegetables. It's good, isn't it? I could get into this vegetarian thing. You made me look at things I hadn't seen at the market. It knocked me out of my comfort zone. That's good for me.")

I tried to remember when someone had last cooked for me—just me—and it seemed like it was a very long time ago. There was something so touching, so intimate—the specialness of the act of preparing all this food reminded me suddenly of Sister Claire and how she had wanted each of us girls to be able to make a meal for the people we loved. I thought of making plantains with Rosario. I wondered, with a pang, where and how she was.

I stood around drinking wine and watching Molly cook. She talked a lot, which was a relief, as I had come to her place more preoccupied than I wanted and had stood outside for a ridiculously long time, debating whether or not to even cross the threshold—as if I were a vampire who needed to be invited in and then might take more than was offered. The search for wine had distracted me, then the sense memory of the delphiniums had thrown me off again. But Molly's delight in both had helped. I realized that Molly had eased me out of the claustrophobic world I'd been living in even before I'd seen Grand. That trigger-warning space I'd inhabited really since I had gotten back from the DRC.

Molly was luring me into her world—one full of food and texture and language and most importantly, no killing. Molly's apartment was a horror-free space. It had been so long since I'd been in one of those, I suddenly thought, because my own apartment was the locus of horror now, for me. But here, in Molly's apartment, there would be no jars on the uppermost shelves, no surprises like Shihong had introduced me to, no nightmare images springing from behind a curtain. Whatever arrived for dinner would not have been carved out of a body. In fact, she had emphasized how she had worked hard to keep the entirety of the meal flesh-free. It was a relief and yet part of me still feared opening her refrigerator and finding slabs of meat and still-pulsing organs stacked there. When would I ever be able to relinquish such thoughts?

Not until Grand was in custody. Or better still, dead.

The aura around Molly was redolent of calm. As Keiko had told me, "She's very Zen. You could use a little of that, you know? Hell, you could use a *lot* of that."

It was soothing, watching Molly cook. She clearly loved it—preparing the food, cooking this special meal for me. I could sense how deeply personal cooking was for her. It wasn't the foodie craze, even if she used the language of it and joked self-consciously about it. Her cooking for me felt like some primordial gift women gave to those they cared for—the gift of sustenance. The gift of survival.

I was surprised at how eager I was to accept it. Not just the food, but all that came with it. But the food itself was delectable and allowed me to talk about something with her that had nothing to do with my fears about what lay in wait for me outside her door. She talked about how cooking had felt like poetry to her, that it was a different layering of imagery and sensations and that it was a different language as well. ("I think women talked to each other with food over the centuries, that it was a code. Like that language of flowers, only with food. You can see a woman giving another woman something she cooked for her or baked for her and no one would know it was a sign of lesbian love, you know? To everyone else it would just be food. But to her? To her it would be a gift from the heart."

Molly was obviously proud of the food and as each course appeared at her little drop-leaf table, I admitted to being impressed. I cooked, but not often. And the foodie craze had mostly passed me by, although I admitted to her that I would occasionally watch cooking shows on TV when I needed to decompress. I could see that cooking had a clarity to it. Maybe I needed to take it up in earnest.

After all the bite-sized tapas, Molly brought us small white bowls of a ginger-carrot consommé with a single red nasturtium floating in it. That led to her telling me about the history of edible flowers. Her mini-lecture made me feel surprisingly unknowledgeable. ("Watercress is also in the nasturtium family. Some afternoon I will make us nasturtium and watercress tea sandwiches—imagine how beautiful they will be!") I joked that I not only needed to stop and smell the roses, I needed to stop and eat some as well. She laughed, and as she cleared our bowls away, she walked toward the kitchen quoting, she said, Anne Brontë, "But he that dares not grasp the thorn, should never crave the rose."

Molly had no idea how often I had grasped the thorn and how rarely I had even considered the rose. I was re-thinking that, now.

The edible floral soup was followed by a complex vegetable curry, with some flash-fried ginger sticks, which I had never eaten before. I wasn't a big curry fan, and yet this was so good, I thought perhaps I hadn't given curry enough of a chance. There were no literary quotes to go with the curry, just my own story about staying in an awful hotel in London where my room was over the kitchen and everything smelled of curry, right down to the towels. Maybe that was what had put me off it.

We sat for a while after the curry. She didn't take the plates away and we talked about our work and Keiko and how they had met and how Keiko and I had met. We talked about the small town that was lesbian life in New York and how grateful she had been that her ex had taken a position at a different college in Boston, leaving her, as she said, "Able to walk to the corner without tripping over my past."

Oh, how I could relate to *that*.

"At some point you are going to have to tell me more about *you*, you realize. Keiko warned me about you. I am now going to ply you with my most exquisite course. If this doesn't get you talking, I despair."

Dessert was indeed amazing—two quenelle of pistachio custard and chocolate sauce with smoked salt. Had I even known there was a thing called smoked salt? After that mix of savory and sweet I was as close to sprawled as I ever got on her sofa, feeling—what was I feeling?—like I had been here often. Everything terrible seemed so very distant. I wished it could stay that way. I wished I could remain here, immersed in the spicy, sensual aura Molly had created for us with her cooking and her stories and most of all, *her*. I'd grasped enough thorns. I was ready, more ready than I had known, for the rose.

Molly's living room opened off the space she'd made for dining and was lit with several low amber lights. Three fat candles sat in a flat earthenware dish on a table in front of the sofa that was stacked with books. I felt sated in the truest sense and said so, thanking her for the spectacular meal. "I would offer to cook for you, but while I can make a few decent dishes, the word *quenelle* is not in my lexicon. And I would have to research where to find an edible flower."

Molly walked over, handing me a small glass with a dark amber liquid. "Zwack," she said. "It's a test. If you love it, you'll be invited back."

I set in on the table, untouched. "That's not a test I'd want to fail."

She set her glass down next to mine and sat on the arm of the sofa. She touched my hair, lightly. I could feel the tentativeness.

"So we are doing this, then, aren't we?" Her voice was low and soft.

"I think so, yes," was all I said, taking her hand, kissing the palm, then letting it go.

"I was right, you see," Molly said, putting her hand against my cheek. "You do need to stay in more. I think you should stay in more with me. Because that texting thing—we may be a little old for that, being post-adolescent and all. I was embarrassed for us both. But I have to confess—I called Keiko first thing to tell her we'd texted until we fell asleep. Or at least I did. So I just solidified how adolescent it really was, by calling my bestie and telling her." She laughed a quick little laugh and I pulled her toward me, onto the sofa. She smelled of curry and flowers and burning leaves. She smelled alive and I could not wait to kiss her.

❖

It was nearly three a.m. when I left Molly's, not wanting to leave, but knowing I couldn't stay. It wasn't just work that forced me to get up off the sofa where we'd had surprisingly quick and incredibly intense sex. It was everything that waited for me back at my own apartment. Luring Grand and capturing him was a plan still in its formative stages. I needed time to think. I needed time alone.

But it was difficult to leave her, and when she walked me to the door, barefoot and mostly naked, I had felt torn, kissing her, pushing her against the door, fondling her. She had opened herself to me and soon I was touching her again lightly, teasingly, before I left, until she pushed my hand hard against her, whispering what she needed.

Molly had been warm and supple. She had an earthy softness and openness that seemed very different from the women I'd had sex with in the past couple of years. She was as sure of herself as she first straddled my lap on the sofa and put my hands where she wanted them as she had been in the kitchen. She liked to talk and I found it a welcome change from silent butches and femmes whose passion had sometimes seemed more performance than true unbridled pleasure.

We had stayed there, on the sofa, my arms around her, not talking, for a while after. Then I told her I had to leave, even though I didn't want to. She hadn't asked me to stay—she seemed to know I couldn't. But I hoped she also couldn't have misunderstood the intensity of what I'd felt all evening. I told her, and it was as true as it could be, how I felt, how I hadn't felt so close to anyone, so open to anyone, in a very long time.

"How long?" she'd asked.

"I couldn't tell you—too long. Longer than I can remember." That was true. It had been years since I'd felt this open, this unaccountably open, this willing to risk my *self*. Because the openness I'd felt with Shihong was different; it was dark and not a little violent.

I wondered again, as I kissed and stroked Molly's black hair, could I really start over, from here, not looking back, only looking forward? I let out an involuntary sigh.

"Something's wrong." It wasn't a question.

"Yes. No. Not here, not this. I just need to get back. Stuff. You know. Always stuff." I'd tried to make it seem unimportant, just nuisance, but she knew better.

"Sort your 'stuff,' Faye. I'm not a 'stuff' kind of girl, in case that's not clear." Her tone was harsh. She had reached for her sweater and I had pulled it from her hand, wrapping my arms around her.

"I *am* sorting it. But it's not another woman. There is no other woman. The only other woman in a while"—I was thinking of Shihong—"we are friends. Close friends, but not with *those* kinds of benefits." I had tried to lighten the mood, but it had darkened and she wasn't in the mood now to go along with my attempt. How had I managed that, to make everything dark, again? Would darkness always follow me? Was this a legacy I could never fully escape, even with someone like Molly?

I had left soon after, after the sex by the door, after one final kiss, after I'd made it clear that I wanted more of her. After I'd made it clear that what needed sorting was me, not her. Or at least I'd hoped I'd made that clear. I'd told her I'd call tomorrow. Maybe I would call sooner.

❖

I decided to walk home, although it was quite a long walk and still surprisingly cold. But the night felt comforting and I could smell the end of winter in the chill air. It was almost over. The season of all that was dead. The season of parents burned alive in cars. The season of monsters. I was ready for spring. Ready for March to go out like a lamb. A sacrificial lamb.

The walk was good for me. I *did* need clarity. I'd passed on the Swack. Bitters didn't entice me. I was glad I had not passed on Molly, but as I walked, I wondered how I would keep from lying to her. Lying over and over. I didn't want to start this—whatever *this* was—lying. But I also couldn't tell her the truth. Or at least not all the truth. But telling her nothing? Lies of omission were just as bad as lies of commission. Every Catholic schoolgirl knew that. And a lifetime of lies of omission had taught me just what they cost and how confession never felt like absolution.

I was a little over a block away from my apartment when I saw him. Thought I saw him, Was sure I'd seen him. He was suddenly there, across the street, standing in front of the little twenty-four-hour greengrocer run by the Phan family. Had he been waiting for me outside Molly's? Had he been waiting here for me to come home? I felt the adrenaline course through my system. I felt light-headed, my heart pounding. Was this it? Was this the climax to our long cat-and-mouse, with its near-thirty-year hiatus? What would I do now? How could I end this?

The questions ran fast—too fast to be coherent or even helpful— through my head. Was I, who had spent the twenty-seven years since I had last seen Grand, who had spent those years refusing my genetic legacy of killing, was I now thinking about how to murder an old man?

I was.

I stared at the doorway to the Phans' shop. At this hour it would be the son, Ly, working, his parents home sleeping until they came in at six.

I blinked. Stared. He was no longer there. Had he gone into the store? Should I go over? Ly would protect me. He'd call the police. I knew that. But what if Grand hurt him first? I couldn't risk one more innocent life. One more person dying to save me from my own grandfather.

My mind was racing as I walked purposefully toward the corner, planning on crossing at the light. But then I changed my mind. I started running. My building was in the middle of the next block. I knew I could get there before him. After all, I was thirty-three, he was what? Late seventies, maybe older. He'd been a runner when I was a child, but now? I sprinted to my building, keys in hand, the little Swiss Army knife on the key ring, just in case.

Finally, finally, I was in, heart pounding, blood rushing in my ears, the door locked behind me, when I thought I saw him again, still on the other side of the street, in a different doorway. So much closer.

Or maybe it was just a shadow. Maybe I'd never seen him at all. Nevertheless, I locked all the locks on my door when I got in. There could never be enough locks to keep mayhem at bay. Never enough.

It was late. I needed a shower and sleep. I would see this monster again, of that I was certain. Our dénouement was still to come. And when it did, only one of us would be left.

Chapter Four
Savagery

I was finding the weekends especially difficult, now. The work week was full—too full, really. But the weekends yawned wide for me in a way I couldn't remember them doing before. Maybe it was because I had been traveling so much in recent months and also preparing for the show. I was still pushing the Afghanistan trip, trying to add Syria into the mix. But the upheaval with ISIS and the recent beheadings of journalists had made the paper wary of a story that was not being done by one of our bureau people. Photojournalists in the region were uniformly male and I understood I was not part of any local team, but I would continue to push to do the story. I had made a number of connections, I knew what direction I wanted to take, where I wanted to go.

I'd renewed my argument for the story three days ago at the editorial meeting, explaining that it was more important than ever, with ISIS kidnaping women and girls, with that side of the ISIS tale being largely untold. I'd highlighted two paragraphs from a story by one of our bureau reporters there, which had referenced the crimes against women—women tied to stakes and gang-raped, then left for dead by ISIS "troops." But there were two paragraphs only. Grisly, brutal paragraphs, but ones which meant there was much more story to be told. And this story, more than most, was definitely one to be told in pictures. Everyone in the meeting knew this. They just didn't want to risk me being the next person in an orange jumpsuit, the beheading knife at my throat. Or have me be the woman tied to the stake. I wasn't an adrenaline junkie—I wasn't arguing for the thrills. I was arguing to tell the story. But it got tabled again, to be revisited in a week or so. Vaguely open-ended.

The meeting had left me unnaturally sulky and I had decided to take a couple of days off, not really caring if I looked as sullen as I felt. Molly was going to a conference and I wanted to spend time with her before she left, so maybe I would be back Monday in a better place than I was in. I had another idea, away from the Middle East, but still dangerous enough, still risky. I would pitch that, see where it went.

The past few weeks I had felt every nerve on edge. I had been taking Xanax to sleep, Xanax to get through every difficult bit of the day. I'd started counting them out for the day so I wasn't taking too many, but I already knew I probably was. I hoped when everything was resolved, when Grand was out of my life, out of everyone's lives, that I wouldn't have to check into a rehab center to detox. My doc knew I was still dealing with the aftereffects of the DRC trip, so she was being lenient with the pills. But I knew that wasn't going to last forever.

With Molly out of town, I was trying to distract myself, trying to prepare for a master class in event photography in the late spring I'd been asked to teach at NYU, but wasn't sure I ever actually would teach. I'd gone out for a few hours to see the Vivian Maier documentary. I'd walked to the Strand and splurged on some books, reminding myself I had money, now, since the success at the gallery. Saul Leiter's *Early Black and White* was pricey, but gorgeous. I looked for my own book and found it, but resisted the temptation to ask if they wanted me to sign it. I was grateful for a used copy, still barely touched, of *Intimate Visions*. I'd always loved Dorothy Norman's photos—such an underrated voice in that whole Stieglitz-O'Keeffe crowd. I was ready to leave when I saw the Tina Modotti book, which had been put back in the wrong place. I grabbed it. I needed beauty today. I needed photographs that took me out of myself, away from my own work, into a different place. I wasn't sure what that place was, but I know I needed to get there—because it wasn't where I was, despite the success, despite my job, despite Molly.

Back at the apartment I immersed myself in reading, setting the new books out around me like talismans, as if their combined powers of genius could protect me from what I knew was lurking somewhere close, somewhere nearby. Maybe I'd been photographed myself as I walked through Manhattan, through *my* city, *my* neighborhood, *my* home. Since the opening, I'd become a paranoiac, imagining him everywhere, camera around his neck, pretending to be a tourist instead of a killer. I envisioned him going up to young women, asking for directions, looking safe, because he was old now, asking them if they would mind showing him, if they'd like to have a cup of coffee, getting a taste for new victims.

Taste. In his case, it was literal. *How long could I live with these images and not go mad?*

Now I wondered every time I went out if he was there, lurking in a doorway, waiting like any stalker to chart my every move. I'd had a stalker for a while. I'd only been at the paper a little over two years when a man had sent me a couple of nice notes there, about my work, which had pleased me at first. But then he'd begun sending them to me at home, and I didn't know how he knew where I lived. He'd fixated on one magazine piece I'd done and kept sending me commentary about it, hand-written in the kind of precise script I'd come to know was Catholic-school handwriting, which made me wonder if he was somehow connected to St. Cecilia's, or to someone I had known there. He'd told me he wanted to know more about me. He'd followed that up by telling me he'd been searching for clues to who I was—who I *really* was.

I didn't think anyone could find out who I really was. Even *I* barely knew who I really was. But it had set off a slew of alarm bells for me. Ever since Mother Superior had warned me about what might happen to me when I left the protection of St. Cecilia's, I'd worried about the possibility of someone making a connection between me and my grandfather.

But it had never happened. Sister Anne Marie's murder had pre-dated the Internet by nearly a decade, keeping me relatively safe from Google searches that pre-dated my job.

Then there was that stalker. When the photos started coming—me in various places, sometimes working, sometimes with friends, often alone—with notes telling me what he would like to do with me at those various places, I knew I was at some kind of risk. I'd let it go on too long—I'd been afraid to go to the police because I'd been afraid of what they might discover about *me*. My name somewhere in a police report from the murder of Sister Anne Marie. I couldn't risk a connection, no matter how unlikely.

But eventually I had called a detective I knew. We'd gone to have a drink and I'd turned over a small shopping bag full of envelopes and photographs. He'd looked at it, taken out a few of the photos, read a couple of the notes. He'd asked our waitress for another beer before he said anything to me. I'd sat there in the noisy bar full of cops and reporters and no one else and waited for him to speak. Finally he said, "Jesus Christ, Faye. Were you waiting to become one of those stories 'ripped from the headlines' on a freakin' episode of *Law & Order*? This guy's a fuckin' psycho. I know you're used to doing all that crazy shit you do, but you *had* to know this guy was nuts. He's not going to stop, you know. These guys never stop unless someone makes them stop. I mean, Faye—these notes? Jesus."

We'd had a few more drinks while he explained what he could and could not do about the situation. He'd offered to go with me to get a restraining order. I hadn't wanted to, but I did. A day lost to New York's municipal bureaucracy, sitting with battered women and women whose ex-boyfriends and ex-husbands refused to let go. When it was finally my turn, it was clear the judge wouldn't have granted me the order if my friend the cop hadn't been there with me.

"No actual physical threats of violence or assault? What about to your family? Any threats to them?" The bored-looking judge almost seemed to wish I'd had a black eye or split lip or chunk of hair missing from the back of my head like some of the other women awaiting their turns at protection.

I had no family.

My friend the detective had spoken up. "The guy's taking pictures of her, Judge. I gotta whole stack—he's following her and he's photographing her and I've seen this before. She needs the TRO. She's a news photographer—he's obviously stalked her from her job to her apartment. One of those guys who thinks he knows somebody whose name is in the paper and thinks he has a 'special' relationship with them. He's not gonna stop—not unless somebody makes him."

The judge had looked annoyed for a moment, like his authority was being questioned, since, of course, it was. But the judge granted the order. Two weeks later, when I got an envelope of photos that included me leaving the court, they picked the stalker up. He got probation, but the letters and packages stopped. I guess he hadn't wanted to go to prison. I guess he hadn't wanted to be on the receiving end of stalking. And yet I knew he would find another victim. Of course I knew.

I hadn't thought about the stalking in a while. Now, like then, I knew my stalker was out there, following me, photographing me, thinking about killing me. I was, after all, the only person who could identify Grand, the only person who could trip him up. I was the reason he'd had to leave, with my grandmother. Leave his nice little Brooklyn abattoir with its retro-fitted basement and darkroom and ready retinue of victims from which to choose. He couldn't risk my doing that to him again. Not now. He was too old to start over. He'd want to stay wherever he was until he died. After all, it was just me to trip him up.

Just me.

I'd become hypervigilant—probably seeming suspicious myself as I looked over my shoulder and peered into shop windows to see who was reflected behind me. There were still plenty of real cameras in New York; not everyone used a cell phone to take pictures. A block from the Strand I'd somehow heard the whizz and click of rapid-fire photos being taken behind me. I'd whirled around, only to scare a student doing exactly what I used to do what now seemed a lifetime ago—taking pictures of his new life. *His* life, not mine. I muttered an apology and headed home.

❖

I paged through the Norman, but couldn't focus on the text. I went online, checked my email—nothing from Grand. *Did I think there would be?* I did a few Google searches and immersed myself in a *Vanity Fair* article about the photographs taken with the last roll of Kodachrome film to come off the assembly line at Kodak a couple of years ago. I got up, found the disc, put it on. *So suggestible.*

Paul Simon's "Kodachrome" blasted through the apartment. There was some dark irony, I was sure, in the jaunty tune with its raucous beat juxtaposed with the grim lyrics. I leaned back, closed my eyes, singing along, I wasn't even sure why. How did I even know this song?

I played the song a few times and then turned it off. It resonated a little too deeply. That was part of what was wrong—Paul Simon was right. Everything indeed looked worse in black and white, all these books of photographs aside. Instead of Tina Modotti's lush body, or Dorothy Norman's evocative hands, all I could see were bits and pieces of women's bodies. I could see the black and white photographs in my grandfather's darkroom. I could see the black fan, the red light, the white enameled pans with the black edges laid out, the neat row of opaque bottles of developer with their black labels and the little black skull and crossbones in the corner. I could see the clothesline and the tiny pins and more than anything I could see the women in our basement being tied with clothesline just like that, those small clothespins pinching their nipples, biting into their flesh. The images were pulling me into their stark vortex, repeating over and over and over on an endless film loop I couldn't bear to watch.

I put on more music, trying to obliterate the images in my head, but I was already in that dark space, spiraling into the darkroom with my little flashlight, sliding back the bolt on the basement door, my six-year-old heart pounding in my chest, going down the stairs, down to the smell of mice and women's hair and the dead meat of carved-up humans. I turned up my go-to play list, an eclectic mix of tunes that made me sad, sadder, saddest. Ella Fitzgerald and Tony Bennett. Adele and the Wu-Tang Clan. Pink and Eminem. Marianne Faithfull and Pet Shop Boys. Maria Callas and Evanescence. A whole lot of Rihanna. What I called music-to-slash-your-wrists-by. I needed music to match my mood, and Simon's upbeat tune with the downbeat lyrics was too discordant. *West End Girls* felt more like it.

Was I *mad*, like the lyrics queried? Or just *unstable*? There was no way of knowing. Not since the gallery opening. Not since I'd seen Grand. Not since I'd imagined his life running parallel to mine, here, in my city, the same place where he'd killed Sister Anne Marie, where he'd fed me bits of his victims, where he'd read to me and given me my first camera and touched me with a mark of Cain, an original sin I could never, ever wash off or be absolved from no matter how many times I went to confession or blessed myself with Holy Water or just sat in the back of the church and cried silently through Mass, walking home not with some hymn in my head, but the chorus of Wu-Tang Clan's "Life Changes" repeating in my head. Was I pretending? Of course I was. I suddenly realized that the only truly real thing about my life was my work. The photographs were real, Susan Sontag's treatise notwithstanding.

Grand had told me about how it was all art and he had been right—he'd just perverted it all. I had tried to right his wrongs by photographing women who'd been taken apart by men. I'd tried to put the pieces back together by exposing what men had done to them. I had peeled away the layers of euphemism and shown the bare, raw, bloodied truth.

But what of *my* truth? My truth was so inextricable from Grand's truth that I couldn't imagine ever being able to reveal it, ever being able to expose where it was I had come from. "Life Changes" felt like my anthem. Could time change *my* ending? It hadn't so far.

❖

Other people's photos were a distraction, like that last Kodachrome roll Steve McCurry shot. He'd taken so many fantastic photographs when I'd been at NYU—had put together a photo-essay of the pictures he'd taken with that roll, all rife with meaning. The roll he'd asked Kodak for. I had a copy of his iconic *National Geographic* photo of the Afghan girl in one of my scrapbooks of photographs I loved. The magazine had labeled it the most memorable of all its covers. His array from the final 36 of the Kodachrome began, I thought, as an omen for me—a portrait of Robert De Niro in an empty theater with the simple caption, "New York, New York, USA."

I viewed all the photos online at McCurry's gallery site and they were magnificent. Lush and full of deep, rich, expressive color. They paid homage to the little yellow roll of film. They left a legacy. They were history.

I realized, as I read about him, that he was just slightly older than my father would have been, had he lived. I thought, briefly, what it would be like to have him as my father, instead of the man I barely remembered, burned alive in the snow. What if McCurry had been my father, training me to follow him around the world, photographing all those things that hadn't been photographed before. I fell into the photographs, thought of my young self as part of a father-daughter photography team. What would my life have been like, then, with no bodies in the basement or without the things in the jars or the slashed neck of St. Cecilia?

I'd read a quote from McCurry somewhere—"If you wait, people will forget your camera and the soul will drift up into view." I imagined the two of us, cameras around our necks, waiting for each soul to appear, but overriding the fantasy was Grand, capturing the abject terror on the faces of his victims in shot after shot after shot.

The work I did was pieced together out of sackcloth and ashes and penitence. Mine wasn't the lush painterly palette of McCurry. Mine was—

Then I stopped thinking about it. *You think you're mad, too unstable. You think time can change the ending.* I needed to change the ending. A plan was coming together in my head. If Grand was going to play cat-and-mouse with me, I was going to have to treat him like I would treat any other story. If I wasn't going to Afghanistan and Syria, maybe I needed to go back to Brooklyn.

I took another Xanax, washing it down with a half a glass of wine that was sitting on the kitchen counter, left over from the night before. Then I went back to work.

It was impossible, of course, to read these stories and not think of him. Of the parallel existence I was leading, had been leading since that night at the gallery. I went through my days pretending to live my life as if nothing had changed, except that I was now a lot richer, due to the sales at the gallery which had made Nick so happy. But in fact *everything* had changed. My life had been transformed that night, only a small part of it for the better.

It wasn't just the critical response. Or even Molly. Molly had altered the interior landscape of my life in ways I could never have imagined. And yet *that* hadn't disrupted anything. Molly seemed as if she had always been a part of my life. Like when I started taking pictures seriously when I was first working for Angelo de Luca. Molly had fitted seamlessly into my life, just like that, like the spot had always been there, empty, just waiting for her to fill it.

But there was no spot for Grand. I'd spent close to thirty years trying to sew up all the places where I'd been torn apart by the knowledge of who he was and where I'd come from and what he'd done. Being in the DRC had ripped a lot of those places open again.

And sometimes when I looked at Molly, when I stroked her face, I saw Sister Anne Marie. All of that was why I needed Xanax to sleep, to get through the days.

Molly knew I had secrets. She'd said as much the first night we'd been together. But she hadn't pushed for information, she hadn't insisted I peel back the layers. There was a patience in her that was perhaps the thing that reminded me most of Sister Anne Marie. Molly wasn't in a hurry. She had her own work, she had her own place, she was single, more than a year out of a long-term relationship. Molly was centered, as Keiko had said. "She'll be good for you, Faye. She'll get you on track."

Molly was Zen, while I had a metaphorical gun at my head, thinking I would indeed be better off dead than in this terrorizing limbo place where I didn't know what was next. Knowing Grand was out there made me worry for every woman who was close to me. My grandfather was a rapist, a murderer, a maniac. It didn't matter that he was now an old man. Nazis were still being captured in their dotage. Because they were still Nazis.

Grand had that dangerous charisma. Nothing could be put past him. He'd said as much to me that night he'd found me in the kitchen and instead of denying that the photographs were his, instead of soothing my traumatized, frightened, orphaned, six-year-old self, he'd described his rampages as art. He'd told me I'd find my way to the same place he had.

At some point I would have to tell her. I would have to tell Molly the truth, *my* truth, such as it was.

And how could I ever tell her any of that?

"Secrets can be sexy," Molly had said to me after our first week together. We were lying in bed, half-watching TV. "Secrets can also be devastating. Don't devastate me with any secrets, darling," she said and looked at me, her eyes gone dark in the half-light of the TV. "I've had enough of that kind of secret."

She had kissed me then, and I had told her not to worry, we were good.

I was lying right to her face. But there was no alternative, was there? I hadn't been able to parse one in my mind so far.

Molly was one of my distractions, the best one, one of the things to keep my mind off my secrets. There was no other way to get through the days, now, except by distracting myself every minute that I was awake. Because I woke up in a near panic every day, now that I was waiting and watching. Now that I was trying to figure out a plan to catch him, to lure him in, to bring him to me and then—and then, *what?*

I had no idea. I just knew I had to snare him. Not just because of all he had done and would continue to do, but because I could no longer live with the threat of him. I could no longer live with his history like a scrim over my own life, so that everything I did was occluded by what he had done—the things I knew of and the things I didn't. He had to be locked up. And my grandmother, if she were still alive, she too had to be locked up. Being party to his crimes made her a monster, too. There was nothing benign about her silence.

And so I was always close to panic as I waited for him to know I knew. I was sure he did, of course. Sure he had seen me and in fact was stalking me. Sure that soon he would turn up, that he would come to claim me.

And so I waited and watched, and if I were honest with myself, feared. Definitely feared. I knew my grandfather was out there, I knew he might even have been—probably had been—at the gallery opening and I just missed seeing him in the crush of people and questions from critics and buyers and the curious. I'd convinced myself that was what had happened when I had seen him in the cab outside the gallery. He'd already been there. Already touched my work, admired his own, admired the photographs of mutilated women he had taken and that I had taken, even though my photos came from a wholly different place than his. But I could imagine him thinking when he saw my work that I had followed in his footsteps, that somewhere I had a basement full of secrets. I could imagine him thinking that the end to us both would be for him to meet me there, to share one last meal of mayhem with me.

I had been sure it was him that first night I had walked home from Molly's apartment. Lurking outside the Phans' grocery. Leaning into a doorway. I was sure. Just not sure enough to be able to tell anyone what it was I was sure *of.*

As I waited for him to show himself to me again, or for me to find him first, I was stymied. Even as I knew that he was there, knew it right to the core of my being, there was nothing I could do about it. I couldn't go to the police. What would I say? "My grandfather, who I haven't seen since I was six, but who is a serial killer who used to feed me and my grandmother cannibalized organ meats from his victims, came to my gallery opening, probably to kill me."

No, I couldn't go to the police. I had no actual proof. Just a glimpse of him in a cab in traffic. Another in a doorway. The sense of him following me.

And going to the police would only expose *me*. It would undo all that Mother Superior had done for me—it would reveal me as the orphaned child of cannibals in this era of *The Walking Dead* and brain-eating zombie lore. Going to the police would make *me* the monster, not him. And I had spent my whole life trying to escape that past that Sister Anne Marie had died to save me from. I was not one of those people who wanted to reveal their harrowing past to the world. I wanted mine buried as deep and dark as possible.

I had to be able to actually turn him over to the police before I could say anything to anyone about him—even to Shihong, who was the only person in my life, other than Mother Superior, who even knew about him. Would she tell me to call the police? I doubted it. She'd been hiding from authorities her whole life as well. One of the things we shared was our illegality. The police were not our friends. Not when the lives we had built were upon such fragile foundations.

The Nazi hunters knew there were Nazis still living. But until they were actually able to find them and deliver them to the justice they had evaded for decades, there was no proof, nothing but the ephemera of what you knew in your gut to be true—that the kindly old man down the street was a butcher.

And now I was left to wonder the same about Grand.

Had he been here all along? Had he and my grandmother simply moved, gotten an apartment in Manhattan with one of the fake IDs I knew you could buy in Jackson Heights, Chinatown, and even the Lower East Side? If you could get them so easily now, with immigration issues as tricky as they were, surely they would have been even easier to get in the 1980s? Plus, he had that charm, the charm that had lured how many women to their deaths? Seventeen that we knew of. And he'd also had my grandmother—my elegant, middle-aged grandmother who no one would have questioned.

Yes, I thought now that they had been living here all along, my grandfather like Dennis Rader, the BTK serial killer who had stopped murdering—or at least had not been caught murdering—for nearly twenty years before he started taunting police again. He'd lived in the same neighborhood as his victims. He'd worked at the same company as two of his victims. He'd been a Cub Scout leader and a church leader and the only reason he'd been caught was because he sent a floppy disk instead of an actual letter to the police as he taunted them, not realizing the disk had the church's imprint encrypted on it.

Where I had steered clear of stories about serial killers before, now I was obsessed with knowing as much as possible, hoping that there would be some clue embedded in the stories of other men who had made a career of killing. But many of these killers had never been caught. I was sure that unless I caught him myself, in some kind of snare, my grandfather would live out what was left of his days torturing and killing women. I was just as sure that I or someone I knew and loved might be one of those women. My greatest fear was that it would be Molly.

It was different for me, all these years later, thinking about my grandfather and his crimes, crimes I could hardly stand to think about, they were so horrifying. It was more than a quarter century since I had found the photographs, nearly thirty years since Sister Anne Marie's death. I had grown up shadowed by Grand's crimes. I had come of age wondering when I, too, would begin to kill.

I knew what torture and killing and all the ordinary mayhem in between were about. I knew there were no lengths to which men would not go and I had witnessed the aftermath up close when I'd been in the DRC. The story Martine had told me of the men she had seen at the checkpoint every day for a year who had suddenly dragged her from her jeep one day and gang-raped her. That story was not a singular story. That story was repeated every day, all over the globe. Just yesterday a woman had been beheaded in her London garden by a man who had stalked her. She was eighty-two. How had she come to be his victim? Just this morning I'd been reading the news. A young woman had been shot in the face overnight in Queens. She wasn't expected to survive her injuries. Police were searching for her boyfriend. Neighbors said they argued a lot.

Grand was still living in New York, swallowed up among the millions of different lives. It was easy to live a dark life, a shadow life, here in New York. Night was alive, day could be hidden beneath layer after layer. All the things needed for depravity were here in this city. Everyone who lived here knew that. We just didn't talk about it. But we all had the locks—not one, not two, but many. We all knew there were things to be kept at bay. Monsters walked alongside us here. Not with the obviousness of zombies, or even the deathly pallor of vampires. But looking like everyone else. Just like Grand. Just like me. Because every day I felt a little closer to madness, a little more enveloped in paranoia and fear. Nothing felt solid, now. I was so unmoored by Grand's return to my life.

I'd thought, briefly, about buying a gun, but I'd always been anti-gun and there was enough mayhem in the world. I couldn't see myself training at a range and keeping a gun under my pillow. There'd been a woman when I was in graduate school, fifteen years older than I, who I'd met at a photography symposium. We'd met at the end of the spring semester and spent most of the summer together. She called herself a sportswoman, which I took to mean she liked killing things. It didn't last long, in part because the air around her was always redolent of gun oil, or so I thought. One day I'd gone to lie down in her guest room, my head throbbing from a sudden headache. The pillow was hard and hurt my head more. When I'd picked it up to fluff it, there had been a small silver handgun with a brown wood handgrip lying there.

I had stared at it, at the incongruity of a pistol under a pillow—*was* it a pistol? Was that even a word people used about guns outside of novels? I didn't know. That was how little I knew about guns.

Yet, like a small child, I'd picked it up, curious about what it would feel like in my hand. It was neither heavy nor light—just a smallish weight in my hand and it felt comfortable there. Surprisingly, unsettlingly comfortable. The woman had come in then, suddenly, looking for me, and I had automatically pointed it at her. It felt reflexive, and it shocked me.

"Don't shoot," she had said, laughing, and putting her arms up in fake surrender, like we were playing some new sex game, this time with guns. I'd dropped it on the bed just as reflexively. And known that was both my last gun and my last day with her.

She'd urged me to pick the gun up again and had talked to me about it, how it worked and how to use it, and I could tell she was excited by the idea of my touching it, touching her gun. That in turn had touched something in me that had both frightened and repulsed me. It had not turned me on, and yet I had let her put the gun in my hand again and I had let her stroke my cheek with it.

What had I been thinking when she was doing that? I could remember the scene vividly, even remember what we were wearing, and how the curtain had fluttered as a breeze had riffled through the window. But I couldn't remember what I was thinking. At that time I was still finding my way, often putting myself in situations that were destructive or even dangerous. My way out of St. Cecilia's had been through a door very different from the one in that long-ago Audrey Hepburn film, *A Nun's Story*, but it had felt just as final and just as unmooring.

The woman had said we could "go shooting" if I wanted to, but I didn't want to. I didn't want to be lured into killing anything. I could tell just from holding the gun so briefly—she'd told me it was a Jennings J-22 and had told me it was "easy handling" and I had felt a wave of nausea—that I could kill with that gun. I could kill her. I could kill myself. I could go out on the street and walk up to a stranger and kill them.

Not only could I tell that *I* could kill, I could also tell that *she* wanted someone to kill things with. *Why did she have guns under the pillows? What did she have in the basement? What was I doing with a woman who was stroking my cheek with a little pistol and running her hand up my thigh at the same time?*

That incident had been one of the only times I had thought about those things—about my family history of killing—since I'd first gone to the public library when Theresa and I had come to Manhattan from St. Cecilia's. I'd worked hard at obliterating that part of my life. Or at least walling it off. In that era of confession, I was stoically silent and unrevealing.

I was also not my grandfather. I managed somehow to take photographs every day and not think, *When will I start taking women home and killing them and serving their organs for dinner?* I wasn't part of that legacy. Mother Superior had said so, but even if she hadn't, I'd known that. I knew what my legacy was and where I came from: I was the orphan daughter of the people who had been burned alive, I was the orphan girl who had grown up behind the iron gates of St. Cecilia's. I was blameless. *I was blameless.*

But being with a woman who liked to kill was too threatening, too dangerous, too tempting of fate and the gods and whatever else might conspire to pull me into the maelstrom of my grandfather's world. I remembered all the little animals I'd put on their leafy pyres behind the grotto at St. Cecilia's. I was someone who paid homage to the dead, but I was not going to be someone who killed. After a night of disturbingly hallucinogenic and incredibly exciting sex that I could still remember years later with amazing clarity, I had gone home. I had left the woman's magnificent apartment at 86th and Lex—I had been at least as in love with that place and its terrace and big airy rooms with amazing windows and spectacular light as I had been with her. I had convinced myself that I could provide whatever she needed and accept whatever she offered as long as I could lie in that big white bed in that white room with the view of what had once been a tenement building, I supposed, but which was now something exquisite and outside my window.

But after the gun, after the sex and the gun, I had to leave. I left dishonestly, as if I would be back, as if I were doing what I did a couple of times a week—go back to my own place, get things I felt I needed, tell myself I was still independent, since I still *had* my own place.

That day, my place became my only place, once again. I was done with the Upper East Side and its lure of wealthy eccentric lesbian artists who offered me more than I was willing—or dared—to accept. Back to the studio apartment I lived in then that was a dank, fifth-floor walk-up on 10th Avenue in Chelsea back before it was hip, back when no one really wanted to live there. It was nothing like the tiny but sweet apartment Theresa and I had had on Spring Street and Mulberry that was some sleight of hand from Mother Superior, or maybe her brother, Angelo. It was so close to school for me, and Theresa didn't mind taking the train to Fordham—or so she said. I think the idea of living in the Bronx terrified Theresa. She wanted to be downtown, with me, in our safe, if tiny, little apartment above the patisserie. She had read me a couple of lines from the guidebook for new students at Fordham about traveling.

"Listen to this, Faye," Theresa had said, making her voice deep and Jesuitical—but I could tell she was nervous. "'While the half-mile walk up Fordham Road to the D train can be quite enjoyable, it is safer during the day than at night. You are encouraged to take the bus or car service during the night hours.' So in other words, you're encouraged to not get raped or killed. Okay, then. Expect to take me with you to the library at night. I'm going to take their word for it and not do much traveling after dark in the Bronx."

I'd loved our apartment and I'd liked living with Theresa. I'd loved coming home to the smell of baking bread and pastries. Sometimes I would stand across the street and just take photos of the street, the network of fire escapes that crawled up our building and all the other buildings on the block. I took photographs of everything that symbolized my new life, the life away from my history, away from St. Cecilia's. The things Angie had kept telling me to record, so I would never forget. I was cataloguing my own life. The one I'd been waiting to have.

One night I had said to Theresa when we were making dinner, "It's like we got out of prison, you know? I never thought of St. Cecilia's as a prison, but it feels like we left one. Like we're on parole. Sometimes I feel like I might make one wrong move and then—then I'll be back there. And not here."

Theresa had stopped stirring the sauce on the stove and had looked at me for a few seconds before she said, softly, "Oh, Faye, are you kidding me? It was *always* a prison. Everyone thought so. We just didn't have anywhere else to go. My mother *was* in prison—she's *still* in prison. You were just too busy sucking up to Mother Superior and being the perfect little angel we were all supposed to model ourselves after to notice."

It had felt like a slap. I had actually put my hand to my face, because it was that visceral. I hadn't spoken for a moment, then I had said, "But they did *everything* for us, Theresa. They *saved* us. What is *with* you? What don't you get about that?"

I had been unaccountably angry. But then it came over me in a wave—Mother Superior, all the nuns, even the ones I didn't like—they were my only family. I had no one but them and the girls I knew from St. Cecilia's. I was an *orphan*. I was a character out of some nineteenth-century novel. I was the girl from the *home*, as Rosario had put it. All these other girls *had* family. Maybe they had family that was in trouble, but they still *had* family. The nuns had family, too. Mother Superior had Angie—if he really was her brother. And I? What did I have? I had two dead parents who had been only children, two dead grandparents, and two other grandparents who were criminals, who might also be dead.

I had me. I had the apartment on Spring Street above the patisserie. The scholarship to college I got because I was an orphan. I had the things in my closet. The box Mother Superior had given me. Nothing else. Nothing but whatever I was trying to build. Whatever a barely-eighteen-year-old orphan with a box full of terrifying history can possibly build.

Theresa felt bad for upsetting me. We were both surprised by the tears running down my face, but I made no sound, made no protest. I just walked out of the kitchen and into my room, took my camera, and left the apartment.

❖

That night was the first night of the rest of my life. That night—a cold, dark, numbingly beautiful night in early November in midtown Manhattan—I knew that whatever happened in my life from that night on was solely my responsibility. I could be invisible the way orphans had been in the nineteenth century with their matchboxes, their begging, their ragged, threadbare clothes, and their workhouses, or I could be the orphan who defied all those odds of centuries before.

From that day on, I was driven. Driven to notice and be noticed and to leave St. Cecilia's and the grim darkroom of my childhood behind, while I worked to become the photographer whose photographs everyone wanted to see, the photographer telling stories no one else was willing or able to tell.

If I hadn't been pushing myself past every boundary and limit, I never would have ended up with the woman, playing sex games with a gun. That was how I had come altogether too close to the edge of my own history, close enough, almost, to fall into its treacherous void.

Climbing the five floors to my apartment had felt impossible and intolerable after the woman's beautiful place in the building with the doorman and the room where I had been studying and listening to music and feeling productive and calm and mentored by the woman. It had felt like going backward, and yet staying with her would have meant a different kind of backward. It would have meant returning to those years when the killing was all around me. Maybe she wasn't like Grand, but how could I ever know for sure? What if the next week or month or year she took me to see her trophies? What then?

There had to be a space for me between where she was and my own apartment, but I didn't know how to get there. Not yet. My place had a horrible bathroom that had initially reminded me of my grandfather's darkroom and I had almost decided against taking the apartment because of that. But the beautiful large window in the room that served as my living room/bedroom/dining room/studio had mitigated the awful bathroom with its strange manila color, single lightbulb like some noir film, and endlessly running sink faucet. But her place? My own bathroom at the woman's place—because I had my own bathroom there—had six shower jets and a bench to sit on in the shower. One day after running I had just lain down on it, the water coursing over me. It felt like the most decadent thing I had ever done.

When I got home that day, hot and out of breath from climbing the stairs in the heat, but really, it had been more than that, I had washed my face and changed my shirt. I'd remembered that day in the shower. Then I had lain down on the daybed and closed my eyes and said a whole rosary in my head, counting on my fingers for each decade.

I'd repeated the Hail Holy Queen prayer over and over at the end, *Hail, holy Queen, Mother of mercy, our life, our sweetness and our hope. To thee do we cry, poor banished children of Eve: to thee do we send up our sighs, mourning and weeping in this valley of tears. Turn then, most gracious Advocate, thine eyes of mercy toward us, and after this our exile, show unto us the blessed fruit of thy womb, Jesus. O clement, O loving, O sweet Virgin Mary!*
Pray for us O Holy Mother of God.

I sent up my sighs, over and over as I lay there, flat and still, much as I used to lie on my narrow little bed at St. Cecilia's. I had never realized with such clarity how alone I was until that day as I lay there, the late-summer sun waning, tears rolling down the sides of my face, wetting my hair and the little throw pillow under my head. I wasn't sobbing, but I also couldn't stop crying.

I knew I could have told the woman about my grandfather, about the life before St. Cecilia's—not that anyone except Theresa even knew about *that*, about my growing up in a *home*—but if I had told the woman, what would have happened to me? I think I understood when I left her place that the reason I *had* to leave there was because she was capable of destroying me. Not with some gun-play gone awry, but with who she was and what she liked to do. With what she might entice *me* to do.

I'd lain there until it had gotten dark, not moving, still crying, trying not to think, but unable to keep from thinking because there was too much roiling in my brain, too many images and thoughts and concerns. For the first time, I wondered what would happen to me. I realized that while I had friends, and Theresa and I were still close, I had no family, biological or borrowed. St. Cecilia's had been my family. The nuns had been my maiden aunts raising me. All that protection and care that I hadn't even been aware of and that Rosario had sneered at when she referred to "the home"—all of that was gone. It had been gone for a while, but I had somehow not realized it, between college and work and living with Theresa and being with Keiko. But now, now that I was completely on my own—it was different. It was a void, a darkness, a space that left too much to chance. And in that space I had done what many of the other girls had done at school—fallen in with the wrong crowd. The woman was the wrong crowd. The layer she had peeled back, albeit accidentally, that layer took me too close to Grand and too far from St. Cecilia's.

Had I sought her out? Had she sought me out? As I lay there in the dark, hearing the fan and the endlessly dripping faucet and the muted noises from the streets below, I wondered if I had magnetized a killer to me because she could smell my legacy on me, she could somehow tell that I had a genetic predisposition to mayhem.

I'd fallen asleep, finally, and dreamed of the long curtain fluttering in the white room in the woman's apartment. I'd dreamed the curtain had become tangled somehow and I had turned to see the woman, covered in blood, her face blue, the curtain wrapped tight around her neck.

Not for the first time, I'd been awakened by my own screaming.

CHAPTER FIVE
SNARE

I couldn't spend all my time in bed with Molly. I *could*—I could fold myself into her for an eternity of longing. But, as she had said as she'd left two days ago after breakfast, to get ready for her conference, after I had asked her to stay and spend the day in bed with me, after I had tried to pull her back to me, "We have lives, darling. Really. We have lives."

We have lives.

I hadn't felt that way in a long while—like I had a life, or at least a life that included another person who wasn't tangential or ephemeral. I wasn't sure how long it had been since I had felt, for lack of a better word, *connected.* I felt like I could remember every single woman I had been in bed with since St. Cecilia's and that first night with Rosario nearly twenty years ago. And yet in all the years since that night in the purloined space at St. Cecilia's, every night with every woman had felt like *that* night—borrowed, stolen, someone else's, not mine. Maybe that was my legacy as an orphan: dislocation, displacement, distance.

Certainly enough women had accused me of that last. But was that fair?

Maybe it was something else. No one knew who I was. Where I had come from. Mother Superior knew, and she was still alive, though retired to Cape May, New Jersey, and the seaside retreat the nuns had there. I'd been to see her once. She was unchanged except now the twenty-first-century habits were really just severe navy blue dresses with short little veils with a bit of white in front. She'd been very tanned and it registered with the adult me that she was Italian, maybe Sicilian. Like Angie, of course. Her brother who had changed my life almost as much as she had. But while Angie and I shared some secrets, we did not share that one. As far as I knew, Mother Superior had told him nothing about my history. As far as I knew, Mother Superior was the only person who knew where I came from, who knew that gruesome, bloody history. She was the only living person, other than my grandparents, who knew that secret, the totality of that secret, who knew, like my grandfather did, like I did, that I was responsible for Sister Anne Marie's horrific death.

Although I had told Shihong some of my story, I hadn't told her everything. The only person I had told everything to was long dead, Sister Anne Marie herself. My telling her had killed her. How could I ever tell anyone else that story? How could I risk another death on my conscience that could never be confessed into absolution?

The harsh reality of my life was that I was a cipher in it. Among my friends, my lovers, my colleagues, there was no one who knew anything of my history. When Theresa and I moved in together when we left St. Cecilia's, we had made a pact that we would never tell anyone about where we'd come from. It was a schoolgirls' pact—a remnant of our years living behind the iron gates—but it meant something to both of us. She was eighteen, I was still seventeen. Mother Superior had had to co-sign on our lease. We were still, to a degree, children. But children without parents, children who would never be going home on vacations or be visiting family. Leaving our old lives behind had meant kicking over the traces of our past. We made the pact. We never mentioned St. Cecilia's outside that apartment.

But now I missed Theresa. I missed having no one to whom I could whisper, "I want to tell someone about my past." Yet I knew what Theresa would have said: "Don't do it, Faye. They'll want to know *everything*. And you can't tell them everything, can you?"

If only she'd known just how much there was that I could not tell.

I wanted to tell Molly. As each day went by and I failed to come up with a strategy, I realized how important it was becoming to me to share things with her. She had talked about her childhood—her big Irish immigrant working-class family, many of whom still "had the brogue," as Sister Anne Marie had said. Molly wasn't the first to go to college—an older brother had been the first. But she was the first to get advanced degrees, to teach, to become, as her uncle had told her "our very own Yeats." She loved her family, had managed to elicit only a minor skirmish with them when she'd come out as a lesbian. They all lived in Queens, the whole extended family which she called "gigantic, really gigantic." She was the only renegade to Manhattan, the only unmarried one, the only one with no children. She went out frequently to visit and had invited me to go at Easter, but I had declined. We both knew I wasn't ready. "Soon," I'd said, but I'd known she was disappointed. "We should do this when it's not such a big holiday. Besides, I spend Holy Week suffering," I had told her. "I do the whole three hours on Good Friday, the Easter Vigil, all of it. I was raised well by the nuns, you see. Your people will like that about me when they finally meet me."

She wasn't sure if I was joking or not. I decided it was best that way. There were so many conversations I wasn't ready to have, that I wasn't sure how to have. I wondered if I could give her bits and pieces of my history, serve it up in consumable, palatable bites, like that first meal I'd had at her place. She knew I was Catholic, knew I'd gone to Catholic school. Would it be that hard to just tell her I was an orphan? Or would a flood of questions come with that reveal? I ached to be honest with her. I just couldn't figure out how. The more time passed, the more I knew she'd see my failing to be honest with her as another betrayal.

It wasn't that I hadn't been in love before. I had, a couple of times seriously. I'd been a little in love with Rosario the entire time we were at St. Cecilia's together. I had been in love with Keiko when we lived together in college. I'd been in love with the woman—in thrall with her. And I'd been in love with two other women in the past twelve years or so. But Molly felt different. Such an intensity of work had filled up the past few years of my life. The days, months, years had been full of traveling, of pictures to be taken, of stories to be told. I had watched friends settle down, straight ones getting married, lesbian ones having babies and talking about when marriage would be legal. Getting married when it finally was. Molly herself had been engaged to her former partner. They were planning on marriage right up until Molly discovered the affair. She'd moved out of their apartment and severed all ties within a month. It had, she said, come close to breaking her.

They'd been together seven years. "I thought this was my *real* family," she said.

The truth was, *I* hadn't *wanted* to settle down. The most settled I was, was having this apartment, the same space for a decade. It wasn't like that magnificent place the woman had had, but then I wasn't rich like she was. But it was so much more than my first little studio. And it was mine. A space that felt permanent. When I was traveling, it was the thing I came back to. Solid.

Now there was Molly. Now there would be Molly to come back to.

For the first time I felt as much of a pull to another person as I did to my work. For the first time I wanted to tell the truth, reveal myself, come out of the shadows. For the first time I felt so trapped by my own history that I couldn't sleep without drugs. For the first time I felt like my whole life was a careful construct of lie after lie and that there was no one who knew me. And for the first time, I wanted to be known. Dear God how I wanted to be known.

❖

I hadn't been to Brooklyn in years. I had friends there, but they always came into Manhattan to see me, I never went out there. Everyone joked that Faye couldn't cross the bridge, and that was partly true. I had never gone back to St. Cecilia's after I'd left. I'd seen Rosario in the city a few times when she'd come to visit me and Theresa. But I couldn't go back to St. Cecilia's. The latch had clicked shut on my time there. And today, when I had driven past, not stopping, I remembered with a gutting pang that the nuns I loved were, except for Mother Superior, all gone soon after our class left. Sister Claire had died suddenly of an aneurysm no one knew she'd had—Theresa had sent me the obit. I was shocked to discover she was only forty-eight. She had been so young when she cared for us, teaching us about love through food. Sister Mary Margaret had died, too, though she at least had made it to sixty. Breast cancer. The only other nun who mattered to me was Mother Superior. So there had been no reason to go back, no reason to cross the bridge and return to a life that no longer existed. I didn't know what had happened to Rosario and I had made no effort to find out, because I was afraid to know. Because I was afraid she was dead. And I didn't think I could bear to know that.

Theresa and I had sent each other the obligatory Christmas cards for years, but we never called each other, never saw each other. We both knew we had moved to different worlds when we left St. Cecilia's. It was only a matter of time before we moved to different worlds from each other, as well.

I'd gone to Brighton Beach one weekend, maybe eight years ago, thinking there might be a story for me there—the place screamed pictorial, after all. But the story that was there wasn't a story I could tell. I'd walked along the same avenues I'd walked that day with Angie, when he was teaching me how to see everything, how to put it all in my photographs, the day we'd seen the Russian mob guy gunned down in the street. But being there felt a different kind of foreign than it had that day. It had made me deeply sad and I hadn't stayed long. I'd walked to the ocean's edge, I'd stopped and had some blini, and then I'd gotten back on the subway home. That had been the last time I'd been in Brooklyn.

Until today.

I'd rented a car for *this* trip, unwilling to rely on buses and subways, unwilling to share this journey with anyone else. Needing to know I could escape quickly, if I had to. I was surprised to be able to find a place to park across the street from my grandparents' house, but an SUV had been pulling out as I drove up the street and I had been able to drive the little subcompact right in without having to hold up traffic to park. Without having to draw the slightest attention to myself. I sat there, in the car, staring across at the house, unsure what it was I was hoping to find. Did I think he was back there? Did I think my grandmother was down the street at St. Brendan's playing bingo with her old friends?

I got out of the car, crossed the street, walked toward the house. I'd taken two Xanax before I left the city, yet I was anything but calm. My heart raced, my mouth was dry, and I felt queasy. I realized I was scared, but I didn't even know of what. There was nothing here, now. Just a house. Just a house where I had discovered my grandfather was a rapist, a torturer who could have put the Nazis to shame, a killer, a cannibal.

Sister Anne Marie had been raped and mutilated and murdered, like some medieval saint there in that house, that house I had sent her to, not knowing, because I was only six, that when she told me she would "get to the bottom of things," that was her death knell. A wave of loss crested over me and I suddenly thought I might start screaming. *I should never have come here. There are no answers here.*

And yet I kept going, because something kept telling me that there *were* answers here. Answers I needed.

I opened the little wrought iron gate in front of the house. I used to swing on it when I lived there. A Big Wheel was abandoned in the front yard, a soccer ball next to it. I guess other children lived here now. I guess it was a normal house, again. I guess some priest from St. Brendan's had come and blessed it and made it habitable.

Or maybe the basement was still full of heads in vises and the smell of putrefaction and dead hair and murdered women—

I rang the doorbell, rehearsing what I would say when, if, someone answered.

A young woman, answered the door. She looked about my age and was wearing a dark green T-shirt with *St. Brendan's* printed across it in gold with the obligatory Irish harp beneath. She looked somewhat frazzled. As she pushed light brown hair out of her eyes, I saw she had blood on her hand. Wet blood. Red blood. There was also blood on her grey sweatpants. I felt faint. I was back here, at the house, and the woman answering the door had blood on her. *Blood.* I needed to leave. I made a half turn away from her. I couldn't look at the blood. Not here. I just couldn't.

"Hey," she said, looking past me as if there might be someone else with me in the little garden. "Are you the nurse? It's been hours since I called. Please, come in, right away." She held the door open. I hesitated.

"I'm not the nurse," I said, thrown off my prepared speech. *What had I been thinking, coming here?*

"Oh. I'm waiting for the nurse. My—" She stopped talking then and folded her arms in front of her, streaking her upper arm with more blood. "If you aren't the nurse, who are you? What do you want?"

This was the Brooklyn of my childhood. Suspicion always just below the surface. It somehow calmed me. It felt normal.

"I'm sorry," I said, summoning my professional self. "I see this is a bad time. Can I do anything to help?" I could hear a child crying weakly inside the house, the sound of a mewling kitten, not a boisterous baby. Crying a ghost-cry inside the house where I had so rarely cried, even though there had been so much for me to cry about.

"My son's got cancer," she said flatly, then, the crossed arms now dropped defeated to her sides. I saw the same look on her face I'd seen on the faces of those parents in the Central Valley. I could see her story written on her face. I taken many photos of that story. Her child was dying, she couldn't save him. There was, the doctors had told her, no hope, just whatever could be done to minimize suffering. And now she felt guilt for wanting him to die, for wanting his suffering to end, for wanting her own suffering to end. There was another child, a healthy child, to take care of. She couldn't lose them both. She'd only survive if she had the other child to care for, the other child to keep her from shattering into a trillion pieces she would never be able to piece back together.

"I'm waiting for the nurse," she repeated and started to cry. "He's vomiting blood. It's a lot of blood."

"Let me help," I said, pushing open the door. I had no idea what I was doing, but as I stepped back into the house where my entire life had careened off course twenty-seven years earlier, it seemed as if I was supposed to be back here, after all.

❖

It was late when I got back to the city. I'd spent the afternoon in that house, the house where so many women had met a grisly end, where there had been blood and suffering and killing. But it was different now—the house looked nothing like it had when I was a child. It didn't even smell like death, even though Kaitlyn McGinty's three-year-old son was dying.

I helped her bathe him—"Connor. His name is Connor."—and managed to unclog the morphine pump for her and swabbed out his mouth with a damp cloth, the little mouth torn and ulcerated from the chemotherapy she had stopped a few weeks earlier when she realized it was just hurting him, but not saving him.

I stood in the kitchen at the stove—not the same stove, a newer stove, but in the same place—where I had put my hand in the flame when I was not that much older than the boy dying in the room upstairs that had once been my room. I prepared a soft gruel of rice and butter, which Sister Claire had taught us all was the best thing to eat when someone was sick and vomiting and she had meant, I knew now, people who were doing drugs and had stopped eating because they'd forgotten everything else but the drugs.

I fed him a little at a time while Kaitlyn took a shower and changed her clothes and got the smell of death off her so she could be fresh for her boy, in case this was his last day. And as I fed him, I talked to him and told him that a long time ago this had been my room and that sometimes I had been scared here, too, but that he should not be scared because everyone loved him and everyone wanted him to be safe and he had said the "soup" was good and I had said he could have more later, but now he needed to sleep and I had stroked his head, his soft, bald head with a big scar at the back the shape of a scythe, and I had told him I was going to pray and he was going to go to sleep to the prayer and I had made up a little prayer for him, "This prayer is for Connor McGinty, so he can have a nice sleep, and good dreams, and wake up to kiss his mother and have more soup and not have the bad hurt he says he hates a lot. Thank you, Mary, Jesus, and all the saints. Amen."

Kaitlyn had come in at some point while I was stroking her son's old man head and reciting the little prayer. She said, "Oh, so you're one of the nuns. I haven't seen you before, so I didn't know. Thank you, Sister. Thank you so much. I'd been praying to Mary, praying all morning, because I thought, I thought—"

She had walked out of the room and I had tucked the covers around her now-sleeping boy, around Connor, and hoped that Mary and Jesus and the Holy Spirit would forgive me for all the new lies I was about to tell.

I found her in the kitchen, her head on her arms, sobbing soundlessly, her shoulders heaving. Her hair was still wet from the shower and she smelled like cucumber and peaches as I knelt on the floor next to her and suggested we go out back and sit in the sun for a while. "He'll be sleeping now, from the morphine. He's not going to vomit again. That was from the pump being clogged. You need to come outside in the sun for a bit while he sleeps. When does your other child get home from school?"

We'd gone outside and just sat on the grass in the yard where the vole had been electrocuted in front of me. She talked to me as if I were her priest, as if I were the only person she could be honest with, because I was the only person who would never breathe a word of what she told me. She knew about the sins of hubris and despair. Weren't these the first sins we learned about, intuited?

Kaitlyn told me about her husband on his final tour of duty in Afghanistan and how he'd tried to get home sooner, but was coming home in only two more days, maybe less, if the flights all worked out, on compassionate leave. He was already in transit, but she would never be able to forgive the government if Connor died before then, what if he died before then, how would any of them live with that? How could she forgive God if that happened? How could she believe in anything at all, if that happened?

I had told her that there was so much that could be lived with, so much more than we ever thought possible, and that she already knew that because she got up every morning as if nothing was wrong.

"Thank you, Sister," was all she said, and when she touched my hand, I felt like Sister Anne Marie was there with me, telling me that this time God would forgive the lies, this time I was actually redeeming myself, if such a thing was truly possible.

"This time, Faye, but don't do it again. You mustn't do it again."

The nurse called, but never came. Someone else would come later that night, around nine or ten. There had been a problem with the order. Everyone was sorry. Everyone was very sorry.

I hoped they could keep Connor alive long enough so that his father, who had already seen more horror than he would ever be able to tell his wife or the child who survived, could see the little wizened, scarred body with the blue-black shoulder from the port in his upper chest. I wondered how many dead or dying children Kaitlyn's husband had seen already. But it was different, when it was your own. All the dead bodies I had seen over the years—none of them were like the body of the dead man in Brighton Beach. Or how I imagined my parents. Or Sister Anne Marie.

I made Kaitlyn an omelette and sat and drank some tea while she ate. I wished I could make her something delicious, instead of just serviceable. Something like the little tapas that Molly had made for me. I thought about how Molly and Sister Claire had both told me in different ways that food was a gift we gave women, but the omelette was the best I could do.

I asked Kaitlyn what else I could do to help—some laundry while she lay down? Her daughter was staying at a friend's after school so Kaitlyn could rest. I told her I could stay another couple of hours, "till Vespers," since I was perpetuating the lie of my nun's status. She told me I could use the computer in the basement if I needed to do any work. She still hadn't asked why I was there. She had just assumed the church had sent me. I wondered if St. Brendan's would have been that kind, and then felt guilty for the thought. Lie upon lie, sin upon sin. I hoped the good I was doing would mitigate the betrayal.

I sorted through the blood-stained laundry. While it churned in what was once my grandfather's darkroom, as I stood with my hand on the door to the basement, as the smell of mango-scented laundry detergent dissipated the smells of blood and vomit and death, I knew I'd be able to go down those steps, down to the catacomb tomb of Sister Anne Marie, whose very being I had been channeling for three hours in the home of a stranger, which was also my home.

And so I did. I turned the knob, I opened the door, I felt—strangely—more calm than I had in weeks. This was the exorcism I had expected from the gallery opening.

The basement, the killing room of my childhood, was now a combination home office and children's playroom. The most grisly thing was a stack of unpaid bills next to Kaitlyn's computer. It was a big cheery room, now, painted a bright yellow, with brightly striped café curtains at the basement windows near the ceiling, the windows which had been covered in blackout paper when I was a child to keep in the secrets of my grandfather's horrifying crimes. Toys were scattered across the end of the room where Sister Anne Marie's body had been found, raped and mutilated, like St. Maria Goretti or St. Lucy, St. Perpetua or St. Felicity. This place was now the antithesis of a crime scene, let alone the scene of many crimes.

I sat down on the floor where the bed had been. A Muppet toy lay nearby, staring a goofy stare up at me.

It was over. Or nearly over. By the time the boy upstairs was being buried, Grand would be gone as well. I could feel it. I could feel it as strongly as if Sister Anne Marie were standing next to me, telling me that we would, together, get to the bottom of things.

❖

I'd decided to keep the car another day. I wasn't going back to the house with the dying boy, but I was going to be searching for Grand.

I would have liked to go back another day to help Kaitlyn. It had felt good, doing that kind of work, being taken that far out of myself. But I couldn't perpetuate those lies another day. It had been happenstance that I'd been there when Kaitlyn was so desperate, desperate enough, she had told me, that she would have smothered Connor with a pillow rather than watch him suffer for another hour. "You saved me, Sister," she'd said. "I would have killed him. I couldn't stand to see him in so much pain. It's not right. It's not right. God shouldn't do this to children."

It would be best for her to remember me as some artifact of mercy, appearing at her door when it was most needed. Better for her to wonder, when she called St. Brendan's to look for me, describing me to whoever answered the call, that I was ephemeral, maybe even a figment of her exhausted imagination. Even when Connor would ask her about the lady with the soup that made his mouth feel good, she would doubt herself.

The truth was, the day had helped *me.* I was clear now, about what I had to do. And the clarity buoyed me. For the first time in weeks I knew what I had to do and was prepared to do it. For the first time I felt like my life was not in stasis, but that I was moving forward after all.

❖

I was tired when I unlocked the door to my apartment. Tired in an honest way, though. Not just the exhaustion of anxiety and fear. I realized I hadn't had a Xanax since I'd left my grandparents' house, now Kaitlyn and Connor's house, although I'd given a handful to Kaitlyn and told her not to take more than three, but when Connor died, she would want to sleep and need to sleep and that might be the only way. I hadn't given her enough to kill herself. But she'd been grateful to have them.

It was the smell that hit me first, when I opened the door to my apartment. What was it? Two smells, really. One of cooking, except I hadn't cooked anything that morning before I'd left, and one of a woman's perfume. Something crisply floral. Beautiful, really.

In my tiredness—it was almost nine and I'd been gone for more than twelve hours—I thought Molly was there, that she'd come and cooked and maybe fallen asleep in the bedroom while she waited for me. My phone had been off the whole day. I hadn't wanted interruptions, hadn't wanted to be startled while driving, and had forgotten to turn it back on when I left Brooklyn.

The low light on the little table in the hallway where I threw my keys and bag and phone when I came in was on, but I had left it on. I could tell the light was on in both the kitchen and the bedroom. I had not left those lights on. I walked toward the kitchen.

She was sitting on the sofa in my living room. She was wearing a short black skirt, a black leather bustier, and a tight little jacket. Her lips were lipsticked an impossibly dark red. Under any other circumstances I would have found her hot, very hot, and she had planned for that, I could tell. But under these circumstances I felt my breath stop. My heart didn't race. I didn't feel any adrenaline surge. I wasn't sure why— weren't the autonomic reflexes coded for exactly this kind of situation?

I was amazed I recognized her after so many years, but she looked the same—just an adult version of the girl who had come into our dorm room late one night, standing slightly behind Sister Mary Margaret. Yes, she looked the same. Ethereal, angelic. The hair was still long and massive and that pale blond color only the Russians and Scandinavians seemed to have. She looked like a model, maybe she *was* a model. I was pretty sure I would never be photographing her, though.

I understood now. It had been slow, the realization. So very, unhelpfully slow. He'd had a partner all this time. Grand had had a partner. That was why I hadn't seen him before this. Because there had been no need. I wasn't sure what the need was now, but the partner he had found would not have liked it, his having a need for someone else, someone other than her. His partner, who had held a grudge for more than twenty years, because that was what psychopaths did, would not have liked it at all.

He had a partner, a girl who had been born with the taste for killing that his own granddaughter had not. A girl who had started early, a girl who even the nuns who feared nothing, had feared. A girl who had been taken away and put somewhere where she had learned to lie and cheat and find her way to someone who would hone and appreciate her very special skill set. A girl who would tell him how she had killed her own mother when she was nine, turning her into an icon like St. Sebastian, stabbed all over with wooden spikes from the banister she had pushed her through when she'd told her she was going to have a new brother or sister. A girl who would recount the tale of how she had sliced open the vein of a nun when she was only ten and had nearly killed another girl of whom she was jealous when she was just eleven. A girl who would talk about the other girl, the girl everyone said was the good one, the nice one, the one who never left the home, the one all the nuns talked about, the one who had secrets no one knew. A girl who would talk about the other girl, the good girl, the one the nuns were so protective of and talk about how she wanted to kill her, how she hated her in a way she'd hated almost no one else.

I wondered briefly how they had met—if he had found her or if she had found him. It didn't matter really, how monsters found each other. It only mattered what happened when two monsters came together.

Mayhem.

"Laryssa." It was all I said. I was standing there, immobile, not knowing what to do. Somehow I knew running was a mistake. Somehow I knew my only chance was to behave as if she'd been invited in, as if we were old friends, as if this scene, whatever this scene was, happened all the time. Where was *he*, I wondered? Had she killed him? Did he know she was here? Was this a pact they had together?

I decided to sit down. Someone was going to be telling a story. I wasn't sure if it would be her or me. All I knew was that it would be a long night—if I was very, very lucky.

Chapter Six
The Final 36

I was frightened. If I hadn't been so tired, I would likely have been terrified. And terror was still in the wings, of that I was sure. I was trapped here, in my own apartment, my one safe space. I was trapped in a city where the anonymity of being one of millions had offered me refuge and sanctuary. But the other side of that anonymity was that people had been ignoring the screams of women in danger forever, here. I had a brief flash of Kitty Genovese, one of New York's most famous victims. She had been just a few years younger than I was now when she was raped and stabbed to death outside her Queens apartment while her partner slept upstairs in their bed. A friend of mine had written a piece about Genovese for the paper—the fiftieth anniversary of her murder had passed mere months ago.

What would happen if I screamed? I'd screamed with night terrors for months and not one neighbor had so much as slipped a note under my door asking me to keep it down. Mine was one of those buildings where everyone valued their privacy. We gave the nod of acknowledgment, we said *good morning* or *good evening* or *hot isn't it* or *can you believe this weather* or *so much snow for the city*, but that was where it stopped. Maybe people knew I was *that* photographer, maybe not. In the nearly ten years I had lived here—since after my studio, since after the woman, since after I got hired at the paper—I had made no actual friends here. We were not that sort, those of us who lived here. We were ships passing at the mailboxes or in the elevator. And now, that anonymity might mean I would die here, I would be killed not by my grandfather, as I had been expecting for weeks and weeks, but by the beautiful sociopath who sat across from me on my own sofa. Now I would be bled out—I somehow knew Laryssa had not lost her taste for blood soup—by this preternaturally calm woman who had probably killed a dozen women and maybe men, too, in the years since I had seen her led away from St. Cecilia's when we were children.

I didn't speak. I was trying to figure out what would upset her, what would mollify her—was it even possible to mollify a creature as feral as she? I was about to ask her how Grand was, when she spoke.

"I've been watching you for a long time, Faye. A long, *long* time. So many details, your life."

The Russian lilt was still there. Her voice was deeper than I would have expected. Smoky. A voice calibrated and cultivated for sex and luring. Everything I had believed about my grandfather since the gallery opening, since I had started thinking about him night and day, had been wrong. He hadn't acted alone. Laryssa had been his dazzling—for she *was* dazzling, with her long legs and long hair and full, lush lips—lure, his pilot fish, his daddy's girl. I could envision her in clubs, that hair flying, skirt barely covering her, flashing every teasing bit she could, to entice her imminent victims. Sitting still, she was a photograph. Sitting on my sofa she was *merely* breathtaking. But moving, in action? Then she would be impossible to resist. Even now, unspeaking, calmly immobile, she was still trying to lure me—her legs provocatively spread, her breasts full above the bustier, her lips that dark, arterial red.

I am going to die tonight, I suddenly thought. *Laryssa is going to kill me.*

Was there a way out? Did I have any options at all? I decided if I was going to die, I was not going to do so silently. I was going to speak. I was going to get answers, if I could, and as many as I could.

"Where's Grand, Laryssa? I was expecting him, not you." I waited. My heart was starting to pump now. I leaned forward in my chair, ran a hand through my hair. I wasn't sure what impression I was giving her, but the only one I didn't want to give her was fear. I'd been known for my calm demeanor, even when I was anything but, since I was six. I was not going to abandon that affect now, not when it might serve me best, no matter that I *felt* like screaming and crying and begging for my life.

Laryssa shifted. Her legs closed. She gave a little lizard lick to those lips. The hair moved almost imperceptibly.

"He sent me," was all she said. I had no idea if she was lying. I had no idea if she even understood the concept of truth. Everything I knew about her was from our time at St. Cecilia's. And what I remembered made me shudder involuntarily.

She stood up. I tried not to flinch. We were not going to have the conversation I wanted, it seemed. We were going to do something else. What, I didn't know.

❖

"Come." It was an order of the sort I imagined prison matrons in Russia might give. It was delivered like a shot. I stood. She was taller than I was by about four inches, but all of that extra height was from the black leather booties she wore—the heels were high. But she clearly wore such heels all the time. It was unlikely I could knock her off them, like I might be able to with some women.

"Where are we going?" It seemed a reasonable question.

"To eat, of course," she said, sure enough of her control over me, over the situation, to not even turn toward me when she said it. I scanned the room for something close to hand that I could hit her with. There was nothing within reach. "I have made you a meal. I know you will love it. *Dedushka*—your grandfather—he loves it. He says I am a *brilliant* cook."

I was unaccountably stung by her words. A memory—more than one, actually—flooded back of Grand coming up behind my grandmother in the kitchen and putting his arms around her waist, nuzzling her neck, and saying, "That smells delectable, darling. But then you are a brilliant cook."

I remembered asking my grandmother what *delectable* and *brilliant* meant and she had said delectable was another word for delicious and brilliant meant you were really good at something. Then she had said, "You, my little Faye, are a *brilliant* granddaughter. The best granddaughter there is." And she had put her arm around me and squeezed me and I had felt safe.

And so I knew. I knew from what Laryssa said that this was not another nightmare from which I was bound to awake eventually. This was real. Grand and Laryssa were in some hellish partnership. I dreaded what awaited me in the kitchen.

But now, more than ever, I needed answers. "What about my grandmother? Where is *she*?" I tried not to sound as demanding—or frantic—as I felt. That memory had made me want to see her, made me feel protective of her, for all her fault in staying with my murderous grandfather.

Now, Laryssa turned in the doorway to my kitchen and looked straight at me. Her eyes were as I remembered them from our fractured childhood—that pale, nearly translucent blue, like husky dogs or wolves. Predatory. Rimmed in black, which only made them look larger and bluer, with long lashes that looked real, not fake.

"Accident," was all she said and I felt tears prick behind my eyes. *Accident* to me meant *burned alive.* For all her collaboration with my grandfather, I hoped my grandmother's death had been swift. I imagined Laryssa had met her one day at the top of some stairs. It was, after all, her *métier.*

She added, "Don't be sad. She had outlived her usefulness. It was better she left us when she did. Before she could become a burden."

The words were delivered in her melodic lilt, but nothing could soften the harsh brutality of those words. Laryssa still hadn't learned how to behave like a human being. Maybe the nuns could have saved her, had she stayed at St. Cecilia's, like they had saved me. But at what cost?

My kitchen was not the galley kitchens of many New York apartments. I had no dining room, but I had an eat-in kitchen. It had been remodeled by whoever had renovated this building sometime in the 1980s to create a charming little French-style country kitchen nook. I had always loved it. If I survived the night, I wondered if I would still be able to love it.

When I entered the kitchen I saw that the table, which was capable of seating six in a pinch, was set for four.

"Are we expecting company?" I asked, worried by those other place settings, as I slid into my usual seat which faced both the window and the stove.

"Yes," she said as she walked to the stove. I saw my cutting board and some leafy things and some of my spices were out, but I wasn't sure which ones. I did not see a knife, the one thing I had hoped to see.

She said, "Of course we will have guests. Meals must be shared."

This had become surreal. Me sitting at my own table, a table now set for some macabre dinner party—plates were laid out, as well as wineglasses. My good cloth napkins were also out, but no silverware. I guessed that would come later, with the food. Laryssa had thought of every detail—and had not wanted a knife in her back or a spoon taken to one of those eerie, too-blue eyes.

Laryssa stood at the stove, a pot each on three of four burners. I didn't want to imagine what was in them. The smell in the room was of meat cooking—like I was in a steakhouse. Meat had never been in this apartment since I lived here, let alone cooked here. The pots would all have to be given away. Or buried. Or turned over to the police as evidence.

I was finally thinking now, I was out of my initial torpor. I was thinking about how I was going to best her, how I was going to survive. Was Grand here? Was he napping in my bedroom, waiting for his little *kukla* to lure me in? Had they planned to kill me together? Because this was definitely a plan, a well-orchestrated plan.

But who was the fourth place setting for?

"I would ask what we are having for dinner, but I'm pretty sure I don't want to know," I said. "So since I don't want to know *what*, why don't you tell me *who*?"

"I think it should be a surprise," she said, busying herself at the stove. Then she turned toward me. "What shall we do first? Have some wine or have a guest?" She held up a bottle of red. It wasn't one of mine.

I needed a drink of some sort, but I also needed to know what was going to happen next. I was also afraid to drink or eat anything she put in front of me. My throat was dry, my heart was beating fast. Any effects of the Xanax from earlier in the day—was that even this same day? It felt so long ago, the young mother, the dying child, my grandparents' house—had worn off.

"I don't suppose I could have some bottled water you haven't poisoned? I've been out all day and I'm really thirsty. I'm not ready for wine, especially if we are having guests. I haven't eaten and it will go straight to my head." I wanted her to think she had me in her control, more than she actually did. I wanted to figure out a way to surprise her, to overpower her.

There was no point in my trying to suss out whatever was the right way to approach her. I remembered well when Sister Claire had tried to do that with the child Laryssa and had nearly died anyway. Laryssa was unreadable. That was the thing about sociopaths. I thought of Martine passing the same checkpoint for a year, only to have those same men gang-rape her one day, out of nowhere. Sociopaths were unpredictable. Laryssa hadn't been predictable at ten. How could she be predictable at thirty-four?

"You may drink," was all she said, still standing at the stove.

"The bottles are in the cabinet under the sink," I told her, knowing I wouldn't be allowed to get one on my own.

She reached for the cabinet, bending over. She wanted me to know she was not wearing panties. This just got creepier all the time. I'd never understood the pleasure in combining sex with pain, with humiliation. After my trip to the DRC, seeing the women ravaged by such unspeakable violence, all of it with that grisly sexual edge, telling the stories they wanted told about rape as a weapon—I never wanted to learn what linked sex and violence together. I'd escaped my grandfather's legacy. But clearly Laryssa was cut from his same repugnant cloth.

I could see Laryssa tear open the plastic around the case of water, taking one of her perfectly manicured nails and slitting the package open as I imagined she had slit actual flesh.

I thought it would be safe to drink it when she handed it to me, still silent.

I opened the bottle, searching for tiny pinpricks from a syringe, but saw nothing.

"I have not poisoned you," Laryssa said. "That is not my way."

Good to know, I thought, not wanting to think about what her way might be, since there were no stairs in my apartment to push me down.

"And now we will have a guest, yes?"

As soon as she said it, he appeared, slightly behind me, almost like an apparition. It was shocking how youthful he still looked. Some men aged so well. Grand was one of them.

When you are six, you have no sense of adult height. Everyone seems gigantic. Grand had always seemed especially tall when I was six—I could no longer remember if he had been taller than my father or not, because I could no longer remember my parents without looking at photographs. The only vivid memories I seemed to still have from the pre–St. Cecilia's part of my childhood, I realized, were tattered shreds of nightmare. Things I would rather not remember.

Grand was tall. Over six feet. Age had not wizened him at all. He stood erect, no hunch in his shoulders or back. He still looked tanned as he had when I was a child. He obviously saw a skillful hair stylist—or his young lover or faux granddaughter or whatever it was Laryssa was to him took care of this—because his hair was artfully dyed so that it was greying, but still dark as well. It looked natural, but I knew it wasn't. His hair hadn't been this dark when I was a child, but had been a ruddy chestnut color. His eyes still pierced and sparkled. He didn't wear glasses, so vanity also demanded contact lenses. He looked closer to sixty than late seventies. As Laryssa went to him and he draped an arm around her with a casualness born of familiarity, they suddenly looked like typical New York lovers—a handsome older man, a striking younger woman. There was forty years between them at least, but he'd diminished the gap with various cosmetic tricks. And I could see from how they were together that she was not a manqué for me. She was something completely different. She was his partner, his soul mate—if either of them had had a soul, that is.

"This is the best part, Faye. This is the best part."

His voice was the voice from my childhood. The voice from nearly thirty years ago. The voice that had read to me, instructed me, comforted me, and now, terrified me. The voice was remarkably unchanged—strong, vibrant. And now, as an adult, as a grown woman who knew voices and timbre and understood what tone meant, I heard what I presumed all those women had heard over I-didn't-know-how-many years. I heard the deep, sensual warmth. The want-to-go-have-a-drink-and-maybe-something-else-ness. I heard my grandfather the man, rather than my grandfather the grandfather.

I knew now that he'd only been middle-aged when my parents died—a full generation younger than my mother's parents, both of whom were dead before I was five—my grandmother of cancer, my grandfather two years later of a loneliness-inspired heart attack.

Grand.

I didn't move. There was no reason to. This was one more in the long series of nightmarish hallucinations I'd been having since I was in the Central Valley, except it was real. Once again it seemed to me there could only be one response: *scream.* Scream loud and long until someone in the building called the police, someone said, even for New York, this is too much.

Scream.

But I couldn't. Instead I had to turn in my seat. I had to look—at him, at her, at them together. It was ingrained, genetic maybe. I was a photographer. My life was looking. I always had to look.

They stood there, in the doorway to my kitchen, in my apartment, in my *home,* and he had his hand on her waist, slipped up under the bustier, touching her flesh. For her part, Laryssa had her arms around Grand, one impossibly long leg wrapped around his. It was nuanced, but disturbingly sexual. For me, the actual granddaughter of this man, it felt pornographic. I fought the urge to say something, to yell, to rush at them both and break free of the apartment. I knew now I could not possibly overpower the two of them. If I had counted on his age being in my favor, I had been wrong. Apparently killing women with your young lover was an elixir of youth, a real-life form of vampirism.

"It's so good to see you, Faye. All grown up. I saw your show, you know. I wouldn't have missed it. I obviously taught you well."

My stomach lurched. *He* had *been there.* Was there nothing of mine he hadn't tainted?

He didn't come toward me. The two of them stood there, together, entwined in that creepy, suggestive embrace, looking at me. Laryssa seemed pleased Grand hadn't approached me. He was hers, not mine. What she didn't realize was I was fine with that. I wanted no part of him. Seeing him didn't confuse me. I wasn't overwhelmed with past feelings of love for him. I wasn't sure what I felt.

I could think of nothing to say. The flood of years. The day spent at the house—his house, *our* house—with the dying child. Images flashed through my head like an Eadweard Muybridge flip-book—each one bringing me to this moment, now, facing my own death in some eerie tableaux.

I suddenly realized I was sitting at a set table just like the women in Grand's photographs. All that was missing was my organs on the plates. Was I really going to just sit and wait for that to happen?

I wondered if I had time to lunge for a pot on the stove and toss it at them both. I was certain I didn't. There wasn't enough space between them and me. Plus, Laryssa was cat-quick. My only chance, I thought, was to separate them. But how?

It was time to speak.

"I'm hungry. I haven't eaten since lunch. Are we eating, or is this set table just another prop? Because if it is, I am getting up and making myself a sandwich. I'm a vegetarian, Laryssa, so I'm not going to be having whatever it is you are making. I don't eat meat. I haven't since I was six. Grand knows why."

I hoped my voice sounded dismissive. I wanted to give the impression that I wasn't expecting to be killed here tonight, in my own apartment, likely with one of my own kitchen knives. I wanted to at least appear to have some control, even though all of us knew I had none.

I started to get up and Laryssa was next to me in a nanosecond, blocking me from moving. "You should sit down, Faye. *Dedushka* and I—"

He interrupted her. "I don't think we have to worry about Faye, my sweet. After all, this is her home and we are really the guests."

I felt the hairs on the back of my neck go up. I was so out of my depth. *Two sociopaths vying for control.* I felt tears sting my eyes. I was truly terrified, now. As many times as I had contemplated suicide in the past few months, now I wanted to live. I wanted to live for my work. I wanted to live for Molly. I wanted to live for that dying child and his mother and for the dead Sister Anne Marie. I wanted to live for all the victims of these two monsters before me. And yet there was no scenario I could imagine in which I got to live, in which I got to walk out of here alive. Because even if I was able to kill one of them, the other would finish me off. This I knew. They were enraptured with each other. They would kill anyone who came between them—and likely already had. Even my grandmother had been one of their victims.

"Would you like to see my studio, Grand, while Laryssa finishes whatever feast she's preparing?"

Pretending normalcy seemed the only feasible approach at this point. I still believed in some small part of me that if I could separate them, I could survive this. I wasn't sure how, but I had to try. I stood again and this time Laryssa did not block my exit from the table. She moved back to the stove and the pots that were simmering low with God-knew-what.

I turned to go toward my studio. Maybe I could push him out the window. Maybe there was something in there I could hit him with, even though he was so much taller than I. Well over six feet, I realized now, standing near him.

I wasn't prepared for what came next. And yet I should have been.

"We have to learn to forgive the people we love, Faye." His voice was so much the voice of my childhood, then—the comforting, soothing voice that tucked me in at night and read to me and made me feel safe in that time between my parents' deaths and my trip to the basement. His voice took me back so far, was so resonant, that I closed my eyes for a second, less than a second, hearing him, feeling a swift rush of emotion for *that* man, the one I had loved, then.

Involuntary. And, possibly, fatal.

For when I did so, just as quickly, in that instant, his arms were around me. He was holding me tightly, repeating the line about forgiveness.

"We have to learn to forgive the people we love, Faye, don't you think so?" He was stroking my hair. His voice was in my ear. "I know you can forgive me because I know you love me. I just saw it on your face. After all these years, the work you have done, it all says it—you still love me, as I love you. We are part of each other. I know you see that now. I saw it in your work. I see it in *you*."

I said nothing, could say nothing. I could neither object nor assent. I couldn't breathe in his embrace. I was suffocated by the knowledge of all he had done, of the way in which I had been forced to live all these years because of him, his sickness, his crimes, all of it. This was not my grandfather, not some long-lost avuncular relative with whom I could spend Saturday afternoons at photography exhibits and talk about old times and for whom I could feel love. This was the man who had kept

• 247 •

me from love for years, who had kept me hidden from my own life as surely as if I had been a prisoner in that basement since I had first gone down there. This was a serial killer, wanted by police since I was six for the seventeen murders they knew of and who knew how many others they didn't know of. I wasn't in the arms of my grandfather, the man who took care of me after my parents were incinerated. This was a killer—a torturer, a rapist, a murderer—and he was holding me and I couldn't breathe. The weight of his violence was all around me, like a vise, like the vise in the basement with the lady's head in it.

I felt sick, a wave of intense nausea passing through me.

He said, "Remember when I would read to you? From the little books you brought with you to our house? I know you remember."

And I did remember, but I couldn't breathe and I was feeling faint from hunger and fear and the smell of meat in my vegetarian apartment and how close he was, how tightly he was holding me.

"I used to read you all the fairy tales. All the stories about magic. The night at the gallery was magic. All those images. All those remarkable images. Laryssa and I—well, we were very proud of you that night, weren't we, my sweet? We had a real celebration afterward."

Laryssa said something in Russian, but I had no idea what it was she said. She felt far away.

Grand had not let go of me and I felt the air going out of me, yet I felt incapable of struggling against him. I was immobilized, like some small creature caught by a cat. *How had I let him touch me? Why couldn't I escape?*

"You need to let go of me," I said, hearing the weakness in my own voice, knowing it doomed me.

But he kept talking and holding me and Laryssa was doing something now at the stove that made a sizzling sound and he was telling me about fairy tales and taking photographs together when I was small and how we could do that again and do our own final 36—the last pictures on that Kodachrome roll—and I couldn't breathe, I really couldn't, and he was stroking my hair and talking to me and then I heard her voice, Laryssa's, far away, but just really at the stove as she said, "But *Dedushka*, in the original fairy tale the Evil Queen asks that Snow White's liver be brought back to her so she can eat it."

And that was the last thing I heard.

❖

There is always the point in a mystery where the detective loses consciousness and we are left to wonder what happened while he or she was out cold. They wake up in a dire, life-threatening predicament. Always. The suspension of disbelief for the reader is wondering why they weren't killed outright by the murderer—why the sloppiness of leaving the protagonist alive, when they were *almost* killed anyway?

I knew why Grand hadn't killed me. I knew as soon as I woke up in my own bed and it was dark and the smell of burned meat was in the air. I knew they were still here, and they were waiting, and that we were nowhere near through the final 36. I could hear the shutter clicking as I had that day coming home from the bookstore. I could hear the low susurration of voices, a small brittle laugh from her.

What were they doing in my apartment? Who was the fourth person? How was I ever going to survive whatever it was they had planned?

Maybe Laryssa *had* drugged the water, after all. Or Grand had done something when he held me, when he was stroking my hair and had touched my face. I had been drugged—I knew the signs. And when I tried to get up, get off the bed, to go see where they were and what they were doing, I felt myself reeling, falling, and just before I lost consciousness again, I thought maybe this time I would not wake up. And that maybe that would be okay.

❖

There is that place between sleep and waking where we are in a heightened state of consciousness. Dreams are most vivid right before waking. I felt like I was in that state for a long time—aware, yet not aware. They were both there, Grand and Laryssa, in my dreams, their arms around each other, looking at me, talking about me, laughing to each other. And there was Molly. I saw her, but she was in the distance and I couldn't reach her. I kept trying to call out to her, but she couldn't hear me. The little boy was there, Connor, lying in my old room, and I was telling him not to be afraid, that I would take the journey with him.

And then there was the scream.

How many months had I been awakened by screaming? By my own screaming? Screaming from the horrors of my work over the last year, the discovery that Grand was still alive, that he was still hovering on the periphery of my life. Screaming from the guilt I felt about his victims, about Sister Anne Marie. It had all taken such a toll on me. Molly had rescued me. Without her realizing it, because I had so many, many secrets, she had pulled me back from the brink—literally. I no longer took my walks to the river, no longer contemplated the plunge into its welcoming darkness. Her dinners and her late-night texts and her long Saturdays in bed with me had anchored me. Molly had made me feel normal, whole. She had made me think that I could move forward without ever looking back.

And now that would never happen, because I would be dead. Because my grandfather and his young lover were going to do something that defied description. *To me.* I was going to be their quintessential victim.

Had I really screamed? Or just dreamed I had? Wouldn't they have come to me, one of them, if I *had* screamed? Come to retrieve their plaything?

I was fully awake, now. It was still dark in my bedroom, so I must not have slept that long. A couple of hours. It had been somewhat after nine when I'd been in the kitchen. I'd seen the little clock on the stove. Now? Maybe midnight or one or even two, but nowhere near dawn.

I turned on my side. I was dizzy, but not like before. I thought I could hear noises, voices, in another part of the apartment, but low, very low. They would want to be quiet at this hour. They wouldn't know that my neighbors didn't care about screaming. I was certain now that I'd been drugged somehow. But they'd misjudged. They didn't know what a tolerance I'd built up since returning from the DRC for drugs that made the world go away. If they'd thought I would wake up, surely I'd be bound and gagged and I was neither.

And yet it didn't matter. I had no landline, my phone was in my bag, which was on the table by my front door. It might as well not exist. Plus, I was pretty sure I had never turned it on, so it wouldn't even be ringing. I didn't keep a pistol under my pillow like the woman had. I looked around the room in the darkness. There was nothing. I kept the bedroom spare, because sleeping was so arduous. There was nothing but the bed and the dresser, which held only clothes and a few knickknacks on top, all tiny, nothing I could hit someone with. The room I used as my studio was the larger room in the apartment. The bathroom opened onto it, so I couldn't even grab something caustic.

Think. There has to be something. I cursed the reliance on my phone for everything—watch, alarm, computer. I should have a landline. I should have a watch—I'd never put mine back on after Martine had told me to take it off with her unsettling dictate, "Here is it always the same hour."

I had to find something, anything, to give me even the slightest edge. Next to me was the little night table with a small stack of books, a box of tissues, the lamp. I leaned over, feeling a wave of dizziness. I carefully and quietly slid open the drawer to see what might be there. An unopened bottle of water which I took out, twisting the cap with the edge of the pillow to muffle the sound. I drank most of it, more grateful for untainted water than any time since I'd been in the DRC.

I felt around to see what else was there. A broken silver chain I used to wear all the time that I'd been meaning to get fixed. Some gum—I put a piece in my mouth and found it surprisingly difficult to chew. Two small votive candles and a couple of packs of matches from two different bars I'd been in during my most suicidal period a few months back. I slid those into my pocket. The rosary Mother Superior had given me. A small bottle of hand cream from some hotel. A little notebook. A couple of pens—I put those in my pocket as well. And then, at the back of the drawer, there it was. A crinkly slip case with negatives inside and its usual companion, a splicing blade—what were they doing in this drawer? Had I been looking at them before bed one night and just put them in there and forgotten? It didn't matter *why*— now I had weapons. Two pens from my local bank and the thin, sharp, blade. I held it. I slid the drawer shut. I lay back down. Should I wait for them or should I surprise them? Were they even capable of being surprised? They might be; after all, they had miscalculated how long I would stay unconscious and neither had checked the drawer. But if it was so difficult to chew the gum in my mouth, could I walk? And would I have the strength or even be able to make myself stab either of them in the eye or the neck with the pens? I doubted it.

I spit the half-chewed gum into a tissue. I held the blade in my hand and lay back. They would come for me soon. And when they did, I would be ready. We were nearing the end of the roll, I knew. This was Grand's and my final 36. One of us would survive this night. I was now determined it would be me.

CHAPTER SEVEN
THE DARK BOX

When I worked with Angie, years ago, my first real job, my first true understanding of how photography worked, the first thing he had done was introduce me to the dark box. When you open a can of film, it's the most dangerous time. Any light and the entire roll will be ruined. He had shown me on test film. But the dark box helps you cheat light. The can goes in, you pull the little tab out, stick the leader card on it, put it in the processing machine. Angie always told me if I wasn't sure, to use the dark box. "You don't want to lose anyone's memories, Faye. Those are irreplaceable. Our memories are our lives, you know."

Now my apartment was the dark box and I was that roll of film. I was being pulled out, frame by frame. Grand was a torturer and he was torturing me. This was not a reunion, as he had intimated in the kitchen as he held me. This was a dénouement. And at the end of the roll I would be the one to be spliced. Or so he intended.

Had I dozed off again? It seemed so. This time when I heard the little scream—for it was small, thin, not piercing—I knew it hadn't come from me. But it *had* come from my apartment. I sat up slowly. The dizziness was less. I took a quick slug of what remained of the water and tried to stand. Wobbly, but steadier than I expected. I thought about taking off my shoes, but decided I needed the protection they offered if I needed to kick. I moved toward the door, slowly, carefully, trying not to make any sounds. It was still dark. But now I saw no light under my door like I had before. *What did that mean?* The scream—if that was what it was—that had awakened me was not repeated. Now there were no sounds at all.

I turned the knob, opening the door slowly, pushing up on the knob, hoping there would be no creaking. I stepped out into the little hallway that led to the living room. It was dark in the apartment, but not pitch black. I knew every inch of this place and often had to walk from the bedroom to the bathroom in the dark. This gave me an edge over Grand and Laryssa. I knew where I was going and knew what would be there. I slunk along the wall, the little blade in my hand. Now I could see a thin light coming from the kitchen. It moved slightly. Laryssa must have lit the candles on the table.

When I reached the living room I could see into the kitchen. The fourth guest was there, sitting at the table. Or rather, slumped over the table. My heart started racing. I looked into the living room—they weren't there. I ran to the kitchen, flipped on the light, no longer caring if they *were* still here, hiding somewhere, or not. I put the blade in my pocket. I blew out the candles.

Shihong was unconscious. I felt her neck for a pulse and found one. It was weak, but it was there. She had a bruise on the side of her forehead—she'd been hit with something. Perhaps that was what had caused the little scream—surprise at being struck. A piece of duct tape covered her mouth. That would have made her scream small. Her wrists were bound behind the chair with one of my scarves. There was blood on it.

I untied her and lifted her gently out of the chair. I laid her on the kitchen floor, knelt beside her, trying to ascertain what her injuries were, talking to her, telling her it would be all right, telling her to stay with me, telling her I was sorry. I pulled the duct tape from her mouth, but she did not move or make a sound. There was dried blood on her lips. There was also dark lipstick—not her lipstick. *What had they done to her?*

There was blood on the front of her blouse and down her arm, blood on her skirt, blood on her legs. But the blood wasn't pulsing. Whatever her wound was, I didn't think it wasn't still bleeding.

I opened her blouse, looking for the source of the blood. The lacy black bra she wore had been cut through in the front. Grand and Laryssa—or maybe just Laryssa, as I was now sure it had been she who had lured Shihong here—had sliced Shihong's right breast, nearly severing the nipple. Yet the cut itself wasn't deep—this was mutilation rather than a view to a kill. The blood had already coagulated around the wound. Below her breast was another wound, long, but also not too deep, this one where Shihong's liver was. Had they been going to cut out her liver and thought better of it? It looked that way.

I suddenly felt faint. I sat back on my heels, closed my eyes for a moment, and tried to calm my heart rate with deep breaths. I knew I had to search the apartment, to see what else was here, to see if they were hiding in my studio or the bathroom, but I was certain they were gone. I had to call 911 and get Shihong to the hospital. Yet even as I knew I had to save her, I knew just as clearly that I had to have a plan, I had to have something to tell the EMTs when they arrived, I had to have an explanation for the police.

And there was the added problem of Shihong being undocumented. Did I dare put her in that kind of danger? What would be worse for her? Dying would be worst. But being sent back to China? That might be just as terrible. I couldn't choose for her.

My mind was racing. It didn't make sense that Grand and Laryssa had left, yet there were no sounds in the apartment. Nothing. They were gone.

What had their plan been? I thought it was to kill me. But I was still alive. Was the plan to kill Shihong in my apartment, put her organs in pots on my stove, and put me in prison for life? If Shihong died— and I had no idea how extensive her injuries were—that could happen. *What would I tell the police?*

I had never called them since that night at the gallery when I had first seen Grand. I had thought about it over and over, but what would I have said? They'd been searching for him since I was six and hadn't found him. And I had to admit, I hadn't wanted to be reconnected to him through old police files, old newspaper clippings, old musings of Detective Tom about what role my six-year-old self had played. I didn't want anyone to know I was his granddaughter. Mother Superior had been so careful to keep me protected. I wanted to stay protected.

But now? Now it was all very different. Now Shihong was bleeding on my kitchen floor and there was human flesh in my pots and I was going to have to call the police, wasn't I?

Yet what would I tell them, now? That my grandfather who had been missing since I was six had teamed up with a sociopathic Russian émigré I had lived with in the orphanage—the *home*—and together they had plotted to kill my friend who is an undocumented immigrant and frame me for her murder? And that the human organs that had been cooked on my stove and which had been partially eaten by them were from one of their other victims, but that really, I had had nothing to do with any of it? I wasn't a killer, just a photographer who recorded mayhem—and of course my photographs would damn me. My story about the DRC would damn me, with the tales of cannibalism. My whole history would damn me.

I had to make sure Shihong didn't die. She was my only witness. I had to keep her alive as much for me as for her. But calling police, calling 911—that seemed out of the question. I needed a doctor. But could I trust my own? *Who, who, who could I call?*

I felt Shihong's pulse again. Slow, yet regular. But she was still unconscious and I feared trying to shake her awake might cause more damage.

I stood up and went into the kitchen. The little clock on the stove read 3:17. So much damage in so few hours.

The pots were still there, covered. I didn't dare lift the lids. Plates—clearly eaten from—were in the sink, along with silverware. This was all so elaborate. Laryssa must have been watching me for months. There would be fingerprints on the silverware, the plates, the two glasses, one with her blood-soup-colored lipstick imprinted on it.

But I could do nothing with them. Because if I called the police, I implicated myself. And Shihong. And I lost everything. Again. I saw that now. The plan was to torture me, to pull me into their crimes and keep me fearful that they would reappear at any time. After all, they had gotten the keys to my apartment, they had lured Shihong. Next time it could be Molly. It could be the little boy and his mother. It could be anyone who knew me. And eventually, it would be me. Eventually.

I felt a wave of rage rush through me. *How? How could Grand do this to me? Haven't I suffered enough for his crimes?* Hadn't my entire childhood been enough? Hadn't my having to keep the world at arm's length and fear that the killing gene was embedded in me been enough? A huge gasp came out of me then and I suddenly burst into tears, slamming my fists on the sink. None of this would have happened if I had just killed myself that night after the gallery. But my will to live—for my parents who had been burned alive before they were thirty, for Sister Anne Marie who had bravely tried to save me, for all those women who had been Grand's victims, for the nuns who had protected me and kept me from becoming a monster, for all the women whose stories I was trying to tell in pictures—that will, that overwhelming will to survive had subverted every plan to die.

And now here I was, with my half-dead friend, mutilated and bloody on the floor of my kitchen, the organs of some other dead woman in the pots on my stove—because what else would be in those pots, but more evidence of *my* crimes?—and me, nearly friendless in the biggest, most anonymous city in America, with nowhere to turn.

I leaned over the sink, splashing water on my face. The water hit the plates, blood running off them. I wasn't washing away evidence. There could be no evidence. Everything would have to be bagged up and taken somewhere and disposed of. Or worse, washed and put back in the cabinets like none of this had happened. Because they would be watching me, just as I had thought Grand had been all these weeks since I had first seen him. Watching and taking pictures of everything. I knew that now. Just as they knew I didn't know how this was done, this hiding of evidence and plotting and all of it. Not the way they did. They were maestros. I was a neophyte. I never intended to become anything more. I was no novitiate, in case they were thinking they could turn their murderous dyad into a triad.

I had to think. I had to have a plan before Shihong died or infection set in or something terrible—more terrible—happened to her.

There was nothing else to do. I had to call Molly. She would be home, now. She'd likely called me more than once. She had a brother who was a fireman, a trained EMT. He would help Shihong. Molly would get him to help her.

But that would never work. I couldn't put either of them in that position, even if I thought it could happen. Besides—there would be too much to explain. There had to be something else, someone else I could call.

Lila. I could call Lila. Lila and Shihong had been the only people I could really talk to since the DRC. Lila understood because she had lived through so much herself, she had experienced mayhem. Lila understood about women who had to remain hidden. It had been Lila who had implored me to go to the DRC to begin with. It had been Lila who had introduced me to Asifa.

I remembered the doctors with Asifa. Lila would know someone who would come, who would take care of Shihong, doctors who knew about women being mutilated like Asifa had been, like Shihong had been. Lila would know someone for whom the only thing that needed to be said was that Shihong had escaped, that she was not legal, that she had been found by someone who had been stalking her, that she had been hurt, and that her life needed to be saved.

I pulled open the drawers, looking for a knife. Everything was just as it always was, as if Laryssa had never been here, never removed every sharp object that could run her through to keep it out of my hands mere hours ago.

They really *had* thought of everything. I was on my own.

I grabbed the biggest knife I had and went to the studio.

They weren't in there. They weren't in the bathroom, either. But I had known they were gone. I peed, washed my face, brushed my teeth. Thinking, thinking, thinking. The clock was ticking.

I got a blanket and spare pillow out of the closet by the bathroom. I knelt down and lifted Shihong's head, putting the pillow beneath it. The bruise had darkened. *Should I try and wake her?* With concussions I knew you were supposed to keep people awake or wake them every hour.

I had brought alcohol and bandages from the bathroom. I didn't touch the nipple—that would require plastic surgery. I didn't want to make anything worse. I put a gauze bandage over it, taping it loosely at the sides. With the laceration above Shihong's liver, I blotted it with alcohol. She stirred, let out a small moan. It must have hurt like hell. I knew that if her pain reflex was intact, she would likely recover.

"Shihong, can you hear me? They're gone. You're safe. I'm going to call someone, a friend, a doctor. I'm so sorry. I'm so, so, sorry. I'm going to take care of you. You will be okay. I'll make sure you are okay."

Looking at her lovely face, her long black hair tangled in her earrings, I felt the tears come back. I stroked her face, her hair, begging her to wake up. She stirred again, but her eyes didn't open. She made a sound, but didn't speak.

I pulled her blouse closed and covered her up to her chin with the blanket. I didn't know if she was already in shock or not, but I wanted to keep her warm. I was grateful they hadn't cut her face. Memories of Grand's photographs with the slashed cheeks and pulverized eyes flashed through my mind. I bent over and kissed Shihong's bruised forehead.

The clock on the stove now read 3:51. There was no waiting till a reasonable hour to call Lila. I got up, got my phone out of my bag, turned it on. I had numerous messages, all of which would have to wait. I walked back to Shihong and called Lila, praying to Mary as the phone rang that Lila would be able to help.

❖

I was waiting at the service entrance for Lila and her doctor friend when a dark SUV pulled up. They had gotten here surprisingly fast— less than an hour. It was that time between night and dawn, the sky mostly dark, but cerulean at the horizon line. It was still chill, but I hadn't put on a jacket. I needed the cold to keep me sentient.

The doctor was not one of the group I had met with Asifa. She was older, maybe in her sixties, and she had an accent I couldn't place. "It is better if we do not exchange names," she said to me when I thanked her for coming. Hugged Lila and thanked her. "We do whatever we can to save these women," she said, putting her arm around me.

I had had nearly an hour to come up with a story and rehearse the telling before they arrived. Now I recited it as if it were the truth. I hoped Shihong would not contradict me when she awakened.

Her eyes were open when we entered the apartment, but she did not speak. I told her I had explained to the doctor and Lila that the man, the snakehead who had tried to sell her, had found her and hurt her. It was partially true—that was her own story, just years old. I explained that they, Lila and the doctor, knew she had no papers, but that they were going to help her. They were going to take care of her, make sure she was safe, make sure she healed.

I hoped she would go along with it.

Shihong spoke. Her voice was barely audible and there was a tremulousness I had never heard before.

"You have no idea how deranged he is, Faye. It was, he was—oh my god, Faye, oh my god." Her face was contorted by pain and fear.

I put my fingers to her lips. "I know, I know. We'll talk when you've been taken care of. I'm so sorry this happened to you. I'm so sorry I couldn't protect you. But I knew you wouldn't want me to call police. I knew that would make things worse."

She stared at me. It was the same look I had seen the first night we had met in San Francisco. A dark look. An unforgiving look. "Yes, you did the right thing, Faye. You were right to protect me," she said. And I knew she meant anything but.

I moved aside and let the doctor examine her.

❖

Lila and the doctor took Shihong away. The three of us had mostly carried her to the car. Lila said there was a safe house in Brooklyn. She would call me later, to tell me where. The doctor explained that she could repair the breast herself, that it would all heal. "The cuts, I mean. The rest, well—" She had waved her hand. The gesture was clear.

I stood outside watching the SUV drive away, wondering if Shihong would ever forgive me, if I could ever forgive myself. For weeks I had thought about killing him or of capturing him, of handing him over to police.

But that fantasy had been about a frail, elderly man. Not the man I met tonight. And of course I had no way of knowing about Laryssa. She was the wildest card in the deck. Her being here had changed everything. Just as she had changed him. Made him worse, somehow. Because they fed each other's sickness, each other's thirst for mayhem.

The sky had lightened now, the sun was nearly up. I turned and went inside. If I had hoped for the elusiveness of closure, I had hoped wrong. There would be no closure. One day Grand would die and then perhaps Laryssa would die, too, because she was so attached to him, because he made her feel real, whole, complete. He validated and excused her every terrible action, even the murder of his own wife. But until that day, his last, which would not be soon, I knew, they would be out there, two monsters stalking prey.

I would never be safe again. Never.

❖

I stood in the shower for a long time, trying to wash the horror of the night off me. I had scrubbed everything with bleach. The contents of the pots had gone down the garbage disposal: the blood soup, the stewed liver, something else I didn't recognize mixed with fluffy light dumplings. The plates and silverware, the glasses and pots were all scrubbed and put on the top shelf of a cabinet I rarely used. At some point in the future all of it would be boxed up and delivered to some charity. But for now it all had to stay here. Another secret.

I had cleaned up the blood on the table, the chair where Shihong had sat, the floor. I'd used paper towels, which I then burned in the sink, disabling the smoke detector and opening the window first. I'd read enough murder mysteries to know that traces remained, but no one would be searching my apartment. Of that I was reasonably sure. Besides, Shihong was still alive.

The water ran over me as I washed and washed. For the past several hours I had been acting like and thinking like a criminal. That's what Grand had wanted—to imprint me with his mark of Cain, and he had done it. I was marked forever, now. Two cannibals had eaten at my little French country table. Two sadists had assaulted my friend, doing who-knew-what to her—I doubted she would ever tell me everything, but I already knew what Grand had done before and I knew what Laryssa was capable of. She had killed her own mother. She had killed my grandmother. She had wanted to kill me.

After the shower I went into my studio, looking for any trace of him, of her.

It was hidden, of course, but in plain sight. That was their style—pretense, subterfuge, a purloined life. I grimaced involuntarily when I saw the box, OPEN IN RED LIGHT ONLY printed on the side. Another image from my childhood. *How unsubtle, Grand*, I thought.

I didn't want to open it. I told myself I didn't have to. It was like the box Mother Superior had given me all those years ago. And yet, as then, I had to know.

The box was nearly full. Photo after photo. Of me. Every one, of me. Not just from the past few weeks, but over years. Over most of my life since I'd seen him last. There were even photos of me with Rosario, me with Angie, me with Theresa, me with Keiko. They went back that far. He had always been there, on the periphery of my life, waiting. No wonder he had found Laryssa. They shared the same obsessions—killing and me.

At the bottom of the box was a note, written in the same strong hand with which he had inscribed my little book, *Now We Are Six*.

> *Dearest Faye—You see now that I have never stopped loving you. You are my flesh and blood. That is a bond that can never be broken by anyone or anything. When I look at your work, I see myself in you. That is a wonderful thing for a father, a grandfather. I had hoped to share that with your father, but he was lost to me. I was meant to share it with you. We will always be part of each other, Faye. I taught you well. I gave you your eye. I helped you to see everything. Remember that day in the garden? When the vole was struck by lightning? Remember when we shared that? Now you see the world like I do. You have to capture the scent of the world, Faye. It's about capturing the scent—it's not always a nice scent, but when you capture it, well, that is when everything opens up for you. That is what makes the blood pump. That's when the artistry begins.*
>
> *I'll see you again. And we will share another meal, another friend, and it will be like you never left me.*
>
> *All my love, Grand*

I closed the box, put it back on the shelf where I had found it. My stomach churned. I thought for a moment, I might vomit. He had killed my parents to get me, to claim me for his own. I didn't know how, but I knew now that he had. I remembered the sparkle in his eye at the grave site, the day they were buried. It wasn't tears, it was glee.

I shut the door to the studio. There was no escaping him, him and the maelstrom he brought with him. I realized now there never had been. I suppose I'd always known that. Ever since Sister Anne Marie left and never came back. I had sent her to hin. She had been *my* first victim. Unwittingly, at only six, I had sent her to her death—her gruesome, ghastly, horrible death. And now there was Shihong, lying in a bed somewhere in Brooklyn, damaged forever by her connection to me. Just as I had lain in my little bed in Brooklyn for more than a decade, damaged forever by my connection to Grand.

And now? Now all there was, was waiting. I could do that. I'd been doing it since I was six. I could go on as if last night and this morning had never happened. That was the thing about ordinary mayhem—it was such minor drama against the backdrop of the world's horrors, you had no choice but to go on. There were many men like Grand out there. I'd seen the evidence. I'd photographed it. I'd keep photographing it. Grand was right—he *had* given me my eye, my eye for men like him and what they were capable of.

I lay down on my bed, my phone in my hand. I thought of Shihong. *The secrets become you.* It was time to call Molly. It was time she knew the truth. I closed my eyes, the phone still in my hand. Maybe in a while, I would call. Maybe.

ACKNOWLEDGMENTS

There are many people who make it possible for a book to be written beyond the writer. This book would never have been written without my friend and editor Greg Herren. For fifteen years Greg and I have had a kind of nineteenth-century-style truly wonderful daily correspondence about writing, writers, politics, the state of the LGBT world, appropriation of lesbian and gay lives by those who aren't, and, of course, literary gossip. We make each other laugh, we push each other in new directions. It's a surprising, but truly fabulous (in all the queerest sense of that word) friendship. Greg's the brother I never had and the gay male friend I've been fortunate enough not to lose to AIDS, as I have so many others over the years.

Greg has pushed and prodded, cajoled and coerced me back into writing fiction when I was solely focused on nonfiction and journalism, leaving fiction behind me. He has inveigled me into writing for every anthology he has edited and sent me numerous calls for submissions to others. He's supported my fiction writing even as it's made him crazy with missed deadlines and bad formatting. But at the end he has always pronounced whatever piece it was "brilliant, as always" and sent me forth to do the next assignment. Greg doesn't just support my writing, as a pro-feminist man, he supports the work of women writers. We first met when he became editor of *Lambda Book Report* and he made it his first mission to bring more women writers on board.

A simple thank you hardly seems enough.

I am now with Bold Strokes Books because of Greg and his support of my writing. That support has been replicated by everyone

I have worked with at BSB. This is a stellar group of women—and Greg—who have welcomed me into their retinue.

First and foremost I must thank Radclyffe, who is the mega-force behind this publishing house, which has nurtured lesbian and gay writers and kept the books flowing. Radclyffe has treated me with such respect and care, I am so very grateful.

The women who keep everything looking effortless also deserve thanks. Without them books don't get finished and don't get promoted. Sandy Lowe, Cindy Cresap, Connie Ward, Kim Baldwin, all helped me along the way. Thank you for making entry into a new publishing house so comfortable and easy and for getting this book, which is so important to me, out there. Stacia Seaman catches the things you somehow haven't despite a thousand re-reads and makes it pretty, too.

Greg was, once again, my editor for this book, and I would never have completed it without his (mostly) gentle prodding. This novel began as a short story, which ended up being entirely too long. Greg published it anyway and cajoled his co-editor Jean Redmann into allowing one story to take up many pages of their marvelous anthology, *Night Shadows: Queer Horror.* My story was listed as Honorable Mention in Best Horror 2012, which was gratifying for me and was a small thank you to both Greg and Jean for including it in the collection.

After she read the story in *Night Shadows*, my friend Nicola Griffith urged me to turn the story into a novel. Thanks go to her for that. I ran various scenarios past her and she was, consummate writer that she is, helpful in suggesting direction.

My "Twitter wife," Andrea Wakefield, has been a consistent cheering section. Our daily discussions about global violence against women, the goals of radical feminism, the fight against erasure and yes, the patriarchy—all these issues have percolated in my consciousness while I worked on this book. Her humor and intellect were a constant for which I can only say, thank you.

My bestie, Roberta Hacker, is always there. We've been best friends since I was seventeen and I have no idea what I would do without her. She's fixed every computer drama, no matter what time it has been or how awful the drama. Two months before this book was due my computer crashed completely and she was able to quell my understandable hysteria by fixing it. She's taken all the kittens of the feral cat we can't catch. She's written checks when I didn't know where to turn. She's sent me cat videos and feminist treatises when I needed them, and by day she saves the lives of abused and addicted women as executive director of Women in Transition, and seriously—how was I fortunate enough to get her as my best friend for life? There aren't enough thank yous.

Judith Redding, family, friend, colleague, constant cat rescuer, member of our "gang of four," is another vital voice in my life who is always around, an intellectual sounding board. She's one of the world's last true readers. All writers need one of those in their lives.

Other people who make my life better for having them in it are my sister, Dr. Jennie Goldenberg, my nephew, Dr. Joshua Goldenberg, my nieces, Shifra and Tirzah Goldenberg. My friends Deborah Peifer, Martha Peech, and Miranda Yardley all add so much, so differently, all the time. Thank you.

Thanks to Michelle Jackson for her endless Zen pronouncements and "just do it!" dictates. Thanks also to that core group of writers always hovering nearby, Diane DeKelb-Rittenhouse, Jane Shaw, Lisa Nelson, and Joanne Dahme. You women have been there forever. Thank you.

Several other editors propel my writing forward every week: Tracy Gilchrist at *SheWired*, Merryn Johns at *Curve*, and William Johnson at *Lambda Literary Review*. My interaction with each of you every week and the work I do for you keeps me in the game in very different ways. Thank you. Noah Michelson at *Huffington Post* has supported my work even when it was controversial.

My partner, Maddy Gold, makes everything possible. If she didn't run our cat shelter (www.ffur.org) pretty much single-handedly in addition to doing her own work and art, I would not be able to write. If she didn't enrage me and engage me and make me laugh with her stellar wit, the days would be so much less enjoyable, the world so much less inviting. I am often thankless for all she brings to me and our life together—so thank you, darling, for all the quotidian tasks you do that you hate so much. You doing them makes my art possible, and I am so, so, so grateful for that and ever so much more, from your lovely face to your stalwart support. So much love for you.

Author's Note

The women whose lives appear in this book are the reason for it. Yes, *Ordinary Mayhem* is a novel, but the horrors here are—regrettably—real. Much of what is written here is culled from my own experience over decades as a journalist, and some of Faye's stories are stories I covered myself, though as an investigative reporter, not a photojournalist.

I have witnessed a lot of the Ordinary Mayhem encapsulated here. The lives of women constantly under threat, endlessly facing extremes of violence and a panoply of struggles, deserve our attention as well as our concern. Women in the developed world certainly have horrors of their own to address, from the omnipresence of rape culture and everyday sexism to the daily imbalance of gender equality that impacts us in myriad ways, from the oppression of no equal rights for lesbians, to the fight for reproductive freedom that attaches to each of us the day we get our first period, to the seemingly endless quest for economic parity.

Yet all that being equal—or not—women in the developing world have all those battles and more. Those women are still addressing sheer survival as their driving force. "Will I live through this day?" is a question millions of women and girls are always asking themselves and it is in no way rhetorical.

In the DRC (Democratic Republic of Congo), where a portion of this novel takes place, getting water and firewood are female tasks that risk assault, gang rape, and death every damned day. When you turn on your tap, another woman in DRC is risking her life to get water for her family. Water. The one thing in life we absolutely cannot survive without.

Speaking with women from DRC is an education no one wants to have. I am, myself, a victim/survivor of two quite brutal rapes, the first of which involved knives, the second of which nearly killed me. The women of the DRC face a replication of what I went through on a daily basis. Many are victims of multiple rapes. The numbers Faye reels off to her colleagues aren't made-up stats for a novel—they are the real figures. And each one represents a real woman. The stories Faye has told here are not exaggerated for fictional drama—these all happened. And Faye responds accordingly.

I quite literally ache for these women. At the time I was finishing this novel, I was interviewing lesbians incarcerated at Yarl's Wood, an immigration detention center that is actually more a prison, some 60 miles outside London in the U.K. When I interviewed Aderonke Apata for *Curve*, she was fighting deportation to Nigeria, which had just passed one of the most restrictive and repressive anti-homosexuality laws in the world. Her former partner had already been murdered when Apata fled Nigeria. Apata's son and brother had also been killed. Apata had a price on her head—she'd received letters telling her she'd be murdered on her return. In March 2013, Jackie Nanyonjo was deported from Yarl's Wood to Nigeria, and she was killed.

Yet in spite of what both the U.K. and the U.S.—which has deported more people, including many lesbians and gay men, under President Barack Obama than at any other time in history—have said publicly is horrific violence and repression of lesbians and gay men in countries like Nigeria and Uganda and the thirty-seven other nations in Africa with anti-homosexuality laws, among others, they continue the loathsome practice of having lesbians and gay men "prove" they are homosexual to fight deportation to certain death. Apata was forced to submit a video of herself in what she described to me as "pornographic" circumstances as proof of her lesbianism. Apata was engaged to another woman, but that was not enough "proof" for the Home Office.

For three decades I have written about the struggles of women, and especially lesbians (as well as gay men, bisexuals, and transgender people), in their fight for equity in a world where women are born into second-class status every day and LGBTQ people are living under the kind of laws not seen since Pol Pot or Adolf Hitler. American lesbians and gay men may think that because we have gotten a few marriage equality laws passed that we are living in some kind of relative state of equality. We are not. For more than twenty years now, the Employment Non-Discrimination Act (ENDA) has been put up for vote in the Senate. It has yet to pass. All this law provides is lack of discrimination in employment, so that lesbians and gay men can't be fired for their sexual orientation and trans persons can't be fired for their gender identification.

These issues are embedded in Faye's story—they comprise the Ordinary Mayhem of the title. As you read this book, keep that in mind. There are no vampires, zombies, revenants, or other supernatural creatures in this horror novel. Those perpetrating the horrors are on our side of the natural divide. And what could send greater chills up anyone's spine than knowing that?

Victoria A. Brownworth
Philadelphia, PA
September 2014

ABOUT THE AUTHOR

Victoria A. Brownworth (victoriabrownworth.com) is an award-winning journalist, editor, and writer, and the author and editor of more than twenty books, including the award-winning books *Too Queer: Essays from a Radical Life*, *Coming Out of Cancer: Writings from the Lesbian Cancer Epidemic*, and *Day of the Dead*. She has won the NLGJA and the Society of Professional Journalists awards and the Lambda Literary Award, and has been nominated for the Pulitzer Prize. She won the 2013 Society of Professional Journalists Award for Enterprise Reporting in May 2014 as well as the Keystone Award for beat reporting. She is a regular contributor to *The Advocate* and *SheWired*, a blogger for *Huffington Post*, and a contributing editor for *Curve* magazine, *Curve* digital, and *Lambda Literary Review*. She is a weekly columnist for the *San Francisco Bay Area Reporter* and *The Independent Voice*. Her reporting, feature writing, and commentary have appeared in the *New York Times*, *Village Voice*, *Los Angeles Times*, *Boston Globe*, *Philadelphia Inquirer*, and *Philadelphia Daily News*, among others. Her collection *From Where We Sit: Black Writers Write Black Youth* won the 2012 Moonbeam Award for cultural & historical fiction. She teaches writing and film and she lives in Philadelphia with her wife, the artist Maddy Gold, and entirely too many cats.

Find her on Twitter at @VABVOX.

Books Available From Bold Strokes Books

Pedal to the Metal by Jesse J. Thoma. When unreformed thief Dubs Williams is released from prison to help Max Winters bust a car theft ring, Max learns that if you want to catch a thief, you have to get in bed with one. (978-1-62639-239-7)

Dragon Horse War by D. Jackson Leigh. A priestess of peace and a fiery warrior must defeat a vicious uprising that entwines their destinies and ultimately their hearts. (978-1-62639-240-3)

For the Love of Cake by Erin Dutton. When everything is on the line and one taste can break a heart, will pastry chefs Maya and Shannon take a chance on reality? (978-1-62639-241-0)

Betting on Love by Alyssa Linn Palmer. A quiet country girl at heart and a live-life-to-the-fullest biker take a risk at offering each other their hearts. (978-1-62639-242-7)

The Deadening by Yvonne Heidt. The lines between good and evil, right and wrong, have always been blurry for Shade. When Raven's actions force her to choose, which side will she come out on? (978-1-62639-243-4)

One Last Thing by Kim Baldwin & Xenia Alexiou. Blood is thicker than pride. The final book in the Elite Operative Series brings together foes, family, and friends to start a new order. (978-1-62639-230-4)

Songs Unfinished by Holly Stratimore. Two aspiring rock stars learn that falling in love while pursuing their dreams can be harmonious—if they can only keep their pasts from throwing them out of tune. (978-1-62639-231-1)

Beyond the Ridge by L.T. Marie. Will a contractor and a horse rancher overcome their family differences and find common ground to build a life together? (978-1-62639-232-8)

Swordfish by Andrea Bramhall. Four women battle the demons from their pasts. Will they learn to let go, or will happiness be forever beyond their grasp? (978-1-62639-233-5)

The Fiend Queen by Barbara Ann Wright. Princess Katya and her consort Starbride must turn evil against evil in order to banish Fiendish power from their kingdom, and only love will pull them back from the brink. (978-1-62639-234-2)

Up the Ante by PJ Trebelhorn. When Jordan Stryker and Ashley Noble meet again fifteen years after a short-lived affair, is either of them prepared to gamble on a chance at love? (978-1-62639-237-3)

Speakeasy by MJ Williamz. When mob leader Helen Byrne sets her sights on the girlfriend of Al Capone's right-hand man, passion and tempers flare on the streets of Chicago. (978-1-62639-238-0)

Myth and Magic: Queer Fairy Tales, edited by Radclyffe and Stacia Seaman. Myth, magic, and monsters—the stuff of childhood dreams (or nightmares) and adult fantasies. (978-1-62639-225-0)

The Muse by Meghan O'Brien. Erotica author Kate McMannis struggles with writer's block until a gorgeous muse entices her into a world of fantasy sex and inadvertent romance. (978-1-62639-223-6)

Venus in Love by Tina Michele. Morgan Blake can't afford any distractions and Ainsley Dencourt can't afford to lose control—but the beauty of life and art usually lies in the unpredictable strokes of the artist's brush. (978-1-62639-220-5)

Rules of Revenge by AJ Quinn. When a lethal operative on a collision course with her past agrees to help a CIA analyst on a critical assignment, the encounter proves explosive in ways neither woman anticipated. (978-1-62639-221-2)

The Romance Vote by Ali Vali. Chili Alexander is a sought-after campaign consultant who isn't prepared when her boss's daughter, Samantha Pellegrin, comes to work at the firm and shakes up Chili's life from the first day. (978-1-62639-222-9)

Advance by Gun Brooke. Admiral Dael Caydoc's mission to find a new homeworld for the Oconodian people is hazardous, but working with the infuriating Commander Aniwyn "Spinner" Seclan endangers her heart and soul. (978-1-62639-224-3)

UnCatholic Conduct by Stevie Mikayne. Jil Kidd goes undercover to investigate fraud at St. Marguerite's Catholic School, but life gets complicated when her student is killed—and she begins to fall for her prime target. (978-1-62639-304-2)

Season's Meetings by Amy Dunne. Catherine Birch reluctantly ventures on the festive road trip from hell with beautiful stranger Holly Daniels only to discover the road to true love has its own obstacles to maneuver. (978-1-62639-227-4)

Courtship by Carsen Taite. Love and Justice—a lethal mix or a perfect match? (978-1-62639-210-6)

Against Doctor's Orders by Radclyffe. Corporate financier Presley Worth wants to shut down Argyle Community Hospital, but Dr. Harper Rivers will fight her every step of the way, if she can also fight their growing attraction. (978-1-62639-211-3)

A Spark of Heavenly Fire by Kathleen Knowles. Kerry and Beth are building their life together, but unexpected circumstances could destroy their happiness. (978-1-62639-212-0)

Never Too Late by Julie Blair. When Dr. Jamie Hammond is forced to hire a new office manager, she's shocked to come face-to-face with Carla Grant and memories from her past. (978-1-62639-213-7)

Widow by Martha Miller. Judge Bertha Brannon must solve the murder of her lover, a policewoman she thought she'd grow old with. As more bodies pile up, the murderer starts coming for her. (978-1-62639-214-4)

Twisted Echoes by Sheri Lewis Wohl. What's a woman to do when she realizes the voices in her head are real? (978-1-62639-215-1)

Because of You by Julie Cannon. What would you do for the woman you were forced to leave behind? (978-1-62639-199-4)

Criminal Gold by Ann Aptaker. Through a dangerous night in New York in 1949, Cantor Gold, dapper dyke-about-town, smuggler of fine art, is forced by a crime lord to be his instrument of vengeance. (978-1-62639-216-8)

The Job by Jove Belle. Sera always dreamed that she would one day reunite with Tor. She just didn't think it would involve terrorists, firearms, and hostages. (978-1-62639-200-7)

Making Time by C.J. Harte. Two women going in different directions meet after fifteen years and struggle to reconnect in spite of the past that separated them. (978-1-62639-201-4)

Once The Clouds Have Gone by KE Payne. Overwhelmed by the dark clouds of her past, Tag Grainger is lost until the intriguing and spirited Freddie Metcalfe unexpectedly forces her to reevaluate her life. (978-1-62639-202-1)

The Acquittal by Anne Laughlin. Chicago private investigator Josie Harper searches for the real killer of a woman whose lover has been acquitted of the crime. (978-1-62639-203-8)

An American Queer: The Amazon Trail by Lee Lynch. Lee Lynch's heartening and heart-rending history of gay life from the turbulence of the late 1900s to the triumphs of the early 2000s are recorded in this selection of her columns. (978-1-62639-204-5)

Stick McLaughlin by CF Frizzell. Corruption in 1918 cost Stick her lover, her freedom, and her identity, but a very special flapper and the family bond of her own gang could help win them back—even if it means outwitting the Boston Mob. (978-1-62639-205-2)

Rest Home Runaways by Clifford Henderson. Baby boomer Morgan Ronzio's troubled marriage is the least of her worries when she gets the call that her addled, eighty-six-year-old, half-blind dad has escaped the rest home. (978-1-62639-169-7)

Charm City by Mason Dixon. Raq Overstreet's loyalty to her drug kingpin boss is put to the test when she begins to fall for Bathsheba Morris, the undercover cop assigned to bring him down. (978-1-62639-198-7)